A
MAP
TO
PARADISE

NOVELS BY SUSAN MEISSNER

A Map to Paradise
Only the Beautiful
The Nature of Fragile Things
The Last Year of the War
As Bright as Heaven
A Bridge Across the Ocean
Stars over Sunset Boulevard
Secrets of a Charmed Life
A Fall of Marigolds
The Girl in the Glass
A Sound Among the Trees
Lady in Waiting
White Picket Fences
The Shape of Mercy

A
MAP
TO
PARADISE

SUSAN MEISSNER

BERKLEY

NEW YORK

BERKLEY
An imprint of Penguin Random House LLC
penguinrandomhouse.com

Copyright © 2025 by Susan Meissner
Penguin Random House values and supports copyright. Copyright fuels creativity, encourages
diverse voices, promotes free speech, and creates a vibrant culture. Thank you for buying an
authorized edition of this book and for complying with copyright laws by not reproducing,
scanning, or distributing any part of it in any form without permission. You are
supporting writers and allowing Penguin Random House to continue to publish books
for every reader. Please note that no part of this book may be used or reproduced
in any manner for the purpose of training artificial intelligence
technologies or systems.

BERKLEY and the BERKLEY & B colophon are registered trademarks of
Penguin Random House LLC.

Title page and part title ornament by Essl/Shutterstock

Library of Congress Cataloging-in-Publication Data

Names: Meissner, Susan, 1961- author.
Title: A map to paradise / Susan Meissner.
Description: New York : Berkley, 2025.
Identifiers: LCCN 2024016554 (print) | LCCN 2024016555 (ebook) |
ISBN 9780593332863 (hardcover) | ISBN 9780593332887 (ebook)
Subjects: LCGFT: Novels.
Classification: LCC PS3613.E435 M37 2025 (print) | LCC PS3613.E435 (ebook) |
DDC 813/.6--dc23/eng/20240419
LC record available at https://lccn.loc.gov/2024016554
LC ebook record available at https://lccn.loc.gov/2024016555

Printed in the United States of America
1st Printing

"I know you are tired but come, this is the way."

—Rumi

A
MAP
TO
PARADISE

PROLOGUE

Malibu, April 14, 1966

T he view from the car window is both calming and startling.

New eucalyptus, queen palms, and jacaranda trees stand on what had been charred earth. Bird-of-paradise and sea lavender hug the footprint where a house once stood. A rose garden at the back of the lot pulls the gaze of the woman inside the vehicle like a magnet. It is much bigger than the one the fire nearly crispened into nothingness. Roses of every shade beckon, and this makes her smile. So does the park bench that offers a wispy glimpse of the cobalt sea a half mile down the hill.

The bench is also new.

She reaches for the garden shears at her feet, freshly purchased from the Nurseryland on Sepulveda Boulevard, and frees them from their packaging.

"I'll only be a few minutes," she says to her husband, sitting in the driver's seat.

The man nods and kills the engine anyway so that she won't feel rushed.

She approaches the garden tentatively, as an intruder might, suddenly second-guessing herself. But when she reaches the multihued blooms in all stages of opening, the roses seem to welcome her forward, lifting on the breeze as if to bare their necks to the blades.

Minutes later the woman is walking back to the car with enough flowers for two bouquets, their petals releasing a honey-sweet fragrance. She left the snipped thorns to decompose where they'd fallen.

The woman turns before opening the car door to gaze upon the Eden-like setting, knowing she might not see these rosebushes again. But she also knows she cannot linger here at the top of Paradise Circle. Traffic into Los Angeles is always difficult at this time of day.

DECEMBER 11, 1956

Ten Years Earlier

1

The last thing Eva Kruse wanted to do was risk drawing attention to herself, and yet she'd done it anyway.

She'd stayed overnight at Melanie Cole's house. Spent hour upon hour there instead of leaving at three in the afternoon as she usually did. Slept in the guest room bed as if an actual guest and not a paid-by-the-hour housekeeper who'd vowed to spend zero extra time at the actress's house.

Zero.

Yet there she stood, at daybreak in a borrowed nightgown.

When Melanie had told Eva she needed her to arrive that morning at six a.m. instead of nine, Eva had explained the best she could manage was a few minutes before eight. The two-bus commute from Los Angeles to Malibu was well over an hour. There was only one bus earlier than the one she picked up in Santa Monica, which still wouldn't get her there in time.

"It's just this once," Melanie had pleaded, as though Eva had said instead that she didn't want to start her workday when it was still dark. "I've an important call from the East Coast at seven thirty. I need my breakfast and a good pot of coffee and my dress ironed—even if no one is going to see me. I need to look and feel confident and poised, Eva. It's an extremely important call. I need you to come at six. Please. Just this one time."

"I am sorry, Miss Cole. The other bus does not come to my second stop until after seven." Eva had enunciated each word carefully so that her accented English couldn't be misunderstood.

She'd hoped the actress would call Marvelous Maids and at last, *at last*, ask for a different housekeeper—one who had a car or a husband who could drive or who lived closer or who had access to better bus routes. She was being paid at the top level for this posting—the most she'd been paid for any housekeeping job since arriving in America four years earlier. No one quits a plum posting without it raising questions. But if Melanie had asked for another maid, it would've solved all Eva's problems.

The most pressing one, anyway. The one that often kept her up at night.

"Then just stay over tonight," Melanie had said. "You'll already be here when my alarm goes off in the morning, so you can make sure I get up. It's a very important call."

"I don't know . . ." Eva's mind had spun with possible excuses. Staying over was a bad idea if Melanie was being watched. It was probably a bad idea even if she wasn't being watched. Sometimes Eva cried out in her sleep. And not in Polish.

"What don't you know?" Melanie had asked, brows knitted. "Is it the money? I'll pay you for the extra hours, even though you're not going to be doing anything while you're sleeping."

"No, it is . . ." Eva's voice had fallen away as words for the reason for her hesitancy fought to take shape in her mouth; a reason she had no intention of giving.

She shouldn't be working for Melanie Cole, plain and simple.

The Hollywood starlet had been suspected of communist ties six months earlier and been blacklisted. No studio, big or little, would hire her now. Melanie Cole didn't need anyone in her orbit who might reinforce the idea that she wasn't a patriot. The actress hadn't been singled out; Eva knew that. There were plenty of other Hollywood people caught up in the long and ongoing hunt to rout out socialist sympathizers, including that famous actor Melanie had starred alongside and who was paying the rent on this house.

And who slept over when he was in town.

That film with heartthrob Carson Edwards had apparently been Melanie's first big role, and audiences had adored her. This Eva had learned from her landlady, Yvonne. Eva herself hadn't seen the movie. Fans and the tabloids had loved even more that Melanie and Carson were "an item," but when he'd been named a suspected communist and summarily blacklisted, Melanie had been, too. Guilt by association. The adoration of the public had evaporated as quickly as morning dew. Yvonne had told her all of this, too.

Everything Melanie Cole was doing or had done was now being scrutinized. Or so Eva surmised.

An overnight stay would draw unwanted attention to both of them if anyone were in fact spying on Melanie, taking notes on who she spent time with. And if those government men poking into Melanie's personal life pried next into Eva's, they might discover she wasn't, as she claimed, a displaced Pole who refused after the war to return to what was now communist Warsaw. They would discover who she really was and instantly assume the worst, because that's what people did.

Eva would not only lose her job with the agency, but she'd likely be deported for having lied on her immigration papers. And Melanie? The actress would probably never work in Hollywood again, which was Melanie Cole's worst nightmare. Eva had heard her talk about it with that screenwriter Elwood who lived next door. That man never came out of his house, but Eva had heard the actress talking with him—both through an open window and also on the telephone. Eva knew all Melanie Cole had ever wanted was to be a film actress. She had finally made it as one, and suddenly that life had been taken from her.

Melanie was no communist; Eva was certain of that, and she would know better than anyone. But she also knew it didn't matter what a person said about themselves; it mattered only what others said about them.

Eva hadn't learned of Melanie's predicament until two months after she started working for her, and it wasn't until a full month after that she came to understand Melanie's associations—that is, who she spoke to, spent time with, had over to the house—were likely being scrutinized, too. People like her. Eva had known then she needed a different posting. Producing a good reason for asking for one was tricky, though. She had a highly desirable assignment. When she'd asked her supervisor, Lorraine, for a change due to the hour-long commute each day—a rather good excuse, she thought— she was told that Mr. Edwards had expressly chosen Eva. She was the preferred Marvelous Maid for Melanie Cole, and so she'd now be compensated for the two hours on the bus each day as well as for her bus fare.

Lorraine had beamed when she'd said this. No Marvelous Maid had ever earned the hourly rate while riding a bus to get to work, let alone been reimbursed for bus fare.

"I have extra nightgowns, if that's what you're worried about," Melanie had added, her tone having warped from expectant to an- noyed. "And it's just one night. I really don't think I'm asking too much, Eva. I will pay you the extra in cash. The agency doesn't have to know."

In the end Eva had agreed. It *was* just one night. There was at that moment no stray car on the cul-de-sac with a strange driver sitting inside it, peering at the house. And the extra money? If she was going to need to start over again with a new job, the extra money would sure help.

She'd slept fitfully in Melanie's spacious guest room and risen before the sun to make the requested coffee and breakfast and to rouse the actress if she slept through her alarm.

But when Eva emerged from the guest room, the actress was already up. Melanie stood now in the dark at the slightly open sliding door that led to the back patio, smoking a cigarette.

"Oh! Good morning, ma'am," Eva said, startled.

The actress turned to her. Dawn was only just beginning to steal across the sky, and the actress looked beautiful in the gleaming light of the still-visible moon. Melanie Cole had all the features a camera surely loved. Golden brown hair that fell in soft waves past her shoulders. Eyes the same verdigris green as meadow grass in springtime. Slender legs and a small waist and nicely proportioned everywhere else.

Even with her hair tousled and no cosmetics on her face, Melanie was stunning. Eva had the same build and nearly the same hair color, but she knew she was merely pleasant-looking.

"I couldn't sleep," the actress said, as though replying to a different comment than Eva's morning greeting.

"I . . . Would you care for your coffee now, ma'am?" Eva asked.

"Can't you just please call me Melanie? I feel like an old woman every time you call me ma'am. I'm only twenty-five."

"Certainly, ma'am. I mean . . ."

"Melanie."

"Yes. Melanie."

Eva waited for an answer about the coffee, but there wasn't one.

Instead, the actress brought the cigarette to her lips as she turned back toward the glass doors. A dry breeze instead of the usual morning coastal mist was ruffling the sheer curtains. Melanie tipped her head back, drew in a breath, and then exhaled. Smoke swirled above her head and out the narrow opening at the door like a streamer made of gauze.

She pointed to the neighbor's house with her cigarette. "Elwood's sister-in-law is out there digging up his roses. Why in the world is she doing that?"

Eva fumbled for an answer. "You mean, so early in the morning?"

"No. I mean, why would June tear up his rosebushes? Elwood is very fond of them. He told me so. They're not hers."

"I . . . I don't know, ma'am. I mean Melanie."

"Come look."

Eva closed the distance between them and looked out toward the neighbor's backyard. The patio lights were on, and Eva could see the head and shoulders of Melanie's neighbor, June Blankenship, just over the fence, bending out of view every few seconds as she drove a shovel into the ground. The woman lifted what appeared to be a rosebush, took a few paces, and then disappeared from sight as she bent forward with the bush and lowered it to the dirt.

"I think . . . I think she might be planting rosebushes," Eva said. "Or moving them around maybe?"

Melanie shook her head. "Elwood is going to flip. He is very particular about those bushes. I don't think she should be doing that."

Eva didn't know what to say to this. She'd never actually met the next-door neighbors, though Melanie had told her that the writer who lived there, Elwood Blankenship, had been in a bad accident some years back and now never came outside. His twin brother's widow, June, lived with him and did his grocery shopping and laundry and all that. Eva also knew that when Melanie had been blacklisted and Carson Edwards moved her from Hollywood to Malibu to get her away from the press and prying eyes, she'd found a friend and unlikely confidant in Elwood Blankenship. Elwood was an accepted member of the Hollywood universe Melanie had been kicked out of, and therefore on good terms with all the people who now refused to hire her. He was additionally, near as Eva could tell, good at giving advice. She hadn't meant to overhear their telephone or over-the-fence conversations, but Melanie wasn't one to whisper. Especially when she was upset.

The last conversation Eva overheard had been a little over a week ago when she'd been in the backyard, shaking out a rug. Melanie was at the side of the house, talking with Elwood across the fence as he stood at an open window on his upper story. It would have been impossible not to hear them.

Melanie had been telling Elwood she'd gotten a letter from Washington laying out for her what the government's expectations were if she wanted to prove her innocence.

"I'm not un-American!" Melanie had been shouting up to the window. "I was a Girl Scout, for heaven's sake. I sang the National Anthem at my high school football games! I have done nothing wrong, Elwood. Ask anyone at the studio! Anyone."

"But this isn't about what you have done or not done, Melanie," Elwood had said, his voice gliding down unhurriedly to Melanie's side of the fence. Eva got the impression he didn't often raise his voice. "It's about who they think you are. And who you associate with."

"You mean who I sleep with," Melanie had shot back, and only slightly less loudly.

"Especially who you sleep with." His voice had still been gentle.

"Even if Carson *is* a communist—" Melanie had begun, but Elwood cut her off.

"You should probably just assume for the moment that they know something about him that you don't. I would."

"Why? Why should I do that?"

"Because word gets around in Hollywood, especially in the writers' circles, where there once were quite a number of Party members. And because you're only on the list because he is."

"But even if Carson *is* a communist, that doesn't mean that I am one!"

"I think perhaps those men in Washington suspect that you're not."

"Then why is all of this happening to me?"

"They suppose, if you are guilty, that you must know a great many people who *are* communists. Because you are in an intimate relationship with one. And that must mean you sympathize with a communist and what he believes in. Communist sympathizers are as great a threat to national security as communists. Maybe worse. That's how they see it."

"That's not what I am!"

"But this is what they see."

"They are wrong!"

"I am inclined to agree with you. The problem is not that they are wrong but that they are in a position to make your life difficult because they think they're right. They have power that you do not."

Eva had stopped shaking the rug but was glued to the spot as she listened.

"So I should do nothing?" Melanie had sounded on the verge of tears. "Is that what you're saying?"

"You can only do what is in your power to do, of course. That's all any of us can do about anything. But you can begin to do something by adjusting what they see."

"And how am I supposed to do that?"

"Well, for one thing, you can stop sleeping with a man they say is a communist."

"But I don't think—"

"*They* think he is. That's what you need to remember."

"He's paying my rent."

"And you don't see that as an additional problem here?"

"I can't afford this place without his help."

Elwood had sighed. He'd sounded tired to Eva, very tired, and it had been only a little past ten in the morning.

"And he's not even here right now," Melanie added.

"But he'll be back at some point, right? Don't you have family in Nebraska?" Elwood had asked wearily but still kindly.

"I absolutely refuse to go back there."

"If you're asking for my advice, stop associating with Carson. And if you can't afford to live here in Malibu without his support, then consider living somewhere you can afford to live. Nothing will change for you until *you* make changes first. I can pretty much promise you that." A long pause followed. "I really need to get back to the script I'm working on. Okay? Think about what I said."

The conversation had ended, and Eva rushed back inside the house so as not to be seen.

Eva hadn't yet met the woman named June whom she and Melanie were now watching; Melanie never had neighbors—or anyone, really—to the house except for Carson and her agent, Irving. But from Melanie's front window Eva had seen June Blankenship opening and closing the garage door and sweeping the walkway and porch. She guessed the woman to be in her late forties or early fifties. It was hard to tell from so far away. June was of average height and build, with mousy brown hair strewn with silver that she kept perpetually swept up into a twist at the back of her head.

Melanie pulled on her cigarette now and blew the smoke over her shoulder. "I need you to do me a favor," she said to Eva. "You're dressed and I'm still in my nightgown. Go over there to the fence and tell June that I need to speak with Elwood before I take that phone call this morning. There are things I need to ask him that I didn't think to ask last week. Tell her it's important. Ask her if I can come over in a few minutes. Or if I can call him. Tell her I know it's early but I can see his light is on. Make sure you tell her it's important."

Melanie then swiveled to look at Eva, who had not moved.

"Did you hear me?" A thin current of agitation rippled in Melanie's voice.

"What? Yes." But Eva couldn't quite recall all that Melanie had asked her to say. She was stunned at being asked to speak to a neighbor she'd not yet met—at dawn, no less.

"Well? Go ask her."

"Ask her . . ." Eva's voice trailed away.

Melanie huffed. "Ask her if I can speak with Elwood for just a few minutes. It's important. And he's up."

"What if you just telephoned—" Eva began, her face warming at her boldness. Brashness. But Melanie cut her off.

"I already tried that. He's not picking up. Now please do what I ask. You work for me, you know."

"Yes, ma'am."

"Melanie."

Eva nodded and slid the door farther open. She crossed Melanie's patio and then the bit of lawn to the fence line. On the other side of it, she could hear June Blankenship grunting and breathing heavily as she worked. It seemed a very bad time to be asking the busy neighbor a question. Especially the one that Melanie insisted she ask. Eva neared the fence as quietly as she could to peer through one of the slender openings between each wooden slat.

June appeared to be putting one last rosebush in place and tamping the dirt all around it. Then she shoveled mulch over the fresh planting. Eva could see that half the rose garden, maybe six or seven of its dozen bushes, had been freshly dug. Overnight, it seemed. The scene too easily conjured a memory, one that she thought she'd finally hidden away in a dark corner so deeply she'd never have to think of it again.

She shook the image away and watched as June Blankenship stepped back from the bushes and onto the patio flagstones. Watched as June set the shovel carefully against the house. Watched as June lifted her gaze to an open window on the second story, and then a moment later as she dropped her gaze and murmured, "How could you do this to me?" seemingly to no one.

Eva pulled back quickly and silently from the slats.

She knew she had to make her presence known in that odd moment and ask the question she'd been commanded to ask, though she would've much rather crept back into Melanie's house, unheard and unseen.

She cleared her throat.

"Mrs. Blankenship?" Eva said.

2

Melanie crushed out her cigarette and watched with aggravation as Eva stealthily approached the fence, tiptoeing as if what she'd been asked to do was scandalous. Did neighbors not talk to one another where Eva was from?

Melanie found that hard to believe. Poland wasn't Mars. Surely Polish women spoke to their next-door neighbors across the fence, even that early in the morning if both were up.

Eva was now bending slightly to peer at June Blankenship through the slats.

"Just ask her!" Melanie whispered to herself.

It wasn't often she wished Marvelous Maids had sent over a chatty American to be her housekeeper. Most of the time she was glad the person they sent was a quiet foreigner. Eva didn't know enough about Hollywood celebrities to be starstruck, and she didn't have American siblings, cousins, and old high school chums pumping her for information about the actress she worked for. Eva was an outsider. Calm, competent, and unimpressed, it seemed, by Melanie's notoriety. Melanie liked that. Her agent, Irving Ross, liked that. So did Carson. So did the lawyer Carson had hired for her. Eva didn't ask questions, didn't initiate unwanted small talk, didn't take things as souvenirs, didn't gawk or gush or giggle. Sometimes Melanie longed for more interaction from Eva—it was lonely being stuck in the house day after day—but if she had to choose between annoyingly talkative and absurdly quiet, she'd still choose the latter.

It had been Irving's idea to bring in Eva as her housekeeper when Carson insisted she have one.

Irving had specifically wanted someone for the job who hadn't grown up reading fan magazines. Nor did he want someone from an agency typically tapped by Hollywood elite. It had to be someone outside the studios. Someone they could trust. Carson agreed.

When a friend had suggested he contact Marvelous Maids in Wilshire Park, he thought that was still a little too close to the movers and shakers on Sunset Boulevard. But when this person said a polite young Polish woman named Eva Kruse had expertly and oh-so-quietly cleaned their trashed home after a particularly wild party, Irving made the call and Carson plunked down the money.

It was the Polish part that had motivated them both. Melanie knew this because Irving had told her.

"I've found you a housekeeper," he'd said, not long after Carson had moved her into a furnished house whose owner was on a two-year assignment to Cairo. "She'll be perfect for you. She's a DP."

"What's a deepee?"

Irving had given her a quick *Are you joking?* look and then replied, "You know. A Displaced Person. From Europe. From the war. A DP. She's one of those people the American government brought over after the war because they couldn't go home or didn't have a home anymore."

"Someone from one of those horrible death camps?" Melanie

had been ashamed to say the mere thought of being that close to true suffering scared her.

"No. No, she's Catholic, I think. Polish. That doesn't matter. She's not from around here. That's what's important. She'll be perfect."

"But I can't afford a housekeeper," she'd said.

"But Carson can. And he wants you to have one."

Carson was already paying her rent, and her lawyer's fees, and buying the groceries that were delivered every Saturday. And now a housekeeper? Carson could indeed afford it; he was rich. And he'd just snagged a great role on Broadway despite being black-listed, too. Apparently, plenty of theaters in New York didn't kow-tow to congressional hotheads. But still. Carson was being too generous.

"Why is he doing that?" Melanie had asked.

Irving shrugged. "Why do you think?"

It wasn't because Carson was in love with her; she knew that. Their off-screen romance had been for the gossip columnists—who'd eaten it up like free candy. She hadn't minded the pretense, though; the post–movie release exposure had been good for her popularity. And then when she and Carson had realized they actually enjoyed each other's companionship in spite of the studio-arranged affair, she hadn't minded that, either. Or Carson's gifts or the fancy dinners or the limo rides. Carson was a fun date.

But he didn't love her. He'd told her early on he wasn't one to fall in love, though he was awfully fond of her.

"I'm asking you anyway," she'd said to Irving.

"He probably feels guilty. You're in this heap of a mess because of him. If you two hadn't been seen around town, you'd probably be working right now. I would have had all kinds of offers lined up for you if you hadn't taken up with him."

She'd bristled at the inference that this was all her fault. "An arrangement you told me would be good for my career."

"Yeah, well, if it weren't for this witch hunt, it would've been. He wants you to have a maid. At this point what difference does it make? He's paying for everything else, and you already know how I feel about that. Do you really want to do your own laundry and scrub your own toilets if he wants to pay to have it done for you?"

It hadn't been that long ago that she was doing her own laundry and scrubbing her own toilet. But a maid for six days a week? For six hours a day? What kind of a slob did Carson think she was?

It occurred to Melanie now as Eva peeked into the Blankenships' backyard that perhaps Irving was wrong and guilt had nothing to do with it at all. Maybe the real reason Carson had been happily paying for a maid was that Eva had actually been hired to watch her. To make sure she wasn't letting reporters into the house or taking phone calls from them.

To make sure Melanie was sticking to her promise to keep her mouth shut and to sound the alarm if she wasn't.

She frowned. That new explanation didn't square at all with what she saw in Eva every day. Eva didn't come across in the least as a spying snitch. Eva didn't hover, didn't linger in the room, didn't seem to be interested in any phone call Melanie made or took.

And it wasn't because she didn't understand English. She did. Eva's accent was pronounced, to be sure, but she could answer any question Melanie posed. Could speak to anyone who came to the door if the bell rang. Could ring up the grocer if Melanie wanted something added to the list. The only time Eva engaged with Melanie was when Melanie initiated it. Eva was like a ghost the rest of the time, a specter who floated from room to room with her broom and feather duster, cleaning a clean house without a sound.

Melanie knew she was only five years younger than Eva, but the maid seemed much older. Her eyes, her demeanor, the way she stared off into space. It was as if sometimes she was back in her homeland and running from the Nazis or whatever or whoever it was that had made her a Displaced Person. Even when she was cleaning in the same room as Melanie, she often seemed far away and certainly not snooping or eavesdropping.

Eva wasn't a spy.

But how hard was it to obey a simple instruction?

Melanie was just about to rush across the lawn in her nightgown to ask June herself when at last she saw Eva straighten and speak to the woman.

She couldn't hear Eva but she saw June jump. Saw the woman nearly knock her shovel to the patio in surprise.

Melanie watched as June listened to Eva's next words, saw June lift her head to gaze at her brother-in-law's window, and then return her attention to Eva. Saw her shake her head.

Eva said something else.

June shook her head again.

Damn it all! She should've known better than to think June would take Eva's request on her behalf seriously. June was like a cross between a fairy godmother and a general when it came to Elwood and his care.

Melanie pushed the door open all the way and strode across the patio and the grass. She was wearing a thin negligee and matching robe, but the early morning air was surprisingly dry and hinting of coming warmth. A frolicking gust kicked up the opaque fabric and swirled it about her ankles.

As she closed in on them, Eva was swiveling to return to the house, obviously unsuccessful, and June was moving away from the fence, too.

"Wait!" Melanie called out. "Wait, June. Please."

June turned back around.

"I won't need more than just a few minutes of Elwood's time. It really is quite important. And he's the only person I trust. He's the only person I know right now who can help me. Please?"

June's countenance seemed to soften a bit. "He's . . . he's just not been himself lately, Melanie. And he's not . . . he's not been taking calls. I can't force him to speak with you."

"Yes, I know he has his bad days and all, but—"

"It's worse than usual, actually." June rubbed a bit of soil on her face with a dirty hand, making the smudge even bigger. "It wouldn't be kind of me to insist he take your call. It just wouldn't. My first responsibility is to him. I'm sorry."

June turned from her, and Melanie rushed a step forward and grabbed at the fence, as though that would keep her neighbor from going back inside the house. A splinter slid its way under the skin of her ring finger, but Melanie barely noticed.

"I have an important call this morning, June! From the people in Washington who are ruining my life. They are going to ask me questions. They're going to want information from me. They're going to insist I tell them what they want to hear! I need to know what I should do. I need Elwood to tell me what I should say."

June pivoted back around, a slight frown etched on her face. "Shouldn't your lawyer be the one telling you what to say?"

"My lawyer isn't thinking about how to win back my career. He is only concerned with keeping me out of trouble."

"More like keeping that Edwards fellow out of trouble, you mean."

Melanie stared at her, wordless.

"I'm sorry, but it's been impossible not to overhear your conversations with Elwood. Carson Edwards chose your lawyer, right? And is paying his fees? Even I can see how that looks."

Melanie was taken aback for a moment. June had never so much as even hinted that she had an opinion regarding Melanie's dilemma. But then she didn't speak to June much. It was only Elwood she'd ever sought counsel from, not his sister-in-law.

"I can't afford my own lawyer," she said after a beat. "The only movie that ever made me any real money isn't playing anywhere anymore. Please, June. Let me talk to him."

June inhaled deeply and then let the breath out. She gazed up at Elwood's bedroom window again. Her face seemed to shift from tired annoyance to something like compassion or sadness, and for a moment Melanie thought she'd won her over. But when June turned to look at her again, Melanie could see that she had not.

"If I asked him about this, you and I both know what he would say," June said. "He'd tell you to share what you know if you want those people to know it. He'd say whatever information you have belongs to *you*. If you want to give it to them, give it to them. If you don't, then don't."

"It's not that simple!" Melanie gripped the fence harder. "They want names! They want me to turn on the people who can help me get my career back when all of this is over. No one likes a traitor, June! What studio will want to cast a lying snitch no one likes or trusts? What actor will want to work alongside one? I'd never get another role. Never!"

Tears began to sting the corners of Melanie's eyes. With her years as an actress, she could have summoned faux tears if she'd wanted to, but these were real. Being a movie star was the only career she'd ever dreamed of having.

June looked at her thoughtfully for a moment but then shook her head. "But we don't always get to have what we want, no matter how much we want it. No matter how much we might even deserve it."

Melanie wanted to scream in the direction of the barely open window; yell Elwood's name to see if he'd come to the glass, raise the frame, and speak to her. She didn't care that she might wake the entire street. She turned her head toward the upper story, and June must've thought she was actually going to do it.

"Fine. I'll ask him for you," June said. "I'll let you know later if he has any advice for you."

"Later will be too late! I need to know now. They're calling me this morning."

June again took in a breath and let it out slowly. "Then I'll go in now. If he's awake I'll ask him. If he has anything to say to you about this, he can tell me, and I can tell you."

"Please just have him call me. Why can't he just call?"

"Because he won't right now!" June shouted. "All right? He can't. You're not the only person in the world with troubles. Now please just go back inside your house and if he has something to say, I'll let you know."

June spun away, opened the patio door, and stepped inside her house.

The air around Melanie instantly became hushed.

She suddenly remembered Eva was standing next to her. "I'll take that cup of coffee now."

The two of them went back into the house.

Melanie paced and smoked as she drank her cup of coffee, waiting for June to call her. She drained a second cup the same way. When she could no longer put it off, she hopped into the shower. Done only minutes later, she toweled off quickly, opened the bathroom door, and learned from Eva that June had stopped over with a note while she was under the spray.

"Of course she had to come then," Melanie grumbled as she took the small, folded piece of paper from Eva.

She read it. She took a seat on the closed commode and read it a second time.

And then a third.

> *All I can tell you is the truth will reveal itself, Melanie. It always does. You can bring it into the open yourself now if you want or you can wait for someone else to do it. Right now it's your choice. But in the end, it will eventually find its way out.*
>
> *You must live with what you decide however, so be sure you can.*
>
> *Elwood*

3

The call from a member of the House Un-American Activities
Committee lasted only ten minutes, if that. When Melanie
phoned her lawyer afterward, Walt told her the interviewer had
merely been fishing.

"Fishing? Fishing for what?" she'd asked.

"To see if you'd be helpful. The HUAC doesn't have anything on
you except for your close relationship with a suspected communist."

"Of course they don't have anything. Because there's nothing to
have."

"Except for what you know and who you saw, Melanie. They'd
like to have that."

The interviewer hadn't wanted to question Melanie on politics.
What mattered was who she'd seen with Carson Edwards. Who
were his closest friends? Who did he spend the most time with?
And what did they talk about?

The conversation had been short because Melanie didn't answer
the man's questions with specifics. She'd answered them the way
Walt had told her to. With ambiguity.

"You were on a sailboat with Carson Edwards in April of this year. Who else was on the boat, Miss Cole?"

"I don't recall. They were Carson's friends."

"You don't recall?"

"I'm afraid I don't."

"You're an actress who routinely memorizes hundreds of lines of script and yet you plan to tell this committee you can't remember a few names?"

"I remember what I want to remember. I want to remember my lines in a script."

"Who was with you and Mr. Edwards at the Trocadero the last time you were there?"

"I don't recall."

"And would you give that same answer under oath, Miss Cole?"

She'd shivered before answering. *"I don't recall who was there, sir."*

The man had told her she had not helped her case. If anything she'd made her predicament worse. Walt had told her the interviewer might say something like that if she refused to name names. Her heart was pounding when she hung up.

She couldn't wait to talk to Elwood to see if she'd done the right thing. The thing he would have done had he been in her shoes.

Melanie reached for the handset of the phone and dialed the Blankenship house. After eight unanswered rings, and thinking she'd rung the wrong number, because she knew June was back inside the house, she hung up and dialed the number again.

No answer.

That made no sense. Elwood didn't answer the phone much these days, but June did unless she was out. But she wasn't out. It was only a little after eight in the morning.

She put the phone down and headed for the front door, calling out to Eva, who was washing up her breakfast dishes. "I'm going over to Elwood's. They're not answering. I want to make sure they're okay."

She stepped across the grass, aerating both her lawn and the Blankenship's with the heels of her pumps. She was dressed in a champagne-hued linen skirt and emerald green silk blouse that someone had once told her matched her eyes perfectly. The blouse, which had cost her more than she'd ever paid for a simple shirt that buttoned down the front like any other shirt, had been bought during the all-too-short window when she had money.

She reached the Blankenship porch and rang the doorbell. "June?" she called out. "June, it's Melanie. Are you all right?"

She waited a moment and then pressed the doorbell again, twice this time. "June! Are you two okay?"

Still no answer.

Melanie pounded on the door with an open palm. "June! Elwood? Are you all right? Should I call for help?" She jiggled the locked doorknob. "Are you hurt? Do you need a doctor?"

Finally there was the sound of a turned lock and the door opened. June stood at an awkward angle, as if miming a Quasimodo pose.

"What do you want?!" she spat angrily.

Melanie was taken aback by this uncharacteristic greeting. In the five months Melanie had lived next door, June had only ever been poised and polite. Her wonder, however, was quickly replaced by concern.

"I phoned here. Twice! I wanted to talk to Elwood about my call. You didn't answer. I thought something terrible happened to one or both of you. I was worried."

A second or two slipped by before June seemed to revert to her usual neighborly civility.

"I . . . I couldn't get to the phone. I've hurt my back and so I couldn't . . . I just decided to let it ring, that's all. I'm fine. We're fine."

Melanie peered at her. "What do you mean you hurt your back?"

"I was doing some gardening this morning," June said dismissively, "and I guess I pulled something. I'm sure I'll be fine." The woman winced as a spasm of pain shot across her spine.

"You don't look like you're going to be fine."

"It's nothing."

"I can tell it's not nothing. How are you going to take care of Elwood like this?"

June's tone turned gentle. "It's kind of you to worry, but I'll manage. Thanks for coming over to check."

She started to close the door but Melanie put out a hand to stop her. "You hurt your back digging up Elwood's roses, didn't you? Does he know you were out there doing that?"

"Excuse me?"

"Why were you out there digging in his rose garden, June? He told me he doesn't like anyone to touch his rosebushes but him. Not even you. Why were you doing that?"

June studied Melanie for a moment before answering. "Elwood has his challenges. You already know this. He's not been able to go outside lately to tend to his roses. So I do it. And I do it when he's asleep so it doesn't alarm him."

"But you were digging them up. Moving them around. My mother never did that with her rosebushes."

"Well, this is California, not Kansas, so—"

"Nebraska."

"What?"

"I'm from Nebraska."

Another cramp appeared to leap across June's spine and she bent forward in a rush, nearly losing her footing. Melanie reached out to steady her.

"Here, let me get you to the couch." Melanie stepped inside and began to slowly move June toward the living room. The downstairs rooms were empty, near as she could tell. Unless Elwood was around the corner in the kitchen, perhaps.

June gritted her teeth in pain as they walked. "I can do it."

Melanie ignored her and continued to lead her farther into the room, then helped June lower herself to the couch. Once she was situated, Melanie turned to the staircase that led to Elwood's bedroom and office and then back to June.

"I insist you let me send Eva over to give you a hand. You can't possibly take care of Elwood like this. You wouldn't make it up the first step to his room."

June gazed at the staircase, too. "He won't want a stranger in the house. It will upset him."

"Then let me help," Melanie said. "I'm not a stranger. And it's not like I have anything else to do."

"He won't want that, either."

"Too bad, dammit. It's either Eva or me."

"El's having a really rough time right now and I—" June began but Melanie cut her off.

"Elwood's having a rough time? *Elwood* is? Have you looked at yourself in the mirror? Is he even coming downstairs these days? Will he be able to get his own meals? Or is he going to be up there starving himself to death while you writhe around on the couch?"

"We'll be fine," June sputtered.

Melanie made a move toward the staircase. "Elwood?"

June sprang off the sofa with a yelp. "Will you please just leave us alone?! Please? This is not your problem. We will manage just fine. We always have. I'd like you to go now."

Melanie turned back to her. "You call this managing just fine? Elwood's not been outside in *years*. Have I got that right? Years! How is that managing just fine? That is not normal."

They were words Melanie had been wanting to say for weeks. June made it seem the way she and her brother-in-law lived was perfectly acceptable. Maybe the march of time had made what was not normal normal to June, simply because it was what happened every day. But it wasn't normal. Healthy people didn't live the way Elwood was living.

"Look," June said carefully, as if she'd heard Melanie's unspoken thoughts. "I understand Elwood's condition. *I* do. I've been caring for him since you were still in bobby socks. Now, please: Go home."

Melanie stood silent for a long moment. "So you admit he's sick. You admit there's something terribly wrong with him."

"That's not what I said. I—"

"You said I don't understand his condition. Explain to me what I don't understand."

"He was in a car accident," June said wearily.

"I know about the accident."

"It was bad, all right? Someone got killed and he was at the wheel. He felt responsible. It . . . it messed with his mind. His sense of safety. Home was the only place he felt safe after that. And he doesn't have to answer to you for the way he feels. You're not family. We barely know you."

Melanie was quiet for several moments as she took June's words in.

"That may be true," Melanie said calmly when she finally spoke. "But you need help. And, yes, I've only known Elwood a little while, but he's the only friend I have right now and I care about him. You let me send Eva over until you're better or I'm calling whoever it is that makes sure caregivers aren't causing more harm than good. There's got to be somebody to call. A county person or something. I'll find out who it is and I'll call them."

June's eyes flashed anger and she opened her mouth to perhaps tell Melanie to go to hell but then shut it.

The woman closed her eyes for a second to formulate better words, no doubt.

"I'm sorry," June said a moment later. "You're right. I do need help. No one's ever offered and frankly Elwood wouldn't have allowed it. And I never really needed it before. I know I do now. You may send Eva over to let me talk with her. If I feel she's a good fit for us I will allow her to help me with the meals and housekeeping and such until my back is better. And I'll need to know how much to pay her."

"You don't have to pay her anything."

"I insist."

"No, I am saying you really don't have to pay her anything. I have her for six hours a day nearly every day. I don't create many messes. She never has enough to do. You'll be doing us both a favor, honestly. You can have her for half the time. Noon to three. Okay?"

"Who is paying for those six hours a day?"

Melanie's eyes narrowed the slightest bit but she went on as if the question hadn't been asked. That was none of June's damn business. "I'll send her over at twelve." Melanie turned for the door.

"Is she a trustworthy person, this Eva?" June asked.

Melanie pivoted back around. "She doesn't snoop if that's what you mean. She does what she's asked to do without any questions. You won't have to lock up the silver, either. And if Elwood doesn't want to see her, he doesn't have to. She can set a tray outside his door."

31

"And where is she from?" June asked. "I can tell she's not from around here."

"She's from Poland. A DP. She lost her home and her family—I guess everything—in the war. The American government brought her over back when they were doing nice things for people instead of destroying them like they are now."

"How? How did she lose everything?"

Melanie shrugged. "I don't know. I've asked her a couple times. I don't think she likes to talk about it. Noon, then. Okay?"

"All right."

Though the conversation seemed clearly finished, Melanie lingered on the welcome mat. She wanted so very much to talk to Elwood. She was about to ask, very kindly, if she could have just five minutes of his time, when June picked up on the reason for her hesitancy to leave.

"So. How did your call go?" June asked. "Elwood . . . he'll want to know."

So. There was to be no short visit. At least not today. "You can tell him I didn't give them anything. What they really wanted were names and I said I couldn't provide any."

"What kind of names did they want?"

"The names of Carson's friends. His acquaintances. Anyone I had ever seen with Carson even if I had never heard them speak about anything political. But I promised Carson I wouldn't do that to him. Or his friends. So I didn't."

"That's very generous of you. Considering what it's costing you."

"Those men in Washington don't control the blacklist; Hollywood does."

"But aren't the studios paying attention to who is eager to clear their name and who isn't? That's what I've read in the papers."

Melanie bristled. "I've been given no promise that spouting out names will clear me. Besides. If I go back on my promise, I'll have nothing. Absolutely nothing, and Carson would never forgive me. I'd have to go crawling back to Omaha. I'm not doing that. This hell I'm in can't last forever. It can't. I've done nothing wrong."

In the next second Melanie recalled the words Elwood had written to her earlier that morning: *"You must live with what you decide . . ."*

"Were those men happy with you telling them nothing?" June asked, intruding into Melanie's thoughts.

"No."

June didn't say it, but they both knew this meant nothing was going to change for Melanie. Not presently, anyway. She'd remain on the blacklist. Perhaps for a long time.

4

Eva was surprised by Melanie's request that she head over to the Blankenship house at noon but wasn't put off by it. Most days she'd done all there was to do at Melanie's by noon anyway, and she spent the rest of the workday dusting shelves that weren't dusty, cleaning windows and mirrors that weren't smudged, vacuuming rugs that yielded nothing, polishing furniture she'd polished the day before. Her only reluctance in helping out at the Blankenships' was that she was somewhat nervous about being around Elwood Blankenship, the man who never left his house.

Melanie told her there had been a tragic car accident years ago; that Elwood had been driving and someone had been killed. That event had changed him. Transformed him into someone who did not venture out anymore. Apparently this inability to step outside one's own house happened sometimes to people who'd suffered a great trauma. There was a name for the condition, Melanie had said, but she could not remember what it was.

Eva could halfway understand Mr. Blankenship's response to this immense tragedy in his life. She was familiar with immense tragedy. What she'd liked most about her new life in America was that she was far, far away from everything that had happened to her, and if she was honest, being inside the same house as a man who'd dealt with disaster by shutting himself away from the world concerned her. Would she be reminded again and again of what she'd lost when she heard Elwood Blankenship moving about behind a closed door or when she cleaned his bathroom or as she prepared a lunch tray for him?

Melanie wasn't sure she would even see Elwood, but what if she did? What if she had to serve that meal and witness firsthand the haunted look she'd seen in her own eyes?

Then again, maybe it was time to see if she could bear a hearty visible reminder that the world could be a cruel place. Maybe it was time to gauge her resilience. How did a person know how strong they were if their strength was never tested? And didn't she want to know if she was free of the ghosts of her past, even the ghosts of those she had loved?

Yvonne had said only yesterday that it was time for Eva to shed the weight of her old, sad life. Eva wasn't getting any younger, Yvonne had said. Eva was still pretty, still had a lot to offer—whatever that meant. Yvonne was newly single, in her late forties, with a plump figure, and had raised two sons. And while she'd inherited a great-aunt's tiny Los Angeles house, she didn't see herself anymore as desirable. Eva, however, was still a catch.

"Let me fix you up with my friend's little brother," Yvonne had said. They'd been outside in Yvonne's postage stamp backyard, and Eva was taking her freshly dried laundry off a clothesline. "He's nice and about your age. And he needs to come back from a heartbreak, too. Just like you."

"I doubt he is just like me," Eva had said, reaching up to unpin a washcloth.

"I mean," the woman had continued, "he's been dealt a difficult hand, too. The gal he was engaged to suddenly decided she was in love with someone else. He was devastated. I'm just saying he knows the loss you're feeling."

Does he really? Eva had wanted to say. *Does he know what it's like to watch the one you love and who loves you be led onto a transport truck at gunpoint? Does he know what it's like to watch your father and brother and the man you love be taken from you and sent to the gulag while all you can do is drop to your knees in anguish, helpless? Does he know what it's like to be told you will never see them again and to have those who told you this be absolutely right? Does he know what that's like?*

But Eva hadn't said any of this to Yvonne. She had no plans to tell anyone any of that, ever. All Yvonne knew was that Eva had lost her home and family in the war, as well as Sascha, the man she loved. That was all Yvonne knew. That was all Yvonne would ever know.

So Eva had placed a folded pair of slacks in her laundry basket and said she wasn't sure she was ready.

"C'mon, Eva," Yvonne had pressed. "Didn't all that happen a long time ago? The war has been over for a decade. And you had to have been only a teenager when you lost this fellow you cared for, right?"

Eva had instantly remembered a conversation she'd had with the woman who'd slept across from her at the third DP camp, and this woman saying something along the same lines but with far less compassion—as though when she'd pledged her love to Sascha at fifteen she'd known nothing about love or the world.

She'd already known quite a bit about the world at fifteen. Too much, her father had once said. And Sascha had not been some fleeting childhood crush. She had loved him with every fiber of her being. He, though only seventeen, had loved her. And Sascha hadn't left her for someone else. He had been taken forever from her. This heartbroken friend of Yvonne's was not like her in the least.

"I'll think about it," Eva had said. But she'd not thought about it at all.

When she was ready to leave Melanie's for the day and head next door, she found the actress standing by the front room picture window, staring at the Blankenship house.

Melanie had been moody since returning from June and Elwood's. She'd changed out of her nice skirt and blouse into everyday clothes—pedal pushers and a lemon-yellow twin set—but she didn't relax. If anything, she was more on edge since her chat with June, more so than even after she'd hung up with the government man.

Something was bothering her; that was clear.

When Eva reached the front door, Melanie turned from the window and reached out to stop her from opening it.

"I need you to do something when you're over there." Melanie looked to the Blankenship house and then back to Eva. "I want you to make sure Elwood is okay."

"Okay?" Eva echoed.

"I want you to find a way to talk to him."

Melanie's tone was solemn. Anxious. As though she was afraid for the man.

"About what?" Eva asked.

"Just make sure he's not being, I don't know, kept away from people."

"What . . . what do you mean?"

"I mean I want you to make sure he's not being held in his bedroom against his will."

A chill swept through Eva. "Why do you—" she began, but Melanie interrupted her.

"Because I haven't seen him in a few days, that's why. I haven't heard his voice. I haven't seen his shadow cross in front of the window in his room. I haven't heard him cough or sneeze or call June's name and we've all had our windows open because it's been so warm."

"But . . . she brought over that note he wrote this morning," Eva said, the chill intensifying.

"Yes, but how do I know *she* didn't write it?"

Was Melanie being serious? A sudden image of June coming at Eva with that garden shovel filled her mind, and, despite the absurdity of it, she felt the color drain from her face.

Melanie must have seen her pale.

"Look. It's probably nothing," Melanie said quickly. "Probably just my imagination. But I want to make sure, okay? I seriously doubt you'll be in any danger. Just open his bedroom door and peek inside. I'm positive June can't make it upstairs right now. She'll never know you've done it."

"But what if Mr. Blankenship yells at me when I open his door?"

"He won't. He's not that kind of person. Apologize for the interruption and then ask if there's anything you can get for him. Or do for him. See what he says."

"And . . . what if"—Eva swallowed—"what if he's not in his room?"

"Get back here and I'll call the police."

"Shouldn't you call the police *now* if you think—"

"And tell them what? I haven't proof that anything bad has happened. Everyone knows Elwood Blankenship never leaves his house. C'mon, Eva. This isn't that hard. I would do it if June would let me do what she's letting you do. Surely you've done far more difficult things. You *did* survive a war."

The observation stung even though it was spectacularly true.

She had done far more difficult things.

"All right," she said.

"If you see anything amiss, you come back here right away."

June Blankenship was slow to answer the door when Eva rang the bell. When it finally opened, June was bent to one side and her face was pinched in obvious pain. The pinned twist at the back of her head had loosened and tendrils of her hair, flecked here and there with gray, spilled about her neck.

She looked helpless, in pain, and quite incapable of chasing her through the house with the garden shovel.

"Hello, Mrs. Blankenship," Eva said. "I am Eva." She wanted to sound friendly. She hoped she did.

"Hello. And please call me June. Come on in."

Eva was shown into a living room. Slightly open venetian blinds tossed rods of light across a sofa under the front window. Its leather was creased and dull but in a pleasing way, as though hours upon hours had been spent enjoying its ampleness. Throw pillows were scattered about the seats and back, and a matching armchair with the same tired but welcoming look was angled next to it. The magazine-covered coffee table, end tables, and floor-to-ceiling built-in shelves surrounding the fireplace gave the room the look of an aging university library—at least how Eva had always imagined one. Framed artwork of seascapes and African savannas and fox hunts hung on the walls. A dry bar with etched crystal tumblers and decanters hugged one corner, and a floor lamp and yet another leather armchair—this one tufted and with a tall back—sat in another corner. A small console television set sat across from it, and a hi-fi topped with three framed photos stood against the wall directly across from the sofa and next to a doorway that presumably led to a kitchen and dining room. Several record albums were strewn across the floor in front of the hi-fi as though one of the

Blankenships had recently wanted to listen to some music but couldn't decide which album to place on the turntable. Half a dozen cat toys were tossed about the floor. A thin layer of dust lay on all the shelves and tables, and a barely there scent of tobacco completed the decidedly masculine ambience, all of which calmed her.

The room looked comfortable but dated, as though everything Eva could see had been purchased years ago.

"Sorry about the dust and clutter." June waved a hand over the room. "We—I assist my brother-in-law with his scriptwriting. And we've been busy on a new one. Very busy. I was going to tidy this room up today. But I hurt my back this morning."

Eva didn't know how to respond to an apology to a housekeeper for a messy house. She said nothing.

June stared at her for a moment. "Please have a seat," she finally said.

Eva took a chair and June gingerly set herself down on the sofa. The seat cushions squawked as she took her place.

"I suppose Melanie has told you I take care of my brother-in-law," June began.

"Yes, ma'am."

"You don't need to call me ma'am, just June, please. I don't know if you've ever seen Elwood from the window or out in the backyard—back when he was going out in the backyard—but my brother-in-law is a very private person. Did Melanie tell you that?"

"Yes."

"He doesn't like strangers, Eva. He's rather fragile and I need you to understand that if I'm going to be able to let you in the house to help me. It's important that you do not attempt to invade that privacy. His rooms upstairs are the only world he has right now. I will allow you to clean his bathroom and vacuum the stairs and his office but I do not want you disturbing him up there when he's behind a closed door or shut up in his bedroom. Do you understand this?"

The sense of calm wavered a bit. "Yes."

"Thank you."

"And . . . and what about meals? Shall I be putting something on a tray and taking it up?"

"No. No, you don't need to do that," June said quickly. "Neither of us, uh . . . eat much for lunch, and breakfast is easy enough for him to take care of on his own. We eat dinner early, so perhaps you can make something simple just before you go that we can heat up? When he knows you are gone he will come down and eat it. But only if he knows you are gone."

"I understand," Eva said, wondering how Melanie was going to take those instructions. Eva might not make it upstairs at all this afternoon.

"All right. That's good," June said, as though checking off an item on a list. "Now then, about the work. Do you have any questions about cleaning this house?"

"I have cleaned many houses."

"And may I ask where you have cleaned houses? Not just here in the United States?"

"No, not just here. I emigrated four years ago. I worked in West Germany as a maid before."

"But you are not . . . German?"

"No. Polish." The lie had grown much easier to say since Eva had arrived in Los Angeles, where no one bothered to try placing her strange accent. "When the war ended, I was living in West Germany, though. Near Munich."

"How was it that you were near Munich when the war ended?"

"The Reich brought in forced labor from all the countries they

41

occupied." That line had never been a lie and had always been easy to say.

"Oh. Yes, I see," June said. "And you could not . . . you could not return home to Poland after the war?"

Again the practiced answer fell from her lips. Also not a lie. "There was no home to return to. No one to return to."

"Ah. I'm so sorry. That is very sad."

"Yes."

"And how do you know English so well?"

"At the DP camps we were expected to find work. I was able to get a job as a maid with an American woman who had married a German man. She offered to teach me English."

"Well. That was very nice of her."

An image of Louise Geller flitted across Eva's mind. A happy one. But a tortured one replaced it almost instantly and Eva reflexively shook her head to dispel it.

"That wasn't nice of her?" June asked.

"No. It was. She was . . . very kind to me."

A lull fell over the conversation, as though neither one of them knew what to say next.

"Would you like me to get started?" Eva finally asked.

"Yes. I suppose so. Thank you for doing this. Melanie rather insisted."

"I am happy to help."

"It's just until my back is better."

Again, silence stole across the living room. Eva supposed June Blankenship had never had a maid in her house before and didn't know what to do with one. She glanced at the staircase that led to the upper story and Elwood Blankenship's bedroom.

"Is there something for your brother-in-law that I can do right now?"

June looked to the staircase, too. "He's resting now. He had a rough night, I'm afraid."

Eva contemplated this answer for a moment and June's silence. "Would you like me to begin here? In the living room, then?"

"Oh. Yes. Yes, that would be good. The dusters and vacuum and such are in the hall closet."

Eva rose from the chair. June made no move to get up off the couch and Eva realized she would likely have to clean up this room with June sitting there watching her. She retrieved the feather duster and Electrolux from the closet and returned to the room. There was no sense in vacuuming until the floor was cleared.

"The record albums?" Eva asked. "Would you like me to put them away?"

"Oh. Yes. They go in the cabinet under the hi-fi. The magazines on the floor there go in that basket in the corner. The newspapers can be thrown out."

Eva knelt down and began pulling the record albums together. The Blankenships liked classical tunes. And jazz and big bands. Liszt. Bach. Benny Goodman. Thelonious Monk. Glenn Miller. The Andrews Sisters.

June spoke into the silence. "So do you like it here in California?"

"Yes, thank you." This is what Americans expected her to say in answer to this question so she always said it.

"It must be very different from Poland."

"Yes."

"Do you miss it? I'm sorry if that's none of my business. I just . . . We were mostly sheltered from the war here. We were never pushed out of anywhere. Do you mind my asking if you miss it terribly?"

Eva looked up. She'd been asked this question before but those other times the askers had been simply curious. The tone of June's voice was different. Eva couldn't quite name the sentiment behind the question. It was almost as if June needed to know if one could lose everything and still be happy.

"I do miss my home. And my family. But I know I cannot return to what is not there. I have them in my heart, though."

June was silent for only a few seconds. "It must have been awful. What you went through. You must have been very brave."

Despite the sound of admiration in June's voice, Eva shrugged. She had never thought of what she had done or endured as having anything to do with bravery. "I was whatever I had to be."

June nodded thoughtfully. "Hmmm."

Eva opened the hi-fi cabinet doors. A long row of albums greeted her, all in alphabetical order. She replaced the records in like fashion and then reached for the feather duster as she stood. She began to dust the top of the hi-fi, picking up the framed photographs as she did so. One was of a much younger June in a light-colored suit and veiled hat. A corsage of orchids was pinned to her lapel. She stood in between two men of smallish stature who looked very much alike and who were also several years older than June. Both were dressed in dark suits and ties, and both wore boutonnieres. The three of them had their arms around each other's waists and everyone was smiling.

"That's me and Frank on our wedding day. With Elwood," June offered from the couch. "Elwood gave me away. Frank is the one on the right. He and Elwood are twins. Not identical but everyone could tell they were brothers back in the day. Their looks were the only way they were alike, actually. Frank was outgoing, spontaneous, lots of fun to be around, a bit reckless sometimes. And Elwood? The exact opposite. Quiet, careful, and happy to be at home by himself, even before the accident. But that doesn't mean people don't matter to him. Or that he doesn't care about them."

This last sentence June said rather wistfully.

"You look very happy in this picture," Eva said.

June smiled. "I was. That was 1939. The world still seemed like a wonderful place back then, like all our troubles were behind us. At least here in the States it did."

"But you are a widow now?"

"For the last five years. Frank had a heart attack on the studio backlot where he was working. He was a set builder at Warner Brothers. That's where we met. I worked with the cutters."

"I don't know what that means."

"The film editors. They take the day's footage and cut out all the bad takes and loop together the nice ones. The director comes in at the end of the day and views just the good parts. I was the cutters' secretary and girl Friday. Their go-to girl. Anyway, Frank was only fifty-three when he died. His father had a heart attack in his fifties, also. Frank and I were already living here with Elwood, and I . . . I just stayed on to continue to care for him. I was happy to do it. Relieved, actually. Frank and I didn't have our own place anymore. And by then this house felt like home."

"Elwood never married?"

June didn't answer right away. "He dated a number of women way back when," she finally said. "But no. Frank always said Elwood was awkward around ladies. A bit of an odd bird. I don't know that I would say that. He was never awkward around me. In any case, when Frank died, all Elwood and I had were each other. I wanted to stay; he needed me to stay. So I stayed."

Eva could see so easily that grief cloaked June's words. She was still mourning a great loss. And the loss still seemed fresh, as though it had only just happened.

"I am sorry your husband died," Eva said.

"Thank you. Were you . . . married over there?"

"No. But I loved someone. Lost someone."

They were quiet as Eva looked at the other photos. One was of the two brothers in army uniforms from the Great War. They were both smiling—Elwood slightly but Frank was beaming.

"They served together," June said, now in a somewhat brighter tone. "In France and in the same regiment. They were only twenty. So young. Frank took a bullet during an advance and it was Elwood who dragged him to safety all the while getting shot at himself. Frank would have died if he hadn't. At least that's how Frank would tell it."

The last photo was of Elwood in shorts and sunglasses, standing in a desert landscape with a camera around his neck.

"That's El in Palm Springs. He has a little bungalow there. He's done very well for himself. He was nominated for an Oscar once; did you know that? Frank was always so proud of him. I would have been jealous had I a sibling who had so much talent. But not Frank. He would talk about his brother's achievements to anyone who would listen."

As Eva replaced the last photograph, she noticed there were no baby photos in the room, no portraits of tots in rompers or school photos of adolescents.

"Did you and Mr. Blankenship have children?" Eva ventured, shyly. Hesitantly.

A soft sigh escaped the woman on the couch. "We wanted to but after trying for a while we found out the wounds Frank sustained in the war messed with something essential. To fathering children, I mean."

Eva wished she hadn't asked. "I'm sorry."

June shrugged. "Frank and I found other ways to be happy."

At that moment from above them came a soft thud. It sounded like a shoe dropping to the floor, perhaps. Or a small ashtray getting knocked off a bedside table onto a rug.

Or maybe a cat jumping down from the top of a highboy.

Eva looked toward the ceiling and the second floor. So did June.

June cleared her throat. "Elwood must be awake."

Eva turned back to the frames, noticing how in the wedding photo a young, smiling June had her head tilted to the side, toward her brother-in-law, and she sensed great affection among the three of them.

Eva didn't know what to make of the sound she'd just heard. She took her time straightening the frames to see if there would be another thumping sound, followed by another, which could perhaps be taken as a cry for help.

But the upstairs was quiet.

When Eva stepped out of June's house a couple of hours later, Melanie dashed out to meet her, looking over at the Blankenship house to make sure June wasn't at her own picture window, watching.

"Well?" she said when she reached Eva.

Eva shrugged. "June didn't want me to go upstairs today. But I did hear Mr. Blankenship moving about up there. And I don't think . . . I don't know. June seems genuinely nice."

Melanie frowned as though she wished June had seemed like a lunatic.

"She said Mr. Blankenship is having a bad spell and doesn't want to see anyone right now," Eva continued.

"I know what she's saying about him," Melanie replied quickly. "But tomorrow I want you to try again. And the next day and the next until we know for sure. I just want you to see him, Eva. I don't care what you heard or how June seems. I'm telling you, something doesn't feel right."

5

Melanie didn't hear from Carson that day until well after midnight New York time.

She'd assumed he'd want to hear right away how her phone conversation had gone that morning and that he'd call before heading to the theater for wardrobe and makeup. When her West Coast afternoon passed without the telephone ringing—the quick calls from her lawyer Walt and then Irving had taken place just minutes after she'd hung up with the government man—she'd then expected Carson to phone her from inside his dressing room immediately after curtain call.

But he'd gone back to his rented Chelsea apartment before picking up the phone to call her. Melanie didn't know if that was because he really did trust her not to spill names or because he'd called Walt much earlier that day to see how it had gone.

This latter notion annoyed her. She wanted Carson to want to hear from her what that man had asked her and what she'd said in response, not from Walt who wasn't even on the call. She spent the early part of the evening before Carson called telling herself it was because he trusted her, even though she didn't quite believe it.

Melanie was in bed sipping a martini, worrying about Elwood, and watching *The $64,000 Question* on the little TV set in the bedroom when the phone finally rang.

"Hey, doll." Carson's voice was smooth, deep, and sensual, as if in character and reading from a script.

"Hey." She'd wanted to sound nonchalant but then quickly realized she'd answered on the first ring. Damn.

"So. You doing all right?" he asked.

"Sure. Are you? It's a little late back there, isn't it?"

"I'm always keyed up after a show; you know that." He laughed as though she'd forgotten something everybody knew about Carson Edwards.

"No. I mean, I thought I'd hear from you before now."

"I wanted to call when we were both alone, and could talk as long as we want, and say whatever we want."

At these words Melanie felt a pang of longing. Carson hadn't been back to see her since his show opened in October, and she missed him. She missed his hand on the small of her back when they were out or that same hand on her knee as they sported about Hollywood in his convertible. She missed the sex, too, but it was his little attentions she missed the most. Carson Edwards had a way of making someone feel like they mattered to him, like his life had more meaning because they were in it. Deep down she knew it was probably all just his forward-facing persona and had little to do with how he really felt about her, but she didn't care what she knew deep down. She missed being held, embraced, kissed. Touched. Elwood Blankenship telling her to distance herself from Carson's affections was easy for him to say; he obviously didn't need anyone.

"I wish you were here." The words fell too easily off her lips. She knew in an instant they were exactly what Carson wanted her to say.

"So do I. But the show's doing well. They're already saying it's going to be held over. Maybe into the spring even."

She took a sharp breath at this response of his. He'd met her deep yearning for him with news about the show. His show. His show that was keeping him gainfully employed on Broadway while her career languished. Carson seemed to sense what she'd really needed at that moment was for him to say he longed for her, too. It was a mistake he probably didn't make often.

"But I will miss you terribly of course if that happens," he said.

"Will you?"

"Absolutely. Now, tell me how your day went, hmm? I want to hear all about it."

She hesitated before answering as she could tell in his tone that he wasn't all that curious. "But you already know how my day went, right? You talked to Walt. Hours ago."

"Melanie."

"What? You already know. That's why you could wait until now to call me."

"Mel."

"What?"

"Yes, I already talked to Walt. But he only gave me details. Information. The gist of what was said. And what wasn't said. That's not what I care about when it comes to you. I want to know how *you* felt about that phone call. I want to know how the day was for you, not how it was for that man in Washington. I couldn't care less about him."

Melanie let those words sink in. Maybe he actually meant them. She wanted to think he did.

"I kept my promise to you," she said. "They wanted names and I told them I didn't have any names to give them."

"I know you did. I don't need you to tell me that. You're not that kind of person."

"What . . . what kind of person?"

"The kind of person who would subject people you barely know to accusations of treasonous activity just because they know me."

"You mean like what happened to me."

"Well, yes."

"I'm not a communist, Carson."

"Of course you're not."

"Are you? Elwood said I should probably assume you are. Should I?"

"Elwood? You mean Blankenship?" The timbre of his voice took on a slightly rattled edge. "Elwood Blankenship doesn't know me. I've never even spoken to the man. You've been talking to him about this?"

"I've been asking him for advice now and again about what I should do. You're not here."

"But you already know what you should do. What you are already doing. Saying nothing. Because you know nothing."

"Then why am I on the blacklist, Carson? I know nothing and yet I am on the blacklist. No one in Hollywood will hire me!"

"I am on the blacklist, too. Nobody in Hollywood will hire me right now, either."

"But you don't have to live like I am living. You're working. You're acting. And you're rich."

"I got lucky, Mel. You know that. If I didn't have a good friend as the director of this play, I probably wouldn't have a job right now, either."

Tears of frustration had sprung to her eyes, and she blinked them back. "That man told me it's likely the committee will sub-poena me to testify, Carson."

"I'm sure he said that just to scare you."

"You don't know that! They have summoned others."

"Hey. Let's not jump ahead of ourselves, doll. Okay?"

"I don't want to spend the rest of my life on the blacklist!" Her voice sounded panicked in her ears. "I won't."

"You won't have to," he said calmly. "I promise."

Melanie wanted so very much to believe him. It had taken her five years of fruitless auditions and disappointing callbacks and seconds-long walk-ons in low-budget films to finally be asked to screen-test for a major film for a major studio. It was, in fact, Carson who had seen her in *The Seven Year Itch*—in which she spoke one line, just the one—and insisted she be tested for the role of his love interest in his next film, *This Side of Tomorrow*. She'd excitedly called her parents in Omaha when she was chosen for the part, and then had to assure them repeatedly she wasn't going to have to take her clothes off and that her looks weren't the reason she got the role. Before she'd hung up she told them MGM was paying her for one film as much as her mother made in an entire year teaching un-grateful fifth graders. She quit her day job at the glove counter at The May Company the very next day and sent her parents an ex-travagant box of French chocolates a week later for their wedding anniversary.

In the weeks before the premiere of *This Side of Tomorrow* and during its run in the theaters and even afterward, MGM all but insisted Carson and Melanie be seen together. The studio heads were convinced that not only was the film going to be a hit but that there was a chemistry between Melanie and Carson they were relying on for future films. This confidence, which Melanie felt every time she was on the sound stage or on location, was exhilarating.

If that wasn't wonderful enough, the months on the set and on Carson's arm, and even in his bed, had been nothing short of magical.

She'd found measures of happiness after that one disastrous relationship with a talent scout whose only aim had been to get her naked. But none of the men she'd dated since had the charm or the class—or the money—that Carson did. None of them made her feel desired like he did. When the movie premiered and Carson ushered her down the red carpet like she was the headlining star rather than him, she'd never felt so valued.

Her parents had in fact changed their tune when the film was released and their Omaha friends and neighbors began raving to them about it. Her parents had gone to see the film—twice, like many people had—and they admitted how wonderful it was to see Melanie's name on the big screen like that even though Kolander was her real last name, not Cole, and how convincingly she had played her part, and how very dead she looked in that crashed car. It was scary how real it looked.

Melanie had thanked them. Said she was glad they enjoyed the movie enough to see it twice. Told them the makeup people were exceptionally good at making someone look lifeless.

When Melanie had hung up with her parents, she realized with a start that she finally had everything she wanted. And more. After so many long, hard years of working and hoping and yearning, she had it all.

She would later think of that shining moment in her life as a beautiful but fragile dream, one capable of being torn in two with just a word.

Because it had been. With just a word.

Blacklist.

"Let's talk about something else," Carson said now, so gently, so persuasively. "Tell me what you're wearing. Or not wearing."

Ten minutes after they'd hung up, Melanie realized Carson hadn't answered her question.

She'd asked him if he was a communist and he'd dodged it.

6

Melanie awoke in the middle of the night and lay in the dark for a long time before sitting up in bed and reaching for a cigarette.

Her words to Carson from their conversation hours earlier echoed in her head, over and over.

I don't want to spend the rest of my life on the blacklist!

And his reply back to her. *You won't have to. I promise.*

They were the same words that had kept her from falling asleep after she'd hung up the phone and were now keeping her awake because the truth was Carson could not promise such a thing. The blacklist was out of his hands. He had no control over it. None of them did. And it had already been around a long time.

She was still in high school when the list first materialized. Her father announced at dinner one night that the names of ten Hollywood writers and directors were now on a do-not-hire list. They were the same ten men who'd refused a congressional request to testify before the House's Un-American Activities Committee—a committee formed when Melanie was even younger, just seven, in response to the ballooning dread that America had been infiltrated by communists who wanted to turn the Land of the Free into a Soviet state.

But Melanie Kolander, as she was known then, wasn't paying a great deal of attention to the so-called Cold War. Indeed, her idea of the war against cold—beginning every October in Nebraska and lasting through Easter—was the battle to stay warm and fashionable until the snow melted and she could wear pretty shoes again. Her schoolteacher parents, Wynona and Herb, felt knowledge of current events was important, however, and many evenings they tried to engage Melanie and her older brother, Alex, in dinner conversations about world affairs.

Especially as they related to the evil empire that was the Soviet Union.

Melanie found those discussions depressing, useless, and of little importance to her daily existence. Life in Omaha went on week to week as if there was no threat lurking in the shadows. Moscow was a world away, as was its malevolent reach. And for heaven's sake, the terrible war in Europe and the Pacific was over. Couldn't people just enjoy peacetime when they'd worked so hard for it? What bothered sixteen-year-old Melanie that November day more than the threat of a Soviet takeover was that she'd been promised Alex's bedroom when he went away to college. Her brother had been at the Cleveland Institute of Music three months already—on a full scholarship that her parents were outrageously proud of—and yet Melanie was still in the little room at the top of the stairs instead of in the big one.

And yet, even so, she was missing her brother terribly. Alex was no fan of table talk about world affairs, either, but he did love a good debate. Melanie had long admired Alex's pluck—and his insights. Her older brother was also wildly gifted on the violin—an instrument he'd once told Melanie he actually didn't care for and that it was hard to be so good at something you didn't like—but she knew Alex had a clever mind in addition to musical ability. And he wasn't afraid to tell it like it is, so the saying went. Or to play the devil's advocate just for the fun of it. On an evening just before Alex had left for Ohio, when the dinner conversation had again wound its way to the monstrous enemy across the globe, Alex had reminded Herb and Wynona that the U.S. and Russia had been allies in the last war. Herb replied that the wartime alliance had been entirely strategic. The two vastly different countries merely had a common goal at the time: to defeat Germany.

"We were temporarily united against a common foe," Herb had said, in his flannel-soft voice. "We weren't allies; we were allied."

Alex had said that was the same thing. Herb said it wasn't. They went happily back and forth with neither one conceding until Wynona finally ended the contest of wills with offers of seconds on cabbage rolls.

It actually wasn't until after Melanie had arrived in Los Angeles to try to make it as an actress after one year of college—a decision Herb and Wynona hadn't been happy about—that she recalled her father having told her several years earlier that there were communists in Hollywood.

She'd been in a crowded hallway, waiting to be called in for her first real audition, when she remembered. Another young woman in that collection of hopefuls mentioned the blacklist—by then in its fourth year—and Melanie heard her mother's voice in her head, asking Herb if he was sure about there being communists in Hollywood. That didn't make any sense. What did actors and actresses know about politics? What did they care about politics?

"It makes perfect sense," Herb had replied back then. "And we're not talking here about just actors and actresses but the writers and directors, the very people who are creating what people watch. It's a perfect way to influence the American mindset and way of life. Through the arts, you see."

He'd tapped the day's newspaper folded at his elbow on the table and then shared that ten writers and directors had been subpoenaed to testify and they'd refused. The Hollywood Ten, as they were being called, had been found in contempt, fined, and now faced jail terms. And shockingly, a number of movie stars had flown to Washington the month before to protest the hearings before which their colleagues had refused to testify: Humphrey Bogart, Lauren Bacall, Danny Kaye, and John Huston, to name a few.

"And that's not all," Herb had said. "The studios—all the big ones, mind you—have responded to this unpatriotic audacity with a blacklist. All ten names are on it."

Wynona had nodded as she plopped a dollop of mashed potatoes on her plate. "Serves them right."

"I quite agree. Bogart and Bacall and the rest should count their lucky stars their names aren't on that list, too," Herb had replied, and Melanie asked what a blacklist was.

Melanie's father had been pleased with her interest. "It's an informal register of people who aren't to be trusted, supported, or employed. A blacklist means these men won't be able to find work anywhere in Hollywood. Actions like theirs must have consequences, you see. You can't blatantly disrespect and disregard all that America stands for and expect to carry on as usual. Anyone who hires these people will find themselves on the blacklist, too."

"But . . . but what did they do?"

"I told you, sweetheart. They were summoned to testify before Congress and they refused."

"No, I heard that. I mean why were they asked to do that? What did they do?"

"They'd been identified as having communist ties and proclivities and they were summoned to address those allegations."

"So . . . they hadn't actually done anything?"

"What they did was refuse a summons. The accusations against them are quite serious, Melanie."

She'd wished Alex had been at the table that night because the conversation moved on to another topic, and Melanie felt like there was more to be said but she didn't know what questions to ask. Alex would have known. And Alex would have asked them.

Clever, unafraid Alex . . .

It was Alex whom she really wanted to talk to now, there in the dark of a Malibu house that wasn't even hers.

Not Carson.

Not poor, damaged Elwood Blankenship.

Alex would know what she should do the next time the Washington witch-hunters came calling.

Alex would know.

Too bad she had no idea where her brother was.

Six years had passed since Alex Kolander had dropped out of college and run off with the girlfriend known to Melanie and their parents only as BJ. She'd heard from her brother only a handful of times since. There had been a postcard from Alex from London not long after he first disappeared telling Melanie all was well and to tell their parents not to worry.

The police had used that postcard to try to convince Wynona and Herb that their son hadn't been kidnapped or sold into servitude or been hit on the head to wander the streets forever as an amnesiac.

Melanie could guess and perhaps even understand why Alex didn't want their devastated parents to know initially where he was. He had walked away from a full scholarship. A full scholarship!

Alex probably hadn't wanted to bear the weight of their parents' immense disappointment. But Alex had abandoned Melanie, too, when he ran off with BJ. And to maintain that distance from all of them for six years? That part she couldn't understand.

When Melanie's movie had come out—was it really only eleven months ago that her name was up in lights?—she was sure Alex would see that she had indeed finally made it and would want to reunite. There had been only a few scattered moments of connection up to that point. A phone call or two. A couple letters.

But there had been no word from Alex when the film released. No flowers delivered. No telephone call. No telegram. Not even a postcard from anywhere bearing a simple *Congratulations* or *I told you you'd make the big time.*

Perhaps because he *had* told her. He'd always believed she'd get to Hollywood someday and find her destiny there.

Melanie knew then, propped there in the darkness against a stranger's bed pillows, that this was the reason she hung on to Carson even though he did not love her.

Even though he could not help her.

Even though letting him pay her rent, her lawyer's fees, her grocery bill, and her housekeeper was a bad idea, just like Elwood had said it was.

Carson was all she had.

Her Hollywood friends, if that's what they had been, had deserted her. What was it her housemates Nadine and Corinne had said when they asked her to move out? *We know you wouldn't want us to jeopardize our own acting careers. We'd do the same for you. Of course we would . . .* She didn't have that sweet shared house in Hancock Park anymore or any savings to speak of—she'd already blown through much of what the studio had paid her to make the film.

And she couldn't go home. Her mother and father were appalled by the accusations that had landed her on the blacklist, despite her tearful insistence she was innocent. Her parents were convinced—because they'd feared it all along—that a naïve Melanie had mixed with the wrong crowd, aligned herself with bad company who had promised her success. Herb and Wynona had believed from the get-go that moving to Hollywood was a terrible idea, not because Melanie was a terrible person, but because it was a terrible place.

But it wasn't too late to come home to Omaha and return to her abandoned university studies, they'd said, perhaps a better major this time around?

"Everybody makes mistakes," her father had written in his last letter. "If we can learn something from them, they're not a complete waste, are they? Come home and we'll help you get back on the right track."

She *wouldn't* go home.

A delicate tube of ash fell onto Melanie's nightgown from the cigarette she was holding but not smoking. Melanie flicked it off, and it came apart and fell to the floor beside the bed, shapeless.

She ground out the cigarette in an ashtray on the nightstand and turned on the lamp. She sat up, grabbed her wristwatch, and squinted to make out the tiny hour and minute hands.

Four a.m. and she was wide-awake.

She may as well just get up and make herself some coffee.

Melanie rose and walked over to the chair by the window where she'd tossed a thin robe. Through the sheers she could see that someone was awake next door as well. Lights were on downstairs at the Blankenship house and also on the back patio, just as they had been early the morning before. Melanie pulled on the robe and made her way to the sliding doors in the living room, opening one quietly. The air was still unseasonably warm and dry. If Elwood was perhaps in his backyard, she didn't want to scare him back inside. She still wanted to speak with him since asking Alex for advice was nothing short of impossible. Elwood was the next best. And she still wanted to make sure he was all right.

Melanie stepped out into the sultry night, walked across the barely dewy grass to the fence, and peered through the fence slats, as Eva had done.

But it was not Elwood in the Blankenship backyard.

It was June. She was sitting in her pajamas at a scrolled metal table on the patio, a tumbler of melting ice and amber liquid at her elbow. A fountain pen rested between her fingers, which were poised over a tablet.

The hand that held the pen was frozen in place inches above the paper, as if the words just wouldn't come.

"Can't sleep?" Melanie asked.

June jerked in her chair and immediately put a hand to her back. "Oh. Melanie. You startled me."

"Sorry. I couldn't sleep, either. I thought maybe Elwood was out here."

"It's just me."

"You working on something?"

June gazed down at the tablet of paper. "Just helping Elwood with the screenplay he needs to finish. It's . . . uh, been hard for him the last few days. As you can imagine. I was just noodling on some ideas for him."

Melanie looked up at Elwood's window. The shade was down and the room within was dark. June glanced up there as well.

Melanie brought her gaze back to her neighbor. "I guess Elwood is sleeping okay tonight?"

June regarded Melanie before dropping her eyes back to the tablet in front of her. "Nice that one of us is, hmm?"

Melanie took another step forward, bringing her body as close to the fencing as she could. "I'm actually quite worried about Elwood." She watched June carefully as she waited for a response. It came quick and effortlessly.

"Well, you don't need to worry, Melanie. He won't always be this way."

"How do you know?"

"Because I've been caring for Elwood for a long time."

"But maybe this time it's different. Maybe this time he actually needs people around him, rather than the other way around. I mean, it's not like you're a doctor."

June tucked in her bottom lip and then gathered up the tablet, pen, and glass, and stood, grimacing as she did so. "That's true, but it's not like you are, either. And while both Elwood and I appreciate your concern, the decisions he makes regarding his personal life are none of your business. They're not even any of my business. Besides. You have enough to worry about with your own troubled life, don't you?"

The question stung and left Melanie momentarily speechless.

"You know," June added when Melanie said nothing, "I think I might try to get in a few hours of sleep after all. Before Elwood awakes. Good night."

While Melanie was still trying to formulate a reply, June turned from her and went inside the house, closing the patio door softly behind her.

DECEMBER 18, 1956

7

In the week that Eva had been helping June she had, among other things, made several meals for Elwood Blankenship, washed and dried his laundry, cleaned his bathroom, and tidied his writing room, which was upstairs and across the hall from his bedroom—the door to which she had never seen open.

She hadn't minded the extra work, though Melanie's charge to find out if Elwood was being properly treated wasn't ever far from her thoughts. Unlike Melanie, June—who spent most afternoons on the sofa with a heating pad—had truly needed help with the house. Eva had even offered to come in on Sunday, not one of her usual working days. She hadn't gotten bored once or found herself at any point cleaning a room that was already clean.

In truth, she liked working for June, despite the lingering question of whether all was well inside the Blankenship house. She liked the recipes June had her make for Elwood's meals, written on spotted, fading recipe cards that had belonged to June's grandmother. She liked the music June listened to. She liked the loved homeyness of the Blankenship furniture and décor.

She liked Elwood's cat, Algernon, who often sidled up to her to rub his whiskered face on her ankles—an unexplainable phenomenon to June. The cat apparently usually excelled in grouchiness and in swatting earrings and water glasses off tabletops.

And Eva could not help but like June, too, who, though in obvious pain, didn't complain about it. She didn't complain about anything.

It was hard to imagine June was the kind of person to intentionally harm someone. Eva had witnessed firsthand the kind of person who could do that.

Yet every afternoon when Eva left the Blankenship house, Melanie would catch her before she headed down the hill to the bus stop to ask her if she'd actually seen Elwood. Every afternoon she told her no. For all her lovely qualities, June was adamant that Eva not bother Elwood. At all. The couch where June spent her afternoons offered an unobstructed view of the first half of the stairs that led to the second story. Eva went up those stairs only the few times June told her to, and if she'd tried to contact Elwood through his closed bedroom door, June would have heard it.

But Eva did tell Melanie she'd seen evidence that Elwood was moving about the house during the many hours she wasn't inside it. Socks and underwear lay tousled in his laundry hamper. Damp towels hung on the rungs in the upstairs bathroom that he used. His bedroom slippers lay askew by the back door. Pipe ash rested in the tray that sat on a little table by the corner armchair. Two dirty dinner plates from the night before were always sitting in the kitchen sink when she arrived, along with two wineglasses, two coffee mugs, two cereal bowls, and two spoons. Two of everything, really, waiting to be washed.

"That doesn't prove anything," Melanie had said on Day Three.

"You need to try Elwood's bedroom door before June's back improves and you're done there."

"She told me not to disturb him."

"For heaven's sake," Melanie said in an exasperated voice. "Elwood is not some kind of madman who can't handle seeing a stranger! He just doesn't go outside. And it's not a disturbance to ask someone if there's anything you can do for them."

So on the fourth afternoon, and while June was sitting on the couch with pages of Elwood's current screenplay to proofread, Eva did attempt to make contact from the hall side of his bedroom door, behind which she heard the sound of a radio playing and the whirring of an oscillating fan. She tapped on the door as lightly as she could and said softly, "Mr. Blankenship? Is there anything I can get for you? Mr. Blankenship?"

There'd been no answer.

With a trembling hand and a whispered prayer she'd tried the doorknob. It would not turn.

Melanie hadn't liked that when Eva told her this an hour later.

"But maybe he couldn't hear me knocking or my voice," Eva said. "I had to be quiet or June would've heard me. He had music playing and there was a fan on in the room, too. I could hear it. And if he really doesn't want to be disturbed, he would in fact lock his door, wouldn't he?"

"You need to try again tomorrow," Melanie said. "Wait until June is going to the bathroom and is behind a closed door. Knock louder."

Eva said she would try.

But by that next day, the fifth day, Eva was beginning to wonder if the problem wasn't that Elwood Blankenship was possibly locked behind his bedroom door and perhaps chained to his bed.

It was that Elwood Blankenship wasn't inside that house at all.

Yes, there were plenty of dishes stacked in the kitchen sink for two people. Yes, there were his clothes in his hamper. Yes, his office chair was often pulled out, there was paper waste crumpled in the little trash can under his desk, and freshly typed pages routinely lay in a little folder by the typewriter. Yes, his opened mail lay strewn about and there was the pipe ash and the slippers . . .

But she never heard the creak of floorboards above her.

Never heard the toilet flush upstairs.

Never heard a cough or a sneeze or the clearing of a throat coming from the second floor.

Never cleaned razor leavings out of either bathroom sink. Not one whisker.

Never caught the faintest whiff of shaving cream or toothpaste or foot powder or any kind of odor at all in Elwood's bathroom.

If the telephone rang and the person on the other end of the line wanted to speak with Elwood, June didn't go upstairs to ask him if he'd like to take the call. Her standard answer was that her brother-in-law was indisposed and could she give him a message, even though the afternoon calls were becoming more frequent.

But the most telling observation? Elwood's clothes and towels that Eva had twice been instructed to wash didn't smell or feel like they'd been worn or used.

Eva had cleaned many houses in which men resided. She was familiar with the daily residue of their existence. There was nothing about the Blankenship house to indicate that a man lived inside it, only signs that a man once had.

She knew Elwood's departure had to have been recent—sometime after she'd overheard him speaking to Melanie earlier that month from an upstairs window.

But she also knew how unlikely it was that he had left the way most people leave a house: by getting into a car or taxi or even just by walking away from it. Elwood had made a practice of not stepping outside his front door. It had been nearly a decade since he'd been anywhere, she'd been told.

Eva spent the entire afternoon of the fifth day pondering if it was possible Elwood had suddenly decided he needed a change of venue and had called for a midnight taxi when the cover of darkness could perhaps mimic the feeling of being inside a closed room. Maybe a longing to see some of the world again had outweighed his longstanding desire *not* to see it.

But then why would June feel compelled to lie about that and go to such elaborate lengths to give the impression he was in the house? Wouldn't it be a wonderful sign of improvement if Elwood Blankenship had finally left his house? Wouldn't June be celebrating her brother-in-law's triumph rather than hiding it?

It made no sense. Elwood's absence didn't seem possible, except for one explanation that seemed too absurd to consider.

The rose garden. The shovel. The wee morning hours.

When she imagined telling Melanie any of this, it sounded ridiculous—as ridiculous as Melanie thinking June was keeping Elwood a prisoner in his own house.

Because June did not seem like a terrible person. She came across as kind and caring. Not only that, but Eva was fairly certain June loved Elwood in a deeper way than just as his sister-in-law, and maybe had for a long while. It explained why she continued to care for him after she'd become a widow. Eva could see it in the way June talked about Elwood and when she looked at his photograph on the hi-fi, at his slippers by the back door, and even at his pipe in its tray. It was a look of longing, as though June *missed* Elwood. Somehow, the Elwood she had long loved was gone from her life. Eva knew that look. She'd seen it in the mirror every morning since she was fifteen. Elwood's absence was not something June was happy about.

Because June loved him.

The mood inside the Blankenship house was a heavy mix of sadness and longing.

Eva could feel it.

It was a feeling with which she was all too familiar.

But it still didn't explain where Elwood was.

"I want you to remember, Little Sparrow," Eva's father had whispered in the last few seconds before the men of her neighborhood were taken, "that there was a time when we didn't have to run or cower or hide. We were home and weren't afraid. We will find each other again in that same kind of place. But right now you must run."

It was late August of 1941. Eva was a few weeks shy of her sixteenth birthday.

His next words were a quick command to Irina Prinz, Sascha's weeping mother, to pull her away from him. A Russian soldier had unshouldered his rifle and was using its barrel to push Eva's father toward a large truck and a misshapen queue of other men. Her brother Arman was also being prodded to that terrible cluster. Sascha was apparently already in it, though because of the crowd she could not see him.

The men were all ethnic Germans, just like her father, Arman, and Sascha were, and the truck they would be forced to climb aboard was bound for the Saratov train station. From there they would ride like cattle for hundreds upon hundreds of kilometers until those who survived the grueling trip reached the gulag, a wasteland of numberless labor camps near the Arctic Circle, and from which, it was said, no one ever returned.

The soldier yelled at Papa to move, and Eva caught a glimpse of Sascha in the group of men at the truck. She untangled herself from the arms that held her and dashed toward him, screaming his name. The next moment she was on the ground, and the side of her head felt as though it had burst open with the piercing light of a thousand stars.

Arms came around her again, pulling her back, pulling her away, the light of those stars becoming less brilliant with every tug.

Irina, still weeping, was dragging Eva from a second soldier who'd rammed the end of his rifle stock against the left side of her head.

When her vision fully cleared, the now-loaded truck was being thrust into gear to drive away with its human cargo. Irina and Sascha's little sister, Tanja, were huddled beside Eva for the moment on the warm pavement just outside the glass factory with other weeping wives, mothers, sisters, and daughters.

"They will be coming for you," Eva's father had murmured to Irina just moments earlier. "They've already taken the men from the neighboring towns on both sides. Today or tomorrow, they will come for the women and the children; everyone else in the neighborhood. Don't stay here, Irina. Take Tanja and Eva and go . . ."

Germany had declared war on Russia, and Stalin wanted ethnic Germans living in Russia nowhere near the advancing armies of their ancestral countrymen. Never mind that the Volga Germans like her father, brother, and Sascha had been self-governed Russian citizens for two hundred years. Deportation to labor prisons and resettlement camps at the farthest reaches of the empire would take care of any possible collaboration with Hitler's forces, Stalin had reasoned, and if they died along the way, so be it.

Eva and her father and brother had just sat down to breakfast when they suddenly heard shouts up and down their street, pounding on doors, cries of distress, and commands in harsh Russian for the men in the neighborhood to assemble in front of the glass factory at the end of the block. They had five minutes to pack a bag. Anyone disobeying this direct order risked being shot.

Papa and Arman had been eating the oatmeal Eva had made; she'd been cooking for her father and brother since Tante Alice had passed away when she was twelve. She'd loved that part of her life. Sascha had whispered to her once that she was a better cook than his mother, and she'd adored him for saying it even though she did not think it was true.

"Can they do this?" Arman had asked after the soldiers banged on their door, verified his and Papa's identities, and personally announced the edict. Arman was only a few months shy of his eighteenth birthday, plenty old enough to be included in the roundup of sixteen and older.

"I . . . I think so," their father had answered.

"So we have to go with them?" Arman's eyes had been wide with alarm. "Where?"

"For how long?" Eva asked.

"I'll find out," Papa had said. "Stay here. Pack a bag, son. Eva, you pack mine. I'll be right back."

With shaking hands, Eva had placed Papa's pajamas, clean socks and underwear, a change of clothes, a comb, a toothbrush, and her mother's framed photo—which had been on her father's nightstand for as long as she could remember—into a travel bag. Because they'd not had time to eat, she hurried into the kitchen and put the remainder of yesterday's loaf of bread inside the bag, along with two small apples and a wedge of cheese. It was at that moment she realized if all the men and older boys were being taken, that meant Sascha would be taken, too.

Sascha, who lived three doors down, had long been Arman's

best friend. Eva had grown up with him and his sister, Tanja, who was four years behind Eva in school. When she was much younger, Sascha had joined in with Arman's roguish teasing, running from Eva with glee when she tried to play with them. But that was when they were children. Their feelings for each other changed when Eva was thirteen and Sascha fifteen. Six months earlier they'd pledged their love to each other and secretly vowed to marry when Eva was old enough.

The thought of losing Papa and Arman to an unknown future was bad enough; losing Sascha was unthinkable. She was to spend the rest of her days with him. He was her destiny. Where he went, she was meant to go.

Eva had dropped her father's bag and run to the door, throwing it open to dash over to Sascha's, but her father had been returning to the apartment that same moment and his frame filled the door-way. Behind him on the street Eva could hear women crying, babies wailing, men shouting.

She had fallen back a step as her father stepped inside.

Papa's gaze had sought Arman standing in the small living room with a rucksack over his shoulder and cap askew on his head.

"They are taking us to a labor camp, Arman," Papa had said, his voice empty of strength and falsely calm. "I don't know for how long. Perhaps a very long time. And it's far. Quite far. It will not feel like August there. Get your coat. And get mine." Then he turned to Eva. "Listen to me, Eva. You need to stay with Irina and Tanja now. Do whatever Irina says. Promise me you will."

But Eva could not speak. Papa had not included Sascha's name in his instructions to her. They were taking him, too, just as she feared. Bile rose in her throat.

"*Spatzi*," her father had said. "You must stay with Irina now. You need to tell me you understand."

But before she could answer, an armed soldier on the street shouted into the house from the open door. *"Seechas!"*

Now!

When Papa and Arman had hesitated, he bolted up the four steps to stand on the threshold. He repeated the command with a shout.

Her father had reached for his coat over Arman's left arm and his travel bag on the floor by Eva's feet. He nodded to his son, and Arman took a trembling step toward the door.

"Follow us down to the glass factory, Eva," her father had said over his shoulder as he paused on the threshold. "We need to find Irina."

"Idti!" the soldier commanded. *Move!*

Eva's voice had finally found its way back to her throat. "What about Sascha?" she yelled, but Papa didn't answer her. He raced out the door to catch up with Irina and Tanja far ahead of them in the human flow filling the narrow street. She scrambled after him.

"You and the girls must get out of here," he'd said to Irina when they reached her and as they closed the distance to the glass factory. "Don't wait and don't sleep tonight at your apartment. Take my vehicle and put the bicycles in the back. Stay off the main roads and drive west until it runs out of gas. Abandon it somewhere where it won't be found for a while. Then use the bikes. Stick to the countryside. Speak only Russian. Finding the advancing German Army is your only hope—do you understand? You must go to where they are. Try to get to your sister's place in Kyiv. The German Army will have to take it before they try for Moscow. You must try very hard to get there. Do you understand?"

Irina had nodded, wide-eyed with fear.

This was when Papa had finally turned to Eva, called her *Spatzi*, his little sparrow—a pet name that she'd long since outgrown—and told her they would surely meet again, as though he already knew he'd never see her again this side of eternity.

A split second later the soldier was cracking her on the side of her head with his firearm and a weeping Irina was pulling her away.

When Eva discovered the awful truth weeks later that tens of thousands of ethnic Germans who were put on trains bound for the gulag perished en route or died within weeks or months of arriving, and when she finally understood there was no plan to bring the Volga Germans back home, not even if the Red Army was successful in driving out the Nazi forces, and when she learned executions of political prisoners were as regular an occurrence at the gulags as cold gray skies, what haunted her most was having been denied the chance to speak to Sascha once more before he disappeared from her life for good.

She never got to say goodbye to him.

And because of that, her love for Sascha was forever still in motion, still spinning, still reverberating within her.

Like a bell that could not stop ringing.

Eva was certain now the same was true of June with regard to Elwood. Her love for him was swirling madly around inside her, too, just as strong and real; but unlike Sascha, perhaps Elwood did not reciprocate the feelings of love.

And it was this truth that troubled Eva the most when she mentally listed all the other things she was certain of:

Elwood never steps outside the house.

If Elwood suddenly stepped outside the house, June would be happy, celebratory.

June is not happy.

June is pretending Elwood is in the house.

Elwood is not in the house.

Melanie had said something didn't feel right, but in actuality it was worse than that. Something was terribly wrong.

And Eva didn't know what to do about it.

8

"No more excuses," Melanie said as she held the front door open for Eva. "You have to see Elwood, today. And I mean physically see him. It's been a week. If you get any trouble from June, tell her I insist you see with your own eyes that Elwood is all right or I'm calling the police."

"Oh, but, Melanie, I don't think she will like that and—"

Melanie cut in. "All right, then. I'll stand in my backyard and yell Elwood's name at the top of my lungs until he opens his window or the neighbors call the police. Think she will like *that*?"

What Eva said next made no sense to her, but she found herself wanting to protect June, at least for the moment. "Let me try another way, Melanie. Please? Let me try to be her friend. Let me try with kindness?"

Eva had spent several sleepless hours the night before contemplating that list of things she knew to be true and could not help but conclude that one of three scenarios had to have taken place. Either Elwood had indeed miraculously left the house and made June promise she would tell no one, and because she loved him, she promised. Or Elwood and June had left the house together and something had happened—an accident perhaps—and only one of them came back. Or June had done something she never thought she'd do and there was no way to reverse it. Eva knew firsthand how the deepest of passions can sometimes express themselves in a regrettable act.

One of these *had* to be true, unless Elwood was in the house like June said he was and Eva was simply mistaken about the lack of real evidence that he was there. But if she discovered she was right and Elwood wasn't in that house? She wasn't yet sure what she would do then. It would go badly for June if Melanie were to come to any of the conclusions that Eva had, and Eva suddenly realized she didn't want that.

Perhaps because she understood better than anyone that life doesn't always hand a person good options at the same time it is handing them terrible circumstances.

Maybe because Eva owed her life to someone who once stepped in for her when the situation seemed just as dire.

Or maybe because not blowing the whistle was the wisest thing she could do for herself. If she said nothing and just let the situation reveal its truth down the road and in its own time, she might be able to escape what would surely be a glaring spotlight on this cul-de-sac. Maybe by the time that happened she could be at a new job and far away from Paradise Circle.

Melanie huffed a breath of annoyance. "All right," she said. "You try your way. The kind way. But if June *has* done something terrible to Elwood, your way is not going to work."

At June's, Eva looked for a way to inquire about Elwood her way, as Melanie had put it, and decided to offer to decorate the Blankenship house for Christmas. It was only a week away, though with the outside temperature in the seventies it felt more like summer. She hoped that a bit of gaiety would lighten the atmosphere in the house and maybe endear her to June a little. Decorating the house might even lighten Eva's own mood, as she'd found out that morning Yvonne would need for her sister the room Eva had been renting. She was going to have to find a new place to live at the first of the year. Trimming the house would be a nice distraction from that looming chore also, as well as afford her a chance to get June to open up about Elwood.

When Eva mentioned the idea, June frowned slightly but then seemed to quickly change her mind.

"Wait. Yes. That would be nice, actually," she said. "Elwood would like that. He has a little artificial tree in the garage made of goose feathers dyed green. It's surprisingly pretty."

She told Eva where she could find the boxes in the garage and Eva brought them in, stacking them in the living room so that June could direct from the sofa where she wanted everything to go.

Eva placed the little tree in a corner by the hi-fi. She'd seen trees like this one before. They'd been popular in Germany, and the Gellers had one. She saw it now in her mind's eye, decorated with tiny snowflakes Louise Geller had made from shiny white paper using miniature scissors shaped like a stork. For a second she heard Louise's voice singing an American Christmas carol as she hung the little snowflakes on a tree just like this one. But then she heard Ernst's voice, too—he was not singing—and she shook the image away.

Eva opened the first cardboard box of ornaments and pulled out tins of tissue-wrapped baubles, all glittery, glistening, and fragile.

"These are beautiful," Eva said.

"They belonged to Elwood and Frank's mother. They're Italian, I think. Frank was so fond of them."

Eva hung a couple on the feathery tree. "Was your mother-in-law Italian?"

"No. I think she just liked pretty things."

"Were you and your mother-in-law"—Eva cast about for the word Americans used to describe a loving relationship—"close?"

"I never got to meet her. She died before Frank and I met. The way he and Elwood talked about her, I think I would have liked her, though."

"I am sure she would have liked you, too."

June laughed. "Maybe. It would have been nice to have a mother in my life who was just a regular mom. I didn't really have one of those. My mother died when I was ten and let's just say she wasn't your typical mother." June laughed again, though this time less happily.

"Not . . . typical?"

"She was her own person, very unpredictable, I guess you could say. She didn't treat me like my friends' mothers treated their daughters. She'd let me stay up all night if she stayed up all night. She'd take me to the outdoor bars down at Kinney Pier or the dance hall or arcade long after dark, or she'd keep me out of school for days if she wanted to drive down to Mexico with someone she'd just met. Sometimes we had food to eat, sometimes we didn't. Most of the time we lived in a one-room cottage in Ocean Park, but sometimes we stayed in mansions up in the hills with men who seemed to only have first names. Sometimes we slept in a neighbor's car."

"What happened to her?"

June paused a moment before answering. "There was a terrible flu the autumn I turned ten. Scores of people died from it that year. I don't even know how many. My mother caught it and was gone four days later. I went to live with my grandmother and aunt in Pasadena after that."

"I'm so sorry. You could not go live with your father?"

"I never knew my father."

"Oh." Eva sensed immense disappointment in those five words. She at least had her father and brother and Tante Alice when her mother died.

"My grandmother was good to me; so was my aunt, my mother's older sister," June continued. "But I was never sure that I truly belonged with them. They'd been at odds with my mother. It was hard for them both when she died, I know that. But they saw me as an extension of my mother and all her poor choices, I think." June stared off into space for a moment, as if floating back to a place in her mind. "I went to secretarial school after high school. I wanted to work in the offices of a Hollywood studio because of all the movies that had kept me company on Saturday afternoons. I didn't even care which studio. I missed my mother during the rest of my growing-up years even though I didn't understand her. The cinema helped me imagine a different world, I guess. One without the ache of losing her."

June brought her gaze back to the present moment and to Eva.

"My mother died when I was eight," Eva said. "She was sick from cancer. I only have a few memories of her when she wasn't ill. They are good memories, though. My father always talked about her like she was a gift from heaven. And my brother Arman was a little older—ten, like you—when she died. Arman remembered her far better. He would tell me things about what she was like when she didn't have cancer, memories he would try to give me as if they could be my own."

"What a kind thing to try to do. You must miss your father and brother."

Eva unwrapped a glass orb striped in red and gold. "I do. I loved them both very much."

"Did they fight in the Polish Army? Is that how they died?"

Eva sat back on her heels contemplating how best to answer that question. "No. They weren't in the army."

The two of them were quiet while Eva hung two more of the ornaments.

"That one is made of walrus ivory. Elwood brought it back from Alaska," June said, nodding to a creamy white six-pointed star Eva held in her hand. "He was stationed there in the Second World War."

This surprised Eva. "Elwood served in the last war?"

"Both he and Frank did. If you were a man between the ages of eighteen and sixty-four, you had to register for the draft. And if you were under the age of forty-four you were answerable for service. I could hardly believe it when they told me. They were forty-three in 1942, healthy and prior military. Of course the army wanted them back."

"I would not have thought at that age . . ." Eva let her sentence dangle unfinished.

"I wouldn't have, either. I hated that time when they were gone. Frank served in the Army Corps of Engineers, and he said before he left he'd just be building things, that's all. As though he wouldn't be in danger. But he was, nearly the whole time. And Elwood assumed he'd get a public affairs post and sit at a typewriter all day long in some war office. But he didn't. He was assigned to Army Intelligence on the Aleutian Islands and he fought frostbite, trench foot, booby traps, and snipers while the army tried to take back the islands of Attu and Kiska from the Japanese. He could've easily come home in a flag-draped casket, too. It was hell knowing I could have lost them both. Absolute hell."

This was the moment to be certain of June's true feelings for Elwood; Eva was confident of it. But how to frame the question?

Certainly not by asking June, out of the blue, how long she'd been in love with her brother-in-law.

June would no doubt ask how Eva dared pose such a question and then show her the door.

She needed a different approach.

What if she were the first one to be honest? What if she told June the truth about herself? Perhaps June might in turn do the same.

But then again, there was risk in doing that.

And yet, as Eva thought about saying frank words that she'd not said aloud to anyone in years, an unexpected calm came over her. What was the worst thing that could happen if she told June who she really was? June could blab it to someone, yes, but there was no benefit to June in telling anyone. And June clearly had her own problems.

"May I tell you something?" Eva said, the decision made.

June's eyes widened slightly. "Yes?"

"It is something I have not told anyone."

A slight pause. "All right."

Eva considered what she was about to do, and June waited. Then she spoke.

"I'm not Polish. I've never even lived in Poland."

"Oh?" June looked surprised but not concerned. Not irritated for having been lied to.

"My people all came from Germany," Eva continued. "They were all farmers from Hessen decades ago. They left Germany with many, many others—tens of thousands—when Catherine the Great offered them land near the Volga River."

June slightly furrowed a brow. "The Volga River. But that's . . . that's in . . ."

"Russia. Yes. That is where I was born. Norka, Russia. It is where my father was born, too, and his father and his father. Eight generations. We all learned to speak Russian of course, but we always spoke German at home. We still felt German—even more so after the Revolution when things got very bad for us. And then when I was fifteen Germany was suddenly at war with Russia, see? It was not safe for Germans to be there anymore. My father and brother and fiancé were taken from me and sent away to labor camps far away in Siberia. No one ever comes back from the gulag. I fled first to Kyiv when the Germans occupied it and then to Berlin with Sascha's mother, Irina, and his sister when the Red Army was marching back to recapture it. We spoke only German to each other. Irina forbade me to even think in Russian. When the war was over I didn't want to go back to Russia. I was afraid to. A Ukrainian roommate and I were moved to a new DP camp near Munich at the start of the American occupation. We told everyone there we were Polish and that our papers had been stolen. I was given new papers that said I'd been born in Warsaw."

"But . . . you are Russian?"

Eva thought for a moment. "I don't know what I am. Sometimes I feel like I am nothing. The whole time I was in Germany I did not feel German. I know I am not Russian, either, even though I was born there."

"And you were engaged to this young man? Tell me again how old you were?"

"I did not have a ring. But Sascha and I loved each other. We wanted to marry. It didn't matter to me that I was only fifteen and he was only seventeen. I knew he was the only man I would ever love."

June was quiet for a moment while she thought. "It doesn't matter to me what nationality you are, Eva."

Eva smiled. "Thank you. But . . . all of this might matter to Melanie. You see?"

A look of understanding stole across June's face. "Oh, my. Yes, I do see. Because of the blacklist."

"I am not a communist. I never was. It was very hard for us

Volga Germans after the Revolution. That's why when the war was over people like me in the refugee camps begged not to be repatriated to the Soviet Union though it was demanded we be returned. That's why some of us lied about where we were from so that we weren't forced to go back."

"And you haven't told any of this to Melanie?"

"When I first started working for her I didn't know she was on this thing called a blacklist. And then when I learned of it, I did not know what to do. I knew if I told her the truth she would fire me, and then the agency I work for would fire me, too, because I lied on my immigration papers. They might report me and I'd get deported. Back to the Soviet Union. It would not go well for me there. I have tried looking for other employment but nothing has come of it."

"But why do you think Melanie will find out about this when no one else has?" June asked.

"I have heard her talking to Mr. Edwards and her lawyer about that committee in Washington. They all say those men are looking at who she knows. Who she spends time with. I am no one to her, and I can only hope I am no one to those men. But I am with her almost every day. For several hours."

"Yes, I see."

"I know I should quit," Eva said. "But Marvelous Maids would want to know why. I can't say why."

"Can't you just tell them you are tired of cleaning houses?"

"But what else could I do? This is the only job I have had here in the States."

"Do you have any other skills?" June asked.

Eva shrugged. "This is all I have ever done for work."

"Maybe you could train for another job."

"That takes money, yes?"

June nodded, looked away for a moment, then turned back. "Say. Do you know how to type?"

The question surprised Eva and immediately brought to mind the cheerless office in Kyiv, its rows of clacking typewriters, and the stern Wehrmacht officers plunking down documents for her to translate from Cyrillic and then oftentimes retype in German.

"I do. It has been a while, though."

"Were you fast? Accurate?"

The Nazis had demanded accuracy but she had not been fast enough for them. No one in that room had been.

"Not really."

"I could help you there. And I know people at the studio where Frank and I both worked. If you catch on and can do it fast and without mistakes, I might be able to help you get a spot in the typing pool. It's not great money, but it would pay more than a maid's wages. And then you wouldn't have to worry about this anymore."

This was the last thing Eva thought she'd get from June—help—and she stared at her agape.

"You would do that?" Eva said after a moment's pause.

"Why not? It's not your fault what happened. You didn't ask for any of this. It was a tragedy for you."

June's words clanged in her head as Eva fought for words of reply. She wanted to serve those words back to June and ask what tragedy had fallen on her that she had not asked for. And what had she done about it? Where was Elwood?

And yet . . .

She wanted far more in that moment to do something with her meaningless existence besides cleaning up the messes of other people's lives.

"June. I . . . I don't know what to say," Eva said.

"How about you finish with that tree and we can start today.

And we don't have to say anything to Melanie about any of this. When you're ready to quit you can just give your notice."

Tears of gratitude stung Eva's eyes. Here she'd wanted to cajole June into opening up about Elwood, and instead June was extending an offer of help. June was surely no callous brute.

Accidents happen. They happen. She knew this.

"I don't know how to thank you," Eva said.

June waved a hand. "It's nothing. I'm happy to do it. You're a good worker, Eva. And you don't need to worry about what you told me. I'll keep your secret. I promise. Melanie will never hear it from me."

Eva was about to say she'd forgotten what it was like to have someone show such kindness to her when the doorbell rang.

June peered out the window with its view of the driveway. She drew in a sharp breath. "God in heaven. That's Max's car!"

"Max?" Eva sat up on her knees.

"Elwood's agent. He's been calling every day. I keep telling him Elwood isn't taking calls right now." June's voice, now panicked, wasn't much louder than a whisper. "Damn him for just showing up like this."

The doorbell rang again.

Eva got to her feet. "Do you want me to take care of it?"

June stood, too, confusion etched on her face. "What?"

Eva took a step toward the door. "I can take care of it if you like."

"He's going to want to see Elwood."

"I can tell him another time?"

"But what if he insists on coming inside?" June made her way awkwardly to the door but then turned to Eva. "I think he thinks . . . that I'm . . . that Elwood isn't . . ." June did not finish.

Eva hesitated only a moment. "Elwood isn't what?"

June's countenance shifted in that moment from agitated to suddenly worn and weary, and for several seconds Eva thought she was going to spill every secret she had to be hiding. But then her features grew hard and controlled again.

"Nothing. Never mind."

"I can tell this man you are giving Mr. Blankenship excellent care if he asks," Eva said. "He can't insist on coming inside. This is not his house."

The doorbell rang a third time.

June put her hand on the doorknob, closed her eyes, and exhaled what seemed to be a calming breath. Then she opened her eyes and looked at Eva. "This is indeed not his house. It's Elwood's and my house. I'll handle it." She started to turn the knob but then swung back around one last time.

"But I do want you to do something for me," June said.

"Yes?"

"Don't let him go upstairs."

9

June swung the front door open wide.

Eva saw a man on the welcome mat dressed in a nice suit. His receding hairline was strewn with gray, and he looked angry. "What the hell, June?" he shouted.

"Hello to you, too, Max," June said.

June sounded surprisingly at ease, and the man named Max stared wide-eyed at June, perhaps stunned by her calm greeting.

"You probably should've called," June said when Max said nothing.

"I *have* been calling!"

"I mean you should have called before coming all the way out here. As I have been telling you for the last week, Elwood doesn't want to see anyone right now. He's having a rough spell. He's not up to it."

"I want to talk to him."

"But he doesn't want to see people right now, Max. Not even you. Nothing personal. It's just how he is sometimes. You know that."

Max exhaled heavily. "*This* is not how he is sometimes. I want to talk to him, June. And I'm not leaving until I do."

He stepped past June and into the entryway. Eva immediately moved behind June to stand closer to the staircase, nearly blocking it.

"Who are you?" Max said to Eva.

For a second no one answered.

"This is Eva." June finally said, a slight edge to her voice. "I am borrowing her from Melanie next door. Eva is her housekeeper but she's been helping out here because I hurt my back."

"Hello," Eva said.

Max nodded to Eva and then turned his attention back to June. "I want to see him."

"Max, I just don't think—"

"This is insane, June."

"No, it isn't. Elwood trusts me to make sure his desires are known and honored and right now he does not want company. We need to respect his wishes, Max. It's unfair of you to demand more from him than he is able to give you."

"But I need to talk to him! It's important."

"I can't force him to speak with you. That would be cruel. I won't do it."

"Damn it, June, this is no way to conduct yourself in this business. He knows this."

"And you should know better than to insist on something Elwood is not currently able to give you."

"This is not acceptable," Max said after a moment's pause. "I think it's time we got a shrink back in here. He's never been this bad. You know he hasn't."

"I've been thinking that, too," June said slowly, and Eva wondered if she was making up the comment on the fly. "But when I

91

mentioned this very thing to Elwood he said no. I think we should give him a little more time before I do something he specifically asked me not to do. And I'll have you know he's not behind on the screenplay. It will be finished on time by the end of the year, just like he promised. He knows how important it is. He works on it every day."

"What am I supposed to do in the meantime?" Max groused. "I have things I need to discuss with him."

"You could always send him a letter, you know. You have a secretary. He's still reading his mail, Max."

"I've been his agent for twenty years!"

"Yes, but maybe that's why he doesn't want to see you," June said. "You knew him before all this. Before . . . you know. The accident."

"That accident was almost a decade ago."

"For you and me, yes. But not for him. He feels it in his soul like it was yesterday, Max."

Max swiveled his head to look at the stairs once more and for a moment Eva wondered if Max might charge past her, bolt up the stairs, and kick open Elwood's bedroom door.

Half of her wanted him to. The other half was afraid something big and awful would come crashing down around them all if he did.

But Max turned back around. "I'll give you a week. One week, June. If he's not better, I'm calling a doctor myself. You tell him that."

"I quite agree, Max. I do. Let's give it until Christmas Eve, then. Or how about the day after Christmas? We don't want to make the holidays difficult for anyone, especially for Elwood, right?"

"Fine. The day after Christmas."

Max glanced up the stairs one more time before moving past June to walk toward the still-open door. "What does he do up there, holed up like a hermit all day long?" he grumbled.

"He writes, of course," June said.

Max turned halfway back around to look at Eva as he stood on the threshold. "A pleasure to meet you." He directed his gaze back to June. "If anything changes, good or bad, I want you to call me. Day or night, I don't care."

"Thank you, Max. That's very kind. And do write Elwood if you like. I promise you your letter will be read. And answered if you need an answer."

"Yeah, yeah." He stepped out.

"Oh, and, Max?" June said. "Might you let the studio know Elwood is taking some time away from the phone and visitors? Perhaps tell them he's focused on finishing the screenplay and doesn't want to be disturbed?"

Max nodded. "I'll take care of it. You take care of him. And I'm serious. If anything changes, call me."

"I promise."

Eva and June watched Max walk out to his vehicle. It was a convertible and he had the top down. It had probably been a lovely drive out to Malibu that afternoon, and the man likely wouldn't mind the jaunt back to LA now, despite not having been able to speak to Elwood. It was that beautiful a day.

When he was gone, June closed the front door and turned to Eva. "I need a drink."

Eva followed June into the decoration-strewn living room, not knowing what else to do.

At the dry bar, June opened a decanter of whisky and poured a healthy amount into a tumbler. She tipped her head back, swallowed, and then poured more. She took the glass in one hand, and with the other she massaged her back as she made her way to the sofa and sat down.

"It's true what you heard me tell Max just now," June said.

"About Elwood feeling like the accident only just happened." She took another sip of her drink and then leaned back against the couch. Her gaze landed on the half-decorated tree in front of her.

Eva moved to the sofa and sat down next to her. "What happened in that accident?"

June took a deep breath before speaking again. "Elwood was dating the woman who was in the car with him that night. Her name was Ruthie. I think they might have been in love with each other. Anyway. Ruthie didn't survive and she left behind two little boys whose father had been killed five years earlier at Pearl Harbor."

"Oh my! That's so sad."

"It was awful. El felt like he made those children orphans. He told me he'd been driving too fast and he'd had drinks before he got behind the wheel. He blamed himself for killing that young woman. It's guilt and regret that kept him chained to this house all these years. And neither of those two things left any room for him to feel anything else. That's the sad, honest truth."

"I'm so sorry."

"When Frank and I moved in here to care for Elwood we both tried, for years, to convince him it was an accident. That's all it was. But he wouldn't listen to us. And then Frank died, and he wouldn't listen to me."

"How sad."

"As sad as it gets," June said, turning her gaze to the photo of her, Frank, and Elwood on her wedding day. Her eyes were glassy, shining with ache.

For several long seconds, neither one said anything.

"Would you like me to finish with the Christmas decorations?" Eva finally said.

June didn't answer right away.

"No," she said, several seconds later. "No, I don't." She tipped her glass back into her mouth, emptying it, and set the tumbler on the coffee table. "You can finish with that later. Or tomorrow. I don't care. Let's go up to Elwood's office and see about your typing skills."

"Now?"

"Yes, now."

"You can make it to the second floor all right?"

"Well, I'm not going to race you, that's for sure, but, yes, I think I can manage."

They started for the staircase.

"Elwood won't mind my using his typewriter, will he?" Eva asked, curious to know how June would answer.

"I can assure you without hesitation that he won't."

Her tone was so final and definitive that Eva felt her eyes widen.

"It's been a very long time since Elwood has been able to write anything well," June continued. "And even longer since he's sat down at the typewriter or even stepped inside his office. I've been writing his scripts for years."

10

Melanie stood at the picture window in the front room and watched as a man in a convertible pulled up to the Blankenship house.

He got out of the car and she recognized him. He'd been at June and Elwood's before, though it had been a while. Max Somebody. Elwood's agent.

The man strode purposefully toward the Blankenships' front door.

For a long moment she wished she were sitting on the passenger side of that shiny red car with its top down, waiting for him to complete his business at the house and come back out to his car. He'd then be on his way back to Sunset Boulevard. Or maybe Beverly Hills. It didn't really matter. She'd want that passenger seat if Max Somebody was headed next to Skid Row, so hungry was Melanie for a break from the tedium of her exile.

She hadn't been back to Los Angeles since Carson had brought her to this house. Irving and Walt—and Carson, too, for that matter—had all advised her it was wise not to be seen in public, especially back in Hollywood. She didn't need the press hounding her or asking her questions and then printing things about her that weren't true and that she hadn't said, and she certainly didn't want to make it easy to be served a summons by coming back to LA.

But oh, how she missed the life she'd had to flee. No, the life from which she'd been banished! She'd worked so hard to make it. Given up so much over the last five years. Gone to countless open calls. Accepted stupid, minuscule roles she hated, just to get noticed. Allowed womanizing Neanderthals to patronize and grope and use her just so that she'd be remembered. And to have achieved the career of a lifetime after all that only to have it torn from her grasp?

Melanie pivoted from the window and then sat down under it, for no reason other than she'd not done that yet. She leaned against the wall and tipped her head back. Some days, the unfairness of it all was unbearable. Truly unbearable.

The hoopla surrounding the rooting out of Hollywood communists had been decidedly waning the last few years. Those who'd earlier worried they might be targeted surely felt safer, Carson Edwards especially, though when Melanie had started dating him, she had no idea he probably believed he'd dodged a bullet.

In the months she'd been hiding out in Malibu, Melanie had learned that when Carson's career was just getting off the ground, he'd dated a folk singer who happened to be an American Communist Party member. There was no reason Melanie should've known this; that had been eight years ago and Carson Edwards had dated a lot of people since then. He was famous for it.

But while the newest Hollywood Red Scare was indeed in decline, the studios' blacklist was still very much intact. Everyone in Hollywood knew that. If a person's name was on the list, the only way to get off was to testify before the HUAC to clear their name.

Clearing a name had become synonymous with naming others. That was something everyone in Hollywood also knew.

Carson had found out right after they'd both been blacklisted that a screenwriter whom Carson was only marginally acquainted with, who'd been on the Hollywood blacklist a long time and who was desperate to reclaim his career, had suddenly decided he'd had enough. The man wanted his life back and to be seen as a part of the solution, not the problem. He'd volunteered to testify. He'd flown to Washington and told the HUAC he'd been naïve and uninformed—for that brief time in this life—when he was a Party member. He'd gotten caught up in the crusade for equality, not just in the workplace but everywhere, but he learned quickly communism was not the answer to America's socioeconomic problems. He'd repented for his socialist leanings years earlier. Left the Party. The HUAC could ask anyone who knew him; he'd been open about his leaving. And when the HUAC had next asked him who else had been influenced as he had been by communist thinking, he named names—fresh ones—including Carson, and, by association, Carson Edwards's current love interest and his closest friends. This testifier said he had seen Carson at Party meetings back in 1948 when he was also there, and several times, not just once. And while he had publicly turned his back on the Party, Carson Edwards never had.

The controlling belief among the members of the HUAC was that there were no good reasons why an American went to meetings of the Communist Party, only unpatriotic, dangerous ones— even if said person didn't actually become a dues-paying member. In other words, it was safe to assume Carson had gone to those meetings because he'd wanted to be there.

Likewise, there was only one reason why someone like Melanie

Cole would become intimately involved with a communist thinker like Carson Edwards.

It was because, as HUAC logic went, she was a sympathizer.

Carson had gotten the phone call that changed everything for Melanie the same day the testimony of this man was made public and every Hollywood studio either read it or heard about it. Melanie was on Carson's patio that June afternoon, lounging by his pool. Their blockbuster movie had been out for six months, and the studio was putting the final touches on a new script for Carson and Melanie for a film that was supposed to begin shooting on location in Honolulu in three months.

He'd just taken a dip in the pool when he heard the jangling of the telephone, and he'd gone inside to answer it after toweling off, leaving the sliding glass door open behind him.

Melanie had heard him pick up the phone, greet one of their producers by name, and then go quiet. For the next few minutes and until he came back outside and told her what had been said on the other end of the line, all she heard were his words in reply.

"I was only dating a gal who attended those gatherings; that was it," he'd said in a peeved voice. "She was the one who brought me."

Short pause.

"I went to a bullfight in Tijuana that year, too," Carson had said derisively. "That didn't make me a matador!"

Melanie had sat up in her chaise to gaze at the half-open patio door and at Carson standing just inside in his slightly dripping swim trunks and bare feet. Bullfights? Some girl he dated? What were he and MGM talking about?

She'd watched as Carson ran a hand through his wet hair. "But I wasn't a member!"

The conversation had gone back and forth with Melanie being

only seconds away from learning that in 1948 Carson had attended multiple meetings of the American Communist Party. He had never publicly disavowed his attendance at those meetings before the HUAC. He should have. He'd had plenty of time and opportunity—and reason—to contact them and do so. But he hadn't, which suggested he was hiding who he was or at least who he'd been. He'd been named by someone. MGM's hands were tied. There was nothing the studio could do about keeping Carson employed until he also testified before the Committee and set the record straight.

"And name names, you mean." When Carson had said this, Melanie suddenly knew exactly what they were discussing, and a chill slunk through her despite the day's heat. Carson had been tagged a Hollywood communist? A ridiculous notion. Inconceivable.

"This is insane," he'd then said, as though he heard her unspoken thoughts and voiced them himself. "But I was never a member! I told you that. And who cares what I did eight years ago?"

Long pause.

"Are you nuts?" he'd yelled. "Melanie was in high school then! I didn't even know her."

And at these words, the subtle chill in her bones had morphed to ice. They were now talking about her.

For the next few seconds, Melanie had heard nothing but the sound of a low-flying two-seater plane high above her, the neighbor's poodle barking at it, and her pulse thrumming at her temples. Carson was listening, saying nothing.

Then he hung up the phone.

Time had seemed to skid to a halt as she waited for him to come back out. She watched as he mixed two martinis at the bar by the patio door, downed one, and made another in the same glass. He came back outside, the two drinks in hand.

Carson extended one of the cocktails to her but she didn't take it.

"What just happened?" she'd said, her question little more than a whisper.

He'd set the drinks down on the squat table in between the chaises and then sat down on his lounger next to her. He replayed to Melanie the half of the conversation she hadn't heard, and she listened mutely, mouth open in disbelief.

She had kept pinching the inside of her thigh as he went on, convinced she had fallen asleep in the warm sun and was having a bad dream. Her thigh became polka-dotted, and still she didn't wake up and still he kept talking.

And then he'd said it. They'd both been blacklisted.

"It's nothing, Mel. I'm sure of it," he'd quickly added. "I'll call my agent. And my lawyer."

"I don't have a lawyer," she'd heard someone say in a breathless monotone and then realized she'd said it.

"You've got nothing to worry about. You're an Omaha girl as apple-pie American as they come. You're practically a Girl Scout."

Melanie had looked down at her revealing swimsuit and painted toenails, the cocktail at her elbow and the obvious fact that she spent more time at Carson's place than her own, and said, "No, I'm not."

"So what? This has nothing to do with you. I'll fix it."

"How? How will you fix it?"

"Leave it to me. I'm Carson Edwards. I'm not some hapless idiot who doesn't know which side his bread is buttered on."

But she had heard unease in his voice, something she'd never heard before.

Carson had looked away from her and taken a long sip of his martini as he stared at the shimmering water in his swimming pool. He was worried.

And this had scared her. Ever since the day she'd gotten the role of Julia in *This Side of Tomorrow* and she suddenly had everything she'd always wanted, Carson had been the one with all the answers. If she needed advice on how to speak to reporters or bait photographers or ditch overzealous fans, he gave it. If she needed to know how to dress for an event or schmooze with the Hollywood elite or handle studio scuttlebutt, he told her how. If she needed to know what to take seriously, what to have a good laugh over, and what to simply leave at the soundstage door, he told her.

If she'd needed a voice of reason, he was it. If she needed a pat on the back, he provided it.

He had been able to do and give and be what she needed.

"What do we do now?" she'd asked.

He hadn't answered right away. She could tell he was thinking, assessing, still working things out in his head. That was good. He was plotting their way out of this. A modicum of calm had returned to her.

But when he'd spoken, he did not turn his head to look at her, and the tone of his voice was one she didn't recognize. "I really don't know, doll."

She'd wanted to scream at him then.

Hurl his pretty cocktail glass to the ground and watch it shatter.

And yet she had also wanted him to take her into his arms and tell her she didn't have to worry. Of course she was no communist. That was as laughable as saying Minnie Mouse was one. She wanted him to assure her they'd be on Oahu three months from then, just as planned, shooting the new movie and laughing about this.

Carson, however, had continued to stare at the water in the pool, at the play of light on its surface, saying nothing.

"Should I call Irving?" she'd asked blandly.

"He probably already knows but, yes, you should call him."

"Should I go home and do it?"

"Maybe you should. I have calls to make, too."

Melanie had risen from the chaise on unsteady feet. Nothing seemed real in that moment. Not the heat of the patio stones on the soles of her feet, nor the breeze plucking wisps of hair from under her sun hat, nor the heaviness in her chest.

Carson hadn't walked inside with her or helped her gather her things. She was grateful he at least came back inside the house minutes later to call her a cab.

When the car came, he opened the front door quickly, as if needing to be alone with his thoughts as soon as possible.

"I'll call you," he'd said absently.

"You'll fix this, right?" she said, desperate to hear him say this again.

"I'll find a way." His voice had been void of confidence.

Melanie had turned to step outside and then felt his hand on her arm. She looked up at him.

"Don't say a thing to anybody about this. Not to your roommates, not to the cabdriver, not to a neighbor, or your mailman, or the guy that cuts your grass. You understand, Melanie? No one. And God, Melanie, no reporters. You understand? Especially not reporters."

"Why? I've done nothing wrong."

"Because the press loves this kind of dirt. They will only want more of it. Whatever you say, they will use to create more dirt. Trust me. So say nothing. They might even be at your doorstep when you get home. Tell them nothing, Melanie. Not a word. If there are government people wanting to talk with you, say nothing to them, either, not on the phone, not to their faces. Tell them you need to consult with your lawyer."

"I already told you I don't have one. And why should I need a lawyer? I haven't *done* anything."

"Maybe . . . maybe you won't need one. I don't know. I'll find out. Just don't say anything."

She'd paused on the threshold as she looked at him, wanting again his kiss, his embrace, his assurance.

"You should go," he had said. "Remember what I said about the reporters. Just stay at home until I can figure this out, okay? You're not going to want to be out and about right now anyway. Lay low. I'll call you."

When Melanie had arrived home, the neighborhood was quiet; the sidewalks and curbs and her own doorstep were empty. No one was camped outside waiting, and her two housemates were away at their day jobs. She indulged in supposing MGM had discovered it was wrong about her having been named, too, or maybe the HUAC had realized she was not someone they needed to be worried about after all. But the relief was short-lived. By four o'clock that afternoon the doorbell had rung half a dozen times, and each time from her vantage point as she peered from behind the curtain at the front room window it looked like a reporter on the welcome mat, with a photographer standing just behind him. One of these cameramen saw her and focused his lens on her before she could duck away. That picture of a hiding-behind-the-drapes Melanie Cole would find its way to a gossip rag the following day when all of Hollywood was agog about Carson Edwards, his ties to the Communist Party, and the shocking and disastrous influence he'd had on his current love, Melanie Cole. Her dismayed housemate Nadine had brought the magazine home and shown her.

Everything about the photo and the article was wrong. She was not Carson's "current love." He didn't love her and she didn't love him. And she hadn't been hiding behind anything. She was inside her house, looking out the window like millions of other people did every day when someone rang their doorbell.

When Carson had called her the following evening, she told him what the article had said and what the caption under the photo had read. He told her to stop looking at gossip magazines and news-papers.

"But they're talking about us. About me! And none of it is true."

"And that's why you shouldn't talk to the press. Any of them. They don't want the truth from you. They want to keep the story alive. They don't care it's not a true story. Talk to them and you keep the story *they* want to tell alive. You need to trust me on this."

She hadn't cried two days earlier at the pool when the news was fresh and surreal but she cried then. Six months earlier, when the movie had come out, the gossip rags and movie magazines and news outlets had adored her. At least that's what it felt like. It felt like adoration. Tears slipped down her cheeks and fell onto the phone handset as she told Carson this. She tasted salt on her lips.

"That wasn't adoration," Carson had said. "That was greed, Mel, pure and simple. Those people just want to be where the money is. That's all anybody in this town really wants. They know if they stay close to the cash, close to what people will line up in droves to pay for, the money will start falling on them, too."

Money. She hadn't brought up the topic to him yet nor had he to her, not that he would. He had gobs of it. But how long would she last without an income? Without work? How long could she lay low and live off what remained from signing the contract for *This Side of Tomorrow*? There wasn't that much of it left, and no contracts had been signed yet for the upcoming Hawaii movie.

At the beginning of shooting, she'd been careful with what she'd been paid at signing. But Carson and pretty much everyone she knew kept asking her why she was continuing to live like an underpaid glove counter salesgirl. That wasn't who she was anymore. She'd made it to the venerated silver screen with the new film and there would be other movies to follow. Plenty of them. And as a result, plenty of money. Janet Leigh could easily command one hundred thousand dollars a film. Easily. And Melanie, who Carson said outshined Leigh by leaps and bounds, could expect the same in the not-too-distant future.

Enjoy the fruit of your labor, Melanie! Live a little!

So she had.

She'd gone clothes shopping at the expensive stores and didn't look at the price tags. She bought big-ticket jewelry, Italian shoes, had multiple manicures and massages, took taxi cabs instead of the Red Car or the city bus, bought French wine and Spanish leather handbags and Swiss confections. She purchased cashmere sweaters, silk blouses, designer evening gowns, and beaded cocktail dresses. She dined out with abandon and invited her housemates to join her when she wasn't eating with Carson. When he wasn't pampering her and treating her like a princess, she pampered herself. What her mother made in a year as a veteran elementary school teacher, Melanie spent in six months.

She had figured she had enough to pay for groceries and her third of the rent for the next two months and then that would be it. She'd be broke.

"How long is it going to be like this, Carson?" she'd asked him gloomily. "I need to know how long."

He had half laughed into the phone. "You think I don't want to know the answer to that, too?"

His flippant tone had annoyed her. This situation, if it dragged on, wasn't going to hurt him like it was going to hurt her. He was a millionaire. Couldn't he see the difference? Besides, it was because of him she was in this mess. Had he really done all he could to free her from this predicament that *he* had technically caused?

"Why can't you just do what that man did? Offer to testify and clear your name?" she had asked testily. "Do we really have to suffer like this?"

"And lie like he did? He pretty much accused me of being a card-carrying communist. And he accused you of being in bed with one. He named my closest friends in this town. People who have been kind not just to me but to you, too. People who welcomed you into their homes and onto their sailboats and at their beach cottages as my date. Roger. Stan. Al and Jeannie. Brandon and Anita. He's putting them through hell just like us. That asshole gave them names because HUAC wanted names. You telling me that's all right with you? To call out peoples' names just to have names to give?"

She'd clearly hit a nerve. And she had not asked him to lie. "Carson, look. I—"

But he had cut her off. "If I testify, you can bet your bottom dollar they will call you in to do the same. You want to list all the names of the people you saw when you were on Brandon and Anita's sailboat? Or when you went to Al and Jeannie's New Year's Eve party? Or all those times we met Roger and Stan for drinks and other people joined us? You want to list all the names of all the people I had over to my house while you were there? People who have Oscars on their shelves and the respect of everybody in this business but happened to be seen by you in my company? You want us off the list or do you want to do what's right?"

He had been angry, maybe not exactly at her, but her question had made it worse. But still.

"Well, what if some of those people actually *are* communists, Carson?" she had asked.

"Damn it, what if they are?" he'd yelled into the phone. "How you choose to think is your God-given, constitutional right as an American. Didn't you learn that in high school civics? What they are asking people on that stand is a violation of basic civil rights. Read the First Amendment. We have the right to assemble, the right to discuss political ideas, even if they aren't popular. The right to dissent if we so choose. You want to talk about who is being un-American, it's that committee. They have no legal right to ask what they are asking."

Melanie hadn't known what to say to any of this. Carson had clearly given the matter a lot of thought, perhaps long before now. When she said nothing, he took an audible breath and let it out just as loudly. When he spoke, his voice was even and controlled again.

"Do you hear what I am saying, Melanie?"

"Yes."

"Look. We need to agree on this. We need to agree that we're not going to turn on our colleagues, our friends. Right? We're not going to do it. Tell me you won't."

An uneasy silence had stretched between them when she didn't answer right away. She wished she could see his face.

"Mel?" he'd said.

"It's not that I want to, Carson. I don't. I really don't. But I need to work. I need money. I'm not like you. I don't have—"

"Hey. I'm not going to let you starve, Melanie. You don't need to worry about that. You won't have to go back to the glove counter at that department store. Not that they'd hire you now anyway. I'll take care of you. I promise."

"You . . . what?"

"I'll make sure you have whatever you need while we wait this out. Food. A place to live. And a lawyer if you need one. You just need to agree with me that we're not going to volunteer to say anything. To anyone. It's the right thing to do."

"Are you . . . asking me to move in with you?"

"God, no. That would just make things worse for you. We need to be seen together as little as possible right now. No. I mean I will set it up with my financial guy to pay your rent, your grocery bill, a lawyer's fees, and so on."

She had felt her mouth drop open. "For how long?

"I don't know. As long as it takes."

"As long as it takes?" she'd echoed, hardly able to conceive of being as dependent as a five-year-old child on Carson Edwards, and for who knew how long? It seemed distasteful. Like she was his . . . call girl.

"Unless you want to go home to Nebraska and wait it out there," he'd said.

Irving, whom she'd talked with that first day, had told her going back to Omaha for a while wasn't a terrible idea, and advised her to maybe come up with a pretense for heading back home for a spell. A sick parent, perhaps. She'd flat out refused to consider it then and had no intention of changing her mind.

"I do not."

"I didn't think so. And I'm not sure how that would look anyway. Have you talked to your parents? Do they know?"

Melanie had been putting off that phone call for hours upon hours, loath to make it. "Not yet."

"You should call them. They need to know not to speak to the press, either."

"They're in *Nebraska*, Carson."

"Trust me, if this story continues to have staying power in the news, they will find your parents. They will pay them a visit and ring their doorbell just like they rang yours. They need to know not to answer the door."

"You've got to be kidding."

"I'm not. Call them and tell them, Melanie. Okay?"

She had sighed heavily. "Yes."

"The best thing for you and me to do right now is say nothing publicly and do nothing publicly. No running away like we're guilty but not being out in the open, either. Lay low, stay low. Hide in plain sight, as they say. All right?"

Her head had pounded with an ache that made her feel like her skull was locked in an ever-tightening vise.

"Melanie?"

"Yes. All right."

They'd hung up, but rather than make the call to Omaha, Melanie swallowed two aspirin and collapsed onto her bed to lie perfectly still until her headache passed. But she fell asleep.

When she awoke a couple of hours later, Nadine was home early from her job at a boutique clothing store modeling ridiculously priced dresses for wealthy women to fawn over. She was auditioning the next day at Paramount and wanted to run through her lines. Corinne, her other housemate, was also home for the evening after an afternoon of callbacks. Melanie came out of her bedroom to grab a glass of water and found her two friends in a tight conversation at the kitchen sink that halted the second she walked into the room.

"Your parents just called," Nadine had said quickly. "They want you to call back."

"We didn't want to tell them you were asleep at five p.m. in the afternoon so we said you were in the shower. You should probably call them back," Corinne added.

"Now?" Melanie asked.

"I think they really want to talk with you." Nadine's tone had hinted of uneasiness.

"Keep it short, though?" Corinne added with a half smile. "Long distance, you know."

"I know how much a long-distance call costs," Melanie muttered, turning for the phone on its little table in the living room.

"We just know money might be tight for you right now," Corinne called after her.

She had dialed her parents' number, thinking perhaps it was actually better if they had already heard rumblings of what had happened and had called to find out from her what the truth was, because then she wouldn't have to spring this terrible, absurd development onto them from out of nowhere.

They had indeed heard rumblings, and not just rumblings. The news of their daughter's fall from Hollywood notoriety to Hollywood blacklist had been in the *Omaha World-Herald* on page five. National news. A one-column story, but above the fold. Impossible to miss.

They had been shocked and appalled, devastated, and humiliated.

"Is it true?" her mother had asked, distraught. "Are you a communist?"

"Of course it's not true!" Melanie had said. "How can you even ask?"

"Is it that Carson Edwards? Is he a communist?" her father had said from the line's other extension.

"I would certainly know if he was, wouldn't I? This is a witch hunt, Dad. That's all it is. I'm completely innocent."

"Please come home!" her mother had begged.

"I don't want to look like I'm guilty and running for cover, Mom. I'm guilty of nothing."

"Except for getting mixed up with the wrong people! A communist, Melanie!"

She had told them she had to go. Her mother was crying. Herb told her to think of her family, her reputation. Her future. She said again that she needed to go, wished them a good night, and hung up.

Melanie had stood for several long moments reminding herself that she was the victim here, not the criminal. She was innocent.

She'd done nothing wrong.

She loved her country.

She was innocent.

She needed more aspirin.

Melanie had gone back to the kitchen for the drink of water and two more Bayer. Nadine and Corinne were still there but seated now at the four-seat chrome and Formica table set against the wall.

Nadine had nodded to one of two chairs across from them.

"We actually want to talk to you, too," she said.

11

Melanie rose from where she'd been sitting under the window and watched as the little red sports car backed out of the Blankenship driveway. Max Somebody—lucky Max—was heading back to the real world. She then sauntered into the kitchen and reached for a glass out of the dish drainer.

She put her hand on the cold tap to get a drink but the next thing she knew, a shriek had torn its way out of her mouth and the glass lay in brilliant shards on the other side of the room. The hurled cup had responded as glass does when connecting with a solid surface at high velocity. Broken bits now glittered like diamonds on the floor.

Melanie inhaled a quick breath.

She'd just flung one of Mrs. Gilbert's pretty glasses across Mrs. Gilbert's sunny kitchen and it had burst into smithereens like confetti onto Mrs. Gilbert's imported Argentine tiles.

Carson had told her that the Gilberts had been advised she'd be an excellent renter. Quiet, tidy, and careful.

Quiet? Oh, yes, most of the time she was mind-numbingly quiet. Tidy? Not really, but she had Eva. Careful? What did that even mean?

A humorless laugh launched its way out of her. She was absolutely not careful, was she? She'd aligned herself with a communist.

A communist, Melanie!

And now, because she'd been careless instead of careful, she was sweeping up a glass that wasn't hers, hiding out like a fugitive in a house full of someone else's things.

She tossed the bits into the trash and imagined storming through the Gilberts' house, grabbing every breakable thing, and chucking each one as hard as she could against a wall.

It was deliciously satisfying to picture it, but only for a moment.

When the moment passed, Melanie felt only fresh defeat and hopelessness. She wasn't that person.

And this house and the things inside it meant something to someone. It felt like a prison after five months but it hadn't always felt that way. In the beginning, Melanie had been glad to have a place to hunker down in. She was embarrassed, angry, and heartbroken. Irving started bringing her cheap paperback romances to read every week, and her parents—after they'd recovered from the shock—sent her, through Irving, their already-read issues of *National Geographic* and *Better Homes and Gardens*, magazines that she would never have read before but devoured from first page to last. The packages from her parents always included her mother's award-winning butterscotch cookies and the offer of a one-way train ticket back home to Omaha.

She'd made it a point to exercise in the mornings to keep her figure—which she still did—and spent many afternoons after Eva left reading aloud the lines for every character in old scripts. Irving provided those, too—to keep her elocution and characterizations at peak level.

Melanie had been hopeful the first two months at the Malibu house, lunging for the phone when it rang, thinking Walt was calling to tell her the studios had realized her name didn't belong on that list and had taken it off. When Irving brought her mail she grabbed it greedily looking for any official-looking envelope that held within it news of her exoneration. But when fall arrived and Carson left for New York, the monotony of her purposeless days began to wear on her. She felt as though the voice of doom was whispering to her that this was her life now: hiding out in a house that wasn't hers and waiting for vindication that might never come. It took a concerted effort to not listen to that voice.

She had also begun to feel restless with the oh-so-subtle changing of the seasons. Malibu was a sleepy enclave on a twenty-mile stretch of coastline with seemingly nothing but glittering sea and sand on one side and hillsides and canyons of toast-colored chaparral on the other. In between land and ocean and canyons of wilderness were cozy sea-view houses of all shapes and sizes and not much else. A few inns and restaurants, beaches for walking, wave sets for surfing. And always the relentless pull and push of the tides, the rising and setting of the sun, and the call of seabirds. It was a place where you could forget—if you wanted to—that there were hours in a day and chores that needed doing and problems that needed solving.

Melanie had decided one afternoon in mid-October, when she could stand the boredom no longer, to disguise herself and walk the winding half mile down to the beach. It was an easy walk getting down there; the hard part, she knew, was going to be walking back home. Yet Eva walked that route every day from the bus stop on the coastal highway and never complained. She decided not to think about the uphill return trip as she set out, nor that she was having to sneak around with a truly ugly scarf tied around her head—one she'd found snooping in some of the boxes in the master bedroom closet that the Gilberts had left behind—and wearing too-large sunglasses.

When that first little jaunt had proved uneventful, she decided to try a few more.

Sometimes she called for a taxi if she didn't want to walk, and she would ask to be let out on the stretch of peaceful coast six miles away where a hundred or so Hollywood stars had their beach houses. Carson had told her that set designers had been loaned out to build the initial houses in what everyone called the Malibu Movie Colony. At the beginning—more than thirty years earlier—the Colony had attracted such stars as Charlie Chaplin, Douglas Fairbanks, Mary Pickford, and Clara Bow, first as leaseholders and then outright owners of the now famous beach property when its original owner landed in financial trouble and sold the lots.

Barbara Stanwyck had a home there now, Carson had said. And Bing Crosby, Gary Cooper, and Merle Oberon.

On another outing to the edges of the Colony, Melanie dared to go inside the Malibu Beach Café for a cup of coffee, just to see which inhabitant of the movie world she'd been ousted from might wander in. She hoped no headlining name would recognize her under the scarf and glasses. She thought she saw Paul Newman in a booth at the back that day. It was hard to be sure and she didn't want to stare or walk back there to confirm it. Melanie lingered before leaving, gazing at all the framed autographed photos on the walls of movie stars who'd eaten there. It had been a depressing evening for her when she returned home.

The day after that she phoned for a taxi again, this time to take her fifteen miles down the coast to the pier at Santa Monica. She didn't even get out of the car to get an ice-cream cone or a hot dog, though she wanted both. It was enough, at least on that occasion, to see joy on the faces of those enjoying the sun-kissed afternoon.

It was risky being out like that, though. Especially now. The man from Washington who had questioned her had advised her she might be subpoenaed. But she also knew that a subpoena had to be hand delivered. She felt safe at home in that. She couldn't be served at the house because she never answered the door. Ever. That was Eva's job. Not that the doorbell rang that often. And if it did ring after Eva left, Melanie sat in the kitchen, where she couldn't be seen, and waited for the person to leave. The few times this had happened, it was only a delivery of something she'd asked Carson to get for her.

She wasn't even sure those who had the ability to summon her even knew where she was living.

But getting served could happen easily if she was out and was identified.

All a subpoena server had to do was pose as a sympathetic fan, gushingly ask her if she was Melanie Cole, and when she said yes hand her the summons. At least this was what Carson had told her. It could happen that fast. Walt agreed it was probably best to stay out of sight.

Irving, who wanted her working again, was on the fence on this topic. Yes, he wanted her safe from prying eyes and tabloid journalists and heartless shutterbugs wanting to make a quick buck. But a summons to testify could clear her name. Get her off the blacklist. It had cleared the names of others.

After they'd coughed up names, though.

Did he want her to be hated like Lee J. Cobb, and that director Elia Kazan, and the screenwriter she'd never even met who named her and Carson and half a dozen others? Did Irving really want her to join the despised ranks of other Hollywood types like these three men who'd given up, given in, and given names?

When she'd said as much to Irving, he'd told her he didn't think she'd end up being hated. Not after a while, anyway.

It was the "a while" part that she couldn't bear.

Melanie lowered the top of the kitchen trash can after tossing in the pieces of broken glass and put the broom away. She'd have to tell Carson about the glass, she supposed.

Or maybe not.

She walked out of the kitchen into the rest of the main part of the house. It was deathly quiet and clean. Too quiet and too clean. Eva still managed to keep the place spotless even though she'd been spending only half her scheduled time at the house. There wasn't a speck of dust anywhere or a dish in the sink or a spot of soap scum in the tub or so much as one item out of place. Even the sofa pillows were perfectly situated.

On impulse she walked over to the couch, picked up two of the decorative pillows, and tossed them with vengeance onto the just-vacuumed rug. Then she poured herself a gin and tonic even though the sun hadn't begun to set—she'd promised herself from the beginning no numbing cocktails until after twilight—and walked out onto the patio. A cooler ocean breeze was sweeping up the hillside but she didn't want to grab a sweater. She wanted to feel something *new* today, even if it was a slight chill on her skin.

Melanie sat down in a patio chair, took a sip of her drink, and gazed over at the Blankenships' house. A light was on in Elwood's office upstairs; she could hear the faintest tapping of typewriter keys striking their target. It was a welcome sound. He was probably up there writing, which meant she'd let her imagination run wild. She had too much time on her hands and not enough mental stimulation and had jumped to conclusions. June hadn't chained Elwood to his bed. For heaven's sake, of course she hadn't. And hadn't Eva told her she'd been laundering his clothes? Emptying his ashtray? Washing up his dishes? Eva had been over at the Blankenships' every day, observing no evidence at all that Elwood was in danger, only that he was there, living as reclusively as one could.

She took another swallow, surprised that she was suddenly jealous of all the time Eva was getting to spend in that house. June wasn't neighbor of the year or anything, but she seemed like a fairly nice person, completely devoted to Elwood's care and his rosebushes. Melanie found herself wishing she'd taken the time to get to know her better. They might've become friends by now. And God, how she needed one. Since Carson had left, the only company she had was Eva—who obediently moved about the house like the soundless apparition they'd all counted on her being—and Irving for one hourly visit, once a week. If she'd become friends with June, she might've been able to become friends—true friends—with Elwood.

Elwood.

Melanie missed him. How long had it been since she'd spoken to him or seen his face at the window? Ten days? Eleven? No matter what June said, that was not good for a person. She'd meant what she told June last week, that she'd call a county person if she thought for a second June was neglecting Elwood. But if she had become better acquainted with June, she could've voiced her concerns in a better way, not as a threat, but more like advice from a friend who cared about Elwood's welfare.

The kind way.

Perhaps it wasn't too late.

Perhaps she could make up for the lost time by becoming June's friend now. That woman surely needed one, too. She never had other women over. Or men, either. And when she was out shopping for Elwood or running errands, she was never gone long. She probably felt isolated, too, here in this haven of a place.

The ice was melting in her drink. Melanie downed the rest and stood up. She had a fresh tin of her mother's butterscotch cookies that Irving had brought over the day before. They were buttery and sweet and slightly addicting. She could take them over to the Blankenships as a peace offering for having rattled June the week before. She could say the cookies were for Elwood, and perhaps that would create an opening for the two of them to have a discussion about him.

Maybe she could invite them both over for Christmas dinner. She'd have to have the meal delivered from a restaurant, of course, as she wasn't much of a cook. Or perhaps Eva could make something the day before that she could warm up. And if Elwood could not manage the short walk across the lawn, she could bring the food over to their house, and the three of them would have a quiet holiday meal together; and they could play Christmas carols on the hi-fi and drink mulled wine and she could have a few little gifts delivered for them to open.

Yes, she liked that plan. For lots of reasons.

Melanie went back inside the house, grabbed the tin of her mother's cookies, and headed for the front door. It was almost four thirty.

As she opened it and started to step out, she saw that June was backing out of the Blankenship garage, obviously leaving the house.

Melanie frowned. She would have to go back over later. Maybe tomorrow.

She had just begun to pivot to go back inside when she saw that June wasn't alone in the car. For a split second, Melanie thought it was Elwood at long last leaving the house.

But then she saw that it wasn't a man in the passenger seat.

It was Eva.

Her frown intensified. Eva should've finished at three. What had June been having her do all this time? And why? The last couple of days Melanie had been able to see from watching June sweep her porch and pinch off deadheads from her geraniums that her back had greatly improved. If anything, she thought June would need less of Eva's help, not more.

And why was she driving her somewhere?

Unless June had offered to drive her down to the bus stop as dusk would soon be falling.

Which was nice of her.

But still.

Why had Eva stayed so long?

Melanie watched June head down the hill and decided she would stand at the edge of her driveway until June returned from the bus stop, and then she'd give her the cookies and the invitation to Christmas dinner.

She waited longer than she thought it would take for June to drop Eva off and was about to walk over to the Blankenships' to see if Elwood might possibly open the front door if she pounded on it when headlights appeared, coming up the hill.

But the car, when it was fully in view, wasn't June's. It wasn't Irving's or Walt's or Max Somebody's. It wasn't any car she recognized.

It also wasn't headed for June's driveway; it was headed for hers.

Driving up to hers. Parking in hers.

And there she stood out in the open.

She could see in the late afternoon's low light a man in profile behind the wheel and a smaller person in the back seat: a little boy sitting on his knees, looking out the window. A devious ploy to make her drop her guard, no doubt. Who would suspect a summons deliverer would have a child with him?

Melanie turned to rush back inside the house but then the driver turned his head toward her and smiled as he shifted the car into park.

She felt her mouth drop open in disbelief.

Impossible.

The car door opened and Alex stepped out.

12

Melanie stood nearly frozen in place as Alex helped the little boy in the back seat climb out of the vehicle. He turned to smile at her.

Wearing faded blue jeans and a button-down shirt the color of apricots, Alex looked the same and yet completely different. Older, certainly, but it wasn't just the passing of time that had altered her brother. Alex had been changed by years of experiences that Melanie had no knowledge of.

And was one of those becoming a father?

A second later, Alex, while holding the boy's hand, was taking Melanie into a one-armed embrace, the tin of cookies unyielding between them.

"Nellie! Look at you. You look great!"

He smelled of lime, Lava bath soap, and salt. His light brown hair, just touching his collar and longer than she had ever seen him wear it, was scented with sea air, as if he'd just come up the hill from a lazy afternoon on the beach. He felt warm and solid against her.

Melanie finally found her voice. "I can't believe it's you."

He released Melanie, stepped back, and laughed. "We never thought we'd get here!" He looked down at the little boy. "Did we, Nick? Longest drive ever!"

"He's . . . Nick is—"

"He's my kid, your nephew, and he couldn't wait to meet you. It's all he talked about on the drive down from San Francisco. I showed him your picture in *Photoplay* when your movie came out. He insisted on cutting it out and putting it in his pocket. Carried it with him for days."

Melanie glanced down at the child. His hair—wavy and long for a little boy's—was the same honey brown as Alex's, and he had the same nose and sprinkling of freckles that Alex did. His eyes, though, belonged to someone else: a woman Melanie did not know. Not even by a photograph.

The boy was looking up at her with a shy grin.

"You had a baby?" Melanie had so many questions. So many.

Alex let out another laugh. "And here I thought I'd lost all the baby weight."

"No, I don't mean that. I'm just . . . I'm so . . ."

"I know. I'm just kidding with you. I was surprised, too, when I found out I was going to be a dad. But we've had a good time of it, haven't we, Nicky?"

The boy said nothing, but his shy grin expanded and he leaned into Alex's leg.

"Okay if we come in?" Alex asked casually. "I really need to take a piss. Nicky does, too."

"Of course. Absolutely."

"And hey. You don't mind if we crash here, do you?"

Melanie felt numb with equal parts both shock and elation. It took her a second to answer. "Not at all. I'd love to have you. For as long as you want."

"Terrific. Let me just get our stuff." He turned to the boy. "Stay here with Auntie Mel while I get our things, Champ."

Alex peeled his hand away from the little boy and walked swiftly back to the car. He reached into the back seat for a suitcase, a canvas grocery bag full of what looked like toys and stuffed animals, and a battered black guitar case plastered with stickers.

No violin.

A momentary ripple of disappointment pulsed through Melanie at the notion that the surprise visit was going to be short. The suitcase wasn't that big, little more than an overnight bag. Alex hadn't brought much with him—unless what he had in his arms now was all he had? No matter if it was. Whatever Alex or his son lacked, Melanie would find a way to get it for them. She looked down at the little boy.

"Hi, Nicky. It's very nice to meet you."

He smiled at her then, big and wide, and held up his right hand with all the fingers spread out. "I'm five!"

Alex was laughing as he returned to them. "Tuck in that thumb, Champ. You're not five until February."

Melanie reached for the toy bag to lighten Alex's load. "I'm so glad you're here. I can't even tell you how much." The isolation from earlier that day was already falling off like a tossed shawl. Tears of joy were pooling in her eyes. Yes, she had a million questions. But Alex was here. Alex.

She blinked the tears away as she led them inside the house and apologized for there being only one guest room.

"I can take the couch in the living room if you want to sleep in my room and we can give Nicky the guest bed," she said.

Alex waved the offer away. "You don't have to do that. Nicky and I can sleep in the same room. We have lots of times."

The suitcase, guitar, and bag of toys were brought into the pristine guest room, and Melanie turned on a bedside table lamp and noticed the stickers on the guitar case were from places around the world: London, Edinburgh, Amsterdam, Paris, Frankfurt, Lisbon, Rome, Florence, Madrid. So many places.

"Pretty nice digs, Nellie," Alex said, breaking into her thoughts as he surveyed the room. "Is the person who owns this place rich or something?"

Melanie didn't know much at all about the Gilberts other than they were in Cairo. Maybe Mr. Gilbert did have money. She didn't care if he did. There was more important information she was craving at that moment.

"Alex, where have you been? Where's BJ? And how did you find me?"

The questions would have kept coming if Alex hadn't held up a hand.

"How about if we have a bite to eat and I'll tell you everything. We're starving, so I hope you've got food in the house. We'd be happy with peanut butter toast. Or just the toast. Anything, really."

"Sure. Of course."

"Okay. Just show us where the bathroom is and we'll be right out."

Melanie led them to the guest bathroom down the hall and then went into the kitchen. She pulled out the beef-and-noodle casserole that Eva had put together earlier that day for her supper and put it in the oven, and then opened a bottle of red wine. She was setting the wine bottle and two long-stemmed glasses on the kitchen table when Nicky and Alex, carrying a cigar box brimming with plastic soldiers, joined her. They took seats at the table and Alex dumped the soldiers on the floor by their feet so Nicky could play while they sipped the burgundy and waited for the casserole to heat up.

"California is amazing," Alex said as he leaned back in his chair and kicked off his sandals. "Seventy-five degrees the week before Christmas! This is like paradise. I actually saw someone watering their lawn here."

"Yes, it's often warm here in December," Melanie said absently. She did not want to talk about the weather. "There is so much I want to know, Alex. I don't even know where to have you begin."

"Well, first off, you won't believe how I found out you were here," Alex began. "Get a load of this. I was in New York last week—no, more like the week before that—and I was already wondering how I was going to find out where you were living. I'd called the house where I knew you were before and—was it a Norine who answered?"

"Nadine."

"Yeah, so she answered and said you'd moved out and she didn't know where you were. Not back to Omaha, she knew that. Anyway, so I'm in New York because an actress friend of mine has a part in a play on Broadway. So she gets me a ticket and I go, and guess who's starring in the same show she's in? That Carson Edwards fella you made the movie with."

Melanie had been about to take a sip from her wineglass but she paused with the rim an inch from her lips. "You saw Carson?"

"What? No. I didn't see him. But I did see my friend after the show and we went out for drinks and she told me she's stayed over at his place a couple times and—"

Melanie set the glass back down on the table, a little too hard. A blip of crimson sloshed out of it and landed on the table. "She's stayed over at his place a couple times?"

"I guess so. Anyway, this Edwards guy told my friend you're

hiding out in Malibu. I figured this beach town can't be that big so I decided I'd come out and drive around 'til I found you. It's bigger than I thought. But we found you!"

Melanie pressed a paper napkin to the splash of red wine and concentrated on repeating the words *It doesn't matter, it doesn't matter, it doesn't matter* in her head. She didn't love Carson; he didn't love her.

She still wanted to kill him.

"You drove here all the way from New York?" Melanie said evenly, hiding her annoyance well, she thought.

"Oh, no. Nicky and I flew to San Francisco. I've got a buddy there and he loaned me his car. We drove down. Pretty drive but, damn, it's a long one."

"So you just decided"—Melanie didn't know how to finish the sentence—"that you wanted to see me? After all this time?" She couldn't hide from her voice the sting of the lost years.

"Hey. I'm really sorry about all that, Nellie. It's not like it's what I wanted."

"What exactly did you want?" It had been too many years since Alex had ditched college, run off with BJ, and practically dropped off the face of the earth, and Melanie still didn't really know why.

"What I wanted," Alex replied matter-of-factly, but gently, too, "was to live my own life and not someone else's."

"I don't understand. Whose life were you living?"

"I was living the life of that kid from Omaha who could play the violin. The kid from Omaha who was supposed to graduate with a music degree on a full-ride scholarship. The kid from Omaha who was supposed to wear a black tux the rest of his life and sit first chair at the New York Philharmonic. That's who."

"But did you have to leave the way you did?" Melanie knew her own wounds were showing through. "Did you have to leave *me* the way you did?"

Alex looked down at his wineglass and ran a finger gently around its pedestal. "I'm sorry about that, too. I was young and frustrated and if I were to do it now I would do things differently, but I can't go back and change what I did or how I did it. I knew Mom and Dad were going to flip. What they wanted for me wasn't what I wanted for myself. I didn't want to live with their huge expectations anymore and I definitely didn't want to live with their huge disappointment."

"They were heartbroken, Alex. They love you and they've missed you very much. We all have."

Alex looked up at her. "This isn't about love, Melanie. This is about liberation. You can love a bird but still keep it in a cage when all it wants to do is fly free. Birds are born to fly. Even the ones you love."

"But for seven years? You couldn't come back to us? To me? Not even to visit?"

"Look, I knew what I had done. I knew how much I had hurt people. How much I hurt you. I didn't want to face it. It was easier to pretend I hadn't hurt anybody and just stay away."

So you were a coward—that's basically what you're saying? Melanie wanted to say, but she also didn't want Alex to respond by grabbing his things and disappearing again. It seemed a distinct possibility.

"And your little boy?" Melanie said softly instead, motioning with her head to Nicky, who was oblivious to their conversation and setting up an elaborate pyramid of soldiers standing shoulder on shoulder. "You couldn't have told us about him?"

"Don't you get it? The longer I stayed away, the harder it was to share that. The way you're looking at me right now is one of the reasons why I didn't."

They were quiet for a moment.

"Is he BJ's, too?" Melanie asked.

"He is. But I'm not. I haven't been for a while."

Melanie waited in silence for her brother to continue.

"BJ walked out on us when Nicky was just a year old," Alex said easily. "And by that time I was fine with that. The person Nicky thinks of as his mother is named Regina. I met her when I was working at a nightclub in Chicago. We got married when Nicky was two."

"And where is Regina?"

Alex took a sip from his glass and set it down. "I have some ideas."

"You have some ideas?" Melanie echoed.

"Yes, I do." Alex's voice was confident. "But enough about me, Nellie. I want to hear all about you! You were in a big movie with a Hollywood heartthrob! You were terrific, by the way. I saw it. I knew you'd make it to the big time."

Melanie shook her head and laughed lightly. "That movie is not exactly what I'm known for right now."

"Oh, that." Alex laughed and flicked a hand like he was swatting away a fly. "You can't possibly be a communist."

It was such an absurd statement that Melanie laughed, too. "I'm not even sure what one is. I wasn't paying attention when Dad went on and on about how awful the Soviets are."

Alex laughed harder. "Well, do you know any? I hear there's a whole bunch in Hollywood."

"Apparently there used to be. I don't know where they all are now. Converted or in hiding or out of the country, I guess. And no, I don't know any. Not that I'm aware of anyway. It's not like the subject came up in conversation at the Trocadero or Chasen's, at least not when I went."

"So, you're just going to hide out here at the beach while you wait for the hysteria to end? Don't you think it might take a while?"

"It wouldn't if I agreed to name names. But I'm not going to do that."

Alex reached for his wineglass. "Names? What names?"

"If I want the studios to take my name off the blacklist, I have to testify before this ridiculous congressional committee and name every person I ever saw Carson with."

"That guy is a commie? Also hard to believe. He seems kind of too full of himself if you ask me. Hard to be a socialist if all you care about is yourself."

"I don't know what he is. He dated a Party member ages ago. Went to some of the meetings with her. He told me he was just trying to impress her. But because he went to those meetings, these government men think Carson's a communist, and if he is, then his friends and acquaintances must be communists, too, or communist sympathizers. That's what they suspect I am."

"Why would they think that? Just because you were in one movie with the guy?"

"Because Carson and I were dating. We were seen together. Photographed together. A lot."

Alex thought for a moment. "Okay, but don't you think his closest friends *could* be sympathizers? Seems to me they could be if he was once one."

"I don't know who his close friends are! That's the point. It's not right to pretend I know something when I don't know anything. And turning on fellow Hollywood people just because I once saw them drink a martini with Carson or they once shared a table with us at the Brown Derby or stopped by his dressing room to say hello when I was there? I'm not going to do it."

"Ah. I get it now." Alex nodded as if in understanding. "That's why I was able to find out which house was yours when I was down at the beach, trying to find somebody who knew where you lived. A bunch of people didn't know who I was talking about when I asked about you. But there was somebody sitting at a booth in a little restaurant down the highway a bit who did. I'm not sure who it was. I think he's been in the movies. His face was familiar but I just couldn't place him. But he knew you were here and he told me he and others in the Colony—that's what he called it—respect you for how you're handling this, especially since he's convinced you're innocent. He told me where you were living."

Melanie was shocked into silence for a few seconds. "Wait. What?"

"What do you mean 'what?' What part didn't you hear?"

"I heard it all. You don't know who he was?"

"I don't. I was never into movies like you were, Mel. Sorry."

Melanie shook her head in disbelief. "I didn't think anyone in the Colony knew—or cared—I was here."

"Well, I could tell he's impressed with you. And he knows you're trying to stay out of the limelight. He only told me where you lived because I said I was your brother."

The timer for the oven beeped. As Melanie rose to dish up their plates she felt an odd sense of relief. She was so sure she'd been forgotten by everyone in Hollywood except those who'd put her out of a job. The thought that someone down at the Colony was in her court was wildly affirming. It was the first bit of good news about her prospects for acting again that she'd received in a long while.

It was turning out to be a good day after all.

Alex grabbed two thick books off bookshelves from the study beyond the living room and set them on a chair to boost Nicky's height, and they ate the savory dish that Eva had made. Afterward, as they sat on the sofa with a fire going and third glasses of wine, Alex filled Melanie in on where life had taken him since he'd dropped out of college.

He and BJ, who'd aspired to be a news photographer, had run off to Paris together when she inherited a tidy sum from her grandmother. Alex, ready to shed every scrap of his previous scripted life, sold his violin, bought the musical instrument that he'd always wanted to play instead—a guitar—and played on street corners for francs and compliments. Before long, he started getting invitations to entertain at dinner parties. It was 1949 and Paris was still in the process of being reborn, like all of Europe was after the hell of war. When he and BJ tired of Paris, they hitched a ride to Amsterdam, and then West Germany, and then Spain and Italy and everywhere in between. When the money ran out, they returned to the U.S., first to Baltimore, where BJ was from, and then to Richmond because Alex had friends there, getting odd jobs so they could earn money to go back to Europe. But then BJ got pregnant. He wanted the baby; she wasn't sure she did. He told her she'd probably feel differently when she actually became a mother, but he was wrong. After Nicky was born, she felt only resentment. A child wasn't going to let her pursue her career. A professional photographer needed to be able to travel, to live out of a suitcase, to be able to drop everything and go to where the action was. A photographer was not a good candidate for motherhood.

When BJ left, they were in Chicago. Alex rented a room in a friend's house for himself and Nicky, who'd just turned one. He met Regina, as assistant accountant who worked in the Palmolive Building while he was headlining a musical act at a nightclub. They married the day after Nicky's second birthday, and then left Chicago for Buffalo when Nicky was three. And now Nicky was four—almost five—and Regina was probably in Mexico. Most likely.

Perhaps Texas.

Nevada was a distinct possibility.

"Has she left you?" Melanie asked. "Is that why you're here in California? Or did you leave her? Is that why you don't know where she is?"

"It's complicated. But I'm not leaving her. Not exactly. I don't think she's left me. But . . . like I said, it's complicated."

Clearly Alex was unsure how much to share with her, and Melanie didn't want to press. Perhaps in a few days he would feel better about telling her what was going on between him and his wife.

By this time, it was well after nine. Nicky had crawled up into Melanie's lap and had fallen asleep as she held him.

"I knew he'd adore you," Alex said, smiling at his son nestled in Melanie's arms. "He was so funny with that photo of you, showing his auntie Nellie to everyone he met."

"So you've taught him to call me Nellie, too. When you know I don't like it."

Alex grinned. "You were Nellie to me for such a long time. Even when I could finally say your name, I didn't want to. I liked Nellie. And what was it you called me? Biscuit?"

Melanie grinned, too. "Something like that."

Melanie lowered her head to rest it against her nephew's. She couldn't remember the last time she'd held a child like that. Maybe the last time she babysat. When was that? A decade ago in Omaha?

A lifetime ago, it now seemed.

"When are you going to tell Mom and Dad they have a grandson?" Melanie murmured.

Alex sighed and stroked Nicky's socked right foot. "I don't know. They'll be mad I didn't tell them. They'll be mad I wasn't married to his mother. They'll be mad they didn't get to hold him when he was a baby."

"And then they will get over it," Melanie said. "Actually, I don't think they'll be mad, Alex. They'll be sad they missed his first four years but they will get over that, too. In time."

"I know but they just . . . everything has to be their way. You know? And only their way."

Melanie shrugged. "I guess."

"You *guess?* Mel, you know it's true. Were they happy you came to California? Were they happy you gave up college to become an actress? Did they send you flowers and champagne when you got that movie role after, what, years of auditions and bit parts that paid you next to nothing? Are they happy now about everyone here thinking you're a commie? Are they happy you're here instead of there?"

The barb went a little deep. Alex didn't seem to notice.

"No. They didn't want me to come here," Melanie said.

"See? You do know it's true."

Melanie had always thought her brother disappeared because he didn't care about what his parents thought or wanted. But now she understood so clearly that not only did he care about what his parents thought, he cared too much. And damn it all, she did, too. "It matters to you what Mom and Dad think. That's why you've stayed away. It's why I don't like going back there, either. We both care. Maybe more than we should."

Alex didn't say anything.

A moment later Nicky stirred and Alex abruptly stood up.

"I should get him to bed." His tone was impossible to interpret.

"I'm sorry I said that," Melanie said.

"Don't worry about it."

"No. I really am sorry. I shouldn't have said it." Though she knew what she'd said was true.

"You don't have anything to be sorry about. I should get to bed, too. Long day."

"We can talk more tomorrow?"

"Sure."

"Or, better yet, how about we go into Santa Monica and get a little Christmas tree and some decorations? Wouldn't that be fun? Maybe get a few presents to wrap up for Nicky? I'd love for you two to stay for the holidays. Or longer."

"That sounds nice. Nicky would love that."

Alex picked up his sleeping son and Melanie followed him into the guest room to turn down the bedspread.

"If you need anything during the night, I'm just down the hall," Melanie said as she turned to leave the room.

But Alex reached for her, pulled her into a hug, and squeezed tight. "Thank you. It's really good to be here. I'm glad I came."

Melanie returned the embrace. "I am too. So glad. Sleep tight."

She closed the guest room door behind her and went back into the living room. The fire was dying. It wasn't even ten o'clock, early for her, but she turned out the lights, made sure the doors were locked, and went into her own room. She put on a nightgown, got into bed, and picked up the novel she was reading that Irving had checked out for her at the Los Angeles library. *Peyton Place*, a book about, she'd gathered so far, all the turmoil that lies beneath the surface in a picture-perfect town, and three women, each with a secret to hide. Irving's wife had loved it.

Melanie read until midnight and then turned out the light.

In the morning she awoke with a start to the sound of a child's voice.

A little boy.

She snapped open her eyes and then remembered. She had houseguests: her long-lost brother and her nephew.

Melanie rose, used the master bath toilet, washed her hands, and splashed water on her face. She ran a quick comb through her hair, grabbed a robe, and then headed out to the main room. Every toy from the canvas bag was out and strewn about. She heard Nicky's voice in the next room and made for the kitchen.

Her nephew was seated at the table eating scrambled eggs. He smiled at her.

Melanie turned to say good morning to her brother but it wasn't Alex who was also in the room. It was Eva.

Of course. Eva. Today was a Wednesday and it was after nine in the morning. Of course she'd be there.

"I see you've met my nephew," Melanie said. "Thanks for making him breakfast."

"It was no trouble. He was hungry." Eva looked pensive. "I think . . . I think he had been up for a while."

"Oh. My brother is still asleep?" Melanie headed for the percolator and a coffee cup.

"I don't think anyone else is here."

Melanie turned back around. "Beg your pardon?"

Eva looked from Melanie to the boy to Melanie again. She picked up a folded piece of paper on the kitchen table and handed it to her.

Melanie unfolded the note and read:

> Nellie, I'm really sorry to do this to you, but there's
> something I need to do. It involves finding Regina and it
> won't exactly be safe or enjoyable for the kid to tag
> along. I will be back for Nicky. I promise. Just not sure
> when. You're the only person I trust to care for him
> while I am gone. It's obvious he's already smitten with
> you, just as I knew he would be. You'll be fine with him, I

know it. I'll call when I am on my way back, scout's honor.

Wish me luck.

Love, Biscuit

p.s. Nicky hates onions . . .

Melanie looked up from the note. Eva was staring at her. Nicky was happily eating his eggs.

Tossing the note to the table, Melanie ran to the front door, threw it open, and dashed out to the driveway.

Alex's car was gone.

DECEMBER 21, 1956

13

Nothing was going as June had planned—if whatever this was could even be called a plan. When something disastrous happens, and one must deal with it right then with no time to consider the consequences of their next steps, what is that action even called?

She didn't know.

What she did know was that Eva knew something was up. That Elwood wasn't in the house. She was also sure that Eva, who no doubt had been told to update Melanie on her daily visits to the house, hadn't said anything to Melanie about what she suspected. If she had, Melanie would have demanded days ago to be let in to see for herself if Elwood was or was not there.

True, Melanie had been a little preoccupied the last few days with the sudden appearance of her nephew and the likewise sudden disappearance of that little boy's father. But still. If Melanie had been told what Eva had surely figured out, she would've beaten the door down to get in, maybe while that kid sat on the grass wide-eyed and watched.

Why Eva continued to come over each day without confronting

her, June could only guess. There had to be more to it than just her not wanting to give up the free typing lessons. It was almost as if the young woman wanted to help June out of the mess she was in, and there could be only two plausible reasons for that. The first was that Eva understood love and loss, and how tragically complicated it was when the two became entwined.

And the second? Somehow Eva had decided in their ever-lengthening afternoon conversations that this—love and loss, the two together like that—was something they had in common.

June doubted their experiences were all that much alike, but that apparently didn't matter to Eva. Eva's knowing looks and careful questions about Elwood suggested she'd guessed June had begun falling for Elwood long before Frank was dead, and yet Eva didn't seem to care that that was true. How could that not matter? It mattered to June. It was troubling, embarrassing. And unexplainable. It was almost as if deep down June knew she'd been meant to marry Elwood from the very beginning and she had blown it. If she'd gone the way divine Providence had led her, she would have broken off with Frank after meeting Elwood.

It would have been awkward in the beginning, breaking things off with Frank, and maybe Frank would've had to weather a few seasons of anger toward his brother, but in the end Frank would've forgiven Elwood for stealing away his girlfriend. He would have forgiven her, too. Frank was that kind of person.

So much about her life would've been different if she'd been tuned in to what destiny had been whispering to her back then and which she had ignored.

Perhaps the reason Eva had said nothing as yet was because she thought she could somehow help fix the broken mess that was June's life because she couldn't fix her own. Eva had assumed an identity that could get her into heaps of trouble, was cleaning houses for a living—a thankless job if you don't care for the person whose house you're cleaning—and she was still grieving a man who'd been dead for, what, fifteen years?

And yet . . .

And yet, there was more to Eva's grief than just the long-ago death of her fiancé. All she had to do was look as closely at Eva as Eva had been looking at her. Eva was grieving the loss of all that had never been hers, and now never would be—a long and happy life with the man she loved.

Perhaps they were more alike than June first thought.

June remembered everything about the day she met Elwood. She and Frank had been going out for several weeks after a chance meeting at the studio commissary. One Sunday afternoon he'd asked if she'd like to meet his twin brother, the talented screenwriter who lived out in Malibu. June said yes.

She'd wanted to meet Frank's brother for several reasons. June had already seen a photograph of Elwood at Frank's half of a duplex on Vermont Avenue, so she knew they weren't identical, but the brothers were nonetheless near mirror images of each other. She wanted to meet this man who looked so much like the man she was sure she was falling in love with, who had grown up in the same house as Frank, slept in the same bedroom, and attended all the same family gatherings. She also wanted to meet the brother who had, the way Frank told it, saved Frank's life when they were in the Argonne together as infantrymen in the fall of 1918. Frank had taken a bullet in the back during a hasty retreat and Elwood had gone back for him, despite heavy enemy fire, and dragged him to safety.

And yes, she wanted to meet the screenwriter who had found

success in a business that could be as stingy with notoriety as it was generous.

It was a little less than an hour's drive to Elwood's place in Malibu—a town by the sea that June had vague memories of having once been to with her mother for a weekend at someone's beach house.

As they made their way west, June asked Frank how it was that both of the brothers ended up working in Hollywood since Reno was where they'd been born and raised.

"It was all Elwood's doing," Frank said. "He was always the smart one, the planner. He knew he would go to college and get a degree and make a career with his writing. That's exactly what he did, too, when we got back from the war. He was always scribbling in notebooks when we were younger—all kinds of short stories and the beginnings of novels, things like that. College didn't interest me. I liked working with my hands. Making things, figuring things out, taking things apart. You couldn't have paid me to sit in a class-room again."

He told her that Elwood had arrived in Hollywood first, with his brand-new English degree, and got a job at Warner Brothers in the reading room, analyzing scripts. Everyone quickly saw his talent and he was given more responsibility, like working on treatments of movies already in production and then trying his hand at adapt-ing books into screenplays. Elwood had been able to get Frank his job on the Warner Brothers backlot in 1934, just before being lured away to MGM with an offer of a lucrative new contract.

"I don't know where I would be if not for Elwood," Frank said. "Not where I am, that's for sure. And not here with you." He reached across the seat to take June's hand. "I was bouncing around from job to job and poker table to poker table. Elwood could see I had forgotten there was more to life than piddly paychecks and playing cards. He's the one who convinced me to come to Los Angeles and take a job at the studio."

"He sounds like a wonderful brother," June said, and she meant it.

"He is."

"But not married? I would have thought someone like that would have been snatched up years ago."

"Well . . ." Frank paused and furrowed a brow, as though needing to think about his next words. "He's dated over the years, and he's been to plenty of events with a woman on his arm, but Elwood is kind of . . . uncomfortable around the ladies, you could say. He has funny little habits that make him seem a little—I don't know the word. And he got hurt a couple too many times, I think."

"That's so sad."

"I think so, too."

"Is that why he lives way out in Malibu?"

"That, and he likes being away from the noise and the hullaba-loo. He says he writes better where it's quiet. And he likes the beach."

"MGM doesn't care he lives so far out?"

"They'd probably love it if he drove in to the studio every day but they can get what they want and need most from him without him having to do that. They'll send him a novel or a story idea or a terrible screenplay that needs fixing and they'll say, 'How long do you need to turn this into a great script?' and he can make it happen in a month, a little more if he needs to read the novel first. Sometimes they'll send a courier out to pick up his work if they want to see it right away. They're getting the best of Elwood Blankenship without him having to come in to the office much and I guess that makes everybody happy."

"And Elwood is happy?"

"I think so. It's kind of hard to tell with him. He never talks about his feelings. But he's always been that way."

It was now quite obvious to June that Frank and his twin, even though they could probably pass for each other at a short distance, weren't really like each other at all. The way Frank was describing Elwood wasn't like Frank in any way, except for maybe the kindness part. Frank was always looking out for the other guy. He was the most unpretentious and genuinely considerate man June ever met.

"Does Elwood ever go on vacation or do anything just for fun?" she asked.

Frank laughed. "I don't think Elwood has ever been on a real vacation. He and I drove down to San Diego a couple of years ago—right after he bought the Malibu house—and I took him to Tijuana and we had lobster and cerveza on the beach, and a mariachi band was playing and beautiful women waited on us. I had a great time and he couldn't wait to get home. Being that far from home didn't really relax him, I guess."

They made their way west on Highway 10 through the urban stretch of Los Angeles and toward the sea until June finally saw on the horizon the sapphire ribbon that was the Pacific Ocean, and then Frank turned north. Half an hour later they were exiting the coastal highway in central Malibu and climbing a residential street where both big and small houses had been perched at whatever angle might afford its occupants a view of the ocean. Frank took a couple turns on curving asphalt roads and then began to climb a hill. She read the street sign as he made the turn:

Paradise Circle

Frank continued up the road and then stopped at a brown-and-white, two-story Craftsman at the top of a cul-de-sac. Potted daisies graced the covered porch, bougainvillea climbed the fence, birds-of-paradise flanked a matching garage, and a young jacaranda tree in the center of the front lawn still had a few straggling lavender-hued blossoms clinging to its branches. The house looked like an idyllic place to live with its peekaboo view of the ocean. June could smell the sea when she opened the car door.

Frank had no sooner rung the bell when the door opened and a slightly thinner version of Frank stood before them. Elwood was nearly the same height but a good twenty pounds lighter. His hair was the same color—toasty brown flecked with hints of gray—but Elwood's waves had been gelled into submission. The eyes, the nose, the chin, the cheekbones—they were all like Frank's.

Along with a plain white shirt, Elwood wore a bow tie and a sweater vest, two articles of clothing June had never seen on Frank's person. Or in his closet.

Elwood's khaki pants were freshly pressed.

He appeared glad to see them on his doorstep but not exceedingly so.

"Hey, Woody!" Frank crossed the threshold, pulled his brother into a hug, and clapped him on the back. Elwood seemed to startle slightly at the intensity of Frank's embrace.

Frank released his brother and stepped back. He then ushered June into the tiled entry with his arm around her waist. "And here is my Junebug."

June smiled and put out her hand. "It's just June."

Elwood smiled politely and put his hand out, too. "Hello, Just June. It's just Elwood. Only Frank gets away with calling me Woody."

She laughed. Elwood's voice was cashmere soft, and he seemed at ease, other than having paused a second before taking her hand. She wondered what Frank had meant earlier when he said his brother was uneasy around women.

They walked through the main part of the house—nicely furnished and clean—to the patio in the backyard, which was drenched in the September afternoon sunlight. Elwood had laid out pretzels, coupe glasses, and a cut-glass pitcher of a cocktail he called a Picador, a drink June had never had before, concocted of tequila, triple sec, and lime juice. Elwood poured the drinks and then he and Frank fell into easy conversation as they discussed sports teams, studio scuttlebutt, and—when Frank realized June was merely a spectator—their childhoods as sons of a barbershop owner. Frank said she could ask them anything about their growing-up years.

As they talked and sipped the tart and tangy drink, June watched Frank's brother whenever she could do so without being obvious.

There wasn't much about Elwood to notice and assess, she discovered. His was a serene, unremarkable presence. He didn't lean back in his chair and toss his head back and laugh when a funny moment was shared between the three of them; he merely smiled and gave a quick nod of his head, as if to calmly agree that, yes, that was comical. He filled their glasses without comment when they were empty, took in with quiet gratitude the compliments Frank gave him about the latest movie they had seen where the screenplay credit had been his, rose to check on a roast he had in the oven, and easily deflected an offer for help in the kitchen with a simple "Just enjoy yourselves on the patio."

Frank did most of the talking, and Elwood didn't seem to mind. Frank steered every conversation, too, and Elwood didn't seem to mind that, either. When he was asked a question, he answered it without hesitation—succinctly and quickly—and when he posed a question in return, he listened intently to the answer without interruption.

When they moved indoors to eat the supper Elwood had

prepared—beef tenderloin, a green salad, roasted carrots, seeded rolls, all accompanied by a plummy red wine—June decided all of Frank's best qualities Elwood possessed, too, but he simply exercised them with exponentially less volume. She could see where, with Elwood's quiet personality, he might come across—mistakenly—as inattentive or broody or maybe even self-absorbed, especially to a woman who expected to be put on a pedestal.

She wouldn't see Elwood's funny quirks—his need to arrange things just so, the way he liked to play the same record album over and over, not immediately recognizing when she or Frank were sad—until much later. By that time she would see Elwood's peculiarities as just the uncomplicated inverse of Frank's intuitive, highly easygoing nature.

June married Frank in the summer of 1939, and Elwood paid for the small ceremony and their honeymoon on Catalina Island as his wedding gift. June had been surprised and touched by that generosity. When she looked back on it, this gift of his had been the beginning of her deeper affection for him, though at the time she did not know it. Frank's cheerful devotion and happy-go-lucky attitude made for a lighthearted, enjoyable life. But Elwood? His careful, methodical ways made her feel safe. Secure. She'd spent the first ten years of her life not knowing from one minute to the next where home was. Or if she actually had one.

When Frank and June moved into the Malibu house after the accident to care for Elwood, it was the first time she felt she lived somewhere where she belonged.

And yet that she felt that way made no sense to her. No sense at all.

Everything about that arrangement was terrible and unfortunate.

That she loved living in Elwood's house and caring for him set her mind to spinning because she should've loathed what brought her and Frank there.

She should've mourned that Elwood could not bring himself to step out the front door.

She should have hated it.

14

The call from the hospital the night of Elwood's accident tore June away from a dream of her mother.

She'd been back at the little one-room cottage in Venice Beach, inside the closet that, when she was little and her mother left her alone overnight, she'd wished was a time-travel machine that could vault her forward to the moment when Lorena would return. In the dream, Lorena was inside the closet with her and they were both adults. June had been about to ask her mother why she was there when a ringing phone yanked her awake.

June fumbled for the receiver on the bedside before realizing there was no longer a telephone at the side of the bed.

She and Frank had sold his half of the duplex and used the minimal capital gain to buy shares in a land development company that was to have been a sure thing. It had become insolvent, however, three months after Frank invested in it. Frank and June were now living in a lunch box of a place in the Olympic Trailer Court in Santa Monica. It had been a harsh blow, losing all that money, but June couldn't fault Frank alone for what had been nothing short of financial disaster. She'd agreed to both the sale of the half duplex and investing in the company that had all but swindled their money from them.

And she wished to God she hadn't.

She was also back to wishing—now every day—that the time-travel closet at the Venice bungalow had been a real thing, and that she could find it again and use it. She'd crawl inside and go back to the moment Frank showed her that brochure and she'd tell him she had a bad feeling about it. Elwood, who'd had misgivings about the investment opportunity, offered to help them out with a nicer rental after they lost everything, and Frank declined.

These thoughts that plagued her during the day were surely why she'd been dreaming of the closet when she was awakened by the jangling phone.

The house trailer was only fifteen feet across and fifty feet long; so even though the phone sat on an itsy-bitsy shelf by the front door, it wasn't that far away from the bed June and Frank were sleeping in.

"Just let it ring," Frank mumbled. "Probably wrong number anyway."

After eight rings, the phone fell silent only to start up again a minute later.

June pushed back the blanket, crawled across the mattress on all fours since the narrowness of the trailer made it impossible for her to stand at her side of the bed, and made her way through the dimness to the phone.

"Hello?" she said, rubbing sleep from her eyes.

"May I speak with Frank Blankenship, please?" The man on the other end of the line sounded very much awake. And in charge. And serious.

Something was wrong.

June turned to Frank, sprawled across his half of the mattress. "It's for you."

"It's three o' clock in the goddamn morning," he muttered.

"I think something has happened."

Frank sighed. "Who is it?"

June lifted her cupped hand from the mouthpiece. "May I tell him who's calling?"

"Is this June Blankenship?"

Her breath stalled in her chest. Something terrible had happened. She could feel it. "Yes."

"This is Deputy Randall Owens from the Riverside County Sheriff's Department. Your husband's brother, Elwood Blankenship, has been in an automobile accident."

Cold zipped through her body like she'd been injected with it, and she nearly dropped the receiver. Elwood and Ruthie had left for Palm Springs earlier that day. Petite and redheaded, Ruthie was quite a bit younger than Elwood's forty-nine, though June could only guess by how much. She had two young sons, eight and nine, and her husband had been a naval aviator who died in the bombing at Pearl Harbor more than five years earlier. Elwood was the first man she'd dated in all that time.

It seemed they had that in common, too—a very long stretch of years since they'd wanted to be a part of anything romantic.

June liked Ruthie—a lot—but she worried that she would end up hurting Elwood like other women had done before her when they'd break up with him after discovering he was a little eccentric. A little awkward. A little moody. A little strange.

All things she loved about him now. All things that made him precious to her. All things that made her jealous of Ruthie for reasons she could not explain. She was married. To Frank.

Elwood had invited Ruthie to spend the weekend with him in

the desert, and, to his surprise, she'd said yes. She left her boys with her parents in Newport Beach and then they'd left for Palm Springs.

And now there'd been an accident.

"Oh, God! What happened?" June said, breathless. "Is Elwood okay? Where is he? Is he all right?"

"Ma'am, if your husband is there, I need to speak with him."

She looked behind her to the bed. "Frank! Frank, there's been an accident! With Elwood!"

Frank was already clambering off the bed and stumbling toward her. He grabbed the phone. "What's happened? Where's my brother?"

June put her head as close to Frank and the handset as she could to hear the deputy's answer.

"Your brother was involved in a car accident earlier this evening, thirty miles west of Palm Springs on Highway 99."

"Is he okay?"

June had never heard Frank sound so afraid. Tears pooled in her eyes, though at the moment all she knew was that there had been a crash.

"He's been transported to St. Vincent's in Los Angeles."

"So he's okay? He'll be all right?"

"You'll need to discuss all of that with the doctors there at St. Vincent's, sir."

"But you can tell me if he was alive when he was taken there! You can tell me that! Can't you tell me that? And what about Ruthie?"

"All I can tell you is your brother has been transported to St. Vincent's. Do you need the address?"

"Is Ruthie there, too? Did you call her parents? They have her boys."

June heard a slight hesitation in the deputy's voice before he repeated his question. "Do you need the address of the hospital, Mr. Blankenship?"

Frank brought a hand up to his face and covered his eyes, as though he was seeing something terrible and was desperate to stop seeing it. "No. No, I know where it is."

"You'll be on your way, then?"

"Yes, yes. We'll leave right now."

"I'll pass that along. I'm sorry you had to hear this news, Mr. Blankenship."

"Yes. Thank you."

Frank hung up and, for just a moment, he drew June to him and buried his face in her hair.

"We have to go," he said.

She nodded and they groped around in the dark for their clothes until June remembered there were light switches in the trailer. Of course there were. Dazed, they'd forgotten.

There were few cars on the roads at that hour and Frank sped all the way, but it still seemed to take far too long to cover the sixteen miles. They said nothing to each other until Frank was parking the used Chevy he'd bought after the war to replace Elwood's old roadster.

Frank set the brake and then took June's hand across the seat. "We need to be ready to hear the worst, June."

He hardly ever called her June. It was always Junebug or Junie or JuJu. Something fun.

"I know," she whispered.

They sat in the car in silence for several long minutes, June sure that neither of them knew what one did to be ready to hear the worst. But then Frank whispered, "Amen."

He put his hand on the car door. "Let's go."

The hospital emergency room was active: nurses and attendants coming and going, the phone at the desk ringing, the injured in chairs waiting.

Frank tapped his fingers nervously on the reception counter as he waited for a nurse to finish a phone conversation.

The second she hung up, he told her who he was and who they were there to see.

"Yes. So your brother is in surgery, Mr. Blankenship," she said, placidly and yet with a hint of compassion. "If you'd like to head up to the surgical floor waiting area, you'll be able to chat with the surgeon afterward. And it's quieter up there."

Frank's next words came in a rush. "Surgery for what? What happened to him? What's wrong?"

"You can speak to the surgeon when he's finished, okay? He'll come out and talk to you."

The nurse smiled minimally, gave them directions to the elevator and the surgical floor, and then reached for a chart.

"And Ruthie?" June asked the nurse, her voice sounding thready in her ears. "Is she here, too? Is she okay? Her name is Ruthie Brink."

The woman looked up. "Are you family?"

"I'm . . . I am Elwood's sister-in-law."

"I can only speak to immediate family regarding any patient, Mrs. Blankenship."

"You can't even tell us if she's here?" June felt as if she was about to explode and not just because the nurse wouldn't tell her where Ruthie was. She was deathly afraid everything was about to change. Had already changed.

"Junie." Frank gently took her arm. "Come. Let's go see about Elwood."

They arrived at the elevator and Frank pushed the up button. "I'm sure we'll find out soon where Ruthie is. One thing at a time, love. Let's just focus on one thing at a time."

There was no one in the surgery waiting area, and only one charge nurse sitting in subdued lighting at the entry station for the post-surgery patient wards. Frank told this woman who they were.

The nurse picked up a black telephone handset. "I'll let the OR know you're here."

Frank and June took seats in the empty waiting room, the ticking of a wall clock marking off the seconds as they waited. And then waited and waited.

They dozed off and on.

Morning sunlight was filtering in through the curtains at the one window in the waiting room when a man in surgical scrubs finally emerged through a set of double doors.

"You must be the Blankenships," he said. "I'm Dr. Fremont. I'm the surgeon who operated on your brother. He's pretty banged up and the repairs took a little longer than I'd anticipated, but he made it through all right, and while he's got some major recovering to do, I expect he's going to be okay."

"Thank God." Frank closed his eyes and shook his head in what looked like near disbelief that the doctor hadn't just said instead that Elwood was dead. His eyes stayed closed for only a moment. "What was the surgery for? Why did it take so long? What happened in the crash?"

"You'll want to contact the Riverside County sheriff for details on the accident," the doctor said. "I don't know those. I can just tell you that your brother's injuries were significant and he's lucky to be alive. His right leg was broken in a couple of places. That will take some time to heal. He might have a slight limp on the other side of his recovery but likely nothing too debilitating. He's got some fractured ribs, a broken collarbone, some contusions and lacerations, and there was some internal bleeding that we took care of in the OR but I will be watching to see if there are complications

157

post-op there. Like I said, he was very lucky. The internal bleeding alone could have killed him."

Both Frank and June needed a moment to let that thought sink in.

"When can we see him?" Frank said a moment later.

"He'll be in the recovery room for a little while yet and he's going to be very groggy for a while as he'll be on some pretty strong pain medication. Perhaps you'd like to go down to the cafeteria and get some breakfast and we'll look at maybe letting you see him in a couple of hours."

Neither June nor Frank had an appetite.

They stayed in the waiting room as the surgical floor came to life with breakfast trays on rolling carts and doctors making their rounds and another couple, about their ages, taking seats across from them while someone they loved was also behind the double doors leading to the surgical suites.

Finally, a little after nine, a nurse came for them to lead them to Elwood's room, admonishing them as they walked the polished linoleum to keep the visit short.

They entered a room with two beds. One was empty with sheets pulled tight. On the other on a cloud of white, Elwood lay, swathed in bandages. His right leg, in a cast, was lifted and held in the air by a sling and pulley. Bruises and scrapes covered the parts of his body not covered by bedding or gauze. He did not appear to be awake. June grabbed onto Frank at the sight of Elwood this way, her eyes burning with ready-to-fall tears. Frank patted her arm as they approached the bed, saying in a whisper, "It's okay, it's okay, it's okay," seemingly as much to himself as to her. When they arrived at the bedside, Frank leaned forward to lay a hand atop his brother's bruised one. The fingernails underneath were rimmed with dried blood.

"We're here, Elwood," Frank said softly. "June and I are here."

For a long moment there was no movement or sound from the man on the bed. But then Elwood slowly opened his eyes. He seemed to need a moment to recognize who they were, but June would learn later he was merely trying not to yell at them to go away and leave him to die.

"The doc says you're gonna be okay," Frank continued. "You're banged up pretty bad, but you'll heal. He says you're real lucky."

Elwood said nothing as he gave the slightest shake of his head. His eyes turned glassy with moisture.

Frank patted his hand gently. "Did you hear me? He said you'll be okay."

Elwood shook his head again and closed his eyes. Two tears slid down his bruised cheeks.

June felt tears sliding down her own cheeks and she was afraid she already knew why.

Ruthie.

"Woody?" Frank said.

"She's dead," Elwood whispered, eyes still closed.

"Oh, God," Frank breathed.

Two more tears slid down Elwood's cheeks.

Two more slid down June's.

Elwood opened his eyes and looked at them. "I killed her."

Over the next few hours it became clearer to June why Elwood believed it wasn't the car accident that had killed Ruthie, but rather him.

He'd been at the wheel of the car.

He'd had a couple drinks beforehand.

He'd been driving too fast.

He'd dared to think she was falling in love with him, and he with her, and that they might actually have a chance.

The Riverside County sheriff's deputy who showed up that

afternoon wanting a full report on what had happened the night before didn't care about that fourth reason. He did, however, care about the first three. But by the time that deputy was at the nurses' station asking for permission to speak to Elwood, Max was also at the hospital, having arrived an hour after Frank called him.

Max instructed Elwood to let him handle the deputy's questions.

Elwood told him no.

Max, who'd also heard Elwood say he'd killed Ruthie, then said, "I insist."

"No."

Max inhaled heavily and then let the breath out. "El, you're upset. I understand that. But you didn't kill that woman. It's very sad that she died, but it was an accident. An accident that nearly killed you, too, okay?"

Elwood moved his head slightly to look at his agent and then moved it back. "Those little boys are orphans now because of me."

"No. No, they lost their mother in a terrible accident that you had no control over. You didn't kidnap her and put her in that car. She willingly got in it. Everyone who gets inside an automobile to go for a ride knows there is danger in doing so. It's a risk we all take when we head out to go anywhere. And you had nothing to do with the death of their father. You can blame a Japanese Zero for that. They are not orphans because of you."

Elwood said nothing.

"And didn't you tell me you just had brake work done on that car?" Max continued.

"Frank told you that."

"But it's true, isn't it? You just had brake work done and something probably wasn't right. You tried to stop and the car just wouldn't obey."

"I was driving too fast."

"You don't actually know how fast you were going, right? You weren't looking down at the speedometer when that pack of coyotes decided to run across the road."

"It was only two. Three, maybe."

"Oh, so now you're telling me you counted all of them? You don't know how many there were. It was an instinctual response to swerve to miss them. You only did what is natural for any of us when we suddenly see something in the road that's not supposed to be there."

Elwood blinked languidly. "I'd been drinking."

Max sighed. "You had two martinis with dinner, El. You weren't drunk. I'm telling you, you need to let me handle this. I'm trying to keep you out of jail."

Elwood said nothing.

"I'm going to go talk with him." Max started for the door but he'd only taken a couple steps when Frank and the deputy entered the room.

Max put up a hand. "I don't know that Mr. Blankenship is able to answer a whole bunch of questions, Officer. Maybe another day?"

The deputy, holding a small tablet, continued into the room, the implements on his belt bumping against each other and making clinking noises as he did so. "I don't have a lot of questions. I just need to get the details that we were unable to get last night. It's for the official report. And, as you know, there was a fatality. We're required by law to investigate casualties."

The room went silent except for the deputy's boots as he approached Elwood. Frank followed quietly behind him. Max scurried to stand at the foot of the bed.

"Mr. Blankenship?" the deputy said.

He waited until Elwood turned from the window to look at him.

"I'm Deputy Owens. I need to ask you some questions about the accident. I know you're probably in a lot of pain so I'll make this as quick as I can. All right?"

Elwood nodded.

The deputy asked if Elwood knew how fast he'd been driving. Elwood shook his head. He asked if he'd consumed alcohol prior to getting behind the wheel.

Yes. Two martinis.

Did Elwood recall what caused him to lose control of the car?

He swerved to miss coyotes in the road.

This answer was supplied by Max when Elwood took too long to answer. When Deputy Owens asked if that was correct, Elwood nodded once.

"And he'd just had brake work done on that car, so it could easily have been that something was out of whack, somebody forgot to tighten something," Max added. "I can show you the paperwork from the garage. He just had it done."

The deputy wrote something down, asked a few more questions about road and weather conditions, and said he had one last question. "Did you attempt any lifesaving measures on your passenger, Mr. Blankenship?"

Elwood closed his eyes in obvious sorrow and June reached for his hand.

"Mr. Blankenship?"

"She was already gone when the car stopped rolling," Elwood whispered. "She was looking at me. She wouldn't stop looking. She wouldn't stop and I couldn't reach her to close her eyes. I couldn't reach her . . ."

For a moment no one said a word.

Then the deputy closed his little notebook. "Thank you, Mr. Blankenship. I have the information I need to file the report. It will go to the county but my guess is no charges will be filed. I can't promise you the family of Ruthie Brink won't look at a wrongful death suit, though. It happens sometimes in cases like this. I am just telling you so that you will be aware. Do you have any questions for me?"

Elwood shook his head.

"Thank you for your time." The deputy walked out of the room.

Silence reigned for a few minutes. Then Elwood spoke.

"I'd like to be alone now."

June would remember those words of his, said that way, for years to come.

15

Eva's days had been different since Max's visit to the Blankenship house and since Melanie's nephew had arrived.

Now that June's back was nearly healed, Eva spent most of her time at the Blankenships' upstairs in Elwood's office, refamiliarizing herself with a typewriter. Every afternoon June gave her a stack of documents to retype—old scripts, recipes from magazines, articles from the newspaper, handwritten notes and other correspondence from Elwood's many files, and pages from books. The Nazis in occupied Kyiv had expected absolute perfection when she was tasked—as a Russian-speaking German—with translating and typing for the Reich. But she'd never been taught how to do it. She was amazed at how much better she was getting at speed and precision when she was being coached instead of yelled at.

Secondly, her morning hours at Melanie's were finally being spent actually cleaning—life with an almost-five-year-old was messy—as well as helping Melanie keep Nicky entertained and happy. There'd been no word from Alex, not even a phone call to check in and make sure his son was doing all right. The little boy was adjusting fairly well to his new surroundings and caregivers as far as Eva could tell, though there'd been a tantrum or two and several *I want my daddy* breakdowns.

She supposed that was to be expected.

Those first few fits had thrown Melanie for a loop but she seemed to have adapted as well, though she didn't want anyone to know, except for June, that Nicky was there. Especially not Carson. When he'd called a few days after Nicky had been left with Melanie, she'd hand motioned for Eva to take him into the backyard so that Carson wouldn't hear Nicky laugh or yell or maybe throw something. Eva wasn't exactly sure of the reason for the secrecy other than maybe Melanie had an image to keep up when it came to Carson, and mothering a little boy wasn't part of it.

Or perhaps it was because Carson was paying her grocery bill, and now there was another mouth to feed?

Eva had heard Melanie say to Irving when he stopped by with her mail that Carson seemed to be growing tired of financially supporting her. The conversation with the man from Washington the previous week hadn't resulted in additional scrutiny, most likely because Melanie hadn't offered any helpful information. What Carson had wanted and needed her to do she had apparently dutifully done. Eva overheard Melanie tell her agent that Carson wouldn't speculate when he'd be back in California and that he had said maybe she needed to think about going home to Nebraska after the first of the year.

"But I'm not going," Melanie had said, her voice firm.

And Irving had said if Carson stopped paying the rent on the Gilberts' house, she might just have to. She would need money if she wanted to stay in California. No production company he worked with wanted to hire a tainted star, not even that one advertising company for whom she had once done a silly toothpaste commercial. He also didn't want her further destroying her résumé by taking substandard bookings should he even be able to get one for her.

Melanie's going home to Nebraska would take care of Eva's problem, to be sure, but not in a good way for Melanie.

Lastly, it was becoming increasingly bizarre to pretend to Melanie that Elwood was leaving his clothes and mail lying around, smoking his pipe, and—judging by his empty plate in the sink—enjoying the meals Eva was making.

"Do you know how his screenplay is going?" Melanie asked one morning. "I know he's writing one."

Eva, who'd initially looked up from scraping breakfast bowls, dropped her gaze back to the sudsy water in the sink. Melanie clearly had no idea June pretty much did all of Elwood's writing. "I guess it's going fine."

June was now tapping away alongside Eva at a second typewriter in Elwood's office in the afternoons rather than spending hours prone on the sofa with the heating pad. The current screenplay was due to the studio at the end of the year, June had said, and she couldn't be late with it.

It seemed to Eva, however, that June was having trouble with the writing, especially now that a time limit had been imposed on her concerning Elwood. June only had until the day after Christmas before Max would expect to speak to her brother-in-law face-to-face. A week had already passed, and Eva could tell June was worried about that looming deadline, too. She would often stop typing and just stare at the keys, as if willing for them to start moving again on their own. Sometimes June would get up from her chair, excuse herself, and head to Elwood's bedroom for a few minutes. Eva would pause in her own typing at these times, for as long as she dared, to listen for the sound of voices coming from the room down the hall. But she was too far away from that closed door. She never heard anything.

Eva supposed it wasn't just the ticking clock that was impeding June's progress on the script. It was also what would happen when the ticking stopped. If Elwood was indeed in the house, it could get ugly. Difficult. Men in white coats coming to the house and carting him away, perhaps. If he wasn't, June would have to come clean as to where he had gone.

Knowing everything was surely about to radically change was perhaps why June had taken to offering random comments about Elwood a couple times a day, while they were typing and even when they weren't, as if replying to a question Eva had asked about him.

As she did just then, while Eva was rinsing out June's percolator.

June was sitting at the kitchen table with stacks of typed script and a red pen, making marks and notations on the margins as she read the pages.

"You know, there's a name for what Elwood has," June offered from out of nowhere. "It has a name."

"Pardon?" Eva said. The two of them were expecting Melanie and Nicky any minute so that Melanie could go into Santa Monica to buy some Christmas presents for her nephew. The little boy was likely going to have nothing if she didn't. Eva had offered her and June's help with minding Nicky while she went, and June had been amenable. Eva wanted the kitchen cleaned up before they came.

"The doctor that came to the house when Elwood first refused to leave it said there was a term for that kind of reaction to a trauma. Agoraphobia."

"Agora—what?"

"Agoraphobia. That's what doctors say a person has if they can't step outside their own house," June said. "We didn't know he had it those first few weeks after we moved in to take care of him. He was so banged up and so despondent over Ruthie's death, we didn't see it. But after six weeks, when he refused to get into the car to have the cast on his leg removed, we knew we had a problem."

"So . . . did Elwood say why he wouldn't get in the car?" Eva asked, wondering if June actually wanted to continue the conversation.

She apparently did.

"He just said he wasn't leaving the house," June replied. "And he said it just like that. 'I'm not leaving the house.' As in, ever. Frank asked for a leave of absence from the studio but they wouldn't give it to him. That's when I offered to be the one to stay with Elwood until he got over it. I didn't get a leave of absence, either, but I didn't care. By then I really didn't like my job anymore."

"I thought you did," Eva said, remembering June telling her that she loved working in the film editing department and watching what fell to the floor as not-the-movie and seeing what was kept, and what an amazing thing it was to instinctively know what the movie needed for the audience to love the story and what it did not.

"I got to do a lot of the editing during the war years when most of the men were gone, and it was hard to go back to being an assistant who never touched the footage except to sweep up what had been cut out. Anyway, I was a better cook than Frank and it made sense for me to stay at home with Elwood and care for him. And I wanted to do it."

"So may I ask . . . is that when it started?" Eva asked gently, leaving the dish towel she had in her hands on the countertop and taking a seat across from June at the table. "I mean, is that when you started to have deeper feelings for Elwood?"

June smiled weakly. "Ah, yes, I was pretty sure you'd figured that out. I'm surprised you're not appalled that I was in love with my husband's brother."

"It's hard to stop loving someone," Eva said. "Especially if you don't want to stop. And you were caring for Elwood, doing so much for him. And he needed you."

"To be honest, I think it began well before that; I just never wanted to think about it. It seemed wrong. And unkind to Frank, who I did love. I really did. It was a very confusing time when I loved them both."

"So Frank didn't know."

"No." June shook her head. "When Frank was home he wanted to be the one to care for Elwood. He gave him his sponge baths, shaved his beard, and trimmed his hair and nails. Frank would help him get dressed in the morning and get him ready for bed at the end of the day until his injuries healed. Frank would do all of these things thinking I was ready for a break from the nursing and caregiving when I actually wasn't. I'm glad he had no idea."

Eva waited to see if June would continue to lay bare things she had probably never told anyone. After a moment, she did.

"You know, the first time I found myself daydreaming about what it would have been like if I had met Elwood first, I thought, *Who does that?* What kind of woman fantasizes about being with her husband's brother? But those thoughts would return to me whenever I wasn't holding them at bay. It was too enthralling to think that if I'd met Elwood first, this beautiful house by the beach would be mine, not that dump of a trailer Frank and I had been living in at the time of the accident. I could be the one entertaining guests on Elwood's lovely patio and serving them cocktails from that crystal pitcher. And it was impossible not to imagine that if I'd married Elwood instead, I might've had a child. I might have discovered I had it within me to be a good mother even though I wasn't raised by one."

June had been speaking as if to the room just then, but now she turned to Eva. "But do you know what is the most painful thought that plays itself over and over in my mind?"

Eva shook her head.

"If I had married Elwood instead of Frank, he wouldn't have been in that car with Ruthie Brink that night. He would have been home with me. I loved Frank. Honestly, I did. But if I had married Elwood instead of Frank, he wouldn't have been disappearing right before our eyes with no way of stopping it. I could see something inside him was shattered, and those broken pieces were changing who he was. He barely touched his roses after the accident. And he loved those roses. He didn't even want to sit down at his typewriter and write. The producers of the movie took back the screenplay Elwood had been working on and gave it to another writer. They kept asking him when he would return to work. He kept saying he didn't know."

"This doctor who told you the name of this condition—what did he say about how long it lasts? Did he tell you it would never go away?" Eva asked.

"That doctor didn't know. He wasn't a psychiatrist. So we called one in. Elwood was polite to that man but he didn't want to talk about why he insisted on staying inside. The psychiatrist wanted to help Elwood regain a sense of security about being in the outside world and to get back behind the wheel of a car. But Elwood refused. He told him he wasn't going to get back behind the wheel of a car. Or leave the house. Ever. And then that psychiatrist quietly suggested Frank petition a court for legal responsibility for his brother so that he could get Elwood the inpatient care he needed."

"What is inpatient care?" Eva asked.

"It would've meant becoming a patient in a mental hospital. Frank was livid at the idea that this doctor thought Elwood was nuts. The doc didn't say that, but that's what Frank heard. He nearly threw him out of the house."

"How awful for all of you."

"We tried another psychiatrist a few weeks later who wanted to prescribe a slew of medications to alleviate Elwood's anxiety. Elwood said no to that, too. Except for sleeping pills. Those he agreed to. After that, there were no more visits by psychiatrists. Elwood demanded it. It was his life to live as he chose to live it, he said. If Frank and I didn't like it, we didn't have to stay. He'd hire a house-keeper and gardener."

"But you didn't go."

"No. Frank asked Elwood if he wanted us to and he said he didn't. He liked having us there. But he didn't want to live life any differently than how he was living it. It was nobody's business but his own."

"Did he think something bad would happen again if he went out?"

June thought for a moment. "That was really only a small part of it. And the more I was around Elwood and watching him and attending him, the more I understood it was guilt keeping him inside. He had made a prison for himself for killing Ruthie. He saw himself as a murderer and he was serving the time. It wasn't true, Elwood hadn't killed her, but it was no good to try to convince Elwood of that."

"But at some point he did start working again, yes?" Eva asked.

"It was a long while after the accident. MGM continued to call with project offers and Max kept urging Elwood to sign on to one of them. It was a good two years later when Elwood was asked to adapt a bestselling novel about two young girls who meet on an orphan train heading west. MGM didn't want to give this project to another writer; Elwood was who they wanted. But they told Max if Elwood turned it down, they would give it to someone else. And if that happened, they would unfortunately have to cut their ties and be done with him. I remember the day Max came to the house and told him this. Elwood was only fifty-one. He'd made some good money, Max said, but it wasn't going to last forever. Max begged him to take that job. I sat down next to him after Max left and told him he'd be wonderful on this screenplay. I'd read the book it would be based on. He was perfect for it."

"What did he say?"

"He said he didn't think he could do it. And I said I was sure he could. He was born to write. Not only that, but that I would help him. I could type while he spoke the words so he didn't have to feel overwhelmed. I told him I was a good typist, and that I knew from working with the cutters what a great story looks like and feels like. I could be his sounding board there, too. That's when I saw a glimmer of happiness cross his face."

"Ah. And that's when he agreed," Eva said.

"No. That's when I finally understood fully why he'd shut himself away in this house. That joy I saw on his face was the thought of writing again, but then he remembered he didn't deserve to be happy. Because of what he'd done to those boys. Ruthie's boys. I wanted to shake him and yell that he did in fact deserve to be happy but I knew he'd pull back at those words. I had to make this about giving back to those boys somehow. So I told him he could use a portion of what the studio paid him to set up college funds for those boys. That would be a nice thing to do for them. A very nice thing. And he finally agreed."

"He still wanted your help, though."

"He most certainly did. And in truth, he needed it. Elwood was at the top of his game before the accident. He really was. But after it, he struggled creatively. It took him a long while to get back in the groove. I'd thought that the more I helped him, the more he'd settle back into his old life and the less he'd need my help."

"But that's not what happened."

"No. The more I assisted him, the more he seemed to need me to. It was almost as if his well was going dry and with every screenplay we worked on there was less and less water."

"That seems so sad. What did your husband think about all this?"

"Frank was happy Elwood was writing again but irked that I was contributing to those scripts and getting zero credit for them. Elwood wasn't too keen about it either, but when he brought up the matter to Max, he'd said the studio wouldn't want to hear that Elwood's sister-in-law who types his screenplays for him wants a screen credit."

June was quiet for a moment.

"The thing is," she continued, "nobody knew how much I was changing what Elwood was creating. Even he didn't. After Elwood would say we were finished I'd keep the script for a few more days and make all kinds of changes. Elwood never knew I was doing that. He didn't need to know. MGM told Max that Elwood's scripts were getting better all the time and how pleased they were he was finally coming out of his slump. It made me feel so good to know I was writing as well or better than Elwood Blankenship. Everyone was getting what they wanted."

"Were you, though?" Eva asked. It seemed to her that the arrangement was highly unfair to June.

"In a way. Elwood was nearly Elwood again. Except for not leaving the house. And Frank died suddenly a couple of years after that, and when that happened all I had was Elwood, this house, and the writing. I loved them all. In my own way."

"It must have been hard to lose Frank even so," Eva said.

"Oh, it was awful. For both El and me. I know it sounds ridiculous to say it but I was faithful to Frank. I loved his brother, yes, but that didn't mean I loved Frank any less. I felt hollowed out those first few days he was gone. Max helped me make the arrangements and drove me to the funeral since Elwood couldn't. Max stood by my side at Frank's graveside for the same reason."

"And when Elwood asked you to stay on, you said yes."

"Not exactly. He told me I didn't need to waste the rest of my life holed up at his house when I could still have a life outside it. He still wanted my help as a writing assistant, but he'd pay me a decent hourly wage and also my gas money to come out to the house once or twice a week. He'd hire a gardener and handyman to do things Frank had been doing, and a housekeeper for the laundry and cleaning and such. He told me he was grateful for all that I had done for him, but that he wanted me to know I was free to move on."

June looked away from Eva then, to the patio door, open to let in the unseasonably warm air.

"It was hard for me to hear those words," June continued a moment later. "We were both so sad about losing Frank. El was devastated, too, at Frank's passing. The last thing I wanted to do was leave Malibu, leave El. Leave the life I had here. I thought Elwood might beg me to stay. I actually wanted him to. It hurt when he didn't."

"But you stayed."

"I did. El was just being El. Wise and careful. I think he knew that I was in love with him. But in telling me I was free to go, he was saying in as gentle a way as he could that his affection for me was no greater than that for a sister. And never would be."

June blinked and two tears traveled down her cheeks.

"You are sure that's what he meant?" Eva asked.

June shrugged and wiped her face with her sleeve. "It's what I heard in his words. If he'd loved me like I loved him, would he have encouraged me to leave?"

The two of them were quiet for a moment.

"In the end, I really had nowhere else to go," June continued. "I mean, there was nowhere else I wanted to go. So I asked Elwood if I could stay just as we'd been when Frank was alive. He said, 'Whatever you would like, June.' He paid two set workers to move his writing room to the upstairs guest room where Frank and I had slept, and he gave me his former office by the kitchen for a bedroom."

June turned to Eva. "The thing is, my world had shrunk to the size of Elwood's companionship, writing for him, and making this house my home. And I was fine with that, but Frank's death showed me how fragile it all was. I started wondering if Elwood had provided for me in his will as his last living relative and friend. I hoped he had but I didn't know and it's not the kind of thing you ask someone. The only thing I really wanted was this house. It had become my home and I let myself believe surely he knew this. I knew he didn't love me like I loved him, but I thought he loved me as his sister at least, especially after all I had done for him. Given up for him."

June paused a moment and Eva waited for her to continue.

When she did, it was as if a dark cloud had fallen across her.

"But I came across his will not too long ago when I was straightening up the top of his desk. I was just putting everything into neater piles. I didn't mean to snoop, but I saw that one of the sets of papers was the draft of an updated will. Elwood's will. I heard him coming down the hall from his bedroom, and I only had time to glance at it quickly. I saw all that I needed to see on the first page."

Eva stared at June. Waited for her to tell her.

"He left everything—including this house—to Ruthie Brink's sons."

16

Melanie sat cross-legged with her nephew in her lap as she tied his shoelaces. He still smelled of the bath he'd had the night before and the dish soap she'd used to create bubbles that he insisted on having.

Had it been safe to plunk a kid down in a tubful of Joy dish detergent soap bubbles? She didn't know. But he hadn't broken out with hives or boils or been transformed into a cup and saucer. It surely wasn't the worst thing she'd ever done, but still, that was one more thing she needed to get when she went into Santa Monica: real bubble bath.

She added it to the list she'd made, which already consisted of presents for Nicky to open on Christmas, ketchup, Frosted Flakes, grape jelly, Ovaltine, and a tin of Band-Aids and Mercurochrome. Carson hadn't sent her any of what he called "fun" money that month. He'd paid the rent and kept up with the grocery tab, but he hadn't sent anything extra like he had in October and November.

She detested, a little more every day, that she needed him to. She'd be making these purchases today with what she had left from last month's generosity and perhaps some of her own money from her dwindling savings account.

Melanie could feel Carson distancing himself from her now that Washington had called her and yet hadn't followed up with contacting him. He hadn't said it outright but she wondered if he felt Melanie's continued silence wasn't something he had to pay for anymore. She'd proven she wasn't going to be a patsy for the Committee like others had been—others who were now pariahs in Hollywood. She'd made it clear to him she wanted her career returned to what it had been before the blacklist, with her character and fidelity to her coworkers intact.

He'd suggested she return to Nebraska to wait out the HUAC and the studios.

He hadn't said it, but her crawling back home would cost him just a one-way plane ticket—a cheap way to get out of the nearly six hundred dollars in rent and groceries he was paying for every month. He wouldn't have to fork over the fun money anymore, either.

The only obvious way she could see to stay where she was in Malibu was to find a way to make the six hundred a month herself. And that seemed nearly impossible.

She could sell the expensive jewelry and clothes and shoes she'd bought with the movie money, but how did one even do that? It was humiliating to even think about. And how long would the resulting cash last if all she could get for used clothing was twenty cents on the dollar? A couple months?

Did she really want to beg for a job down at the café where actors and actresses from the Colony dined and schmoozed? Would the owner even hire her? Could she handle the embarrassment if he did? And even if she could handle it, would she make enough money pouring coffee and delivering plates to live in the Gilberts' beautiful Malibu house? That didn't seem likely.

Nicky stood up when the laces were tied, anxious to go next door and see Algernon, which was how Melanie convinced him to be willing to spend the next couple hours with June and Eva.

She'd been astonished at both Eva's and June's willingness to help her out with Nicky—June especially. June didn't have children, so had never raised any, but she'd come over that first day after Eva told her what had happened, bringing saltines and peanut butter when Nicky wanted them for a snack and Melanie didn't have either ingredient. And quiet Eva, who hardly ever spoke to Melanie when she was at the house, was suddenly full of words for Nicky—and gently delivered advice when Melanie responded to tantrums with near-tantrums of her own.

While the withdrawal of Carson's care and attention—and soon his money—was soul crushing, the unlikely almost-friendship she was developing with Eva and to an extent June was softening that blow.

The only thing that could complete this welcome addition of having friends again would be if Elwood appeared at his window and started talking to her again.

Well, that wasn't the only thing that would complete it.

There was also the matter of Alex's return . . .

Her brother had vanished for the first time on a Friday.

In reality, he'd been gone for several days when Melanie's parents found out from college officials that Alex, instead of attending classes, had packed a suitcase and left. Herb and Wynona Kolander were advised their son was in danger of failing every class that semester—and losing his scholarship, too, by the way—if he didn't return pronto.

Herb and Wynona's first response had been to call the police.

Alex was a gifted violinist; he'd never voluntarily leave like that. He had to have been tricked into packing his things. Fooled into getting in someone's car. Prevented from asking anyone for help, and likely been threatened with harm if he tried to contact his parents.

The local police in Cincinnati had obligingly considered this scenario until Melanie received a postcard from London: Alex and a girlfriend named BJ were happily on their way to the Continent and could she please tell their parents not to worry? The police assessed the postcard—which Herb and Wynona had Melanie mail to them in Ohio, as they'd left her at home—determined it was Alex's handwriting and not written under duress, and closed the file.

The closing of that file had happened on Melanie's eighteenth birthday.

Melanie had imagined that she'd still be angry when Alex showed up in a few weeks, which she was sure he would do, and she'd give him the cold shoulder about it. A person only has one eighteenth birthday, and Alex had found a way to ruin hers.

But Alex hadn't reappeared after a few weeks. In fact, Herb and Wynona Kolander—who'd returned to Omaha after ten days in Cincinnati—spent the summer after Melanie's high school graduation frantically waiting to hear from Alex again. They took only short breaks from their vigil to urge Melanie to rethink her plan to study theater at the local university in the fall and likewise abandon such an unreachable career goal as becoming a movie star.

As the weeks went by, Melanie's anger toward Alex had softened into longing. She heard again from him only once. A postcard arrived from Calais in July, which was not where he and BJ were planning to stay; it was merely a stopping-off place before heading to the interior of France. Alex did not say where their ultimate destination was to be, nor did he give Melanie any kind of return address.

This was what saddened Melanie the most: that Alex had seemed to have gone to a completely different planet, and right at the time when Melanie needed him most. For the past two years if Melanie wanted to talk to Alex, all she had to do was pick up the phone and call him. She hadn't phoned him that often, but it was knowing that she could that eased her mind. Living in the Kolander house without Alex had been lonely and burdensome. Melanie had been especially looking forward to her brother coming home to Omaha that summer—even though Alex had promised no such thing—and now she didn't know when she would see him again or hear from him.

Melanie could have especially used Alex's insights in mid-August when Herb asked for a serious sit-down talk about Melanie's post–high school plans. He began the conversation by asking Melanie what she envisioned she might do with a degree in theater arts. Teach? Wouldn't it be better, then, to major in education and minor in theater? He also said it was highly improbable a person could become a movie star by simply wanting to be one.

It surely didn't happen as a result of college coursework.

More likely it came about by chance and happenstance and knowing the right people. Melanie didn't know anyone in Hollywood and was fifteen hundred miles from Hollywood. A degree in communications or public relations was the smarter choice because there were actual jobs in those fields. And if a gainfully employed Melanie wanted to perform in community plays in the evenings and the weekends, well, she still could. That made more sense, didn't it?

It wasn't until after Melanie had gone to bed that same night that she'd thought of what Alex would have added to the conversation if he had been there. He would've said something like, "Well, if someone can't become a movie star by studying acting, then maybe Melanie should just skip college altogether and head out right now to Hollywood."

That little thought had made her smile. And ponder.

She'd lain awake a long time wondering what it might be like to just pack a suitcase and head west. To leave it all behind and go after what she really wanted.

To do what Alex had done.

Although not how Alex had done it. Melanie would never do that to her family.

But could she—after she'd kissed her disappointed parents goodbye—hop on a train bound for California with nothing on her side but determination, some high school acting classes, and a couple of senior high lead roles? Is that something she could actually summon the courage to do?

She had known she would need money. Money for the train ticket. Money to rent a room or a little studio apartment until she found a part-time job. Money for professionally produced photographs. Money for nicer clothes to improve her chances at open call auditions. She knew about open call auditions. Her high school drama teacher had told her about them. Open call auditions were how someone like her got acting jobs, got her foot in the door, got noticed. It only took one casting director to decide a person was perfect for a role—even if it was just a tiny part with seconds of screen time—to set things in motion and maybe change the course of a person's life. It could happen that easily. It could happen just by being *in* Hollywood. Lana Turner had been discovered at fifteen, purchasing a soda at the Top Hat malt shop; Rita Hayworth at sixteen while dancing with her father at a Los Angeles club. She'd heard of women with no connections at all—just like her—getting noticed by a studio exec or talent scout while picking up dry cleaning or walking their dog in a park or buying flowers at an outdoor market, and then being asked if they'd like to come in for a screen test.

As the grandfather clock in the hall struck a single chime at one a.m., Melanie had decided she would take less than a full load of college courses, she'd live at home to save money, and she'd get a better job than just running the cash register at the five-and-dime a couple days a week. She'd save every penny she could. As soon as she had enough—and she knew it might take a while, two years, maybe three—she'd pack her bags.

It took only one and a phone call from Alex.

Her parents had left one late summer morning after her freshman year for Minneapolis for an annual teachers' conference they routinely attended. It was a little after two p.m. when the phone rang. She answered it on the third ring.

"Hi, Nellie."

Alex.

Joy and surprise and something akin to sadness had filled Melanie in an instant and she could not find her voice.

"Mel, you there?" Alex had said, when Melanie said nothing.

"Alex . . ." Melanie finally spoke.

"Hey. Mom and Dad aren't home, are they?"

"I can't believe it's you. Where are you?"

"You're alone, right? Mom and Dad have left for that thing in Minnesota, yes?"

Alex hadn't sounded like he was calling from across a faraway ocean, and this replaced surprise with hope. "Yes. Yes, they're gone. Where are you?"

"I need to keep it short, Nellie. I just wanted you to know I am back in the States for just a little while. I've been thinking about you and I wanted to know how you are."

"I'm fine, I suppose. Can't you tell me where you are?"

"You *suppose* you're fine? Why? What's up?"

"Alex, please, can't you just come home? Please?"

"Mel. Omaha isn't home for me anymore. I can't come home because that's not my home."

"Then just come back to visit. You don't have to stay. I just . . . I've missed you."

"I've missed you, too, but Nebraska isn't on the itinerary at the moment. Why do you only *suppose* you're fine?"

"Because . . . because . . . I don't want to be here anymore, either," Melanie had said in a sudden rush of found words. "I want to be in California. I want to be in films. I want to be an actress. In Hollywood."

Alex had been quiet for only a moment. "Well, then I think you should go and be one."

Melanie had laughed. "Right. It's not that easy."

"Going? Sure, it is. What's keeping you? God knows you've got the talent and looks."

"It takes money, Alex. I've saved some but I don't know if it's enough. It won't last forever."

"Is it enough to get there?"

"Well, yes, but—"

"So go. Get a job there. I assume that's what you're doing now, right? Working to earn money? You can do that there. And then you'd already be right where you want to be."

Melanie paused too long and Alex spoke again.

"Look, I promised my friend I wouldn't be on his phone more than a minute. It's long distance. I've got to skedaddle, Mel. But I want you to promise me you'll go to California. Don't give up on your dream. Promise me you won't."

"Wait, Alex!" Melanie shouted. "Please don't hang up! Please!"

"Here's what I want you to do, Melanie. BJ has a friend in LA. I'm going to give you Rich's address and as soon as you're settled in Hollywood, I want you to go over to his place and give him your new address and phone number, okay? I'll get it from him and I'll call you sometime, okay? Got a pen?"

"Alex, wait—"

"You need to get a pen, Melanie. I have to hang up."

Melanie had grabbed a pen next to the phone and the little note tablet her mother kept in a tidy drawer in the telephone table. Alex rattled off a Los Angeles address for an apartment on West Third and Melanie wrote it down.

"You can tell Mom and Dad I called," Alex had said. "And tell them I am perfectly fine, okay?"

"Alex, if you could just—"

"I really do have to go. I'll call you in California. Someday soon, I hope. It's up to you, really, how long it takes. Bye, Mel."

The line had gone dead.

For several long moments, Melanie had only been able to gaze at the piece of paper in her hand. As she stared at the numbers and letters, the images in blue ink seemed to transform into something more than mere scribbles on a page.

It had been almost as if the address were a directional pointing to a door cracked open just far enough to reveal light on the other side.

She'd packed her bags, waited for her parents to return so she could tell them goodbye, and then stepped toward that brightness.

17

June leaned against her kitchen counter and watched Nicky Kolander eat pieces of triangle-shaped cinnamon toast. Her grandmother had always cut her toast and sandwiches like that when she was young. June still liked the way it looked on a plate with the points meeting in the center like four kissing cousins.

It had been Eva's idea to bring Nicky over to the house that afternoon so that Melanie could run into Santa Monica and buy a few Christmas presents for him. June, who had agreed, was peeved, though—not at Melanie but at that brother of hers, Alex.

"You telling me she still hasn't heard a peep from this guy in a week?" she'd said to Eva.

"Nothing."

June had shaken her head, and not for the first time in the last couple of days. She'd done the same when she'd first learned from Eva what Melanie's so-called long-lost brother had done to her, and again yesterday when Melanie sent Eva over to the house before her usual arrival time to borrow carpet cleaner—Nicky had gotten chocolate pudding on Mrs. Gilbert's white carpet—and then three hours later when she heard from across the yard Melanie banging on the front door to be let back in the house. Nicky had locked her out. Apparently accidentally. But still.

Melanie was clearly in over her head. And that brother was as irresponsible as he was heartless and unkind. Who abandons their child a week before Christmas, leaving him with an aunt he's never met and without even asking her first? Who does that?

Despite her own troubles, June felt sorry for her neighbor.

Melanie had looked frazzled and nearly unrecognizable with her pretty hair pulled back under a scarf and wearing big sunglasses when she dropped Nicky off.

"He won't bother Elwood, will he?" Melanie had asked.

"He won't be bothered, I assure you. We'll stay downstairs."

Melanie had nodded and then just stood there on the welcome mat as Eva ushered Nicky into the house and then led him through the living room to June's kitchen.

"I'm sure he'll be fine," June had said.

"I know he will. Eva is really good with him."

Still she'd lingered.

"Is there something else you need, Melanie?" June had asked, supposing Melanie was again going to ask to see Elwood. She readied herself to say no.

"Maybe . . . Um. Did you have little brothers? Or nephews? Do you have friends with grandsons?"

"Oh. I'm afraid not."

"All right. I just . . . I don't know what little boys like." Melanie had sounded lost and young. "I don't know anything about how to care for little boys."

Again, that brother! *What a cad,* June had wanted to say.

"Just ask the clerk at whatever toy store you go into what little boys like," she'd said instead. "Or if you see a mother shopping for her own children, ask her. I'm sure kids his age aren't that difficult to please."

Melanie had exhaled heavily. "I suppose you're right," she said, but she hadn't turned to leave.

The young woman was a pitiful sight.

"I'm just not . . . I—," Melanie stammered. "I don't know what the hell I'm doing. I really don't."

"Look," June said. "This is none of my business, but I think your brother is expecting too much from you. Especially right now. If you want my opinion, you should scoop up that little boy and fly home to Omaha. Take him to your mother and father. They're his grandparents, aren't they? And they *do* know how to take care of a little boy, although it appears to me they've raised a near-narcissist in your brother. Is it true what Eva told me? That your brother hasn't spoken to your parents in years and has instead been gallivanting around the globe?"

"It's a little more complicated than that," Melanie had replied defensively after a beat. "And I don't see how I can just show up at my parents' with him. They don't even know about Nicky."

"Why not? Why don't they know?"

"Alex has his reasons."

"Because your parents were terrible to you and your brother growing up? Is that it? Did they beat you two? Demean you? Neglect you? Withhold love and affection from you?"

"Well, no. It's not that."

"Then it seems to me his reasons, whatever they are, are about him and only about him. If you ask me, that man has no regard for the impact of his actions on other people. That makes him about as self-centered as a person gets. And if you think I'm wrong about that, you tell me what kind of man dumps his child on a sister he hasn't seen in years without so much as asking permission to do so and without any indication at all about how long he's going to be gone. Is he running from loan sharks? The police? An angry husband?"

"I . . . I don't think so."

"Take that little boy home to his grandparents if you're not feeling up to the task. Lord knows, if I were you, that's what I would do."

Melanie had looked past June and toward the kitchen, where Eva and Nicky were. June could hear him asking for cookies.

"But if Alex wanted my parents to be taking care of Nicky right now, he would have taken him to their house, wouldn't he?" Melanie had asked.

What sway this brother has on her! June had thought. He must've long had it. Though he'd been estranged for years, he'd pulled his sister back into his little self-orbiting universe in just a matter of hours. June hadn't met him and she already disliked him immensely.

"It seems to me your brother lost his vote on how to handle this situation the minute he chose to leave you alone in it. Your biggest concern right now shouldn't be making sure your brother gets what he wants. Besides, I think it's cruel of him to have kept your parents from having a relationship with their grandchild."

Melanie's eyes had instantly become rimmed in silvery tears, and June had felt bad at once; she'd said too much. "Look," she tried in a softer tone, "you don't have to decide today. But unless your brother comes back, you do get to decide what happens next with this little boy. I know you feel like you don't get to decide much about your life right now, but you do get to decide this. And I know money is probably a bit tight. If that Mr. Edwards won't buy your airline tickets for you and Nicky, I will."

Melanie's mouth dropped open. "I can't believe you're being so nice to me."

"What is that supposed to mean?" June had said, frowning.

"I . . . nothing. I just don't feel like I deserve it right now. Because, well . . ." Her voice fell away. The two women stared silently at each other for several seconds until Melanie continued. "I'm sure my parents would wire me the money if I asked. I mean, I know they would. And I still have some savings left. But thank you for offering. I'll think about it. I should go call for a taxi. And I won't be long, I promise. You're sure Elwood won't mind Nicky being here for a little bit?"

"We'll all be fine. Do what you need to do. And for heaven's sake, take my car. You don't need to call for a taxi."

Melanie's mouth had again dropped open in grateful surprise. For a moment it seemed Melanie was going to embrace her. The moment passed and June went to get her car keys.

Now as she watched Nicky eat the cinnamon toast—a nice alternative for the cookies June did not have—June could not stop thinking about how dumbfounded Melanie seemed at having someone be kind to her. She'd wanted to linger in Melanie's awe and gratitude. She'd wanted that embrace. That moment had reminded her of what it was like to matter to someone.

There were many moments the first couple years after Frank had died when she'd felt so empty, and Elwood, though he had never been particularly adept at empathy, had somehow been able to figure out when she needed the kindness of another human to make it through another day. He'd lay a hand on her shoulder and allow her to lean back on him as she sat in a chair and he stood behind her. Or he'd kiss the top of her head lightly, so lightly. Or he'd put an arm around her as she sat on the couch and cried. He also seemed to have sensed that moment when her grief over Frank's death had been replaced with lone desire for him. He was careful with his touch after that.

As she watched Nicky eat, it was like getting a glimpse of the life she had not chosen, a peek into a past she'd never gotten to live, a past that was haunting her these days with its possibilities.

If she had chosen Elwood from the beginning, would she have done this very thing in this same kitchen, albeit years earlier? Made cinnamon toast for her little boy and cut it into triangles? Poured him a glass of milk before heading out to shop for his Christmas presents? If she had indeed been the mother of a little boy named Nicky and the wife of a quiet but content man named Elwood, would she and her husband have gotten a sitter for Nicky on a day like this, maybe someone like Eva, and gone Christmas shopping together? Perhaps made a day of it. Gone out to dinner afterward. Toasted their prowess at choosing such fun toys for their son. Come home to kiss their child on the forehead as he lay asleep.

June closed her eyes there at the table and allowed herself to imagine that dream existence was the real one. She marveled at how solid it felt in that moment, not at all like the diaphanous place that was the real world, where everything that made you feel safe and secure seemed made of mere kindling for the tiniest of random flames to consume.

Impossible to protect.

As much as she didn't want it to be true, the countdown to Max's deadline had begun. She had to finish that script and mail it Christmas Eve so that it would be properly postmarked December 24. It would be too late after that. On Christmas Day she'd be driving out to Palm Springs and then returning to Malibu to await Max's promised call the following day.

She'd already imagined and rehearsed that conversation.

Max would call on schedule and he'd ask, *Is he any better?*

And she would say something like, *Actually, I think he might be. I mailed his script for him on Christmas Eve. It's done, Max. Just like he promised. And then he had me take him out to his place in Palm Springs.*

He said he was ready to at last finish the journey he'd begun with Ruthie and then move on.

There would likely be a slight pause. And then, *You're kidding.*

No. I'm not, she'd say. *I think he might be turning a corner. I stayed with him through Christmas afternoon but by dusk he said he wanted to have the place to himself to figure some things out. He asked me to head back home and come back for him on New Year's Eve.*

Max would be incredulous. *You're telling me Elwood left the house after being holed up inside it for nearly a decade? And went to Palm Springs? In a* car? *Just like that?*

No, not just like that, she'd say. *It was a big step for El and not an easy one. He took one of his sleeping pills and lay down in the back seat of the car. I waited until he was out before I opened the garage door. He slept for the whole drive. And when we got to Palm Springs, I waited for him to rouse before I helped him inside. And to tell you the truth, he didn't need that much help. He walked from the carport to the front door pretty much all by himself. He started to get nervous just once. Then he was okay.*

And you left him there? Alone?

He asked me very nicely to leave. It's his place, Max. I couldn't insist on staying. And anyway, I'll have you know we spent much of Christmas Day sitting outside under that big red umbrella you bought in Mexico. The one with the—

I know what the umbrella looks like, June.

Well, he sat under it. Outside. And then we went for a little walk around the property just before I left. Yes, he leaned on me a little, but he was outside. I'd call that getting better, wouldn't you?

Another slight pause would likely occur before Max would speak again.

Perhaps. Have you heard from him since you came home?

Of course not. You know there isn't a telephone there.

Max might then say, *Well, can't a neighbor check on him?*

June would need an answer for that.

That's a good idea, she could say. *I'll see. It's the holidays, though. It might not be that easy to find one at home. And I don't know all the other homeowners in that neighborhood.*

At this point she was sure Max would offer to go check on Elwood himself. He was chomping at the bit to talk to him anyway.

He would probably leave right after they hung up. He'd get to the bungalow, and then he'd dash back out to his car and drive to the convenience store two miles away and ask to use the phone to call the police since Elwood didn't have one at his desert hideaway. Or he might bang on a neighbor's door and use their phone if he could find one at home. He'd probably phone her then, too.

She'd have to sound distraught when Max called and appear doubly so when she met up with him later that day in Palm Springs.

How long would the police search for Elwood?

A couple months? Longer?

That script had to be in MGM's mailbox before Elwood's disappearance was reported: missing men don't finish scripts.

Unless . . .

Unless she turned it in to MGM herself a few days into the New Year when it was looking more and more unlikely that Elwood would be found. That would give her more time. Perhaps she could tell the studio she'd just found the completed script in a desk drawer. That would give her another week, maybe two.

MGM would still be obligated to pay him. The work would have been delivered. She'd tell Max when they gave the check to him that she would deposit it into Elwood's account as usual—Max knew she did Elwood's banking—but she'd actually endorse the check to herself and deposit it into her own account and cross her fingers no one would notice.

And down the road, if Elwood's accountant did notice, she'd inform him Elwood had promised her that money because of all the help she'd given him with that script. He'd left a note stating that. Yes, a note. Easy enough to forge.

It was the most money Elwood had ever been contracted to write a screenplay—ten thousand dollars. And it had to be enough for a down payment to buy back the Malibu house from Ruthie Brink's sons. But she still needed to see about getting her old job back at Warner Brothers. Any bank that loaned her the rest of the money to buy the house was going to insist on assurance that she could make the monthly mortgage payment.

Everything still left to do was all too much to consider at the moment. Too much. She liked far, far better imagining herself Christmas shopping with the Elwood she had loved—the Elwood who should have married her and left her this house. Having a nice dinner with him. Coming home to his bed . . .

Eva touched her shoulder then and June's eyes snapped open.

"Are you all right?" Eva asked.

"Oh! Yes. I was just . . . thinking."

Eva moved away, looking slightly unconvinced.

June looked again at her guest. Nicky was finishing his last triangle. She stared at him for a long moment as she reacclimated herself to the here and now.

"Now what do we do?" the boy said to her.

"That's a great question," June said with a laugh, because it was. *Now what do we do?* was the perfect question.

Eva shot her a quick look, and then said, "We could make brownies."

"Do you want to make brownies, Nicky?" June asked.

He shook his head. "Do you have soldiers?"

"Soldiers?"

"To play with. Green ones."

"I have a chess set."

"What's a chest set?"

"Chess. It's a game on a checkerboard. Moms and dads play it. You could pretend the pieces are soldiers, I think. There are kings and queens and castle rooks. And horses."

"Okay."

June, grateful for the distraction, retrieved Frank's chess set from her closet shelf and took it outside to the patio. It was a beautiful day, high seventies, sunny and cloudless. Nicky followed her. So did Eva. Her back injury nearly healed, June nevertheless carefully lowered herself to a patio chair.

She unclasped the box and opened it on its hinges, revealing the chessboard and the pieces. Nicky picked up a white knight.

"The horse!"

"There are four of them, two white and two black," June said. "If you want, I can show you how they go on the board." June set up all the pieces on the patio table, showed Nicky some basic moves, and told him that the white king and queen were always at war with the black king and queen. He began hopscotching the pieces across the squares and making up all of his own moves. Ten minutes later he had abandoned the board, and now all the pieces were in various states of battle on the grass and atop the planters of alyssum and impatiens that bordered the back fence, and even in the rose garden.

June sent Eva back into the house to fetch a blanket and set it on the grass so that the two of them could sit on it while they watched Nicky.

When he began to tire of playing with the pieces that way, June had Eva bring out a dishpan of water and Nicky gave the chess pieces swimming lessons. When he tired of that, Eva hid them like

Easter eggs in the yard while June made sure Nicky kept his eyes closed until he went looking for them. He then wanted to be the one to hide the pieces. And after that, he wanted to be the one to look for them again.

June lost track of time as they occupied themselves in the backyard. It was the best kind of afternoon, almost like summer, when the days are long and carefree. Again she found herself drifting mentally to that Other Place, the one where she'd married Elwood. It was easy to do, watching that little boy play among the rosebushes.

The daydreaming, however, meant June was not thinking about the fact that, being outside in the backyard, she likely wouldn't hear Melanie when she returned to the house. Might not hear her knock on the front door and then perhaps open it herself when no one answered. Nor was she considering that Melanie might easily see from the kitchen window June, Eva, and Nicky happily playing in the backyard and that Melanie might turn from the window then and head up the stairs to talk to Elwood.

Nor that when Melanie reached his bedroom door, she might tap gently, say Elwood's name, and, upon hearing no response, force open the door.

18

Driving to Santa Monica to go Christmas shopping was the first completely normal thing Melanie had done in months. When she parked June's car near Henshey's Department Store like dozens of other people had already, she nearly cried at the sheer ordinariness of it.

Aside from her hair in a matronly bun, the ugly scarf around her neck, and the too-big sunglasses, she knew she looked ordinary, too: She was just an average woman with a purse on her arm and a list in hand, shopping in Santa Monica.

Melanie was aware that she was still risking being recognized, but honestly, would anyone suspect blacklisted actress Melanie Cole would be perusing the toy aisles at Henshey's today? And even if a fellow shopper identified her, how bad could it be? They might stare, yes. Frown, yes. Whisper under their breath, *Commie!* Possibly.

She didn't care.

It felt too good to be doing something so natural as Christmas shopping.

If they stared, she'd ignore it. If they frowned, she'd smile sweetly in return. And if someone murmured *Commie!* as they walked past her, she'd wish them a merry Christmas.

She wouldn't engage, wouldn't cause a scene, wouldn't draw attention, wouldn't linger. She'd do as June suggested and watch other mothers shop for toys for their little ones. Then she'd pick something up for Elwood and perhaps something for June, too. Maybe a fountain pen for Elwood; he had told her once he thought fountain pens made him write better. That had made them both laugh.

Some fancy bath salts for June, perhaps?

And she'd get something for poor Eva, too. A little bracelet, maybe. Something pretty.

Melanie had been alone, angry, and afraid when the Gilberts' house had become her home, and she'd assumed she'd make no friends living there, secluded as it was and Carson's cautions making her uneasy about meeting new people. It amazed her now as she stepped inside the department store how different she was beginning to feel about the place where Carson had dumped her. The house had grown on her, surprisingly enough.

And not just the house—also a sense of belonging was starting to fill her that she would never in a million years have thought would happen.

That first day completely on her own at the Gilberts' house had seemed like it would never end.

When the sun finally set on that hot July day, Melanie knew she was going to need to make a schedule for herself of what she was going to do to fill her days—and nights—and she needed to do it quickly or she would seriously lose her mind. The following morning on Day Two, she made the list in fifteen-minute increments, from the time she got up in the morning until she clicked off the light for bed. Every activity was on the list, no matter how mundane. She wanted the daily record to be long so that she could feel a sense of accomplishment as each item was checked off, even if it was just teeth-flossing, exercising with Jack LaLanne on the TV in the living room, playing rounds of solitaire, and *not* eating the peach melba ice cream Carson had included in the first grocery delivery.

On Day Three, Carson called, and she wrote in the activity and checked it off:

Talked to Carson.

She watched the paid gardener mow the front and back lawns in diagonal lines, and she shooed a spider outside and plunked out a melody on the baby grand in the far corner of the living room:

Watched the grass being mowed.
Saved a spider's life.
Figured out the notes of "Mr. Sandman" on Mrs. Gilbert's piano.

On Day Four, she added to the daily list to stand on the back-yard patio in the mornings for an hour and recite the lines she still remembered from her high school plays.

It was while she was engaged in this activity on the sixth day of her Exile in Paradise, as she was starting to call it, that she first heard Elwood Blankenship's voice.

She was reciting all of Gwendolin's lines—the ones she could recall—from *The Importance of Being Earnest*. She'd just spoken the words, "Pray don't talk to me about the weather, Mr. Worthing. Whenever people talk to me about the weather, I always feel quite certain that they mean something else. And that makes me so nervous," and was imagining in her mind the character Jack's reply when suddenly that line was floating her direction from across the fence.

"I do mean something else," the voice said.

Melanie was only momentary startled into silence. But she was far too curious and hungry for human interaction to think how strange it was for the next-door neighbor—whom she hadn't even met yet—to be listening in on her, and then, on top of that, playing her little game. She faced the fence and delivered Gwendolin's next line.

"I thought so. In fact, I am never wrong."

Jack's reply glided across to her. "And I would like to be allowed to take advantage of Lady Bracknell's temporary absence."

Melanie took a step toward the fence. "I would certainly advise you to do so. Mamma has a way of coming back suddenly into a room that I have often had to speak to her about."

The next line wafted over the fence as she took another step.

"Miss Fairfax, ever since I met you I have admired you more than any girl . . . I have ever met since . . . I met you."

Melanie grinned at the line everyone always laughed at and took a third and fourth step: "Yes, I am quite well aware of the fact. And I often wish that in public, at any rate, you had been more demonstrative. For me you have always had an irresistible fascination. Even before I met you I was . . . I was . . ."

She couldn't recall the rest of the line. But she was at the fence now and peering over it. She could see a trim, well-dressed man, gray at the temples, sitting in a kitchen chair at the open door to his own patio. The front legs of the chair were just over the threshold. He was as close to the outside of a house as one could be while still being inside it.

This was the screenwriter who never left his house. She'd seen his last name on his mailbox at the curb. Blankenship.

He was leaning slightly forward in his chair, and a cat was rubbing a cheek on his pant leg. The man smiled lightly with a closed mouth.

She smiled back and then tried the line again. "I was . . ."

But the rest wouldn't come.

"Far from indifferent to you," Mr. Blankenship said, finishing it for her.

Suddenly the next part came to her, but only the one sentence. "We live, as I hope you know, Mr. Worthing, in an age of ideals . . ." Her voice fell away.

His smile widened slightly. "We certainly do."

"I can't remember the rest."

"Been a while?"

"Nine or ten years, I guess. How long for you?"

He laughed lightly. It was a nice sound. "Quite a bit longer. But it's a favorite. Named the cat Algernon." He looked down at the cat, who'd plopped down next to his left foot and was now cleaning its face with a paw. Then he looked up again. "You rehearsing for an audition?"

"No. I'm just . . . killing time. It's just for fun."

"Ah."

"I'm Melanie Co—Kolander," she said, catching herself just in time. This fellow was a Hollywood man—even way out here—if he was a screenwriter. She'd promised Carson she would be careful. "I'm . . . I'm housesitting for the Gilberts while they're in Egypt."

"Kolander," he said, thoughtfully. "Ah, yes. Yes. I see." He nodded. "Don't worry, Miss Cole. I won't give you any trouble. You have nothing to fear from me."

Fear prickled all over her body. "You know who I am?"

"I recognize you and your given name from the newspaper and the magazines my sister-in-law likes. But I assure you, you have no reason to be afraid. I have no desire to make things more difficult for you."

"No one is supposed to know I am here," she said breathily, almost as if to just herself.

"There is no one I wish to tell, I assure you. And I will make sure June knows this, too, Miss Cole."

"June?"

"My sister-in-law. She lives here, too. The name's Elwood Blankenship."

"Nice to meet you, Mr. Blankenship."

"Please. Elwood will do."

"And I insist you call me Melanie."

"A pleasure to make your acquaintance, Melanie. I would get up and walk over there to the fence and introduce myself proper if I could, but I can't. I'm sorry."

"Why can't you? Are you hurt? Is that why you don't leave your house?"

His eyebrows lifted a fraction. "Touché. I guess you know who I am, too."

"Not really. Mr. Gilbert said you never leave your house. I don't think he told us why."

Elwood was quiet for a moment. "Yes, I guess in a way I am hurt. For a while I could still make it out to the backyard to tend my roses, but even that is starting to be difficult." He nodded toward an oval of rosebushes across the patio from him. There had to be a dozen different varieties and shades, all in bloom.

"They're very pretty," she said.

"They are, aren't they?" He exhaled heavily. "They are very special to me. I have missed caring for them."

Melanie was incredulous. She'd heard of people being reclusive, but not someone being powerless, though physically capable, to step out their back door. "You don't even go into your own backyard?"

"Not very often. Sometimes at night when there is no moon."

A few seconds of silence hung between Melanie and her neighbor.

"You're a screenwriter?" she asked a moment later.

He laughed lightly. "I am."

"Like, a working one?"

The laugh turned into a lazy smile and he nodded. "On contract with MGM."

"Lucky you," she blurted. "MGM won't hire me right now." She clamped a hand across her mouth, instantly regretting her words.

"I know they won't. I know none of the studios will. I'm very sorry this has happened to you."

"I'm not what they say I am. I am not a communist. I'm not even sure what a communist does or wants."

"I've no doubt you're not. There are a lot of people on the blacklist that are or have been communists but I know there are just as many—more, actually—who aren't. And have never been. Again, I feel badly for you. You were just in a big movie, too, weren't you? With Carson Edwards? Your debut, I believe."

"Yes. I don't suppose you saw it."

"No. But I read the reviews. The critics liked you. And the audiences."

"For the most part. And now everyone despises me. There was another movie in the works for me with an even bigger role and then this happened."

"To you and Edwards both, yes?"

"Yes. And some other people he knows."

"And the two of you are . . ."

"Are what?"

"A couple? My sister-in-law thought she saw Carson Edwards drive up and go inside the Gilberts' house a few days ago and then leave the next morning. I told her it probably wasn't him. I'm guessing now it was. I owe June an apology and five bucks."

"We're sort of a couple," Melanie said. "We're not exactly . . . It's not love—it's . . . I don't know what it is. He's a good friend, the only friend I have right now. He's paying my rent for this house. I could never afford it on my own. He and my agent thought it would be a good idea for me to get out of Hollywood for a while."

"I see. You'll be here until the Gilberts get back, then?"

"God, no!" she exclaimed, instantly appalled by the assumption. "They'll be gone for two years!"

"Of course. That was thoughtless of me. Forgive me."

"I'm sorry I yelled, but I can't live this way for two years. Shut up like this? No, no, no. I'd go nuts."

He laughed lightly, but she could tell he wasn't laughing at her predicament but the words she had used. She'd pretty much said if she had to live the shut-up life he was living, it would drive her crazy. Her face instantly warmed.

"Wait! That's not what I meant! I wasn't suggesting that you—"

He held up a hand, still smiling. "It's all right. Don't worry about it. I've surely been called worse."

"I'm so sorry. I didn't mean anything by that."

"I know you didn't. Please. Don't give it another thought."

He came across as such a genuinely nice man. Kind. Wise.

"You don't seem crazy at all," she said, thinking aloud.

He laughed again. "I'm glad to hear that."

She was about to say how nice it was to talk with someone again when June Blankenship came to the patio door. Melanie could instantly see that June cared for her brother-in-law, was protective of him. It was also clear by the expression on June's face that she'd heard every word that had passed between Melanie and Elwood.

Elwood introduced her to June, but June did not come to the fence when she said it was nice to meet Melanie and that she hoped she would enjoy living in Malibu. She then told Elwood that his morning tea was ready if he wanted to come inside and have it.

"Have a nice day, Gwendolin," Elwood said as he rose to step fully back inside his house.

She waved goodbye and he closed the door and was gone.

When Melanie went back inside the house, she added to her list of activities for the day:

Talked with Elwood Blankenship.

And crossed it off the list.

Carson came over that night and she told him about meeting Elwood and that, despite her being careful, he had figured out who she was but he also promised to keep her whereabouts a secret.

"It'll be nice having a friend to talk to," she said to him as they sat around the kitchen table eating the chicken and biscuits he'd brought for their dinner.

"But you can talk to me," he said, frowning slightly.

"Sure, when you're here. I'm talking about having someone to talk to when you're not here, which is pretty much all the time. It gets lonely here, Carson. This place is like a crypt."

"It's . . . a really nice house, Mel."

"Okay, it's like a really nice crypt. I don't like being alone *all* the time."

"All right, all right." He took a bite from a chicken leg.

"And why aren't you hiding out like I am?" she asked, an observation that had been needling her the last three days. "Why aren't you out here with me if it's so risky for us to be out and about?"

Carson wiped his mouth with a napkin. "Because I can maintain my distance from hecklers and the press and all that. My house is gated. I have my own vehicle. I can afford private security."

"But you still get to be around other people. It's not fair to expect me to speak to no one or to never go out to eat. I'm getting pretty tired of canned soup for dinner. You try eating it five nights in a row."

A few days later he'd hired Eva for six days a week from nine to three, to cook and clean and no doubt keep her company. Having Eva in the house was certainly better than having no one, but it was Elwood she was drawn to for company.

Over the next few weeks, as July eased into August, Melanie would find herself talking often to Elwood either across the fence, as he sat in the patio doorway, or sometimes as he stood by an open upstairs window and she spoke to him from several feet below and on her side of the fence. Twice in September he welcomed her into his house for short visits, and they talked about plays and movies and acting. Both times June served them coffee and seemed to hover. Melanie thought it was perhaps because Elwood had so few visitors, only his agent and a few studio execs and couriers; Melanie was his only outside-the-studio friend. She hoped maybe June liked that Elwood was opening himself up to someone new from the outside.

She came to learn in the first of those two inside visits—and in general terms—of the car accident years earlier that had a lasting effect on Elwood and made him not want to leave his house.

"Because you're afraid you might get into another accident?" she'd asked.

"Something like that."

He'd stood then, signaling that the visit was over, and she intuited this was a topic he didn't discuss. She would not bring it up again, though it bothered her that this good man was stuck inside his own house by choice. She wanted to be his friend. She wanted him to be hers.

When Carson broke the news to Melanie in October that a director friend had offered him a lead role in a new Broadway play and he would be leaving for New York for a spell, she went to Elwood to lament how jealous she was that Carson was going to be working again. He'd listened as she cried tears of frustration and had offered her his handkerchief, but it was the last time he let her inside the house.

Not long after this she noticed it had been a while since Elwood had stood at the open back door, his chair straddling the interior of his house and the rest of the world. When he spoke to her now, it was from the upstairs window or the occasional phone call. Always from within—fully within—his house.

She expressed concern to June about this, but her neighbor told her sometimes Elwood would drift into a melancholy state for a while and would eventually drift back out. She needed to let him be about it. He didn't like people fussing over him or telling him how he should feel.

But weeks had now passed and he hadn't drifted back out at all. If anything, he'd gone further in.

Melanie tucked her shopping bags into the trunk of June's car and hurried to the driver's side. She still needed to stop at the A&P before heading back to Malibu to get the last few things on her list. No one had recognized her at Henshey's as she shopped and then paid for the Tinkertoys and books and farm animals she found for

Nicky, nor when she bought Elwood's fountain pen or June's lemon verbena bath salts or the charm bracelet she'd picked out for Eva.

She'd made good time in the department store, but she didn't want June and Eva to have to be responsible for Nicky any longer than they had to be, nor did she want to tempt fate by staying out too long and having some random reporter figure out who she was and start pelting her with questions.

Besides, while it had been enjoyable at first, shopping in the open like any normal person, she knew the whole time it was all a façade. That joyous feeling of being out had begun to lessen as soon as she'd paid for her purchases and walked back out to the car. The shopping trip had been fun but it had changed nothing.

She was still grieving a lost career.

She was still certain Carson was losing interest in her.

She was still worried about Elwood.

She was still wondering how she could stay in California without Carson's financial help.

Still waiting for Alex to come back into her life and stay there.

She drove to the A&P contemplating that the year would soon end but without the likewise end of her banishment from Hollywood, nor of Carson's wanting to stay in New York, nor of Alex's continued absence.

But even so, she felt a strange calm regarding her situation—at least for the moment—because she wasn't entirely alone.

She had Elwood and June. Sort of. And quiet Eva. She had Nicky.

Christmas wasn't going to be a lonely affair focused on everything she'd lost.

She would celebrate the holidays with her neighbors, Eva, and her nephew. She'd invite Elwood, June, and Eva over for Christmas dinner, like she'd thought of doing the day Alex arrived. If Elwood wouldn't come, and he probably wouldn't, she'd suggest they have a family-style Christmas dinner at the Blankenship house.

There was no way Melanie was going to tuck tail and run home to Omaha with Nicky as June had suggested, and to subject herself to her parents' immense disappointment in her. Not at Christmas of all times.

Besides, she didn't belong there.

Here was where she felt the most at home, if home couldn't be in Hollywood.

After the quick stop at the grocery store for the bubble bath, the ketchup, the Band-Aids, and the other items on her list, Melanie made her way back to Malibu along the coastal highway, listening to Christmas music on the radio with the car window down as far as it would go.

She parked June's car in the driveway, took out her shopping bags, and ran them over to the Gilbert house. She hid away the gifts in the master bedroom closet and put the A&P bag on the kitchen counter. Then she headed back over to June's.

When no one answered her light knock, she opened the door slightly and said June's name. Still no answer.

Melanie stepped into the foyer and heard a laugh from beyond the front door but not inside the house. She made her way through the living room and into the kitchen, and then saw through the window that June and Eva were sitting on a blanket in the backyard in the plentiful sunshine and Nicky was running across the grass with little toys in his hand. At least they looked like small toys.

Everyone seemed to be having an enjoyable time.

She was about to join them when it occurred to her that she'd just been given the perfect opportunity to see for herself if Elwood was truly okay.

Melanie turned from the kitchen, went back through the living room, and began to climb the staircase.

"Elwood?" she said in as gentle a voice as she could from the second step. "It's just me. Melanie. Mind if I come up?"

No answer.

She continued up the stairs. "Elwood? May I just talk to you for a moment? Please?"

No answer.

Now she was on the top step. She could see the door to his office was ajar.

"Elwood?"

Nothing.

Melanie crept down the short hallway to the office, passing Elwood's empty bathroom.

"Elwood?" As soon as she poked her head in the room she could see no one was in it aside from Elwood's cat, curled up on the seat of the desk chair. Algernon raised his head to look at Melanie and yawned lazily.

She turned and retraced her steps to the top of the staircase and the closed door just to the left of them that led to Elwood's bedroom. She knocked on it softly.

"Elwood? It's Melanie."

No answer.

She put her hand on the doorknob. Locked.

"Elwood, are you all right?"

Nothing.

Melanie pulled a bobby pin from her hair and stuck an end into the lock, turning it this way and that, jiggling it, then reinserting the pin upside down and jiggling it again until she heard the mechanism inside the lock turn.

She slowly opened the door.

The first thing Melanie saw was Elwood's bed, stripped entirely of its linens as though it were laundry day.

She stepped into the room saying his name. "Elwood?"

The bookshelves that lined one wall were in order. The bedside table was clean. The dresser top was free of clutter, as was an amply stuffed armchair and the table beside it. There was no sign of Elwood.

Had he dashed into his closet to hide from her?

"Elwood?" She approached the closet and opened one of its double doors. The inside was full of clothes and shoes lined up with their mates, and boxes in neat stacks on the shelf above the clothes rack. But Elwood wasn't hiding in the closet.

Elwood wasn't upstairs.

Melanie dashed to Elwood's bedroom window that overlooked the backyard, hoping that he was outside at last with the others and his roses and that she had just missed seeing him.

Below her, June and Eva were still on the blanket. Nicky was lining up what looked like chess pieces on the top of a low retaining wall on the far side of the yard.

Elwood wasn't in the backyard, either.

Melanie made her way as quickly as she could back downstairs, alarm beginning to make her heart race. She looked for Elwood in June's room, in the garage, in the utility closet, in the laundry room, even in the coat closet by the front door.

But Elwood Blankenship, the man who never left home, wasn't inside his house.

19

For one fleeting moment, Melanie imagined Elwood had been rushed to the hospital with some awful injury while she'd been gone. But that was not possible. Not possible. June wouldn't be relaxing on the lawn at that moment if he'd fallen down the stairs or cut his hand in the kitchen or accidentally swallowed poison.

Had he finally decided it was time for inpatient care to help him deal with his debilitating problem? Or had June decided enough was enough and called for a psychiatric hospital to come get him? Impossible on both counts for the same reason. June would not be sitting on a blanket in the backyard if either were true.

Had he never been in the house at all? Had she been talking to a ghost all this time? June, too? Talking and living with a ghost? Unthinkable. Eva had been coming over to the house for more than a week. She'd made meals for Elwood, washed his laundry. Straightened his slippers. He was no ghost.

Melanie threw open the Blankenships' patio door.

June was still sitting on the lawn, but Eva had joined Nicky to line up the chess pieces atop a brick planter filled with pink and white flowers. Both women turned to the sound of the patio door banging open.

"Where's Elwood?" she said.

June struggled to rise to her feet. Eva left Nicky with the chess pieces and started to walk toward her. Neither woman answered the question.

"Where is he?" Melanie demanded.

June brought a shaking hand to her forehead and brushed a few stray hairs away. "Melanie! I didn't hear you come in."

"Tell me where he is, June."

June looked to Nicky, and so did Eva. The boy had stopped playing and was staring at Melanie.

"You need to keep your voice down," June said evenly.

Melanie swiveled to face Eva, who was now standing next to her. "Have you seen him? This whole time you've been coming over here, have you seen him? Even once?"

Eva shook her head slowly from side to side, eyes wide.

Though she'd answered Melanie, it was plain as day Eva knew something. Melanie wanted to scream at them both.

Instead, mindful of Nicky, she lowered her voice. "I want to know what the hell is going on or I'm . . . I'm going to call the police."

June closed her eyes for just a moment, let out a breath, and then turned to Eva. "I think it would be best if you took Nicky back to Melanie's."

Eva did not move. Melanie saw fear in the maid's eyes. Or maybe dread. June spoke to Eva again.

"Please," June said. "Just take him so that Melanie and I can talk. He can't be here."

Eva looked from Melanie to June to Nicky, clearly not wanting to leave. She hesitated before walking across the grass, bending

down, and saying something to the little boy. He smiled and nodded. She offered her hand, he took it, and they walked back to the
patio.

"Nicky wants some ice cream. We are going to go back home so
he can have some," Eva said, falsely cheerful.

"You want ice cream, Auntie?" Nicky asked Melanie as he approached her with his hand in Eva's.

"Later, honey. I need to talk to Miss June."

Eva glanced up at Melanie and then immediately averted her
gaze.

Eva knew. She knew Elwood wasn't in the house!

She'd deal with that betrayal later.

As soon as Eva and Nicky were gone, Melanie rounded on June.
"Tell me where he is."

June exhaled deeply as she walked to the patio table mere feet
from where Melanie stood and sat down at it. "It's very sweet of you
to care for Elwood as you do, Melanie. Honestly. I've not appreci-
ated you the way I should have all these months. I should've insisted
he visit with you more often. I think he liked talking with you. It
might've changed everything if I had. Well, not everything."

"Tell me where Elwood is. Right now. Or I'm calling the cops."

June closed her eyes and then opened them. "Yes, you probably
should call them. But I think it would be a disaster if you did."

"Why? What has happened? Where did he go?" Melanie said in
a rush.

"Sit down and I'll tell you."

"I don't want to sit down! I want to know where he is."

June shook her head as she said softly, "He's gone, Melanie."

Melanie knew in an instant. She could tell by the tone of June's
voice and that look of anguish what she'd meant. Elwood was dead.
An ache began to throb in her chest. But still she asked.

"Gone where?"

Quick tears had sprung to June's eyes. "He swallowed a bottleful of pills, far too many, and he died."

June leaned forward, put her elbows on the table, and rested her forehead in the well of her palms.

Melanie reached for the back of an empty patio chair to steady herself as shock and sadness somersaulted inside. Elwood!

Dead.

Elwood was dead.

"When?" Melanie murmured. "When did this happen?"

June didn't look up. "Almost two weeks ago."

Melanie pulled out the patio chair and sat down. "Why have you been pretending he's still here? Why would you do that?!"

June lifted her head and gaped at Melanie as though she didn't know how to answer any of those questions. So she didn't.

Which didn't make any sense, either.

"June," Melanie said, her voice thick with emotion in her throat. "Why have you been pretending he's still here?"

"Because he is." June's voice was somewhat childlike, and Melanie felt a chill zip through her. The woman had to be off her rocker. Completely. Because the only other explanation for her comment was . . .

"What do you mean he's still here?" Melanie said again, her throat now thick with unease.

June shrugged and looked away, off toward Elwood's roses. "I didn't think he would ever do something like that. If I had known I would have called for a doctor. I didn't know. So I wasn't ready. I don't even think he was ready. But then he just . . . did it. He took all those pills."

"June, what do you mean he's still *here*?"

"I loved Elwood," June said, her head cocked to one side, two

214

tears tracking down her cheeks. "You need to know that, Melanie. I loved my husband very much. But I loved Elwood, too. He was my best friend after Frank died, my only true companion. And he gave me a home, something I'd never really had before. He gave me work to do, work I loved. And he let me care for him, almost like a wife cares for a sick husband. He gave me everything. Everything."

Melanie's heart was pulsing madly in her chest as her brain embraced the notion that something was terribly off.

"June," she said. "Where is Elwood? Where did you take him?"

"I needed more time," June said vacantly, still staring at the garden. "That's why I did what I did. I didn't know what else to do."

"What? What did you do?"

"He left everything to Ruthie's boys, Melanie. Everything. All his money, all his investments, his royalties. And this house. This house where I had lived with the two people I loved most in the world. It is more than just a place to live. It's my home. I couldn't lose it. I needed more time to finish the script I was writing for him. I needed the money it will bring in. I'm going to beg those boys to sell me the house and I need that money for the down payment. So I needed more time. I needed Elwood to be alive and finishing the screenplay. I can't lose this house."

"So you . . . didn't tell anyone he'd died because you are writing his screenplay?" Melanie said, aghast.

"They aren't really his scripts anymore," June said. "I've been writing them for a long while. A very long while."

Melanie leaned forward across the table. "June. You need to tell me where Elwood is. Where did you take him?"

June sighed heavily. "I told you. I didn't take him anywhere. He's right here."

"That doesn't make any sense!"

June pointed to the rose garden. "Right *here*."

The blood in Melanie's veins seemed to whoosh to a chilly stop, followed by an odd calmness. "Are you telling me that you buried Elwood in the backyard?"

June was staring at the rosebushes, several of them blooming in the summer-like temperatures of a typical Southern California December. "Yes."

"And Eva. Eva knows this, too?"

"She doesn't. At least, I don't think she does. I'm not sure."

"What do you mean you're not sure?" Melanie echoed hotly.

"I think maybe she has suspected it for a few days. Maybe a week."

Anger began to flare. "And she did *nothing*?"

"I think it's because she understands. She lost her home, too. She lost her family. She knows what it's like to lose everything. I think maybe she wanted to help me."

"Help you?" Melanie said furiously. "Help you commit a crime?"

"I didn't kill him! He was dead on his bed when I found him. It's not like I committed much of a crime."

Melanie shot to her feet. "The hell it's not." She turned for the house and stormed through the kitchen, June trailing behind her.

"Where are you going?" June asked.

"Where do you think?" Melanie called over her shoulder as she made a beeline for the front door. "I can't be a part of this. You know I can't. I'm sorry for your loss, June, I am. But this is crazy. I'm going to call the police."

"Wait!" June called after her. "Melanie! You don't understand. I have a plan!"

"A plan? A *plan*? I can't believe you let Eva be involved in this. Honestly, I can't. And by God you're not going to involve me." Melanie was in the entry, her hand reaching for the doorknob.

She'd started to open it and June was suddenly there with the palm of one hand slamming it shut.

Melanie swung around to face her.

"Wait! If you call the police . . . you'll wish you hadn't," June said, as if improvising. Pulling words out of the troubled air.

Melanie stared at her, incredulous. "Are you threatening me?"

"No." June shook her head, her tone and countenance earnest. "No, I swear to you I'm not. I'm just . . . just telling you what's true."

Despite the gratitude for June she'd felt just a few short hours ago, this was nuts. June had buried a dead man in her backyard! Melanie had to get out of that house, out of this mess. Nothing good could come from becoming an accessory to June's actions. There were laws regarding what a person could do and not do with someone's remains. She spoke gently but authoritatively. "You will let me leave, June. What you have done has nothing to do with me."

"I know it doesn't," June said. "But you're already on the blacklist for reasons that have nothing to do with you. If you call the police and you tell them Eva has known for a week, we'll both be in trouble. They will look into her. And if they do that, they will find out about her past."

"So what if they do!"

"Listen to me. If they discover who Eva really is, everything will fall apart! I already know I'll go to jail. But Eva will probably get deported. And if that happens, I guarantee you, you won't ever get off that list."

20

Eva had just started to rinse Nicky's ice-cream bowl when she heard the Gilberts' front door fly open, and then June's voice.

"Melanie, please! Don't do anything rash! Let's talk about this."

She turned from the sink as both Melanie and June rounded the corner and entered the kitchen. Melanie looked livid. Eva glanced quickly to Nicky, who, beyond the kitchen in the open living room, was building a tower with wooden blocks. He'd paused in his play, though, and was looking in the direction where the three women stood framed in the kitchen doorway.

Melanie grabbed Eva's arm and pulled her attention back to her. "How could you do this to me?" she said through her teeth, fiercely angry but controlling her volume. "How could you keep working for me day in and day out all these months, knowing what I am up against? How could you do that? You're a Russian!"

Melanie's words were nothing near to what Eva had expected her to say. "What?" She looked to June.

"I'm sorry, Eva," June said. "I just . . . it slipped out. She was going to call the police. I figured she'd tell them you had known for days that Elwood wasn't in the house. I was afraid they might arrest you, too, and they'd look into how you came to the States and discover who you really are. So I told Melanie why calling the police could be bad for her. I just wanted her to stop and think. That's all. I just wanted her to stop."

"But what about Elwood?" Eva said, dazed.

"He's dead!" Melanie yelled. "And this woman you're protecting buried him in her backyard. The backyard!" Melanie had let go of Eva's arm but her body was still heaving in fury. "And *you*! You've been with me all this time when you knew the backlash I'd get if it came out you're from the Soviet Union. How could you do that?"

But Eva had barely heard Melanie's angry question. Her mind was spinning around the sudden image of Elwood's body below the earth, resting among his roses. She'd known all along, hadn't she? Starting with the day Melanie asked her to speak to June from across the fence—that morning June had been digging up rosebushes in the dark. That scene had called to her mind a memory she'd had to forcibly sweep away so that she could ask the question Melanie had told her to ask.

A memory of a body. The dead of night. A rose garden.

Eva shook it away again as she pictured June burying Elwood in his own rose garden, a man June loved but who had not loved her—a man who'd left June's only home to the sons of the woman he *had* loved.

"June?" Eva said.

"I'm talking to you!" Melanie shouted.

But Eva sought June's gaze. "June, what happened?"

June shook her head and winced as if it pained her to say again the words she'd surely just spoken to Melanie only moments before. "He killed himself, Eva."

Melanie pivoted to June. "And how do we know that's what happened? How do we know you didn't do this to him?"

"Because she loved him," Eva said quickly, not taking her eyes off June. "Right, June? You would not do this and lose the house and your work. You would not do it."

"What are you talking about!" Melanie exclaimed.

June pulled out a kitchen chair and slumped into it. "No. I would not."

"What do you mean by 'lose the house'?" Melanie said.

"In his will Elwood left the house—everything—to the sons of that woman who was in the car with him the night of the accident," Eva said. "And no one knows this, but June is the one who has been writing Elwood's scripts. She has nothing if he's dead, Melanie. No house. No work. And she loved him. She didn't do this."

"But you don't bury a man in his backyard. For heaven's sake, June! What were you thinking?" And then Melanie pivoted to face Eva. "And why didn't you tell me you're Russian? God in heaven, the two of you are going to ruin me!"

"I should have quit when I found out about that list. I should have. But you need to know I am not—"

"What? Not Russian?" Melanie cut in. "Of course you are! I don't care if you think you're German. You were born in Russia! You lived there. Your family was shipped off to a Siberian gulag! That's what happened, isn't it? That's how you lost everybody you cared about. They were hauled off to Siberia. In *Russia*! Tell me everything June just told me about you isn't true."

Eva swiveled to look at Nicky again. He was knocking over his tower with a spatula she'd loaned him from the kitchen, happily uninterested in what the adults were shouting about. She turned back to Melanie.

"What June probably told you is true, but I *am* German. All my family is German. Yes, I was born in Russia, but I am not Russian."

"Then why did you lie to me about it? Why have you been lying to everyone? Why have you told everyone you are from Poland? Why do you pretend to be someone who you are not? Can't you see how that looks? It looks like you have something to hide. It looks like you're a communist trying to pretend that you're not one!"

"I assure you I am not."

"But it looks like you are! Don't you see? That's all that matters!"

Melanie pulled out a kitchen chair, too, and sank down into it, resting her head in her hands.

Eva took the chair beside her. "I'm so sorry, Melanie. I will leave at once. I didn't—"

But Melanie didn't let her finish. "Me firing you doesn't solve anything. It solves nothing. You've already been here for five months. It's too late for that. And you can't leave me with this mess!" Melanie tossed a hand in June's direction.

"I swear I didn't know when I first started coming here what had happened to you," Eva said. "When I found out about the blacklist, I did look for another job so that I could quit. I should have quit anyway. It was wrong of me to stay on. It's wrong of me to stay now."

Melanie sighed. Shook her head as she massaged her temple. "I told you. It's too late. You've already been here all this time. And I don't want you to quit. I . . . I need you right now. For this god-damn mess and for that little boy. I don't know what I'm doing."

"I don't think that's true."

"Hush up and let me think."

"You are wonderful with him and he is so fond of you. I can tell. He feels safe with you."

"That's nice of you to say, but that doesn't solve anything, either."

"What do you mean? What must we solve?"

Melanie pointed in the direction of the house next door. "Elwood is dead and everyone thinks he's alive. Oh, and let's not forget June buried him in the backyard and you and I both know it."

June looked up. "Hey. I wasn't thinking clearly when I did that."

"No shit, June!" Melanie said hotly. "What exactly *were* you thinking?"

"I . . . I just panicked," June said. "When I found him, I knew I was going to have to call somebody. And I knew when I made the call, they would come and take him away and he would be gone from me for good and I would have nothing. I just . . . I didn't want to say goodbye to any of it. To him. To his house. To my life here. To any of it."

"Okay, but why the rose garden?" Eva asked.

A long sigh escaped June. "I needed more time to finish that last script. I wasn't thinking things through when I took him out to the rose garden. I was reeling, I felt so betrayed by him. The day before, he seemed like he was coming out of his bad spell. Honestly, he did. I had no idea he was going to put on a suit, write, 'I'm sorry,' on a piece of typing paper, and then swallow every sleeping pill he had. When I found him the next morning, he was already cold."

"Oh, June." Tears stung at Eva's eyes. Nothing else on earth hurt like the death of someone you loved; she knew this all too well.

"All I was really thinking was how much he loved his roses and that I needed more time," June went on. "I knew—deep down I knew, even when I was shoveling—there would be no digging him up again. I knew I would need to have an explanation for Elwood being missing, and a good one so that no one could ever suspect where he actually was."

"Well, good luck with that," Melanie said.

"I did come up with one, though. It's a good plan and it still might work."

"You can't possibly be serious!" Melanie half laughed.

"I think we should hear her out," Eva said. "Please, Melanie?"

"I can't believe we're actually discussing this." Melanie spoke to the walls of the kitchen as if they were listening in.

"I decided that when the script was done, I would tell everyone he'd asked me to drive him out to his bungalow in Palm Springs. You know, to finish the trip he had started with Ruthie. Because he thought if he did, he would find peace. I was going to say I agreed to drive him, that he'd taken a sleeping pill from inside the car while it was still in the garage and slept the whole way; that's how I'd say he got himself out of the house. And once we were there, I'd say he'd asked for some time to himself, that he wanted me to return to Malibu and come back for him in a week. But when I went back to Palm Springs, I would say I didn't find him. What I would find instead was a note he'd written, and I'd show the note I already had. And then, after Max came by with his ultimatum, I figured he'd want to go out to the bungalow to talk to Elwood and so he'd be the one to find the note. I'm going to add just a little bit to it, which will be easy. I've already mastered Elwood's script for signing his name for banking."

"What are you going to add?" Eva asked.

"I'm going to say that Elwood has chosen to financially provide for Ruthie's boys his way, by ending his life out in the desert, and he doesn't want anyone to come looking for him. But of course the police will be called, and days will be spent in the wilderness searching for him. He won't be found, though, and at some point he'll be declared dead. But I will have already gotten the money for that last script, and I'll convince Ruthie's sons to sell me this house using that money as a down payment. The house will be mine, then. Truly mine. I can then watch over Elwood's beautiful resting place the remainder of my days."

Melanie exhaled heavily. "And I suppose this is the story Eva and I are supposed to corroborate for you if we're questioned about it? That everything seemed just fine at your house before you and Elwood went to Palm Springs? You want us to lie for you?"

June didn't hesitate. "I do. But Melanie, I'm not asking you to. I can't keep you from calling the police if that's what you'd rather do. Maybe I do belong in jail for this. But I don't want anything bad to happen to Eva. Or to you. I don't want Eva getting arrested or deported to the Soviet Union to face whatever kind of hell awaits her there. And I don't want you to never be in another film. I know how hard you worked to make it in Hollywood. And I haven't told you this before, but I drove into Santa Monica back in January when your movie came out. I saw it. You're a wonderful actress. None of what has happened to you is your fault, either. I've made a mess of things, but I don't want you or Eva to pay for it. You've already had to pay."

Eva reached across the table and squeezed June's hand. There had been only a handful of women in her life who'd been this kind and good to her. Four, really. Her mother, Sascha's mother for a time, Louise—dear Louise—and now June.

"Assuming I agree, what happens if the police or Max don't believe you?" Melanie asked. "What if they don't believe us when we're asked to corroborate? What happens then?"

"What's not to believe? I think it's easier to buy the story I plan to tell than the real one. Who is going to believe I had the crazy idea to bury Elwood in his rose garden? And that you both found out about it and said nothing? You and Eva standing by me if you're questioned means there will be no reason to doubt me. Max knew

Elwood wasn't doing well. He'll tell anyone who asks that he'd told me we needed to get help for him, and I'll act remorseful that I didn't. Actually, I won't have to act. I wish every minute of every day that I had called a doctor when I saw Elwood slipping this time."

Melanie seemed to think on June's plan for a moment before shaking her head in obvious rejection. "Why would I do this? This is insane! I am already in enough hot water. If it's that easy to lie, then I'll just lie when I call the police and I'll leave out the fact Eva knew something bad had happened to Elwood. She'll stay out of trouble, and so will I."

"But, Melanie," Eva said gently. "June will go to jail. She will lose the house. She loves this house. It's her home. It's all she has now."

Melanie seemed to ponder this but only for a second.

"No," she said, vehemently. "No, no, no. It's too risky, and I can't manage another catastrophe in my life. I just can't. I won't have a place to live nor money to live on if this goes south."

June furrowed her brow. "Why won't you have a place to live?"

But Eva knew what Melanie was referring to; she'd overheard her talking on the telephone with both Carson Edwards and her agent.

"Carson is already talking about pulling the plug on supporting me," Melanie said. "All he really needs is just a little push and he'll say he's done. This house may not be mine but it's all *I* have now."

There was a second of silence before June spoke, and when she did, it was as if the words had suddenly just come to her. They spilled out in a rush. "You can come live with me. You and Nicky can both move in with me, and you can have the upstairs to yourselves. I'll buy a new bed for that room. You won't have to leave Malibu if Carson stops paying your rent. You can stay."

"What?" Melanie said doubtfully.

"I won't charge you room and board or anything," June went on. "It won't cost you anything to move in here. If Carson stops supporting you, you won't have to leave Paradise Circle. You can stay right here as long as you need to. I'll provide anything you need."

"Why on earth would you do that?" Melanie's voice was not much more than a cautious murmur.

"Because we need each other right now. Please, Melanie. I can't go to jail. I need to finish this last script and get the money for it. It's the only way I can keep my home."

There was a long stretch of silence.

"I seriously can't believe Elwood left those boys this house when it's your home, too," Melanie finally said with a huff. "Do they even need it? Aren't they already living somewhere else?"

"I can't imagine they will keep it," June said. "They'll probably be advised by their grandparents to sell it and split the profit so that they can each buy their own place someday. Two teenage boys have no use for a house in Malibu. I need to be the one to buy it from them."

"So when will you do that? I mean, how long will it take for . . ." Eva's voice trailed off.

"I have no idea how long before Elwood will be declared dead. And I can't ask anyone."

"But if those boys don't want to sell it, where will you go?" Eva asked, knowing intimately what it is like to have a home one day and be without one the next.

"I can't even begin to think about that. I guess I'll have to go back to the city and get what I can afford."

"And you'd just leave Elwood . . . here?" Melanie asked.

Eva saw June shudder. "What choice would I have?" she said.

"But . . . ," Eva began as a new thought sprang to mind, and then she closed her mouth. She was about to say: What if the boys keep the house and decide someday to take out the rose garden?

What if they should decide to dig?

The quiet resting place of a good but troubled man would become a crime scene. The police would come looking for June. She would likely be charged with murder despite her claim Elwood had overdosed on sleeping pills. June would spend the rest of her days in prison as a murderer who had killed no one.

Eva suddenly knew what would need to be done if June lost the house. Perhaps regardless of whether or not she got it.

It was the only thing that could be done, really, though it seemed impossible to carry out.

It would require a great deal of planning.

Still, she was the one who could do it if there *was* a way to make Elwood's last resting place forever secure.

If there was a way, she could do it for June. For all of them, really.

After all. She had done it before.

21

Eva had somehow known from the first day of working for Louise Geller that this woman would change her life.

She wasn't normally given to prescient thoughts but there was no mistaking the sensation when she met her that Louise was going to be the person to set her on a new course. Sascha's mother had done that, too, by fleeing with Eva and Sascha's sister Tanja to Berlin when the Red Army began its march to reclaim occupied Kyiv. But this relationship with Louise was going to be different. With Irina, Eva had been bound by a promise she'd made to her father to do whatever Sascha's mother asked of her. She'd been just shy of her sixteenth birthday when she'd made that pledge, and still seen as a dependent child in the eyes of the world.

By the time she met Louise, however, she was twenty-two.

The war had been over for five years and she was alone in yet another Displaced Persons camp, this time in southern Germany. Irina had long since remarried a Hungarian man she'd met in their second DP camp and moved with him and Tanja to Budapest. Though Irina had been her last link to Sascha, they'd lost touch even before the war ended, when Irina and Tanja relocated to a different DP camp so that she could be with the man she was going to marry.

It was after Irina left that Eva learned southern Germany's new occupiers, the Americans, had been told by Moscow that the Soviet Union wanted its citizens in DP camps repatriated, whether they had a home and family to go back to or not. American camp officials were expected to make that happen.

It had given Eva nightmares thinking what her return to Russia would be like. She'd surely be seen as a conspirator who'd sided with the Reich as its soldiers marched into Kyiv, and a traitor who then worked for the Nazis for nearly two years. Eva knew what the Red Army did to traitors . . .

When a dorm mate Eva had befriended told her she was going to tell the American forces overseeing the camp that she was Polish and that all of her documentation had been stolen from her during the war, she invited Eva to do the same. They agreed to pretend they were cousins who could corroborate each other's claims. Living in the camps alongside Polish women for several years had allowed them to pick up just enough of the language to fake it.

"What if the Americans check the camp records?" Eva had asked her as they formulated their plan.

Her friend had replied, "What if they don't?"

In the end, there had been no camp records to check. At this new monastery turned refugee camp, it was not unheard of for someone to claim his or her few belongings had been stolen from them, been destroyed by warfare, or been lost.

The Americans in charge believed that Eva and her friend were Polish cousins brought by force to Germany to labor for the Reich. They believed it simply because the same was true for hundreds of thousands of other non-Germans who were in Germany at war's end. The Americans believed Eva's suitcase had been ransacked and that she'd been robbed of her identification papers. She was given new ones.

Eva had felt a tremendous sense of control that she'd not only managed that deception but that it had held. She had in an instant become someone else.

And now she felt the same was going to happen with Louise; she was embarking on a new life without camp officials and foreign occupiers forcing her hand or erecting limitations. Her new employer was going to be instrumental in helping her forge a new future. She couldn't explain it, but she could feel it. And she wanted it. She needed it.

Working for Louise hadn't been her first job following the war. Expats in the DP camps were expected from the beginning to find employment. When the camp's job assistance clerk asked Eva what her prior work experience had been, she couldn't say she'd spent nearly two years in a Kyiv government building typing and interpreting for the Nazis. Eva Kruse from Warsaw could not say that. Eva Kruse from Warsaw had never been to Kyiv. She told the woman she had experience cleaning houses and cooking and mending, as those were all tasks she had performed starting at age twelve when Tante Alice passed.

Her first job placement was as a part-time maid at a hotel that housed occupational forces.

When the Americans at last left, the hotel's German owners didn't want camp refugees as employees. While Eva was looking for another job, she heard camp rumors of a congressional bill floating around in America that, if passed, would provide relief for a great many of the six hundred thousand refugees still foundering in the world of the camps. Other nations had already made similar overtures of assistance: Belgium, Australia, and several South American countries. But to immigrate to a country whose language she didn't speak? Eva struggled to understand how a person who did that ever felt like they belonged.

She started working in the laundry room of a hospital, also part-time, the same day in June 1948 that President Truman signed the Displaced Persons Act, which, among other things, made provision for the immigration of two hundred thousand DPs to the United States over the next four years. But the news changed nothing for her. Eva knew no one in America; she didn't know what else to do but continue to wash the worst kind of soiled laundry.

And then one afternoon she heard of another job opening.

There was a woman, American by birth but married to a German man, who was looking for domestic help for her large Munich home. She wanted someone young. Someone who could cook and clean but carry on an intelligent conversation, too, in German or English. Someone she could trust and someone who still knew how to laugh.

"I can do all those things," Eva said to the woman who'd read off the job description. "I can cook and clean. I can speak German. I can laugh."

Two days later, Eva returned to the office to see if there'd been any word regarding her application.

The same woman smiled and handed Eva a card with an address on it and a train schedule.

"Frau Geller would like to meet with you on Monday at ten a.m."

Eva would address this woman as Frau Geller only once, when she met her. Every day thereafter, until the moment Frau Geller put her on a plane to Los Angeles three years later, Eva called her—by request—by her first name.

Louise, tall and auburn haired, was a forty-two-year-old former Bostonian who'd gone to Oxford University for her last two years of college as a literature major. While in England she'd met Ernst Geller, born and raised in Munich, who was also at Oxford, but studying economics. He was from a moneyed Bavarian family, spoke English impeccably, was handsome in a stark way, with ice-blue eyes and sun-blond hair and a near-regal bearing. He was calm, elegant, and methodical, and she'd fallen quickly and deeply in love with him after only three dates. But when he proposed the week of their graduation in May of 1928, her family back home in Massachusetts had been appalled. Her parents had lost an uncle, a cousin, and a neighbor to the kaiser's armies in the Great War only ten years earlier. They begged her to reconsider wanting to spend the rest of her life with a German man. They would never accept him as their son-in-law, and if she married Ernst, she was turning her back on not only her family but her heritage, her country, and everything she'd been taught was good and right. But Louise was in love. She married Ernst Geller in Munich the summer after her graduation. She'd not heard from her parents in the years since.

After Louise told Eva her story, it occurred to her that Louise hadn't said Ernst was a man she still loved, only that she had loved him when he'd proposed and when she'd married him.

Eva wondered if Louise was happy in the beautiful house that had survived Allied bombing, with its tapestries and paneled walls and window boxes full of flowers, and whose grounds featured majestic fir trees and a pond and rose garden. It was a grand home to be sure but there were no children living in it nor any evidence that there ever had been. Louise was easy to work for, always had a neat list of tasks for Eva on the Mondays, Wednesdays, and Fridays that she came. And she insisted on paying for Eva for an extra hour or two every day she worked so that Louise could teach her English to better Eva's chances of getting chosen to emigrate to the

U.K., Canada, or America. She was kindhearted, generous, and maternal.

And because of this, it surprised and saddened her that Louise had no children.

Louise would have made such a good mother.

Herr Geller—for that is what he instructed her to call him—displayed no parallel fatherly instincts. She found Ernst Geller impossibly hard to get to know. He had a prominent position in finance and in the newly formed West German economy. The deutsche mark had replaced the occupation currency, and Herr Geller was somehow integral to the leadership of the banking system and worked long hours in a headquarters office in downtown Munich. Eva wasn't entirely sure what he did. He was almost never at the house when she was there, which Louise almost seemed intentional about.

When he was at home, he was polite around Louise, but not in the way Eva had seen other husbands be gracious to their wives. It was not so much in a kind way as in a mannerly way. He never put his hand on Louise's or kissed her in front of Eva, though she knew some men were not prone to public displays of affection. Louise had described him as a quiet, calm man, and that's what he was. But he was something else, too—something that Eva couldn't quite name. *Aloof* wasn't quite the right word. Nor was *dispassionate*. Nor was *calculating*. Eva was certain Herr Geller cared about something, was devoted to something, and it was probably his marriage, but only logic told her that. She didn't see the physical evidence that he cared for Louise, that he loved her, esteemed her.

But neither did she see physical evidence that the opposite was true.

As the months of the first year of working for the Gellers ticked by, Eva made it a point to remind herself that while she was fond of Louise and grateful that Louise was teaching her English, she'd not been asked to fix Louise's problems or to even identify if she had any.

Her goal instead was to learn English and apply for permanent residency somewhere English was spoken. Louise was certain the United States was Eva's best option, and not just because that's where she was from. Louise had college chums and high school friends up and down the East Coast and even a few on the faraway West Coast that she was confident would help Eva identify a sponsor, which was the biggest hurdle to getting a DP immigration application approved. If Eva mastered English and had a sponsor willing to arrange for a job and a place to live, she could easily be one of the four hundred thousand DPs America was willing to take. Louise even offered to teach Eva how to drive.

These were the activities Eva concentrated on, and when stray concerns about Louise's happiness would pop up, she shooed them away as none of her business, even though Louise did seem interested in *her* happiness.

Eva had tried dating a few men—other refugees on the male side of the camp—at Louise's suggestion that she have a little fun now and then. There were dances and concerts and cultural celebrations hosted by the different nationalities represented in the camp, and Eva was often asked by young men of the camp to attend one as their date. Aside from the momentary distraction of an evening out, Eva didn't know how to empty Sascha's place in her heart so that she could happily date other men. It seemed wrong and unkind to his memory. And it didn't seem fair to the young men who wanted to court her.

Besides, she was priming herself to go somewhere far away from

Sascha's memory. Like America. Or Canada. Or England. Or Australia. What was the point in beginning a relationship in the camp when she wasn't planning to stay? There wasn't.

Late in the following year, when immigration protocols had been formalized, Louise helped Eva with filling out two applications, one for Australia and one for the United States, though the process for immigrating to America was rumored to be slower and more selective.

Louise seemed sad as she helped Eva work through the many questions on the initial forms. Eva realized as she tucked the papers away before leaving the Geller house for the day that she was sad, too. She and Louise had formed a bond over the past two years that had transcended their relationship as employer and employee. Louise had marked Eva's birthdays with sweets and new clothes. She had spoiled her with Christmas gifts and hair appointments and the best present of all—she'd given her the ability to speak English and drive a car. Louise was the first person since her father who'd genuinely cared for her like a parent would.

"You know," Louise said, "if neither of these applications is accepted, I could help you stay. I could help you apply for a permanent place to live right here."

Eva had shared with Louise all that had befallen her—leaving nothing out—and also her desire to put as much distance as she could between herself and those losses. Staying in Germany hadn't been a consideration until just that moment.

"You mean here with you and Herr Geller?"

"Oh, no!" Louise replied quickly. Too quickly, and Louise seemed to sense it. She just as rapidly reframed her reply. "I mean, you would want your own little place in the city center where there are more after-work activities for young people. I could help you get a nice little flat close to a train station so you could still easily get to the house and all the other people you work for. Or I could help you with training for a different job if you wanted."

Again, Louise seemed eager to do the things a parent would for an adult child who needed help making their way in the big world.

It was obvious—and touching—that Louise cared for Eva and didn't want her to go.

She might've considered staying if her world hadn't again been turned upside down, this time by her own hand.

Eva was at the Gellers' later than usual to help clean up after a dinner party. By ten o'clock the last guests had left and Eva was in the kitchen washing the final round of dishes. Louise was going to be driving her back to the camp when she was done, as the last bus had left for the train station an hour earlier. As she rinsed a serving platter, she could hear Ernst speaking to Louise in the hallway on the other side of the wall. When he raised his voice, she turned off the tap.

Herr Geller was scolding Louise for something she'd said to one of his guests.

"It was not your place to say such a thing," Ernst said. He'd had much to drink that night and his voice sounded different. Slightly unhinged.

Louise said something in response but her words were muffled by the thickness of the wall. Perhaps it was, "I was only trying to help."

"You belittled me."

Louise's next words were indecipherable except for their tone. She was pleading.

Something then crashed to the floor and broke, and Louise cried out.

On impulse, Eva bolted from the kitchen and rounded the corner to the hallway.

Ernst had Louise against the wall next to a table where seconds earlier a large vase of flowers had been standing. Water, lilies, and big chunks of broken lead crystal were splayed at their feet. In his hand Ernst held a fistful of Louise's hair.

Eva realized at once that Ernst had forgotten she'd been in the kitchen. The look on his face when he turned and saw her was one of utter amazement. The look on Louise's was one of utter terror.

"Why are you still here?" he shouted at Eva.

"Louise?" Eva said softly, as though unsure her voice still belonged to her.

Louise smiled but it was the grin of a clown, painted on. Completely fake. "Go back in the kitchen, Eva. Go back. I'll take you home in a minute." She reached up a hand to gently ease away the fingers wrapped around half the hair on her head. But even as she did so, Ernst tightened his grasp and Louise cried out in pain.

Eva took a step forward. "Stop! You're hurting her." The words came out of her mouth like a command.

Ernst wheeled away from the wall and toward Eva, Louise's hair still in his fist. Louise cried out again. "How dare you speak to me like that?" he said to Eva. "And in my own house."

This insult was delivered at near calm. If he hadn't had hold of his crying wife by her hair, his tone would have suggested everything was fine and he'd just told Eva to bring him a brandy.

When Eva said nothing in response, he took another step toward her.

"Ernst, please!" Louise screamed, both in pain and desperation.

The realization that she and Louise were both in danger hit Eva like a lightning bolt. She suddenly knew exactly why Louise had never wanted her to be at the house when Ernst was home. Why Louise hadn't wanted her to stay with them when they talked about her remaining in Germany. Why Louise hadn't ever said that she still loved Ernst. Why sometimes when Eva came to clean the house Louise said she had a migraine and spent the hours Eva was there lying on her bed with a cool compress. Why Louise perhaps never wanted to have children, if this brute of a man would have been their father.

Louise had married a monster who was able to look and act like a gentleman when it suited him. And to be who he really was when it didn't.

Ernst closed the distance to Eva. It was the nearest to her he'd ever been, and he towered over her. Louise was struggling to free herself and screaming his name, but he held onto her hair as though it was the easiest thing in the world to do.

"I asked you a question," he said to Eva.

"And I said you're hurting her." Eva was unable to recognize from where these brave words came because fear pulsed through her. She was already imagining her own hair in Ernst's grip when he tossed Louise to the floor and came at her.

Ernst swung the back of his hand like a cudgel. Eva instinctively ducked and his arm swung harmlessly through the air.

He lunged for her and she dodged him again. His face was now contorted in quiet rage, as though no one had dared to challenge his strength and control before. He lunged a second time, but his feet, clad in his expensive leather shoes, slipped on water from the spilled vase, and he went down on his back with a thud.

Eva ran to Louise, who was half sitting, half kneeling on the tile floor, cradling her head.

"Go, Eva! Run! Get out of here!" she wailed.

"You're coming with me." Eva had no sooner wrapped her arms around Louise to help her up when her friend screamed Ernst's name and Eva felt herself being lifted away from the floor as if on puppet strings. Then she was flying. She slammed into the wall and then fell to the floor. Stars burst in her head much like they had when the Red Army soldier smacked her with the butt of his rifle on that long-ago, terrible day.

For several seconds a buzzing blackness filled her mind.

When her vision cleared, she saw Ernst kicking Louise as she lay on the floor at his feet after he'd flung her there, hurling insults at her.

Louise was curled into herself, crying out, begging him to stop, but he did not. Eva knew she had to make him stop. He had to stop. She stood on shaking feet, grabbed the largest piece of the broken vase, the heavy bottom, and swung it hard, cracking the back of Ernst's head.

He went down next to Louise with a groan, but the next second he grabbed his wife's wrist as she lay just feet from him. He dug his nails into the soft flesh of Louise's underarm as he tried to yank her toward him. She cried out in pain.

In that moment, every terrible thing Eva had witnessed since the moment her father and brother and Sascha were taken from her, every cruelty she'd seen in Kyiv, every act of anger and aggression at the camps, every moment she wished she could unsee, smashed into her. She had not been able to save her family or Sascha. She'd not been able to save any of the people the Nazis had executed in Kyiv. She'd not been able to save anyone.

Until now.

She would stop Ernst.

Eva raised her arm and brought the base of the vase down on the back of Ernst's head.

She did it again and again and again until he was still and the vase bottom was red in her hand.

There.

He had stopped.

In the years that followed, Eva would understand completely why June buried Elwood in the backyard. She would understand why a person might decide the best thing to do with a body that needs to disappear is to bury it in a rose garden in the backyard. When one is traumatized and frightened and tired but required nonetheless to address a gigantic problem at that very same moment, one might do an impulsive thing.

No one would believe Ernst might have killed them both, Louise said in those endless minutes after they both realized he was dead. No one was going to believe that Ernst had been violent with Louise since the earliest days of their marriage. No one would believe it because Ernst was an upstanding citizen of fine pedigree and held an important position with the biggest bank in the country. Louise was a nobody American who'd never complained in the past about anything Ernst had done. Ernst's family had wealth, privilege, and influence. She had nothing. If she called for an ambulance, it was likely Eva would be arrested for murder. Louise probably would be, too, as an accessory.

As they dug his grave in the backyard, Louise decided on the story she would tell Ernst's family and the authorities. Ernst had already been planning to go the following morning to Starnberger See, a beautiful lake outside Munich where he liked to row his canoe for recreation and exercise. It was how he maintained his strong physique. Louise would report him missing that evening when he failed to come home. After they were done burying the body and while it was still the wee hours, Louise would drive Ernst's car to the lake's shore, and Eva would follow behind in Louise's car. They would push Ernst's canoe out into the water and let it float away. Then they would return to the house in Louise's car, leaving Ernst's at the lake. Louise would bring Eva back to the DP camp in the morning and Eva would tell her roommates she slept over at her employer's house after working at a dinner party that lasted past camp curfew when the gates were locked.

Eva, numb and in shock, at first said nothing as they dug and Louise spoke their plan into being.

All she could think about was that she had killed a man. A monster of a man but still a man. She'd killed him.

Ernst was dead. Dead. He was dead.

And Louise kept laying out what they would do about it, with tears of fear and perhaps relief slipping down her face as she plunged her shovel into the ground.

When the plan was implemented, Louise was saying, she would play the grieving wife concerned for her missing husband. In a few days' time it would be determined that Ernst Geller had drowned, for there was no other conceivable explanation. "And this nightmare will be over," Louise said. Eva would immigrate to the States just like they'd talked about.

At this point in their digging, Eva found her voice. "I only meant to stop him, Louise. I just wanted him to stop. I'm sorry. I'm so sorry."

Louise dropped her shovel and gathered Eva into her arms. "I've imagined him dead a hundred different ways, Eva. I'm the sorry one. I should never have asked you to stay late. I'm the one who needs your forgiveness."

They clung to each other for several long minutes before Louise whispered they had to finish what they'd begun. They needed to finish digging the grave. They needed to drop Ernst into it. They needed to drive to the lake. They needed to get back to the house so that what happened next would be according to her plan.

All might have transpired just as Louise had intended if not for the neighbor's beagles.

The dogs would not leave the burial site alone. Over the next few days Louise and Eva chased the two dogs away several times. They'd even been digging at it four days after Ernst had disappeared when Louise was sitting in the living room with a police detective, following up on Ernst's parents' claim that foul play had to have been involved. She saw through the window the dogs pawing at the ground as she answered the detective's questions with her heart pounding madly in her chest.

Eva and Louise knew they needed to move the body, and it had to be done quickly and soon. But how and when and where to take it? More people were coming to the house all the time. Family, friends, police.

The evening Louise was asked to meet with the Geller family in the city to discuss who might have had reason to harm Ernst, Eva decided she would do what needed to be done while Louise was gone.

The blanket-wrapped body they had buried on a Friday was not the foul-smelling thing Eva dragged to Ernst's car as soon as night fell on a Wednesday. But she did not think about this.

She did not think about anything as she drove two hours out of the city to a deserted forest road that led to deep woods where there was no trail, and to a ravine where—she hoped—woodland animals and insects would find and devour what was left of Ernst Geller.

When she returned to the Geller home, Louise was waiting for her, near frantic with worry. The police were still of a mind Ernst hadn't just fallen out of his canoe and drowned as there was no body. Divers and dredgers had searched the lake twice.

"Then it's good that you don't know where I've taken him," Eva told her. "You will be able to answer truthfully you have no idea where he is."

They worked together the rest of that night to hide any evidence that anyone had been digging in the garden. Days passed and the body was not discovered. After three weeks, the police finally ruled out any kind of foul play—Ernst Geller apparently had no enemies. After four weeks, it was determined he had likely died of accidental drowning.

His case was closed.

Not long after his memorial service, Louise asked Eva to sit down with her at the kitchen table. A thick envelope covered with foreign stamps lay on its surface.

"I owe you my life, Eva," she said when they were both seated. "In more ways than one. I think Ernst would've killed me that night. He might've harmed you as well. I just wish we didn't live in a day and age where we had to do what we did. And I wish I would've called the police and been believed the first time he was violent with me. I wish I had at the very beginning."

They were both quiet for a moment, each surely aware that the past is always and will always be just what it is.

"Listen," Louise finally said. "After what you've done for me, I wanted to do something for you."

Eva thought perhaps Louise was about to ask her to come live with her now that Ernst was gone. Half of her wanted to be Louise Geller's almost-daughter and make Munich her forever home. But the other half wanted to leave all of Europe behind and never look back.

"I found you a sponsor," Louise went on. "In Los Angeles, in California. A friend of mine attends a Catholic church there that has decided to sponsor ten Displaced Persons. You can be one of those ten people, Eva. They have already chosen you based on my recommendation." She patted the envelope. "I'll go down to the immigration office with you tomorrow and show the American officials all the documentation. You have a job waiting for you and a place to live. You can leave as soon we can get your application finalized."

Eva was so surprised, she found she could not speak. Louise mistook her silence for fear.

"I know it's a big step, but I really do think you will be happy there. You can build a new life in America, far from this one. You will love living in the States, Eva. It's a place of possibilities. Especially California. You need to trust me on this."

Still Eva could not bring words to her tongue.

"I will never forget you," Louise continued. "I promise you. And I will be forever grateful to you. But I don't think we should stay in contact with each other. It would look . . . strange. And it would be dangerous for both of us for anyone to think they need to look closely at us, at what we mean to each other. Do you understand what I am saying?"

Eva nodded. She did understand.

"But," Eva said a second later, "what will happen to you if the body is found?"

Louise shrugged. "The police have no reason to suspect me. Nor do my in-laws. If Ernst's body is ever found, I will act surprised. Because I will be. I need to be done living in fear, Eva. I don't want you to start living in it. I want you to go to America and be happy. Be free."

Louise lifted the envelope off the table and extended it toward her.

"I don't know what to say," Eva said as she took it. "I won't forget you, either. And I'm so sorry. I never meant for this to happen."

Louise's eyes began to shimmer with tears ready to fall. "I know. But you have given me a new life, Eva. And now I am giving you one. But I want you to do something for me."

"What is it?"

"Open your heart to love again," Louise said softly. "Please? Will you do that?"

Eva nodded even though she did not know how to do such a thing.

She knew how to run from the Red Army, how to hop a freight train bound for Kyiv, how to lie, how to survive on crumbs, how to clean toilets and bedding stained with human suffering, how to bury a bad man, and how to dig him up again.

But this other thing—opening her heart to love again?—this she did not know how to do.

DECEMBER 25–30, 1956

22

Eva awoke Christmas morning to a cloudless sky. An accompany-ing summerlike breeze seemed eager to convey a message, so intent was it to fit through the two-inch opening she'd left at her bedroom window.

She sat up in bed and listened to the wind's subtle chant. *Wake up, Eva,* it seemed to say. *Change is coming.*

Eva had heard this California wind before, many times since she'd come to the States. It even had a name. Santa Ana. The first time she'd experienced it was five months after arriving. She had settled into a different rented room, that first one being in the home of an older couple, the Talbots, who attended the Los Ange-les parish that sponsored her immigration. She'd already started her job at Marvelous Maids and was taking the bus each day from La Brea to upscale neighborhoods like Bel Air, Westwood, and Beverly Hills where the well-to-do lived.

She'd awakened on that day in early autumn, not late December, but hearing the same persistent wind. It had been tugging at the Talbots' backyard furniture and scooting it around their small patio as if determined to rearrange the seating options. As the day had worn on, the wind had transformed into a super-heated gale as angry as a swarm of agitated hornets. It had snapped a power line in Topanga Canyon and fanned into flame a resulting wildfire that burned a thousand acres of brush before being extinguished.

"It's a Santa Ana wind," Mrs. Talbot had told her that first time. "It blows in from the desert. They come every year. You'll get used to them."

"This wind has a name?" Eva had asked, incredulous.

Mrs. Talbot laughed. "In Poland you have no winds with names?"

Eva had shaken her head. She didn't think there was such a phenomenon in Poland, but then how would she know?

"A Santa Ana can wreak havoc on your sinuses because it's so very dry, but don't worry, Eva," Mrs. Talbot said, saying Eva's name as *Eh-va*, an ongoing mistake Eva had simply stopped trying to correct. "A Santa Ana doesn't last but a few days usually. It comes and then it goes."

Eva had moved into the rented room at Yvonne's a year later, when her sponsorship had been considered complete. She'd continued working for Marvelous Maids, measuring the progress of time by those winds that came without warning every fall and seemed to disappear by April.

This Santa Ana nudging her awake seemed particularly timely. Everything *was* about to change. The day before, Eva had given notice at Marvelous Maids "to pursue other career goals," June had coached her to say. Marvelous Maids had promptly contacted Melanie Cole to inquire if Eva Kruse had failed to meet her expectations and if she would like them to provide a new housekeeper. Melanie had declined, telling them she'd be contacting Mr. Edwards herself to let him know she no longer needed a maid service. She also told them Eva Kruse had been an excellent housekeeper, which Eva had been grateful to hear, especially since she felt she was owed nothing from Melanie except her indignation. She couldn't help wishing she had quit working for Melanie the minute she learned she was on that blacklist. While Melanie had initially thought the same, her anger had softened over the last three days.

June had told them both if there was something to come on its own from Eva's working for Melanie, perhaps it would've happened already. Eva was not sure that was true. She didn't think Melanie thought that was true, either.

But it was done now. She'd quit, severed the employment tie, and would not be seen going in and out of Melanie's house on a regular basis any longer.

June believed Eva's typing skills were nearly on par with her own. She just needed a few more weeks of dedicated practice, which she'd be able to give herself over to now that she wasn't working with Marvelous Maids. June was planning to telephone her studio contacts right after the first of the year. She was confident a job would be found for Eva in the typing pool, if not in one of the Warner Brothers' many offices.

And in the meantime, June had offered Eva Elwood's bedroom until Melanie and Nicky needed it, and until she got a new job and could find a place of her own closer to the studio; a kindness to perhaps guarantee Eva's compliance as she had brokered Melanie's, though June didn't need to do that. Eva was ready to tell anyone who asked that Elwood Blankenship hadn't seemed suicidal. She was even ready to say she'd spoken with him, albeit only for a moment, while she'd been assisting June. It was a lie, but what was one more compared to all the others she'd told in her lifetime?

Eva rose from her bed and surveyed the room that would soon no longer be hers. The furniture was Yvonne's—Eva had rented the room from her furnished—and in the four years she'd lived in America, Eva hadn't acquired much in the way of belongings. Most of what she owned was now ready to be boxed up and moved to June's on New Year's Eve, the day her rental agreement would be up.

She was grateful for June's offer to let her stay with her a little while. That generosity only strengthened her desire to figure out a way to help June out with what lay beneath the rosebushes. The longer she contemplated how to move the body elsewhere, the harder it was going to be to do. Seventeen days had passed since June had gotten out that shovel . . .

Today, however, it was Christmas.

June had invited her and Melanie and Nicky over for pancakes and presents before June drove out to Palm Springs. Eva wasn't going to think about anything unpleasant. She was glad for June's invitation to spend Christmas morning doing something festive, and she could tell June hadn't wanted to spend the entire day by herself, either, nor for Melanie and Nicky to spend it alone.

Everything was about to change for June, too.

And Melanie as well, for that matter.

Eva rose from her bed and quickly got ready so as not to chance missing one of only two buses at her local stop that ran on a holiday schedule.

She'd bought a few gifts the day before on her way home from work—earrings for Melanie, gloves for June, and a stuffed dog for Nicky—and she placed these in a canvas tote along with a sweater in case the afternoon grew chilly, though there seemed little chance of that.

On her way to the front door, Eva caught a glimpse of Yvonne in the kitchen pouring herself a cup of coffee, and she stopped to wish her a merry Christmas.

"Merry Christmas to you, too," Yvonne said with a sleepy smile. She'd clearly just gotten up.

Eva hitched her tote onto her shoulder. "I don't know what time I'll be back. I'm not sure if Melanie will want company this afternoon or not. If she does, I'll probably stay until the last bus."

"Okay. I'll be at my mom's overnight anyway," Yvonne said. "But I'll leave a light on for you. Have fun and I'll see you tomorrow night."

Eva turned to go.

"Oh, that reminds me," Yvonne added, and Eva swung back around. "You might have visitors tomorrow. They were here yesterday afternoon wanting to see you. They said they'd be back tomorrow morning."

Eva felt a dart of unease. "'They'?"

"Two men. They didn't give their names."

"Two men?"

Yvonne yawned. "Uh-huh."

"What . . . what did they look like?"

Yvonne shrugged. "I don't know. Normal-looking. Nice-looking, I guess. Shirt and tie. Hats. You know. Like businessmen. But not from around here."

The unease doubled in intensity. "And they did not say where they were from or who they were?"

"No. I asked and the one who did all the talking just said they'd come back. He asked if you were going to be home on Christmas and I said I sure hope not. So he said they'd come back the day after."

"Did he say what they wanted?"

Yvonne laughed lightly. "You sound so anxious, Eva! They didn't look like criminals, honestly. And the one fellow sounded very nice."

"But did he say what they wanted?"

"Well, it was the strangest question, really. They wanted to know if you were German. I told them you were Polish."

Eva's breath stilled in her lungs.

A million thoughts began darting like arrows around the confines of her mind.

The lies on her immigration papers had been uncovered.

She would get deported.

She would be sent to Moscow.

She would be sent to Siberia.

Or, worse, the men were there because of the body.

The body had been found! The police had found Ernst's body. Louise was in trouble.

Louise had been arrested.

Louise had told them how Ernst's remains wound up off a deserted road two hours outside Munich . . .

Yvonne opened the fridge to get out a small carton of half-and-half as these thoughts somersaulted wildly in Eva's mind.

"They seemed so friendly, though. Very polite." Yvonne began to pour the creamer into her coffee cup. "Maybe one of them saw you on the bus and followed you home because he wants to ask you out." She smiled as she began to stir. "If I were younger I wouldn't mind going out with one of them. I . . ."

But Eva didn't hear the rest. She'd flown out the front door with her bag to run to the bus stop.

23

Melanie awoke with a heel poking into her back and an arm across her neck. She knew without turning to look that Nicky had crawled into bed with her again.

Her closed lips curled into a tiny grin. Four nights ago when he'd done this the first time, she'd been annoyed by the intrusion of a four-year-old who stole her blanket and splayed his bony limbs across her body. But the last two mornings felt different. She felt different. Nicky was becoming less and less the little kid taking up space in her life and on her mattress, and more and more her nephew. Her brother's son. She was his auntie and she was starting to care for him deeply. And it was because of this, she'd made a decision.

She looked across the semi-dark room at the dresser and the envelope atop it that had arrived yesterday by courier. Inside were two one-way airline tickets to Omaha that she'd bought with the last of her savings. She'd be taking Nicky to her parents' in five days, though they didn't know it yet. All they knew from her phone call to them last night was that she was coming home to see them after Christmas, and for an as yet unknown length of time.

Melanie had considered for a moment telling her parents she was bringing their grandchild with her, but then she'd just as quickly decided she wanted them to meet Nicky the way she had. A surprise could be both hard and wonderful. Better to experience it in person, she thought. And besides, Nicky, too, deserved to meet them face-to-face.

June had been in Melanie's kitchen the previous evening to show Nicky how to make popcorn balls when she told June about the tickets to Nebraska.

Melanie already knew June would approve of the trip home, but she surprisingly still wanted her affirmation. It only took seconds for June to give it.

"I'm sure your parents will be very happy to meet their grandson," June said. "I'm glad you're doing it."

Then Melanie told her she was planning to stay in Omaha for a while, though she didn't know for how long.

"But . . . but I already said you can stay here with me," June said promptly, as though instantly worried Melanie's willingness to play along with June's deceptions—which had seemed to hinge on that offer of a place to live—was now off the table.

But Melanie's attitude toward June—and Eva, too—had tempered in the last few days since she'd learned the truth, not just about Elwood and what June had done about it.

She'd come to realize her own stubbornness had complicated matters for herself; it was not just what both June and Eva had done. If Melanie had listened to Elwood and gone home to Nebraska like he'd first suggested, Nicky would surely already be with his grandparents, because she wouldn't have been in Malibu when Alex showed up out of the blue. He would've had to bring Nicky to her in Omaha. And if she'd simply said no, thanks, to Carson's money as compensation for keeping quiet, she wouldn't have spent the last five months living in a house he was paying for and having it look like that was exactly what she was doing: getting paid to keep her mouth shut.

And if she'd gone home to Nebraska back when Elwood told her to, she wouldn't now be part of this insane scheme to make it seem like he'd wandered into the desert to end his life rather than having done so at home in his own bed.

She couldn't fault June and Eva entirely for the pickle she was in. Part of it was her own fault.

"You don't have to worry about me saying anything to anybody about where Elwood is," Melanie said to June. "I'm not taking back anything I said I would do for you if I'm called upon to do it. And I'm still grateful for the offer to stay with you. I might even take you up on it after a few weeks at my parents' if you're still here, regardless of what Carson does or doesn't do."

"So," June said carefully, "you're not exactly with him anymore?"

Melanie laughed ruefully. "Was I ever? I knew it was all pretend, before the blacklist and even after. It was all for show. His show. Irving says he's heard Carson is in Florida for the holidays. And he's not alone."

"Oh, Melanie, I am sorry."

"I'm not. You know, I can see much better what kind of man Carson is when he's not here, if that makes any sense. For a while there, it seemed like he was my only friend. It . . . it doesn't feel so much like that anymore."

When she'd said this, Melanie realized with a start that she'd felt like she'd been in the company of friends the last two weeks with Eva and June, strange as that was, and that it had been a long time since she'd felt that way.

A long time.

The three of them were unlikely companions with hardly anything in common, yet Melanie had felt an alliance between them based on the one thing they did share: their desire to recover that exquisite feeling of knowing you are right where you belong, and that you can rest there because no one is trying to take it from you. There had been a time once when all three of them knew what it was like to own a happy little corner of paradise. They'd each found it before without a map, and she had to believe they could all find it again the same way. Because there is no map to paradise. There is only the dream that such a place exists, as does the desire to possess it, and the determination to find it again when it's been lost.

And she knew now that the people she'd meet along the way would either walk alongside her as companions or they would hold her back as competitors. Moving forward to recapture her bliss was really just a simple matter of figuring out who was who in her life.

Melanie turned over in bed to look at her sleeping nephew with his thumb half in his mouth and his curly hair tousled about his face.

Devotion to Nicky was already replacing the churning fear of being responsible for him. She brushed a tangly lock off his forehead. How had Alex been able to leave him with her like this? How had he been able to be gone for a week already and not even phone her to talk with his son, tell him he missed him, that he'd see him soon?

But then again, Alex didn't have her phone number.

Still, he could've written. Sent a toy or two in the mail for his boy. It was Christmas morning, for God's sake.

And it was going to be a different kind of Christmas Day, that was for sure. Last year, she had slept in until noon, had eggs Benedict and champagne for breakfast, exchanged gifts with Nadine and Corinne, and then gone from swanky party to swanky party with Carson. She'd worn a lamé sheath that hugged every curve in her body and emerald earrings and shiny Italian stilettos. She'd tasted caviar and drunk expensive French wine and sung Christmas carols while someone with amazing piano skills played an ebony baby grand in a living room with a twenty-foot-high ceiling. The other guests at that party had clapped and told her her voice was beautiful and they couldn't wait to see her new movie. She and Carson had stayed over at the house of a friend of Carson's in Beverly Hills, in a beautiful cabana by the pool that was as big as her grandmother's house in Lincoln.

This Christmas was going to be nothing like that.

Instead, she was having Christmas brunch with a nephew she hadn't known she had, a displaced Russian maid, and a widow who'd buried her brother-in-law in her backyard.

This made her giggle, and Nicky opened his eyes.

"Did Santa come?" he said, at once awake.

"I think he did."

"Are there presents?"

"Shall we go see?"

The boy bounded out of bed.

Eva arrived breathless at the top of Paradise Circle just as Melanie and Nicky were about to ring June's doorbell.

She looked as if she'd run the whole way up from the bus stop.

"Hey. It's not like we would've started eating without you," Melanie called out as she pressed the button, but as soon as Eva had closed the distance to her, she could tell Eva wasn't worried about arriving late.

She was afraid.

"What's the matter? What happened?" Melanie asked.

Eva's breath was still coming in shallow heaves, but she sputtered out the words, "Yvonne said two men in suits came by for me yesterday. They wanted to talk to me. She said they are coming back tomorrow."

A thin burst of alarm shot through Melanie. "Who were they? What did they want?"

Eva shook her head, still gasping. "They didn't tell Yvonne who they were. I don't know what they wanted. They just asked Yvonne if I was German. She told them I was Polish."

"You think they were immigration officials?"

"I don't know!"

The front door opened at that moment and June stood ready to greet them. She was wearing a ruffled white blouse, black pedal pushers, and a red and green chiffon apron sprinkled with smudges of flour.

Her smile quickly turned to concern. "What's wrong?"

"Two men showed up at the house where Eva lives, looking for her. Asking about her," Melanie said.

"Come inside."

Melanie, Nicky, and Eva stepped into the house and June shut the door behind them.

"Who were they?" June asked.

"They didn't say who they were." Eva was still slightly out of breath. "Yvonne said they wanted to know if I was German!"

"And they didn't identify themselves as immigration officials?"

Eva shook her head.

"Did she say they asked about me?" Melanie asked.

"No."

The three women stood in the entryway in momentary silence. It was possible the two men had nothing to do with the blacklist,

Melanie thought. Perhaps Eva's true nationality had at last been uncovered. Perhaps those men were in fact immigration officials who didn't know Eva worked for an actress on the blacklist. Or knew and didn't care.

"I don't know what to do." Eva's voice sounded almost childlike. "There are other things I've done . . ."

"Now, let's just think about this a minute," June said. "Come into the living room and set your things down."

They moved into the next room. Melanie and Eva set their totes of gifts down by the little tree and Nicky ran up the stairs to look for Algernon.

The women sat down.

After a moment June said, "All right. Here's what I think. I think you should stay here in Malibu tonight, Eva. I will take you back to your place early tomorrow morning, before anyone's workday starts. We'll get your things and you'll come back here like you were going to in a few days anyway. Those men won't know where you've moved to, whoever they are, and they'll have to find you all over again."

"But what about Yvonne?" Eva said. "What do I tell her? She knows I was planning to come stay here for a while."

"Do you trust her?" June asked. "Is she your friend?"

"I think so."

"Tell her you don't want strange men knowing where you are. It's as simple as that. Tell her she's not to share your new address with them. If these fellas have a legitimate reason for wanting to talk with you, they will give her their business card or something, won't they? And then you'll know who they are."

"Wait a minute. I think I should take her to get her things tomorrow morning," Melanie said. "I'm not the one just getting over a back injury, and if they happen to be there when Eva arrives I want to see who they are. If they are there because of me, I want to know. And if this has to do with only her immigration, I'll step in if they start giving her trouble."

"Okay, but you're not exactly a lawyer, Melanie," June said.

"I'm an actress. I'll act like one."

"It doesn't make any difference to me, but whoever takes her needs to go early, and I mean early early. Like four thirty or five. Don't you think? It would be best if you didn't see them at all, wouldn't it?"

"I suppose so."

"But there's Nicky to think of. He won't be awake then, will he?" June said.

Melanie thought for a moment. "Could he sleep over here? Just tonight? I could bring him over after you get back from . . . you know. Palm Springs."

"Well . . . I guess I could make him a little bed on the floor by me," June said. "Okay, then. That's what we will do. Now, no more worrying about this. The griddle is hot and ready. Let's eat."

"But what if . . . what if those men know what else I did? What if . . ." Eva's voice trailed away, as though the words that would've completed the sentence were too awful to say.

"For heaven's sake, stop asking 'what if,' Eva," Melanie said. "Nobody ever feels better asking what-if questions. They only feel worse. And I don't want to know what else you did. Keep it to yourself and leave me out of it."

"And it's Christmas," June said. "Time for pancakes."

After their brunch and a time of gift sharing, June put a Mario Lanza Christmas album on the hi-fi and they sipped hot cocoa while Nicky played.

Melanie couldn't stop thinking how good it felt to be sitting in a cozy living room in ordinary clothes instead of gold lamé, sipping a hot chocolate instead of a Manhattan, and watching her nephew enjoy his new toys instead of nursing a hangover.

She hadn't missed her family in the last five years as much as she did just then, and she was suddenly overcome with gladness that she had those airline tickets. In five days she would be home. Home. And her parents would meet their grandson.

She'd be going there as Melanie Kolander, the girl who once had a dream. And yet she wasn't the same girl who had left five years earlier. She was also Melanie Cole now.

She was both somehow.

"What are you thinking about, Melanie?" June asked her, breaking into her reverie. "You look like you're a million miles away."

Melanie looked across the room to where June sat with her own mug.

"I was thinking about what it will be like to take Nicky home to Omaha and to be there myself again, I guess. I never thought I'd be so eager to go back there."

"Home was not a good place for you?" The envy in Eva's words was slight but unmistakable. *You have a home to return to. You have parents . . .*

Melanie considered the question and the underlying tone for a moment. "I'd gotten it into my head that I was someone different now. That Melanie Cole isn't Melanie Kolander, that they are two different people. But they're not. And there is no 'they.' This stage name Irving gave me is just that. It's just throwing together a few letters of the alphabet that sound like the name that is really mine. But I'm still me. I am still Melanie Kolander from Omaha. I hadn't understood that until just these last few days. This thing with the blacklist isn't fair, and none of it is true, but it's still real. It's real and because it's real it's part of who I am now and who I will always be. I need to find a way to make peace with that. To somehow own it without it owning me."

June looked at her thoughtfully. "I wish that Elwood could have heard you say that. That accident took everything from him and he never figured out how to live without the things it took. That accident owned him. And oh, how I wish I had known he'd grown so weary of being possessed like that . . ."

June's voice trailed away.

"Elwood made his own choices, June," Melanie said. "And nobody can know another person's thoughts if they choose to hide them. You didn't know. If I've learned anything from these months on the blacklist, it's that it does no good to wish you could change the past. Or the future. It's impossible."

June smiled softly. "I used to imagine the closet in the little one-room shack my mother and I lived in was a time machine. When she would leave me to fend for myself I'd go inside it and pretend to travel forward to the moment when she'd come back. I hated being alone like that. Especially at night."

"Your mother left you alone at night?" Eva asked.

"She had way too much faith in my ability to handle that much independence."

Melanie cocked her head. "How old were you?"

"Seven and eight. Nine, too, but I was used to it by then. It's funny. Now I wish I could go backward in time rather than forward." She sighed. "I wish it all the time."

"So do I," Eva said.

"All the time?" Melanie asked. "*All* the time?"

June took a sip from her mug and then set it down on the coffee table. "Don't you?"

"Not *all* the time. I wouldn't go back and not make the movie with Carson just so that I wouldn't have met him."

"But it wasn't that movie of his that got you on the blacklist," June said. "It was dating him, right? Wouldn't you go back and decide not to do that?"

"That was the studio's idea."

"But you went along with it. What if you could go back and not go along with it? What if you told the studio you wanted the movie to be the magic, which it already was, rather than some made-up Hollywood romance? Wouldn't you do that if you could?"

Melanie sat back against the sofa cushions. Would she do that if she could? "Maybe," she said.

But she knew she would. She'd go back and make the movie, which she'd loved doing, but not the other things. Nothing about Carson had been about love. Not even the sex. Especially not the sex. What was the good of doing something that had nothing to do with love?

"I would go back those weeks before Sascha and my papa and brother were taken and convince them to leave Russia like other Volga Germans had done. Everything would be different right now if we had."

"Why didn't you do that?" Melanie asked.

Eva shrugged. "We did not have anywhere to go. We should have left anyway."

Melanie turned to June. "What about you? Where would you go back to? The night Elwood took the pills?"

June was silent for a moment, as though unsure she wanted to say what she'd say next. "I guess I'd go back to when I first met him."

Melanie crinkled an eyebrow. "All the way back to then? To change what?"

June looked away from her, toward the tree made of dyed feathers. "I've always wondered what it would have been like to have chosen him instead of Frank. I loved Frank; I did. But I can't help wondering how my life would've been different if I had married Elwood instead."

"I don't think it would work like that," Melanie said.

June turned her head to face her again. "Like what?"

"You going back in time to when you met Elwood. You were dating his brother at the time, right? That's how you met Elwood. Are you saying you would dump Frank to be with Elwood? He would have to fall in love with you, too, wouldn't he? No time machine could force that to happen. Besides, can you see Elwood falling for the same girl who broke his brother's heart? I know I didn't know him as well as you, but I can't."

June frowned in consternation. "Well, I'd have to go back further, then, to before I met Frank. I'd have to meet Elwood on my own somehow. Maybe get a job at MGM instead of Warner Brothers so our paths could cross."

"And then hope for the best?" Melanie asked. "What if you couldn't make it happen?"

June seemed to need a moment to ponder this. "At least I would know, wouldn't I? I could come back to this life and I wouldn't wonder anymore."

The three women were quiet as their wishes for what they would change if they could swirled unseen around the room.

"Wait," June said suddenly, shattering their silence with a word. "No, wait. That's not what I would do. I know it's not. It's not." Her eyes had turned silver with moisture.

"What do you mean? What would you do?" Melanie asked.

"I'd go back to the night Elwood got into that car," June continued, emotion thick in her voice. "Of course I would. And I would keep him and Ruthie from getting into it even if I had to slash all four tires."

"Ah," Melanie said thoughtfully. "For love. Elwood loved Ruthie. And you loved him. You'd use the time machine because of love."

Two shining tears tracked down June's cheeks and she did not palm them away. She smiled. "Is there really any other reason?"

An hour later June's car was packed with food for the Palm Springs bungalow—including everything for a ham dinner June would cook and eat alone that afternoon, as well as Elwood's suitcase of clothes, his pipe, and a few of his books.

Before loading the car, June had taken out to the backyard the handgun that Elwood had long kept under his mattress in case of a home burglary, burying it deep in the farthest edge of the rose garden so that when Max or the police asked her if Elwood owned a gun and she answered yes, she could announce in all truthfulness—after pretending to check—that it was missing.

"You're sure this is how you want to do this?" Melanie asked as June got into the car to leave.

June did not answer.

"What else can she do?" Eva said to Melanie as the two of them stood in the driveway next to the car.

When Melanie said nothing in response, June looked up at her through the open driver's-side window. "I'll be home by six. Bring Nicky over anytime after that."

June put the car in gear, backed out the driveway, and disappeared down the hill.

24

Nicky had long since nodded off on the sofa cushions June had arranged on the floor of her bedroom, but she felt wide awake.

A sense of finality had fallen over her when she'd driven away from the desert hours earlier with all the props in play inside the bungalow. It was almost as if Elwood had died all over again when she left. The next time she made the trip to Palm Springs it would be because Max had gone out there with the intention of finally speaking to Elwood face-to-face but had found instead the note.

Elwood would die a third time then, and she would have to pretend it was the first.

When June had returned to Malibu, she'd gone first to Melanie's for borscht that Eva had made for Christmas supper—the invite had been left for her on an entry table just inside her front door. She surprised herself by consuming two bowls. June had tried to eat what she'd made for the pretend early dinner with Elwood, but she had no appetite then. She instead scooped out enough of all the dishes she'd made for two servings each, dumped it all into a shopping bag, and then tossed this into a gas station trash bin on her way back to Los Angeles. The rest of the meal she put into containers and placed in the fridge as staged leftovers for Elwood.

Except for the music playing on the radio and Nicky's occasional questions, their Christmas supper had been quiet. Melanie and Eva had seemed lost in thought, just as she was. Tomorrow was going to be different for all of them.

Blissfully unaware of any of their concerns, Nicky had been perfectly happy to head next door to June's after they'd eaten. Not only was he intrigued with the idea of a sleepover, but he adored Algernon, and for some unknown reason the cat seemed to have the same affection for him. Melanie had stayed with him until he fell asleep on the makeshift bed, and then she returned to the Gilbert house to get to bed herself. She and Eva would be rising before the sun to drive over to Eva's. Eva would sleep in Melanie's guest room since Nicky wasn't in it.

June now turned over in her bed and watched the curtains fluttering at her open window. The night was warm, oddly dry, and nearly electric with portent. It was as if the very air in the room crackled with anxiousness.

There was nothing she could do about the impending loss of her source of income, nor was she completely confident Ruthie Brink's sons would be willing to sell the house to her. She could only hope they would be. Elwood had been generous with those young men; even their grandparents had said so. How could they not return the kindness and let her buy back her home?

Those boys were getting everything else.

They just had to sell to her.

With her savings and the money from the last script, she would surely have enough to make a down payment. All she had to do was find a bank willing to give her a mortgage for the rest.

Which depended on getting her old job back. Or any job.

And she needed to finish that script. She was close. If she could just concentrate on the story and not be distracted by these other pressing matters, she could have it done in a few days, surely.

But what if she couldn't get it done before MGM asked about it?

What if she couldn't manage all these things?

Stop imagining the what-ifs, June heard Melanie saying in her ear, but she couldn't stop. She fell asleep pondering the worst possible outcomes.

And then June was suddenly yanked out of her hard-won slumber by a hard knocking on the front door.

She sat up in bed, her first waking thought that the police had somehow discovered what she'd done and had come for her.

The pounding continued and her next, more lucid thought was that she'd forgotten to give Melanie the keys to her car the night before. Melanie and Eva needed to leave early for Los Angeles.

But then she smelled a whiff of smoke from the open window. Something was on fire.

Good Lord, could it be Melanie's house? Is that why she was banging on the door?

She sprang from the bed despite the lingering pain in her back to let Melanie and Eva in.

But Max stood on the threshold, not Melanie.

Before she could register this, he stepped onto the entry rug just inside. "Why haven't you answered the phone? I've been calling!" he exclaimed.

"I was having trouble falling asleep last night. I took the phone off the hook," June sputtered, still unable to grasp the fact that Max was inside her house.

He stepped farther in, past June and toward the staircase. "You and Elwood need to get out of the house. There's a wildfire headed right in this direction. Can't you smell it?"

Max had his hand on the banister. He called Elwood's name.

The acrid odor of burning brush somewhere off in the distance was now wafting in from the open front door. Dawn was arriving with a ghostly pallor. June could barely make sense of either fact: Max with his foot on the first stair calling Elwood's name, and the harsh stink of torched earth.

"Elwood!" Max yelled, "I'm coming up!"

He ascended the first step.

"He's not up there." The three words rushed out of June's mouth as if The Plan itself were taking charge of the situation.

Max swung around. "Elwood!" he shouted toward the living room, and then he was moving toward it.

"He's not down here, either, Max. He's not in the house. He's in Palm Springs."

Max spun around to face her. "He's *what*?"

"He's at the bungalow. In Palm Springs."

For a full three seconds Max said nothing. "Since when?" He sounded angry, rather than relieved, to hear Elwood had at last left the house.

"Since yesterday. He wanted to finish the trip he'd started with Ruthie all those years ago. He thought Christmas was a good day to do it. I agreed. So I took him."

The Plan continued to roll off her tongue as if she'd rehearsed it only seconds before.

"And you just left him there?" Max said, incredulous.

"I didn't just leave him. I came home after our dinner because he asked me to. He wanted to have the bungalow to himself for a few days. It's his place, Max."

Max stared at her, eyebrows pinched into consternation. "Why didn't you call me?"

"And tell you what?"

271

He huffed in obvious exasperation. "That he'd finally left the house!"

"Because he told me not to. You should leave him be, Max. He wanted some time alone to think and work."

"But he *left this house*! Don't you think I should have been told?"

At that moment, Nicky appeared from within the kitchen, sleep in his eyes and one of June's crocheted afghans in his arms.

"Who the hell is that?" Max exclaimed.

"That is Nicky my houseguest and I'll thank you to watch your language, Max."

Max gaped at her, his wordless stare a command for more information.

"He's Melanie's nephew. He spent the night here if you must know."

Max took this fact in and then shook his head when it didn't mesh with the other revelation of the last few minutes. "You need to grab anything important, get in your car, and get out of Malibu. The first fire has already spawned a second one."

"I don't have my car. I loaned it to Melanie. I need to wait until she gets back with it."

"Oh, for the love of God," Max said. "You cannot wait until she gets back. You're leaving now with me. Where's the cat?"

"I can't leave now. She and Eva are probably on their way back. Or will be."

"And I'm saying you absolutely are leaving right now. I'm not stranding you and that boy here without a car. Have you not been listening to me? There's a major wildfire headed this way."

"But they won't know where I am!"

"Leave them a note!"

Nicky began to cry. "I want my daddy!" he wailed.

"Now look what you've done." June scrambled over to the child and put an arm around him.

"We are not discussing this, June. You and this kid are leaving with me. Right now. Grab some clothes. Grab whatever is the kid's. I'll find the cat. We need to leave."

June turned to the little boy. "We are going to go with my friend Max in his car. It's a nice car. It's red and fast. Let's get your Christmas presents from my room. We'll leave Auntie Melanie a note. She will come to Max's, too, okay?"

Nicky nodded, pacified, it seemed, at the thought of driving away in a fast red car.

June followed Nicky back to her bedroom and scooped his new toys into a fabric shopping bag. She wasn't sure what to grab for herself. Wildfires in or near Malibu weren't altogether uncommon. She knew that Malibu had been threatened by fire in the past—many times—and that on more than one occasion a blaze had waltzed in on a dry Santa Ana wind and destroyed whatever lay in its path. Elwood had once told her that in the last three decades more than thirty wildfires had broken out in the brush canyons near Malibu. Living in Southern California meant living with the threat of wildfires, and she'd lived all her life in Southern California.

June tossed into an overnight bag her jewelry box, Frank's Purple Heart, and a few pieces of clothing, and also grabbed her purse and the emergency cash she kept in her lingerie drawer. On a notepad in the kitchen on which she usually wrote her grocery list she scribbled a hasty note for Melanie with Max's address. On their way to the front door, she placed into her bag the framed photographs that Eva had days ago replaced on the hi-fi.

June taped the note to the front door with one hand and held on to the wriggling cat with the other.

Then she and Nicky and Algernon climbed into Max's little MG—Nicky on her lap and a disgruntled Algernon on his.

"I stayed last night with a friend in Santa Monica but I'm getting us back to LA. As soon as you're safe at my place, I'm going to drive out to the desert to see Elwood." Max put the car into gear as the angry cat growled at him. "I don't care if he asked for privacy. I need to discuss things with him and I'm tired of waiting."

"All right," June said slowly, picturing in her mind Max arriving at the bungalow in a few hours, knocking on the door, getting no answer, finding a way inside, discovering the note. Dashing back out to his car . . .

The Plan was unfolding far faster than she thought it would.

There was no going back now.

Although that had been true for three weeks, hadn't it? Since the moment she dug a grave in the backyard and rolled the man she'd loved into it.

She wrapped her arms tight around Nicky and the cat as Max sped away into the smoky sunrise.

25

It didn't take long to haul down to the car Eva's boxes of belongings. When the last of her things had been tucked into the trunk of the car, they headed back inside so that Eva could leave a note for Yvonne with instructions not to give June's address to those strange men.

She started to write a vague reason for the request but Melanie stopped her.

"Don't give her any extra information. Trust me. Just ask her to say if they have a business card, they can leave one with her. And that the next time she sees you she will give it to you."

There had been no sign of those men when they arrived, nor was there now as they got back in the car to return to Malibu.

The morning sky on the horizon was refusing to turn blue as Melanie pulled away from the curb, a ghostly coral tinge in its place instead. As the minutes and miles ticked as they approached the coast, the more smoke and the odor of ash hung on the air.

"There's a fire somewhere." Melanie turned on the radio and flipped through the stations until she found one reporting the news.

A fire had indeed broken out in the wee hours of the morning in Newton Canyon, eleven miles from Malibu.

But it was apparently a hungry fire and a generous one. It was now gobbling its way toward the coast, starting new fires along the way and in happy partnership with winds eager to play along. Worse, no roads led into Newton Canyon. Getting ahead of it was going to be no small feat for local and regional fire departments. Evacuations were likely if the winds didn't die down and firefighters couldn't reach the fire's heart.

Melanie stepped on the gas.

"They're okay, aren't they?" Eva said. Surely June and Nicky were okay. Weren't they?

"I think so. But I think we might need to hurry."

"June doesn't have her car."

Melanie exhaled loudly. "I know she doesn't. Stop talking about it. That won't help me get us there."

By the time they reached the Pacific Coast Highway, the air outside the car windows was a gritty, dismal gray. Few cars were rushing north toward Malibu as they were, but plenty were driving away from it, toward Santa Monica.

Eva counted down the fifteen coastal miles they needed to travel. She knew those miles. The second bus she took to work every day traveled them. Melanie was driving fast; Eva could feel it. But each time a pumper truck or fire engine came wailing up behind her, she had to pull over to let them pass, losing what seemed like precious minutes.

Finally they were turning off the highway, climbing a residential street, sometimes needing to wait as homeowners backed out of their driveways and fled. At last they pulled to a stop at the top of Paradise Circle.

Eva and Melanie both bolted out of the car and dashed to the front door. A taped note fluttered there.

Melanie plucked it off. "She and Nicky already left, thank God."

Relief and surprise poured over Eva. "Where are they? How'd they leave?"

"Max came for them. June wrote down his address."

"And the cat?"

"They have him. Come on. I need to grab a few things from my place before we hightail it out of here."

As they turned from June's front door, a fire truck pulled to a stop at the top of the cul-de-sac. Four firefighters jumped off of it, each brandishing a pickax or shovel. One of them made his way over to them as the other three jogged partway down the hill to the next closest house.

The firefighter coming toward them was moving fast.

"This street is being evacuated," he called before he even reached them. "You two need to return to your vehicle and get as far south from here as you can." His tone was urgent. "Is this your home?" He pointed to June's house.

"My neighbor lives here," Melanie said. "I live next door."

"Is she still inside?"

Melanie held up the note. "She's already left."

"All right, listen. We need access to the backyards on this side of the street to dig firebreaks. If you can unlock your neighbor's gate, we won't have to break it down. Are you able to do that quickly before you go?"

Eva felt a cold shot of alarm rush through her as she tried to fit together the firefighter's request with what she knew lay buried in June's backyard.

"You're . . . what? What did you say?" Melanie asked.

277

"If you are able to leave your neighbor's gate unlocked for us we won't have to break it down. Can you quickly do that?"

"Uh. Sure," Melanie said.

"You both need to be gone in five minutes. It's not safe to stay."

He jogged away from them, holding a shovel aloft as he went.

"Melanie!" Eva said as soon as he was out of earshot.

"Shut up. Don't say it." Melanie fumbled with June's key ring, looking for the one that would open the front door. When she found it she thrust it into the lock.

"But they are going to be digging in the backyard!"

"I said don't say it!" Melanie threw the door open.

The two women entered the house and Melanie made for the back door in the kitchen that opened onto the backyard and everything that was in it.

Eva followed her, calling her name.

Melanie didn't answer.

Seconds later in the backyard Melanie glanced at the rose garden for only a second before heading to the gate on the side of the house nearest her own. She turned the lever that released its lock, swung it open, and turned to face Eva and the rose garden.

"We have to move the body," Eva said softly but with intent.

Melanie's mouth fell open. "What did you say?"

"We have to. If they dig a firebreak, they will find Elwood. We have to move him!"

A second of silence hung between them before Melanie pivoted to move past her. "I can't believe you're suggesting this."

"But we can do it. I know we can. I have already been thinking how to do it if June loses the house. Elwood can't stay here if she does. You know that, right? What if the new owners want to take out the rose garden? What if they want to put in a pool?"

"Are you out of your mind? Absolutely not!" Melanie started for the house.

Eva put out her hand to stop her. "Melanie. Those firemen will call the police. And the police will arrest June. Can't you see that? It wouldn't be right. She loved Elwood. She did nothing wrong. Surely you of all people understand how unfair that is."

Melanie yanked her arm out of Eva's grasp. "Now, wait just a minute. June did all kinds of wrong. She broke several laws, I'm sure, not the least of which is burying a man in his backyard!" Melanie punched out the last six words with force.

Could Melanie really not see they were the only ones who could help June?

"But she was not trying to break any laws," Eva said. "She was desperate. She was not thinking clearly."

"Well, neither are you right now. I don't really want to see June go to prison, either, but we're not digging up a dead man, Eva. We're not. We only have five minutes—we'd be caught red-handed, and who would that help? We're not going to compound the mistake June made by making a huge one of our own. She wants this house. I get it. But that's not a reason to bury someone in his backyard. Sometimes you don't get what you want. Surely you of all people understand *that*."

Eva winced but shook it off. She had to make Melanie see reason. "June was grieving and afraid, Melanie. She meant no harm. She's a good person. But we have to hurry. We have to do it before the firemen come back."

For a second Melanie seemed to waver. But for only a second. "You seriously want to dig up a body that's been in the ground for nearly three weeks and move it? Even if we had the time, you want to, what, put it in the trunk of June's car and drive it somewhere?

Did you not study biology in high school? Are you telling me you don't know what happens to the human body when it's dead? Honestly, Eva! And where in the world would we take it?"

"I have already thought of a place. We can bring Elwood to the desert outside Palm Springs. He loved it there, yes? We can rebury him somewhere far off the main road where he will not be found for perhaps years, if at all. He will have a resting place like this one, one that meant something to him. It will fit the story June is telling if the remains are ever found. June need never know where we buried him. If she's ever asked if she knows where Elwood is, she can honestly say she does not."

Melanie was staring at her as if Eva had gone mad.

"What in God's name happened to you in that war that has you thinking this plan of yours is a good one?" Melanie said. "A reasonable one? A feasible one! Eva, this is insane, what you're suggesting."

Was it? Was it insane? Was she insane? Had the war—and everything that had happened to her before it and after it—turned her into a madwoman?

She didn't feel crazy, but was she for wanting to dig up a body like one digs up tulip bulbs? Was she crazy the first time she'd done that?

No. Ernst was not Elwood. And Louise? Had Louise also made a terrible mistake when she wanted to bury that monster of a husband in her backyard?

Eva didn't know. All she knew was that Ernst would have killed Louise. Eva had to do whatever she could think of in that fear-filled moment. And so she had.

There was nothing similar about the two men. Nothing at all except where their bodies had ended up. But there was much that was similar about Louise and June, including what they wanted and deserved to have.

And what they both meant to her.

"Eva," Melanie said in a gentler voice. "Listen to me. You're not thinking clearly. Elwood has been dead for three weeks. That body of his is not the one any of us knew. It isn't Elwood anymore. June should have called the authorities when she found him dead in his room. He should have been properly taken care of. Do you understand what I'm saying? He needed to have been properly cared for. He wasn't."

Eva was tearing up as if she had known Elwood herself, though the two of them had never spoken to each other. The tears were not for Elwood, however. They were for June. They were for the undeserved cruelties of life. They were for the ache of loss that was never far from the surface no matter how many years had passed. "She took him to his rose garden. How is that not taking care of him?"

"Because now June is facing the possibility of his body being discovered by those firemen," Melanie said, still gently but with authority. "If it was caring and proper to do what she did, you wouldn't be worried right now. But you *are* worried. Because it wasn't the proper thing to do. You know it wasn't. You and I are helping her live with what she did when she wasn't thinking clearly, but that doesn't make what she did right."

"But we're her friends!"

"And if she's charged with murder, we can decide if we want to vouch for her that Elwood committed suicide. But it's not always a fair world, Eva. You and I can't prove what really happened the night Elwood died. I know June wouldn't have deliberately hurt him. But I can't prove that to the police or to anyone else. And neither can you."

Eva turned to look at the roses. Smoke in the grip of the Santa Ana was swirling above the bushes like a filmy shawl being tossed about on a clothesline. She could taste ash on her tongue.

"We need to go," Melanie said.

Eva said nothing though she knew Melanie was right. About everything.

"Eva. Come on. We have to go."

"June did not want the house, you know," Eva said, still looking at the place where Elwood lay.

"What?"

"It was not this house she wanted. She wanted to keep her home. That is what she wanted. Her home was this house. She wanted her home."

Melanie at first said nothing, and in that space of silence between them Eva could almost hear the far-off roar of the approaching blaze.

"You and I have lost things we wanted to keep, too, Eva," Melanie said a second later. "It wasn't fair. It wasn't our fault. But we couldn't stop it from happening."

"So we just let it go? Pretend it doesn't matter?" Eva said, the words stinging in her throat.

"It's already gone! And no, we don't pretend it doesn't matter. Of course it matters, but we've done all that anyone can do. *That's* what matters right now."

"But you don't understand. I've done—"

"I don't want to know what you did before!" Melanie shouted, trampling on the rest of Eva's words. "I don't need to know what awful things happened to you or what you did before you came here, okay? That was then; this is now. You are not living that life anymore! *That's* what you can let go of. The fireman gave us five minutes and those five minutes are gone. We need to go."

When she hesitated, Melanie pulled her by the arm and led her back through the house to the still-open front door.

"Do we tell June?" Eva asked as they stepped onto the porch.

"Do we tell her what the firemen will be doing when they go inside her backyard?"

Melanie closed the door behind them. "It won't make these next few hours any easier. I say we say nothing and see what happens. Let's go over to my place. I need to grab a few things. And I need you to gather up Nicky's stuff there."

She and Melanie hurried over to her house, and Eva grabbed Nicky's bag of soldiers and toys and his clothes. Melanie came out of her bedroom a few seconds later with her airline tickets in one hand and an overnight bag in the other.

Before heading back outside, Melanie pulled open a drawer in the kitchen and took out a notepad.

"I need to leave a message for Alex," she told Eva. "Just in case."

On the note Melanie wrote down Max's address and phone number. She taped it to the door and pulled it shut.

They got into June's car. Melanie put the vehicle in gear and they drove into a curtain of smoke.

26

Melanie drove down the hill as one might navigate the densest London fog. Curves that had been familiar before seemed completely foreign now. Usual landmarks she'd relied on in the past to anticipate turns in the road had been swallowed up in a cloak of smoke. Her hands were aching as she at last reached the bottom of the hill and realized her grip on the steering wheel was tighter than tight.

An exodus of other vehicles was already in place when they reached the coastal highway. Some trucks had horse trailers attached, some cars had suitcases strapped haphazardly to their roofs. All were heading south in a caravan of anxious movement. The bilious smoke was less concentrated here, giving Melanie and Eva a better view of the blaze headed their way. The flames were not yet visible on the hillsides but the sienna-hued canopy of smoke that was the inferno's headdress was immense, filling the sky over the mountains and canyons that separated Malibu from the San Fernando Valley and the rest of Los Angeles.

In the five years she'd been in California, Melanie had not seen such a menacing sight.

Horns blared, though no one could drive any faster than the next vehicle in front of them. It could take an hour or more, Melanie guessed, at the speed they were traveling, to cover the miles to Highway 10—an hour to get away from the mountains and their ample kindling of dry brush and scrub.

It wasn't until they were finally heading east toward LA and the heavy caul of smoke began to lessen that Melanie began to feel safe again.

She and Eva had said little to each other as she drove. Melanie was imagining what was happening at that moment in June's backyard, and knew Eva no doubt was, too. And then there were the unwanted images of what Eva may or may not have done before. Maybe someday she'd ask Eva what she'd done, but today was not that day. When they were at last turning into the driveway of Max's spacious home in Westwood, it was nearly eleven in the morning and the monstrous fire was just an immense copper swath on the western horizon behind them.

They were welcomed into the house by a relieved June and a clingy Nicky. Melanie had never had a child grip her neck the way Nicky was holding on to her now. She held him tight but sought June's gaze. Max wasn't in the house.

"He's on his way to Palm Springs," June said tonelessly, as though answering a question.

"When did he leave?"

"A while ago. I suppose he's getting there right about now." June's words seemed simple, but all three of them knew they weren't simple at all.

Eva shot Melanie a glance and June noticed it.

285

"What?" June said.

"It's nothing," Melanie said. "Nothing you need to think about right now."

"Is it the house?" June pressed. "Has the fire reached it? Tell me the fire hasn't reached it."

"It hasn't."

"I don't like the fire," Nicky said into her neck.

"I don't, either." Melanie moved from the entryway to Max's living room and folded herself onto a leather couch with the little boy still wrapped around her middle.

Eva and June followed her into the room.

"I guess we just wait now," June said.

Any other person besides Eva might have thought June meant wait for the fire to be put out so they could return home. But Melanie knew June meant wait for the phone to ring with Max on the other end.

The call came twenty minutes later, a few minutes after Nicky fell asleep in Melanie's lap. June reached for the receiver on the end table next to her.

Melanie listened to the only words she and Eva could hear—June's—but from them they could easily guess what Max was saying.

"Yes, Melanie and Eva are here now," June said. ". . . What do you mean Elwood is missing? . . ." She closed her eyes—perhaps against the performance she was giving. "What note? . . . I don't understand what you're saying . . . Yes, he owns a gun . . ."

The tears that were suddenly tracking down June's face, Melanie had not expected to see, nor did she expect to feel them on her own cheeks at this moment. She'd known for five days that Elwood was dead.

June's tears looked as authentic as her own. There was nothing artificial about them, and Melanie would know. She'd produced plenty of false tears for casting directors who needed an actress who could summon them on cue. She realized that for the near-week Elwood's death had been a secret to be kept, it had seemed like make-believe. A fiction. A dream. But not now. Now word of his demise was coming from the outside world. The world that was real.

"Tell me again what the note says." June's voice broke even though she already knew what the note said. "Oh, God, Max . . . I'm coming. I'm leaving right now . . . I can't just wait here. I need to help look. I need to be there . . ."

Several seconds of silence hovered in the room as Max said something Melanie could not hear.

"I'll be fine . . . I need to be there, Max," June said. "Don't tell me I can't be. I'm coming."

She hung up the phone and reached for a tissue in her pants pocket to wipe her tears. Melanie palmed away the wetness on her own face with the hand that wasn't encircled around the sleeping boy.

"Max has already called the police," June said. "And I need to go up there. It's what I would've done."

June was trembling all over.

"Maybe I should go with you," Melanie said on impulse. "Eva can stay here with Nicky."

"Yes," Eva chimed in. "Please take Melanie with you."

June shook her head. "I don't want you to have to pretend any more than you have to."

"I'm an actress, June."

"I mean, I don't want you to have to pile on lie after lie. For me. Max won't care if you all stay here until the fire's out. Call a cab if you don't want to wait for me and you've found out the fire department will let you back in. I'll pay for it."

"You're not paying for anyone's cab," Melanie said. "Eva and Nicky can wait here. But I'm coming with you. It will look better if I'm behind the wheel when we get there anyway. You need to look too worried to drive."

June let out a long breath, perhaps of resignation, perhaps of gratitude. She stood. "Let's go, then."

Melanie transferred the sleeping boy to Eva's arms.

Melanie and June were silent as they traveled the urban sprawl of Los Angeles to reach the quieter highway that headed east, toward the desert a hundred miles away.

When they were out of the city, June let out a long breath.

"You all right?" Melanie asked.

"Yes. No. I don't know."

"This day had to come, June. You couldn't have pretended forever that Elwood was still alive."

"I know. It's just . . . I feel like it's all slipping away from me now. My home, my work, my life. I feel like I am losing everything."

Melanie gripped the wheel a little harder. "Forgive me for saying so, but I think it's cruel that Elwood hasn't left you a thing in his will. I'm sorry if that's hard to hear. But honestly, June. How could he have left you nothing?"

June shrugged. "He paid me to be his assistant and caregiver after Frank died. I have most of that in savings still. I didn't have a lot of expenses. He knew that."

Melanie cast a glance toward June. "I'm not talking about what you have in your own bank account. I'm talking about what he had in his. And that house? Your home? To give it to strangers? You're family. I get that he felt bad about what happened to Ruthie, but still. You say he knew you had most of your earnings in your savings but he also knew that's all you had. Your own husband left you nothing. Isn't that right? Frank left you nothing?"

June startled as if struck.

"Okay. I'm sorry," Melanie said quickly. "I shouldn't have said that. I'm just trying to . . ." Her voice trailed off. Elwood had been a good friend to her, and a wise one, but she was becoming increasingly perplexed about this side of him. This side he never showed to anyone. The side he kept hidden from everyone. This side that she now found so self-focused and unkind.

"I'm just trying to understand why . . ." Melanie couldn't ask the question; it seemed far too harsh.

"Why I loved him anyway?" June said.

"Yes."

June was quiet for a moment as both of them stared at the road ahead, a stretch of asphalt and white dividing lines that stretched far into the horizon. "It was a million little things, I guess," June finally said. "Or . . . or maybe for no reason at all. It was the same with Frank. I can't list reasons why I loved either one of them. I don't think true love is like that."

"Of course it is. Those reasons are how we know it's love."

June shook her head slowly. "No, I don't think so. Reasons might explain why you're attracted to someone or enjoy being with them or why you like them. But love is . . . it's deeper than that. Higher. Elwood had fallen in love with Ruthie just because she was Ruthie. And if he'd married her, those boys would have been his stepsons. He would have been their stepfather. He would have helped raise them. Loved them. Of course he'd want to provide for them. You understand that, don't you?"

Melanie let June's words sink in. They explained a lot. Still . . .

"His love for Ruthie didn't mean he couldn't love you, too, as the widow of his brother," Melanie said. "He could've provided for you, too, June. You actually *were* his family."

June let out a long breath. "Maybe a healthy person would have seen how to do both. He wasn't, though, was he? He wasn't a healthy person. That's probably my fault. Maybe I should have insisted he try other doctors. Other treatments. But those were things he didn't want to do. If I had insisted, I think he would've asked me to leave, and that's something I didn't want to do."

They were quiet then, and Melanie turned on the radio for Christmas music, but there were only news updates of the inferno to the west.

27

Though she had been to Palm Springs often in the past, the stark beauty of its treeless foothills as golden brown as toasted bread and the larger snowcapped mountains that towered above still took June's breath away each time. The little city itself was an oasis of hotels and mansions and palm trees situated like a shining gem on an immense swath of tawny-hued velvet that seemed to reach forever in all directions.

Elwood's hideaway was at the farthest edge of Old Las Palmas, a neighborhood set against the base of the San Jacinto Mountains and home to dozens of Hollywood elite who'd wanted, like Elwood had, a haven far from the rat race.

Kirk Douglas had a place a mile away from Elwood's bungalow; so did Cary Grant, and Judy Garland, and others. The movie stars' homes were immense and gated, and Melanie now drove past several of these as they motored toward Elwood's place, a little two-bedroom house on an acre of land that was far smaller than the estates they'd driven past, and nowhere near as posh.

But the tile-roofed, white stucco bungalow tucked away behind a stand of acacia trees was exactly what Elwood had wanted.

Elwood hadn't been here since before the accident. After it, June and Frank went only a couple times to check on the place. Once Frank died, only Max and the occasional old friend of Elwood's would ask to use it. June had wanted to come following Frank's passing but she never felt good about leaving Elwood for very long. And especially not for that purpose. Just the mention of Palm Springs could send Elwood into a somber mood that could last for days.

Now, again, she was impressed by the desert's odd grandeur. But then the circular drive of Elwood's place came into view. It was filled with cars and her heart began to beat faster.

One was Max's, two belonged to local Palm Springs police, and two more to Riverside County law enforcement. Three other vehicles parked off to the side June did not recognize.

Uniformed officers looked up as they approached, as did several people in plain clothes—neighbors, perhaps. Max was there, too, watching them pull in. His suit clothes were dusty and dirty; he'd no doubt been out in the brush behind the house looking for Elwood. All of these people probably had been. They'd probably come in anticipating June's arrival to find out from her what had transpired between her and Elwood the day before. What had he said? What had he done? How did he seem when she left him?

As Melanie pulled in behind the parked cars, she turned to June. "You ready?"

"I just want this part to be over," June whispered.

Melanie cut the engine and they got out.

Max hurried over, taking June into a quick hug before guiding her toward a pair of Palm Springs policemen. One of the officers had a clipboard with Elwood's handwritten note attached.

"We'll find him, June," Max was saying. "I promise. We'll find him."

June felt at once like she was floating above the scene in El-wood's driveway, listening in on a conversation between Max and a woman that looked like her but was not her. She felt detached from both the moment and everything swirling about it—the fear, the urgency, the unknown. It was all happening so fast.

She was vaguely aware of Melanie at her other side as they moved toward the officers.

"Mrs. Blankenship, I'm Officer Vargas." The policeman was dark haired and younger than June, with just a hint of silver at his temples. He motioned toward the other officer, a man who was probably closer to Melanie's age, thin and lanky, with short, curly hair. "This is Officer Truett. A search party has already been out looking for your brother-in-law but what we really need right now is help figuring out where he might have gone, all right?"

June nodded mutely.

"And you are?" Officer Vargas turned to Melanie.

"I'm Melanie. I am June's neighbor. And a friend."

"All right. Well, if we could just step inside, please?" Officer Vargas said.

They entered the bungalow, and everything looked just as it had when she'd left it less than twenty-four hours before. The staged dishes in the sink, Elwood's slippers by the back door, the tweed jacket on a hook—all was right where she'd placed it.

Everyone sat down in the open living room. Outside, one of the patrol cars' radios squawked and June jumped in her seat.

"It's going to be okay, June. We'll find him," Max, sitting next to her, said again.

It occurred to June, her demeanor was successfully convincing everyone that she was shocked out of her mind that Elwood had walked off into the desert to end his life.

"Mr. Goldman here has informed me of your brother-in-law's . . .

condition," Officer Vargas said carefully, nodding toward Max. "We understand he hasn't left his house in almost a decade but decided to come here for Christmas and then spend some time alone. Working and thinking, is that correct?"

He looked from June to Max and back to June again.

"Yes," June said. "This is where he'd been headed the night of his car accident. I thought . . . I thought maybe he'd finally turned a corner. I didn't know he would do something like this. If I had, I wouldn't have left him."

"Of course you wouldn't have," Max said, patting her arm.

"And just so I'm understanding you correctly, your brother-in-law asked you to bring him here after not going anywhere, not even out to his own front yard, in nine years?" the police officer asked.

"I . . . he took a sleeping pill before I opened the garage door. He was asleep when we left Malibu. He wasn't awake for the traveling part."

"And when you arrived, what happened next?"

"He struggled a bit to come inside, but it was nothing we could not manage. He wanted to be here, Officer." The lies were tasting bitter on June's tongue. She swallowed hard. The cop didn't seem to notice.

"And Mr. Blankenship gave you no indication at all what he was planning to do after you left last evening?"

"She already said she wouldn't have left him if she'd known," Max said defensively.

"It's all right, Max," June said, her tone sounding as though cloaked in regret. "They're just doing their job." She turned to the officer. "He seemed fine. At peace."

The officer nodded, wrote something down. "Does your brother-in-law have any favorite hiking trails or vistas or spots here in the desert?"

June told him Elwood loved it all. Back in the day.

"Does Mr. Blankenship own a gun?"

June bit her lip and nodded. "A pistol. He keeps it under his mattress at the Malibu house. In case someone tries to break into the house. He's never used it."

"What kind of pistol?"

She had no idea. "It's black."

"Do you know if he brought it with him on this trip?"

"I don't know. He packed his own things."

The questions continued.

Had he ever attempted suicide before? Was he having financial troubles? Had he made any new friends lately? Had there been any suspicious activity in any of his bank accounts? Did he have a passport? Did he owe anyone money? Had there been phone calls to the house? Had she noticed anyone watching the bungalow yesterday?

When all the questions had been answered, the officer rose and thanked June.

"The county might investigate to rule out foul play," he said. "This information will be helpful if we can't find Mr. Blankenship. If you think of anything else that might help, just call down to the station. And when you return home to Malibu, we need for you to see if the gun is still under the mattress."

The officers went back outside to confer with the other authorities and to get an update on the search party's progress.

Max watched them go, shaking his head. "I should have insisted we get Elwood help when I was out at your place the other day. I shouldn't have taken no for an answer."

"I should have insisted," June said. "This is my fault."

Max swung back around. "No it's not. You were too close to him. You weren't about to ruffle his feathers. But I could have made the call. I could've brought someone in. So what if he might've hated me for it? At least he would've gotten the help he needed and this wouldn't be happening right now."

Across from her, Melanie got to her feet. "I'm going to look for him, too."

"I'll join you," June said, also rising.

Max stood as well. "The cops might say leave it to the pros to look."

"I'm going anyway," Melanie said. "Sitting here isn't helping."

"I don't care what they say, either," June said. "You can stay here, Max, if you want, and in case Elwood changes his mind and shows up."

Those in charge of the search weren't in the driveway to tell them to stay at the bungalow if they'd been of a mind to say so, so June and Melanie set out in a different direction than the search team to look for a man whom they both knew was nowhere in the desert.

When twilight began to touch the sky with shades of rose, violet, and peach with no sign of Elwood, Melanie and June drove into town to use a pay phone to call Eva for an update on the fire.

Eva didn't know much more about the Malibu blaze other than multiple fires were still burning and all of Malibu had been evacuated. Nicky had asked about Melanie several times after he awoke from his lap nap, but he was fine now. He'd had fun splashing in his undies on the steps of Max's pool, they'd taken a couple of walks in the neighborhood, played with his Christmas toys, and were now about to eat scrambled eggs and toast with jam for dinner. Max didn't have much else in his kitchen to eat.

"How are things there?" Eva asked.

"The search party is still out," June said. "I guess they're going to continue until midnight and pick up again tomorrow. We're sleeping at the bungalow tonight. You and Nicky can stay there at the house. Max says the sheets on the guest bed are clean and there are linens in the hall closet if you want to change the sheets on the bed in the master bedroom."

"Do you think you will be back here tomorrow?"

"I honestly don't know."

As they drove back to the bungalow, Melanie fiddled with the radio dial until she found a Los Angeles station relaying the latest information on the fire. The news was grim. A man had died that day trying to flee the flames, and more than thirty homes had been destroyed in the Zuma Beach area alone. Hot spots were popping up everywhere. The fire was predicted to burn its way into Ventura County, northwest of Los Angeles. Nine hundred firefighters— including two hundred and twenty-five Navy volunteers—were engaged in battling the flames, and an end was not yet in sight.

The second and third days in Palm Springs ended like the first had, with no sign of Elwood Blankenship despite a twenty-mile radius being searched by both trained professionals and teams of volunteers. June was told that without water, food, or shelter, a man Elwood's age and health was not expected to survive beyond three days. The arrival of the fourth day would signal the end of the official search and rescue. If Elwood had indeed wandered out into the desert without any food, water, or shelter, and if he'd not been picked up by someone or been aided by someone, and even if he'd not used the gun, he'd most likely perished.

At this news, delivered by the search and rescue team captain, June broke down and wept. Both Max and Melanie immediately put their arms around her.

Elwood was alive to no one now. He'd been gone from just her life for almost three weeks, and now he was gone to everyone.

Presumably deceased wasn't the same as officially deceased, though. June was also told it might be some time before Elwood was actually declared dead since no one saw him enter the desert and no body had been recovered.

Max said he'd stay a few more days in Palm Springs; he wasn't giving up just yet. June said she wasn't giving up, either—it seemed the right thing to say—but Melanie and Nicky had airplane tickets to Omaha for the next day. Their flight left at noon. And June was desperate to be reassured that the house was okay. Scores of homes in Malibu had been scorched or severely damaged, but so far Elwood's house hadn't appeared on any list of lost homes published in the daily *LA Times*.

"I understand," Max said when she told him this. "I'll keep looking for Elwood during the day and I'll read the script at night. He had to be close to being done before he did this. And I want him to be remembered well for his last screenplay if it's really going to be his last one. Where would he have put it? I've looked pretty much everywhere in the bungalow and I don't see it."

A jagged bolt of panic darted through June's body at the mention of the script.

"June?" Max said. "Where's the script? You said Elwood came here to think and work. So where's the script?"

In June's mind's eye, she saw herself grabbing Frank's Purple Heart, her purse, the rainy-day money, Nicky's toys, the photographs on the hi-fi, because there was a fire headed in their direction. There'd been no time to ponder what to take. All that was really on her mind at that moment was that she'd just told Max that Elwood was in Palm Springs.

The Plan had been set in motion and everything was about to be different.

She'd completely forgotten to grab the script.

28

Nicky didn't let Melanie out of his sight after she and June returned to Max's place.

Within an hour of their arrival back in Westwood, the radio station updating them on the fire announced the Malibu blaze had at last been contained. Only residents in areas where the fire had fully been extinguished were currently being allowed to survey what the fire had taken from them.

June wanted to leave right then to make sure the house still stood. She'd been quiet on the drive from Palm Springs to Los Angeles, wanting to listen to news stations reporting on the fire. Melanie thought this was due to June's wanting to distract herself from the ruse they'd just driven away from. But now Melanie could see June was very worried about the house—more than she had been the day before or the one before that, when the fire had been much worse.

"I'll drive you out to Malibu, June," she said. "I need to check on the Gilberts' house and pack a bigger suitcase than this overnight bag. I don't have the right clothes for Nebraska."

"I'll come with you," Eva said quickly.

Eva turned to Melanie; her gaze was earnest.

Understanding dropped onto Melanie like a solid weight. The firebreak. Those firemen had said they'd be digging a firebreak in June's backyard.

Digging in June's backyard.

"Has anyone been here? Called here asking for June?" Melanie said to Eva, meeting that earnest gaze with an intensity of her own.

Eva shook her head, her eyes wide.

"Why would anyone be looking for me here?" June said quickly. "Who could possibly know this is where Max brought me?"

"I can't just leave Nicky here," Melanie said to Eva, ignoring June's questions.

"Nicky can come, too," Eva said. *We cannot let her go alone,* Eva mouthed.

"You girls don't need to come," June said wearily, reaching for her purse and car keys.

"We want to," Eva continued. "Nicky and I have been cooped up here too long. June, you need to let us come."

June swiveled her neck to look at Eva. "I *need* to?"

Eva opened her mouth and then shut it. Then she looked at Melanie.

"What is going on?" June said tonelessly to Melanie.

Melanie pulled Nicky tighter into her arms. "Come on, Nicky," she said next as she reached for her own purse. "Let's go for a ride."

Melanie ushered June out the door. Eva followed, and as Melanie pulled the door shut, June asked again what was going on.

"You go ahead and get into the back seat, okay?" Melanie said to Nicky. She set him on his feet. Happy to at last be out of the house, her nephew ran to the car parked in the driveway. Melanie turned to June. "I don't know if you need to know this yet, but maybe you do."

"Know what?" June asked.

Melanie exhaled deeply. "Firemen told us they were going to dig a firebreak in your backyard."

June's eyes widened in absolute shock. "A *what?*"

"A firebreak. In the backyard."

For three long seconds June said and did nothing. "Oh, dear God . . . ," she finally murmured.

"But it doesn't mean they found anything, June," Melanie said. "They told us they were going to dig the firebreak that first day. If they'd found the body we would have heard about it, right? It would have been news. All the law enforcement agencies would have heard about it. The authorities would have come out to Palm Springs. You'd be in jail right now."

The minute the words were out of Melanie's mouth, she wished she could reel them back. June looked stricken.

"I shouldn't have said it like that, June," she went on. "I'm just thinking maybe you don't have to worry about it. They can't have found Elwood's body. I think we would know. It's not like you've been hiding in a cave somewhere. The police would've found you if they were looking. It's been four days."

"I think Melanie is probably right, June," Eva said. "She is probably right."

When June still said nothing, Melanie scooped the key ring out of June's hands. "I said I'm driving."

The drive to central Malibu seemed to take far too long, and when they reached its borders, the first smoldering patches of earth and skeletal landscape were an eerie greeting. The closer Melanie inched the car toward the turnoff for Paradise Circle, the more destruction they saw: buildings with roofs burned clean off, buildings burned only partway, buildings burned to their foundations, and some buildings not burned at all, as though the fire had gone through the seaside community with a pointer and selected what it would devour and what it would not. At the street they needed to take off of the highway, they were stopped at a roadblock by a National Guard patrol armed with rifles and lists of who would be allowed in.

"I am renting the house at the top of Paradise Circle," Melanie told the guardsman when he leaned in to inquire about the occupants of the car. "I've been living there since July."

"Only homeowners are allowed up," he said.

"Well, this is June Blankenship." Melanie motioned to June sitting next to her. "Look on your list. I am sure Blankenship is on your list."

The man consulted his clipboard. "Blankenship. Blankenship. Elwood Blankenship." He turned his attention to June. "You Mrs. Blankenship?"

June swallowed. "I am."

It wasn't a lie.

"Can I see some ID?"

June lifted her purse onto her lap and fished out her wallet. Her hand was shaking as she opened it to where her California driver's license lay framed behind a sleeve of clear plastic.

Melanie took it and handed it to the man.

He looked at it, looked at June, and handed it back.

"All right. You're allowed to view your home only. Understand? No getting out of the car. It's not safe to go traipsing about. You need to be back here in ten minutes. And I'm sorry for your loss."

Melanie felt June startle in the seat and heard her gasp.

"What was that?" Melanie said.

"I said I was sorry for her loss."

"Loss?" Melanie echoed.

"Her house. It's a loss. You didn't know? The new list came out an hour ago. The Blankenship house is a loss. I'm sorry."

Melanie could not bring herself to look at June sitting next to her. "Oh, my. No. She didn't know."

"Remember what I said. Stay in your vehicle. Ten minutes."

"Right. Thank you."

The guardsman moved the barricade and Melanie drove forward several hundred yards before she turned to look at June. Behind her she could hear Eva sniffling.

"June?" Melanie glanced at the half-blackened road ahead and then back at June.

June's face was jarringly void of expression. "It was all for nothing," she muttered, seemingly only to herself. "I did that horrible thing to Elwood for nothing. For nothing."

"June!" Melanie persisted. "Look at me."

But June did not. "I stuffed him into a ball gown bag, zipped him up, and dragged him down the stairs like an ugly old rug I didn't want anymore."

"It wasn't like that!" Eva exclaimed from the back seat.

"A ball?" Nicky said. "I don't see a ball."

They passed a trio of pepper trees that bordered a large fenced-in lot. Two of the trees' feathery bark looked like ebony, their stripped branches lifting themselves to the sky, empty. The third still had its tiny green leaves on one side.

"I want the ball," Nicky repeated.

"There is no ball, Nicky," Melanie said, and then said June's name again.

But June went on. "I dug up his roses. I got blisters on my hands from digging the grave. It took so long. I kept thinking, 'Surely

303

now it's deep enough.' But it wasn't and I had to keep digging. And then when it finally was deep enough. I rolled him into it. Like he was garbage. He's not even face up. He's on his side. I tried to roll him over and I couldn't. I couldn't . . ."

"Don't do this, June!" Eva said. "Do not remember it like this!"

"But this is what I did. This is what I did to him. And it was for nothing. The house is gone. Everything is gone. The script is gone. It was all for nothing."

"June!" Melanie shouted and then immediately lowered her voice. She could see through the rearview mirror that Nicky was staring at the back of her head. "This kind of talk is not helpful. You didn't do it for nothing. It wasn't for nothing. So stop this. And he was going to be buried in dirt anyway. Dirt is dirt. You picked a good spot."

"A beautiful spot," Eva interjected.

"Listen," Melanie said. "Elwood loved those roses. If he's looking down on you right now he's probably wishing you would just re-member how much he did love them."

June was silent as these words swirled about them in the car.

They were passing houses that had partially burned, some that looked perfectly fine, and a few scattered lots where there was no house at all, just an ash-strewn foundation. And then they were taking the last curve, the last turn before the street ended. Trees on either side were robbed of their top leaves and branches. The Gil-berts' house came into view first. It appeared untouched.

And then June's.

It was hard to tell there had been a house. The brick fireplace still stood, blackened but erect, and the stove in the kitchen had made a last stand. But the walls were gone, the second story was gone. In their place was ash and soot and black rubble. In the back-yard, the patio was a pile of cinders but miraculously three of the dozen rosebushes still stood, almost calling out audibly to be noticed.

And there was no firebreak. No part of the backyard had been dug up at all. What used to be the backyard was flat except for the three remaining rosebushes, singed but standing.

The firemen must not have been able to dig the firebreak before abandoning the cul-de-sac as the fire approached.

Or maybe they'd been radioed to attend to another area under greater threat and they never made it back here.

The reason didn't matter.

What mattered was Elwood was still in his favorite place in all the world. And three of his beloved bushes had survived to mark it.

Nicky was anxious to get out of the car and he grumbled when Melanie told him he had to stay where he was.

June stared, unblinking, at the ruin outside the passenger-side window. "What will I do now? I left the script in the house. I have nothing now. Nothing. I don't know where I'll go."

"Look. One thing at a time, June. As soon as power is restored, you can stay at my place, okay?" Melanie said. "I won't be there for a couple weeks at least. You and Eva can both stay there for right now. It's not like Carson is going to find out. Not for a while, anyway. If he even bothers to check to see if I am all right, I'll have Irving tell him I'm fine."

"And after that? And how can I leave Elwood here? Like this?"

"Well . . ." Melanie's voice trailed off. There was Eva's way . . .

"You should buy it anyway," Eva said from the back seat.

Of course. The answer was easy. Melanie wished she'd said it first rather than imagining for a terrible moment Eva's solution.

"Eva's right," Melanie said. "Buy the lot, June. Elwood had this place insured, right? Those boys will get the insurance money for the house as part of the estate. Offer to buy the lot from them.

They're not going to want it anyway. Look at it. Just buy it. Then you can . . ."

June finished Melanie's thought. "Protect it."

"Care for it," Eva added.

For a moment June said nothing, then she put her hand on the car door handle. "I need a minute. I won't break any other rules, I promise." She opened the door, got out of the car, and began walking toward the edge of the ruin.

Nicky asked when they were leaving.

"Very soon, hon," Melanie said.

The two women watched in silence as June stood at the rim of the remains of Elwood's house. Watched as she gazed at the three rosebushes beyond that were boldly extending their branches to the sun.

June looked old and worn and defeated, standing there with her back to them.

But no time machine in the world could have prevented this, Melanie thought. *Not this. You can't go back in time and stop a fire from coming.*

Honestly, what *could* a person actually stop from happening?

Even the strongest of hopes were still as delicate as paper outside the confines of the heart. Choosing to do something differently if she could crawl inside a time machine still meant she'd have to wait to see if messing with the past had been worth it.

And what would happen to the lessons learned from a past she'd erased? Would she get to keep them? Would she be willing to lose them if she couldn't?

If she could go back to the moment she agreed to become more than Carson's costar and decline to do so, would she find herself just wishing for another time machine somewhere farther down the road?

Would the rest of her life just be one constant stretch of regrets and disastrous attempts at do-overs?

What was the good in that? A time machine would be a portal to hell if that's what would happen.

Which meant . . . the past had to amount to more than just the spent years of that one life each person gets. Something weightier.

Maybe the past's allure wasn't that it could be changed if time machines were real but that it begged to be remembered. Maybe it was the ability to hold on to all those years—to remember where she'd been, the choices she'd made, the paths she'd chosen—that made the future something she was capable of stepping into.

Maybe it was the only thing that did.

"Do you think June will be all right?" Eva asked, as though reading Melanie's thoughts.

"I don't know. I guess that depends on her."

"Melanie?" Eva asked a moment later. "Would you mind very much taking me to Yvonne's after this?"

Melanie swung her head around from the front seat to face Eva. "What for?"

"I don't want to live like this. Like she has been living. Is still living." Eva nodded toward June. "She lives now with the fear of being discovered, every day. I have, too, for so many years. I do not want to live that way anymore. I don't want to live afraid. I want to talk to those men. If I must face what I have done to not be afraid anymore, then I will."

Melanie regarded her. "If you're sure."

"I am sure."

29

Eva spent the forty minutes heading back into LA preparing her heart and mind to meet head-on what would come next.

If Ernst's remains had been discovered in ragged woods rather than at the bottom of a lake, the authorities would reopen his case file. Of course they would. They would probably see his crushed skull and have no trouble redefining Ernst Geller's death as a probable homicide.

A homicide meant there was a killer.

Someone with a motive to kill.

Ernst Geller had been a wealthy man. And who benefitted most from a wealthy man's death? His surviving spouse.

Louise.

They'd be at her door, ready to arrest at the slightest discrepancy in her recalled events of that day Ernst failed to come home.

She would either tell the truth or she'd lie and say she'd killed him because God knows she wanted him dead.

And it was knowing this was a distinct possibility that had her now desperately wanting Melanie to drive faster.

It no longer mattered to her that much that the men who wanted to talk to her might know she was Russian born, not Polish, nor that they might be prepared to escort her in handcuffs to the airport with her final destination being Moscow.

It did matter to her that this fact might spell additional trouble for Melanie, and yet this didn't seem to weigh on Melanie as much anymore.

Maybe she, like Eva, was finally ready to live her life in the shimmering light of truth. Yes, suspected communist Carson Edwards had hired a Russian housekeeper for Melanie who was masquerading as Polish. It was true. It also meant nothing.

Living in truth, even if it was difficult, had to be better than living in fear.

As they neared Yvonne's house, Eva felt as though she was about to complete a circle now, one that would take her back to that moment Papa told her he'd see her again in a place where they would be safe, where they wouldn't have to run or hide.

The blazing place of truth.

When the car pulled up in front of the little house, Eva intended to turn and wave goodbye to Melanie and June, wishing the best for them. There were boxes of her few belongings in the car's trunk but she didn't need any of it.

But Melanie would not hear of it when Eva asked to just be let out.

"For heaven's sake, I'm not just dropping you off." Melanie set the brake, turned off the engine, and then swiveled around to speak to Nicky. "You wait right here with Miss June. I'll be right back."

She got out of the car before Eva could formulate a protest.

"You don't have to come with me," Eva said, once out of the car and walking alongside Melanie to the front door. She was suddenly awash with a desire for Melanie to never know about Ernst. About what she had done to him and with his body . . .

She was ready to face what she'd done—all of it—but only as the person she'd been before.

"I know I don't," Melanie said. "But I'd like to know, too, if these men have been back to see you and why they're here. And I want to make sure Yvonne's home and you get in. Plus, you have stuff in the trunk."

Eva was about to say she didn't need anything from the trunk when the door opened and Yvonne stood there in front of them, her face an explosion of surprise and smiles.

"Oh my stars, Eva! I've been trying to find out where you were! I even called your agency to see if they knew where you were. I was worried when I couldn't get anywhere, what with that fire and all. I'm so glad you're here! I have the most amazing news for you."

"News?" Eva couldn't hide the apprehension in her voice.

"Those men came back looking for you yesterday." Yvonne's smile widened. "I told them what you said. That they could leave a note for you and I would forward it to you."

"And?" Melanie prompted impatiently when Yvonne paused.

"I peeked at the note after they left," she continued. "I know I shouldn't have but I did because they said they were leaving tonight to go back to Minnesota."

"Minnesota?" Melanie echoed.

"Eva, those men?" Yvonne said. "They are your brother Arman and that man you loved. Sascha. That's who they are."

The ground beneath Eva's feet seemed to tilt and she instinctively reached for Melanie to keep from falling. Melanie's arm was around her in the next half second.

"That's not possible," Eva whispered. To Yvonne. To herself. To the very heavens. "My brother and Sascha are dead."

"No, they're not. They're alive. They were here."

Eva pinched the soft lining of her underarm. She was dreaming.

She was dreaming and she needed to wake up. "It can't be true," she murmured.

"But it is! Here's the note." Yvonne thrust the note toward Eva but she did not take it. Her arms felt like lead.

Because she was asleep. She was asleep. She had to be. No one survives the gulag. Especially not political prisoners. And especially not Germans.

Out of the corner of her eye she saw Melanie reach for the note.

Melanie began to read aloud. "'My name is Arman Kruse. I am here in Los Angeles with my friend Sascha Prinz and we are looking for my sister Eva Kruse, born in Norka, Russia in 1926. You have the name of my sister but your lady says you are from Poland. Please if you are my sister, call me at Hotel Normandie. I apologize my English is not good. I do not speak Polish. Sincerely, Arman Kruse.'"

Melanie looked up from the note. "There's a number, Eva. At the hotel."

"I told you, Eva!" Yvonne said happily. "I told you I had great news! And why on earth did you tell me you were Polish?"

"I . . ." Eva began, but she could summon no words. Sascha was alive. And Arman, too.

And what about her papa? Where was he?

Eva turned on her heel. "I have to go."

"Don't you want to come in and use the telephone?" Yvonne called after her.

"Do you know where this hotel is?" Eva said to Melanie, who had also turned away from the door and was following her down the two front steps.

"That one will be easy to find. Hotel Normandie is on Normandie Avenue." She turned to wave to Yvonne. "Thank you!"

The woman was still standing there watching them as Melanie

eased away from the curb. June, whose window was rolled down, must have heard the entire conversation.

"I know exactly where that hotel is," she said.

"You okay, Eva?" Melanie asked when they were five minutes into the drive. She was looking at Eva from the rearview mirror.

Eva didn't know what she was. She was afraid to be happy. Afraid it was still a dream or that someone was playing a terrible trick on her. Afraid she didn't deserve this turn of events. Afraid to believe that it didn't matter if she didn't.

Fifteen years had passed since she had seen Sascha or her brother. She'd been a teenager then, little more than a child, though at the time she hadn't felt like one. Now she was a thirty-year-old woman who'd lived through war, internment, starvation, and deprivation. She'd killed a brute of a man and then dug up his disgusting, decaying body. She'd lied to people, deceived them. She'd lived the last fifteen years with recurring nightmares of what she'd seen and what she'd done. On top of that, she'd had everything taken from her—everything.

Was she still the girl Sascha had once loved? Wanted to be with? Would her brother even recognize her?

"Eva?" Melanie said again.

Eva looked up at the eyes watching her in the rearview mirror. "I'm scared."

June turned around from the front seat. "But you're not alone."

Eva swallowed a thickening in her throat and nodded.

They covered the next few miles in silence.

When they arrived at the hotel, Melanie and June did not ask if Eva wanted to go in by herself. They all got out of the car and went inside.

Melanie handed Nicky over to June, and the two of them took

seats in the lobby near a window so that Nicky could watch cars coming and going on the streets outside it.

Eva approached the front desk with Melanie right beside her.

Her palms were tingling with sweat and expectation.

"How may I help you?" The desk clerk's tone was welcoming but Eva could not bring herself to ask for Arman and Sascha. She had not said their names in such a long time.

When she did not speak, Melanie did: "We're here to see Arman Kruse or Sascha Prinz. They are guests at your hotel."

"Certainly." The man consulted a ledger opened in front of him and then picked up the handset of a nearby phone, shiny and black. "And who shall I say is here?"

Melanie opened her mouth to answer but Eva cleared her throat and spoke first.

"Eva Kruse," she said. "Tell them Eva Kruse is here."

The clerk made the call. Said her name. Replaced the handset.

"The gentlemen will be right down," he said calmly, as if it was just a small thing that was about to happen.

Eva turned toward the elevators on the far side of the lobby and began to walk slowly toward them, stopping a few yards from the brassy doors.

She watched the dial above the one that indicated a descent from the fourth floor had begun. Watched the crescent that showed the journey from the floors above to the lobby. Felt Melanie's presence a few feet behind her.

A happy, melodic sound trilled, and the doors slowly opened.

And then it was as if June's time machine really did exist because Sascha and Arman walked out of it.

They had aged, too. Just like she had. They had surely seen things no person should have to see, lived through what no one should have to, had maybe done things they thought they'd never do. Just like she had.

But beyond the outward appearance of fifteen years having passed, they were still Arman and Sascha, the brother she adored and the man she loved. She knew as soon as they enveloped her in their arms that Papa had not survived the gulag. Her tears of elation were those of sorrow, too.

Arman pulled back so that Sascha could encircle Eva in his arms unimpeded. He kissed her neck and forehead and cheek and then her lips.

"I've been looking for you for so long," he whispered in German into her hair. "I was afraid . . ." His words trailed off for a moment. "No matter where I looked I couldn't find an Eva Kruse from Norka," he continued a second later. "From other places, yes, but not from Norka. I finally found my mother in Budapest. She said you'd lost track of each other when she remarried but that you'd stayed in Germany. Nobody I talked to knew where you were."

"I thought you were dead, Sascha," she whispered back. "Everyone said you were dead, that I should let you go. I tried, but I couldn't."

He wrapped his arms more firmly around her and she felt the burden of five thousand days begin to crack and splinter in that tightness.

"Come with Arman and me," he said. "We are heading back to Minneapolis tonight. We are staying with friends who have family there. You will, won't you? Please say you will come with me? Please?"

She reached up to touch Sascha's face.

"I have never left you, Sascha."

30

Melanie watched through the porthole window of the airplane as Omaha came into focus from out of the cloud cover. Nicky knelt on the seat next to her with his face against the glass in jubilant glee.

"See all the little cars on the snowy roads?" she said, tousling his hair gently, already missing having her nephew to herself. It had been surprisingly wonderful to care for him the last two weeks.

The voice of an airline attendant came over a loudspeaker telling the passengers the plane would be landing in a few minutes and everyone needed to check to see that their seat belts were securely fastened.

"Let's get your seat belt on," she said to Nicky as she helped him resettle onto his seat and buckled him in.

Melanie leaned back into the seat cushion and took a deep, calming breath. Flying was still a novelty to her and a bit unnerving. She closed her eyes to picture Eva on her flight the previous evening to Minneapolis, with her brother and Sascha most likely on either side.

How remarkable it was that Eva had been reunited with them. After Eva had introduced her brother and Sascha to Melanie and June, they'd gone to the hotel's restaurant for what seemed like endless cups of coffee so that they could tell Eva what they'd endured and how they'd been released.

Eva had been unaware that the gulag system had begun to significantly change after Josef Stalin's death four years earlier, and that tens of thousands of prisoners had received amnesty and been released—and were continuing to be released.

Sascha and Arman had been amnestied in 1954 and traveled to West Germany as soon as they had the resources to do so. They began the search for Eva, Irina, and Tanja right away. It took ten months to locate Irina and Tanja in Budapest with help from Displaced Persons officials and relief agencies, and many more after that to discover that five women by the name of Eva Kruse had emigrated from the many DP camps in West Germany, and then still more months to find that three of those women had come to the United States: one to Dallas, one to Chicago, and one to Los Angeles.

Sascha and Arman had documents and sponsors in place—in St. Paul—to complete their immigration to the United States themselves, but had been holding back on moving forward until they'd exhausted every effort to find Eva. They thought perhaps they had exhausted every effort.

When Melanie and June had left Eva at the hotel, they'd hugged goodbye as if they'd been friends for decades rather than just a month.

"Stay in touch?" Melanie said as they broke away.

"I promise," Eva said.

"I suppose you'll have a Minnesota address after today?" June asked with a smile.

"I hope so."

Melanie and June had driven back to Max's for the night and then June gave her and Nicky a ride to Los Angeles International that morning.

At the airport curb Melanie had thanked June for the ride and handed her the keys to the Gilberts' house back in Malibu.

"Groceries come every week on Mondays," she had said. "You may as well just let them come. Carson might call at some point, I suppose. If you end up talking to him, you can tell him I'm okay, the house is okay, and you can tell him where I am. And I guess you can give him my parents' number if he asks for it."

"And if he asks how long you'll be gone?"

Melanie had shrugged. "I really don't know. I just want to be home for a little while, you know?"

June had nodded. "I do know."

A couple seconds of weighted silence had hung between them.

"He might kick me out," June had said.

"He might. Worry about that if and when you have to. And, hey, listen. I know you're upset that the script is gone, but you can re-write it, June. Rewrite the whole thing and everyone at MGM will see it was you all along writing Elwood's scripts. They will have to believe you because Elwood's not here to rewrite it. Only you are."

"They will assign it to someone else," June had said. "They won't want to see anything I've written because they'll never accept that I've been writing the majority of the scripts. Max doesn't know how much I was writing for Elwood. Elwood didn't even know."

"Make them read it, June. Don't stop trying until they do."

June had nodded, smiling weakly. "All right. I'll rewrite it. What else am I going to do while I am waiting?"

Melanie and Nicky had gotten out of the car, and Melanie leaned in through the open window to say goodbye.

"You take care, June. And if something happens in the next few days where you need me to vouch for you, I want you to call me, okay?"

June shook her head. "I'm not going to do that to you. I'm the one who made this mess I am in."

"Call me anyway."

June's smile had increased. "I'll think about it."

Melanie had turned to go but then suddenly remembered her brother might show up to retrieve Nicky. She swung back around. "If Alex comes by wanting his son, you tell him where he can find him, okay?"

"Absolutely. And, Melanie?"

"Yes?"

"I could be wrong, I know, but I'm guessing your mother and father care for you very much and probably tried as best they could to be good parents."

Melanie had warmed to those words instantly but nevertheless said, "You've never met my parents."

"But I've met you. I know you. I know the people you care for are important to you. And that you wouldn't let any harm come to them if you could help it. Usually someone has to model that to us."

A car behind June's at the curb had honked.

"Thanks, June," Melanie had said as she stepped away from the vehicle. "I'll be seeing you."

Now, as Melanie watched the ground rise up closer and closer, she knew the hours before she'd introduce her parents to their grandson had shrunk to minutes.

She turned to Nicky, who still had his face as close to the glass as he could get it while still being buckled in. "Remember who we're going to see?"

"Grandmom and Grandpop."

She loved the way he said their names. "And remember what I said they might do when they see you?"

"They might cry."

"Happy tears, remember?"

"Grandmom might squeeze me too hard."

Melanie laughed. "She might."

The plane landed and taxied to a stop. Melanie buttoned up her coat and Nicky's and gathered his bag of toys and her purse. They made their way down the aisle, and then out of the plane and into the overly chilled air of a December day in the Midwest.

As they entered the terminal, it was her mother's face she saw first. She was on tiptoe with her arm on her father's, looking over the heads of the passengers who'd already stepped inside. She waved when she saw Melanie, and then her happy countenance turned to surprise when she saw that Melanie held the hand of a little boy.

"Well, who's this?" Wynona Kolander said, cheerfully after she'd hugged Melanie.

"Hello, Melanie," Herb said, planting a kiss on her forehead. "Made a new friend on the airplane, did you?"

"Mom, Dad, this is Nicky."

Her parents smiled tentatively.

"Hello, Nicky," Wynona said politely a second later.

"I had a visit a couple of weeks ago," Melanie continued. "From Alex."

Herb and Wynona had been looking at the boy but both popped their heads back up to look at Melanie.

"You saw him?" Wynona said.

"I did. For a few hours, anyway. He's married now but I think he and his wife might've hit a rough patch and she left him. Or maybe she's looking for buried treasure and he decided to join her. All I know is he didn't stay. And he didn't say where he was going. If I had to guess, I'd say I won't hear from him again for a bit."

"But . . ." Wynona gazed down at Nicky.

"He left Nicky with me. Nicky is his little boy. And he's your grandson."

For a second neither Herb nor Wynona moved so much as a muscle. And then Wynona was on her knees with Nicky in her embrace, Herb standing over them, touching his grandson's head.

Melanie was quite certain she'd hear from Nicky that Grandmom had squeezed him way too tight.

They'd been at the house for a couple of hours playing with Nicky and Melanie catching her parents up on Alex's visit, the details of the fire, the state of her stalled career, and the fact that she hoped she could stay for a couple of weeks—or more—when the phone rang.

Herb came back from answering it. "It's for you, Melanie. It's Irving."

Melanie rose from where she'd been sitting on the floor of the living room with Nicky and her mother. They'd found a box of Alex's old toys in the basement, and Nicky was happily playing with a shoebox full of little wooden race cars.

She made her way to the phone with an uneasy feeling in the pit of her stomach. Melanie had told Irving where she was going and had made it pretty clear this was to be like a vacation from her Hollywood life, a time of introspection and a refocusing of her aspirations. If she wasn't going to be a movie star anymore, what was she going to do with her life? She needed time away from California to consider such a challenging question. It was the reason she'd extended her trip. If Irving was calling, it was because it was important enough to intrude on this set-aside time with her family.

And that meant it couldn't possibly be good.

Melanie reached for the telephone in Herb's office and picked it up, steeling herself to hear the reason her agent had called.

"Hello, Irving," she said.

"Thank God you're finally in a place where I could call you," he exclaimed on the other end of the line. "Please tell me you've not had to surrender your passport."

"What?"

"Tell me you have your passport."

Carson and other, more notable blacklisted people had been forced to turn in their passports, but not everyone on the blacklist had. Melanie hadn't.

"I still have it."

"Hallelujah," Irving said. "Listen. I've been doing a little scouting that I haven't told you about because I didn't want to raise your hopes just to see them crushed again. But, Melanie, I have news."

"What? What is it?"

"You're wanted in Paris in five days for a screen test. I mean, you're *really* wanted."

Nothing that Irving was saying made any sense. Paris? A screen test? "Irving, what are you talking about?"

"I'm talking about a screen test for an acclaimed French director, baby. Jacques Becker saw you in *This Side of Tomorrow*. I told him you speak French. He wants you to test for his next film."

"You told him I what?"

"You had two years of high school French. You told me that."

"I did, but, Irving, that doesn't mean I speak French."

"It doesn't matter. The film is about a Parisian detective who falls in love with an American tourist who witnesses a murder. You don't have to speak perfect French. He doesn't want you to speak perfect French. You just need to understand filming directions. The role is perfect for you."

"But . . . the blacklist."

"There is no blacklist in Paris, Mel. And the HUAC can't keep you from flying to Paris to make this movie. Melanie, this could change everything for you. You could make it big in French films. Becker said it himself. I already booked you on a flight next week. I want you on that plane."

For a moment, Melanie could not speak. All she could do was look at her parents on the floor, playing with their grandson, racing wooden cars on the curves of the braided rug they sat upon.

Sometimes life was so hard you could barely breathe.

And sometimes it was so sweet you couldn't wait to take your next breath . . .

"Send me the tickets," she said.

JANUARY 5, 1958

31

June folded the newspaper she'd found in the lawyer's waiting room and placed it back on a side table with the Arts and Entertainment section on top so that the photo of Melanie Cole, the newest star of French film, was in full view.

Paris had gobbled up the bright young actress Hollywood had chased out of its studios the year before, and the new film she was starring in was apparently playing to rave reviews in France.

The movie had opened only three weeks prior in Paris and had already filled to capacity every theater where it had been shown. Extra showings had been scheduled. Additional showings had been slated for all of Provence and up and down the Côte d'Azur. And in Belgium, too.

Americans who wanted to see *Ce Qu'elle a Vu* would have to wait a while for a dubbed version to be shown in its indie theaters, though.

Too bad, too, the article had said. Miss Cole's performance was spectacular, and Hollywood was going to regret losing her, especially since they'd apparently lost her over nothing: The blacklisted costar of her previous film, Carson Edwards, had been called to stand before the congressional committee eight months earlier and testified that his costar, Miss Cole, was never part of any conversation in which politics of any persuasion were discussed. The newspaper had reported he'd said his and Miss Cole's off-camera relationship was arranged purely for photographers and fans.

"But you and Miss Cole also had an intimate relationship, did you not?" he'd been asked.

"Ah, that. That was merely for fun and the cameras," he reportedly said. They weren't even good friends.

That might have been the nicest thing Carson had done for Melanie, trivializing their relationship like that.

But he was still an ass.

And they were both still blacklisted.

June smiled at the photo of Melanie and then picked up the paper again, pulled out the Arts and Entertainment section, and stuffed it into her purse. She'd send the article to Eva in St. Paul.

An intercom buzzed on the desk of the receptionist at the front of the room. Seconds later June was taking a seat in the paneled office of Tobias Markham, Esquire. Elwood's lawyer.

"Sorry to have kept you waiting, Mrs. Blankenship. I know this must be a difficult time for you."

"It's all right. I'm not in a hurry."

"How are you? Getting on okay? Staying busy?"

"I'm all right. I'm writing a screenplay. A second one. I couldn't get anyone to look at the first one except for Max. He liked it. Very much, in fact. But he's not a studio man. I'm staying with it, though."

"Yes, I recall Elwood telling me what a wonderful assistant you had been to him since the accident. You must have learned a lot working for him."

June cracked a smile. She couldn't help it. "Indeed."

"And you're staying at Max's house these days, right?"

"Yes. In his pool house. With Algernon."

"Algernon."

"Elwood's cat."

"Ah. Yes."

The lawyer cleared his throat and leaned forward in his chair, a wordless sign that polite small talk was over. "I just want to reiterate again how I'm deeply sorry about the loss of the Malibu house in that fire. It's a terrible tragedy. Not only that, but you could have stayed in it all these months while . . . well, you know. While the estate was in flux."

"Yes."

"Right. On to our business, then. I'm sorry this day has come but it did have to come, as you know. I take it you've been informed the judge ruled for a declaration of death yesterday?"

"Yes. I . . . I was in the courtroom. In the back."

"Of course. So, Mrs. Blankenship, I believe from our earlier phone conversation that you are aware that Elwood left the majority of his estate to Peter Brink and Carlton Brink, sons of the late Ruthie Brink, yes?"

"I'm aware."

"The reason I called you in before I speak to the Brink sons is because I have a letter from Elwood that I was instructed to give to you upon his death and before the reading of his will and the disposition of his assets. With the judge's ruling in the books, I am now free to do that."

The lawyer opened a desk drawer and withdrew a sealed, ivory-hued envelope. He reached across the desk and handed it to her.

June took it with slightly trembling hands. "When did he give this to you?"

Markham hesitated a moment. "A number of weeks before . . . before last Christmas."

They were quiet for a moment. Then the lawyer stood.

"Shall I give you a few minutes?" he said.

"Yes. Thank you."

The lawyer left the room, closing the door behind him.

June stared at Elwood's script on the front of the envelope, at the four letters of her name. At the elegant way he made his *J*s.

She hadn't seen his script in more than a year now. The last time he'd written anything to her it was that note bidding her farewell . . .

In the twelve months since the house had burned down and Melanie and Eva had left, June had felt like she was suspended between two worlds: the world where Elwood was alive and the one where he wasn't. Somewhere in the middle of that she'd been hovering, tethered to neither.

She'd been so naïve to think a missing person could be declared dead in just a couple of months, even with a suicide note. If there's no body, there's no physical evidence of a death. If there's no physical evidence of a death, there is no declaration of death. Four months after Christmas, when she began to cautiously inquire when a person was legally considered deceased, she'd been astounded to hear it was often seven years, and that if any family member wanted it to happen sooner, they had to bring a petition before a judge, which June had done, as Elwood Blankenship's only living relative, a month ago. Everything that had belonged to Elwood, including his cat, had been in estate limbo, the entirety still owned by a man who seemed to have simply vanished into thin air.

What bothered June most when she learned all of this was knowing the three rosebushes that kept vigil over Elwood's grave wouldn't be cared for in a limbo state, and that was simply not acceptable. She'd gone out to the property every Sunday since the fire to water, tend, and nurture them. The rest of the lot was a weed-filled jungle at the twelve-month mark, but not those three rosebushes.

It was because of them and what they meant that she petitioned the court, and likewise it was because of them she would beg those Brink boys at three o'clock today when she met them to let her buy the land.

But first there was this letter.

She could not even begin to guess what Elwood would have to say to her, knowing she'd read it upon his death.

June slit the envelope open with a fingernail and pulled out a single sheet of paper, written on both sides in Elwood's careful script. He'd dated it four months before he swallowed the sleeping pills:

My dearest June,

If you are reading this then I have passed from this life to whatever awaits me beyond it.

I need to tell you why I did not leave you the Malibu house.

If I were a braver man I might have explained my decision in person because you certainly deserve that but I am not that brave man. I did not want you living in the Malibu house after I was gone. It is not a house for the living; it is a mausoleum of memories for us both. Were you to stay in it I think you would come to despise its hold on you. I do not want that for you.

I never should have let you stay on at this house and care for me after Frank passed. It was the most selfish thing I have ever done. And when I came to understand that you loved me like you loved Frank, continuing to let you stay was the most heartless thing I've ever done. You should have been free to begin a new life away from this house and away from me when Frank died. I am so desperately sorry, June.

I have left you the Palm Springs house instead. You can live there if you wish but my hope is you sell it and buy something else in a place that makes you happy. It sits on prime real estate and should fetch a nice price. I also want you to know that I have left a letter to be given to MGM assuring them that you were the strength and sweetness of anything I wrote for them the past nine years, not me. I have written that they would be fools not to employ you as a screenwriter under your own name. I do not think they are fools, but they might be slow-moving. Don't give up on them. They will come around.

I know full well that I owe you more than I can ever repay and have treated you dismally. If you could find it in your heart to forgive me for my many flaws and for the ways I have misused your love and friendship I would be grateful. I want your forgiveness so that you can be done with me and find happiness again.

Despite what Max and you and everyone else has tried to tell me over the years, I did kill Ruthie. I was driving too fast, I was showing off, I had been drinking, and I was reckless with her precious life. I took from her sons their mother and only remaining parent. I did that. This is my confession.

June, you have the biggest heart of anyone I know and within it are such riches to be shared with the world. I know you will do great things.

I loved Ruthie, but I loved you, too. And for far longer. Perhaps you are the only person who can understand how it is possible to love two people like I loved the two of you. First her, then you—in my own way. From the moment she left me you became the brightest star in my little cosmos. I am so grateful to have known you.

Yours, Elwood

June held the letter to her chest as tears fell, dotting the paper like raindrops. "Oh, El," she whispered.

She pulled the letter away from her body and traced her finger on the words *I loved you, too.*

Elwood had been wrong about so many things. He hadn't killed anyone. To kill was to plunge the knife, pull the trigger—want the other person dead—but Elwood had not desired that for anyone. And the taking of his own life did not balance any scales.

But . . .

Elwood had loved her.

He'd loved her.

And in that remarkable, singular fragment of time, that was enough.

EPILOGUE

Hollywood, April 14, 1966

Eva holds the two bouquets of roses like a bride might as she searches the throngs outside the Palace Theatre for her friends. Melanie had told her to look for them beyond the stanchions and past the photographers now pressing their shutter buttons at a frenzied pace. But Eva hadn't considered there would be so great a crowd for the premier of *A Moment in Time*.

June was being modest when she wrote in her last letter that it probably wouldn't be a bad idea to take a mid-morning flight out of the Twin Cities and to get to the theater early.

Eva had assumed half an hour *was* early.

Perhaps she should've forgone the side jaunt to Malibu to gather the roses, but even Sascha hadn't tried to talk her out of the two-hour round trip. Wise, rational Sascha, who knew everything about the rose garden.

And everything else about everything else.

"I think we can make it back to Los Angeles in time," he'd said. "This is important to you."

She'd been relieved Sascha had understood this.

If Elwood's secret grave haunted June at times like Ernst Geller's haunted her, she wanted to reassure her friend that Elwood rested in a beautiful place that he'd loved, as lovely as any memorial garden. And to remind herself that Elwood was not Ernst.

Collecting some of Elwood's roses had seemed the best way to properly celebrate June's and Melanie's new movie. Their first.

It wasn't Melanie's first, of course; she'd been in a dozen French films in the past decade. And it wasn't June's first, either, now that she was finally getting the screenplay credits she'd long deserved. But it was their first project together: the original screenplay being June's, the starring role Melanie's. The story was that of an unhappy woman who uses a time machine to travel to the past but who discovers she's only allowed to convince a younger self to make just one different choice, and only one—all while remaining unseen by that younger self.

The surprise ending was apparently a huge hit with early reviewers and critics, but Eva already knew what the twist was. Melanie, who'd flown to California from Paris for pre-premier publicity, had told her over the phone a week ago after Eva begged her to. Of all the things the unhappy woman in the film can do differently, she opts to save the man she loves even though she knows it means he will choose someone else. When she returns to her own life in the present, though, she finds that she is married to this man. Her sacrifice had changed her future.

"True love conquers all," Melanie had chuckled. "Although it doesn't, actually. But people love a happy ending."

"Because people love hope," Eva had said.

"And they like to imagine the outcome if love *could* conquer all."

"Perhaps it does, though. Or it would if . . ."

"If the world were a different place?"

"If people were different."

There had been a pause then.

"You got the airline tickets, didn't you?" Melanie had finally said.

"We did, thank you. It's very kind of you."

"It's nothing. You need to be there for the premier, Eva. No one knows the inside of this screenplay like you do. My parents and Nick will be there, too. He remembers you, you know. Alex might even show up. He said he would. But I'll believe it when I see it."

"Do you see them?" Sascha now says. He is at her side, and she can see a tiny smear of scrambled egg on the lapel of his suit coat where their five-year-old, Anna, hugged him before they left that morning.

Eva starts to say she cannot, but then she catches a glimpse of Melanie. She is dazzling in a sequined black dress and diamonds.

They make eye contact and Melanie shouts her name. A phalanx of photographers parts to see who the star of the movie is addressing, giving Eva a view of June, standing next to Melanie in an organza gown of fairy-tale blue.

Eva and Sascha inch their way forward as Melanie and June move toward her. A man in a black tuxedo unclips the stanchion rope and allows them to pass through onto the red carpet.

Melanie quickly pulls Eva into an embrace, and Eva holds the bouquets high so that they are not crushed. She turns then to hug June the same way.

The years have been kind to her friends. June looks tanned and radiant; Palm Springs' ample sun has surely been generous. And Melanie, married now to a French designer and the mother of two twin girls, looks like she hasn't aged a day.

When they part, Eva extends the two bouquets.

"I made a little detour to Malibu before coming to the theater," she says. "I hope . . . I hope you don't mind? I think Elwood would be so proud of you. Of both of you. I hope this is okay?"

As a surprised and moved June reaches to take hold of the flowers, one stray thorn pierces her finger and she winces.

Eva opens her mouth to apologize but June raises her hand to stop her even as a tiny bloom of crimson dots her forefinger.

"They are perfect, Eva," June says. "Absolutely perfect."

"That was really sweet of you," Melanie adds.

Eva feels so at home in the company of these people that she wants to freeze time even though strangers surround them and she's wearing a silk gown she will likely never wear again.

How wonderful and curious it is that home is not just the house you share with the people you love and who love you, she muses, but it is also *this*. This sensation, this way.

An usher approaches to lead them inside, telling them the film is about to start.

"Shall we?" Melanie says.

Sometimes you belong only to the moment, Eva thinks as they turn to follow the man, *and that one singular snippet of time owns your fate. You belong only to that moment and to nowhere else.*

And then sometimes the moment belongs to you.

Author's Note and Acknowledgments

A Map to Paradise, like all my previous novels, wouldn't exist without the assistance and insights of so many talented people. I am grateful to my Berkley team, especially Claire Zion, Carly James, and Tara O'Connor, and my gem of a literary agent, Elisabeth Weed at The Book Group. They bring out my best and they don't let me settle for anything less. Thanks, too, to my mother, Judy Horning—the only person who sees my manuscripts before I turn them in—for her careful proofreading, and to my husband, Bob, for putting up with a lot of angst and blank stares with this book. And to God, the One who has given me so much—including Jesus, my family, and a love of writing.

When I began researching the 1950s for this book, I was struck right away by how fearful people were in the early years of the Cold War. Home—not just the place where we sleep at night but that unparalleled sense of belonging and safety—seemed to be hanging in the balance. The anxiety in the U.S. over what would happen if the Soviets and America went to war was real. Dread of both a communist takeover and the Bomb was real. I began to ponder the impact of both the true and the imagined loss of home, also known as "displacement." I asked myself the questions a character would ask if they suddenly found themselves exiled from everything that gave them security. Like, what does someone do when they've no sense of home anymore? How do they live without it? What are they willing to do to get it back? And if the loss of home is imminent, what are they willing to risk to keep it from being taken from them?

Out of those ponderings and more, the three main characters in *A Map to Paradise* materialized: Eva, an immigrant Displaced Person who lost everyone and everything in the war; a blacklisted Hollywood actress named Melanie who was on the cusp of the only career she ever wanted; and June, a widow living with her agoraphobic brother-in-law, who would have nothing if he died. I decided the lives of these three women—who were all facing different stages of displacement—would converge in a most unlikely Paradise: Malibu in 1956.

For Eva's character, I'd read early on that after WWII a million people were living untethered lives in Displaced Persons camps all across Germany, Austria, and Italy—most of them Eastern Europeans who did not want to return home to what were now Soviet-controlled countries. Some, like Eva, were known as Volga Germans. They were Russian born but of German descent, and they'd lived in Russia for generations while maintaining their German way of life and language. When Germany declared war on Russia in WWII, however, things got very bad for the Volga Germans and very quickly. On September 1, 1941, a mass evacuation was announced for the more than four hundred thousand Volga Germans living in Russia, followed by forced deportation to labor camps in Kazakhstan and Siberia. Most were given just minutes to pack up a few belongings and food. It is estimated that tens of thousands perished on the long journey to the gulag, which took place in overcrowded cattle cars and in freezing conditions.

After the war, Displaced Persons who were also Volga Germans, like my fictional Eva, had good reason to not want to return to Russia even though it had been their home for two hundred years.

For Melanie's character, I'd read about the Red Scare in Hollywood and the blacklist that resulted when studios teamed up to keep suspected communists and communist sympathizers from working as screenwriters, directors, and actors. I remember being so surprised that it was the entertainment industry that came under such intense scrutiny rather than, say, higher education, and that it seemed at times to be more of a fear-fed witch hunt than a logical scheme to identify subversives. What happened to people like Melanie who were innocent seemed like its own kind of displacement: to be shut out of any way of making a living in your chosen career field and to also be at the same time labeled by hearsay as traitorous. Unpatriotic. Untrustworthy. A pariah who belonged nowhere because nobody wanted you.

June's story began in my mind as an image of a sad and desperate woman digging up rosebushes at three a.m. to bury her dead brother-in-law—a man she'd secretly loved for years. What she is doing she'll wish she'd not done, but all she is thinking at the moment is that this man who gave her a home and job and companionship and someone to love has just committed suicide, and in his will he's left the house to someone else. If he's dead, she has nothing. Nothing. But, she reasons, her brother-in-law is agoraphobic. He hasn't left his house in nearly ten years. It will be some time before he is missed. And in the meantime she will find a way to hang on to the only house that has ever felt like home to her. She just has to.

The coastal enclave of Malibu as the setting seemed so appropriate. It was coastal-calm, idyllic, and ruggedly pacific in the 1950s. It has also been nicknamed the wildfire capital of North America, which means it is a fragile paradise. You can't know for certain that what you think of as home there will always be around. That to me made it a perfect fit for this story. If you're familiar with Malibu, you may be wondering why I kept the specific location of the Blankenship house a bit ambiguous. Paradise Circle is a street name that I created so that I could control what happened on it. Choosing a real location for June and Elwood's house would've meant having to stick to the actual boundary lines of the two fires that decimated Malibu in December 1956. The larger one, the Sherwood-Zuma fire, was contained a little bit to the north of where it would seem the Blankenship house was located, based on Melanie's little forays down to Malibu village and the Malibu Movie Colony. The smaller Hume fire was contained a bit farther south. With that in mind it was wiser for me to keep the location nonspecific so as not to trample too harshly on historic fact. In the last century, upward of thirty wildfires have burned in Malibu. The most recent Woolsey blaze in 2018 was the largest, scorching almost one hundred thousand acres and exceeding $1.6 billion in property loss and damage.

If you would like to know more about some of the historical events that occur in this book, I highly recommend:

The Long Road Home: The Aftermath of the Second World War by
    Ben Shephard
The Last Million: Europe's Displaced Persons from World War to
    Cold War by David Nasaw
Tender Comrades: A Backstory of the Hollywood Blacklist by
    Patrick McGilligan and Paul Buhle
Hollywood Party: How Communism Seduced the American Film
    Industry in the 1930s and 1940s by Kenneth Lloyd Billingsley
I Said Yes to Everything: A Memoir by Lee Grant

My Fifty Years in Malibu by Dorothy D. Stotsenberg

Malibu Burning: The Real Story Behind LA's Most Devastating Wildfire by Robert Kerbeck

As always, I appreciate you so much, dear reader. Thank you for partnering with me in my literary endeavors. You are the reason I write.